OPEN MIKE

First Published in Great Britain 2019 by Mirador Publishing

First edition: 2019

A copy of this work is available through the British Library.

ISBN: 978-1-912601-79-0

Mirador Publishing
10 Greenbrook Terrace
Taunton
Somerset
UK
TA1 1UT

Open Mike

By

Ade Cory

FEAR

Mike Grimshaw could feel his hands quiver.

He tried to breathe through his stomach, a technique he'd been instructed to employ in times of stress by either his therapist or an online monk. His mouth was paper dry.

There's no way I'm going to able to get the words out, Mike thought, desperately trying to salivate.

He tried to shift the guitar a little so it would sit more comfortably but his leaden arms seemed incapable of movement. Mike's legs were also rooted to the spot; the reliability of his thighs now in question as their consistency morphed from the customary bone and tissue structure into an unsupportive, gelatinous mush.

And then, his heart just stopped.

It was going at about 200 bpm a second ago – Mike knew this because he could feel the damn thing tying to remove itself from his chest cavity. And now – nothing.

Goodbye cruel world, he silently mouthed.

When he didn't die a few seconds later, Mike assumed he'd been mistaken. With the spotlight still keenly on him, the northern, cross-dressing owner of an unprofitable village shop bizarrely cursed his luck.

Just do it, he demanded of his body. But his body wasn't playing fair.

As watery eyes regarded the sea of ever-hopeful faces before him, his throat suddenly felt like it was swelling up – engorging rapidly as the result of some massive allergic reaction. His windpipe would soon be crushed; he would fall to the stage gasping for air; the crowd would look on in horror; cries for an EpiPen would go answered; his helpless, lifeless body would –

"Get on with it!"

The heckle brought Mike crashing out of his reverie. This was it – the moment! He wanted this – so all he needed to do was strike that first chord. He urgently tried to add some perspective: this wasn't about achieving greatness, it was simply to avoid averageness being thrust upon him.

Sing the goddam song, Michael!

A rasping E rang out across the pub, and Mike was finally playing an open mic night.

MIKE

"Oi really enjoyed yer playen tonight, boi!" The audience member swayed a little as he approached Mike, his eyes somewhat at odds with each other. "And that gingham dress yer got on is smashen!"

Mike tugged awkwardly at an errant pleat in his skirt. The grimace on his face suggested a different opinion of his night's efforts with the guitar but he thanked the well-oiled pig farmer for the compliment nonetheless. With the pleasantries over, the farmer suddenly remembered his rather pressing engagement in the gents.

"Ooh!" groaned the farmer urgently before bundling past Mike and veering headlong into an occasional table, scattering a hitherto untouched pile of local attraction leaflets onto the pub floor in the process.

"S'alroight!" the farmer cried, with one hand in the air and the other firmly affixed to his crotch. "Oi'll pick 'em up in a sec, only oi'm bursten!"

Mike watched the pigman stagger into the toilets before briefly considering the true value of performing in front of this bizarre rural audience. Wasn't it already something of a stretch for the pub's patrons to accept that their quaint village store was now being run by a mostly depressed lad from Lancashire with a penchant for stylish dresses? Did he really need to add insult to injury by throwing in a series of suspect performances on the guitar for good measure?

While mulling over these new-found emotional burdens associated with open mic night, Mike regarded his guitar lying in its case. For a moment, he thought it was whimpering up at him like a small child who'd been refused a favourite bedtime story; it was clearly under the impression it had been harshly treated.

Mike had spotted the instrument on an eBay auction twelve months earlier. It was a *Takamine*, the exact make of guitar the forty-something had set his heart on. More importantly, it was the unwanted gift of someone in Gravesend who'd 'only played it twice', according to the detailed product description. This, Mike decided, would be the guitar he would master and take to the stage in his local. By treating the crowd to sublime covers of classic tunes, Mike would cement his role within the small yet strangely dark community. It would raise the profile of this rather insecure northerner who was so much more than just a vendor of over-priced groceries. At least, that's what he thought.

If nothing else, maybe it would kick-start his life again.

"That's better!" cried the farmer, his face a picture of relieved bliss.

"Um, you're flying." Mike delicately pointed at the gaping chasm in the front of the farmer's mustard-coloured trousers, a space that was neatly embellished by spots of splash-back.

"Ooh, ta!" said the farmer, and yanked up the zip. He noticed he was stood over Mike's guitar. "Noice axe. Yer 'ad it long?"

"Not long enough," Mike replied rather meekly, and the pair looked down at the wounded animal.

The race for ownership of the guitar unravelled across the early hours of a September morning. Mike had logged onto eBay after a late-night stock take, determined to get his guitar-playing career underway once and for all.

With interest in the instrument gradually gaining momentum after a slow start, Mike watched the first few optimistic bids change on his laptop and settled in for the long haul. A selection of dips and antipasti, plus a number of tins of Red Bull, were on the table beside him to help keep his energy up and his mind alert during the crucial moments of the auction. In preparation for battle, Mike had a Foo Fighters playlist looping on the *Sonos* and had donned a cosy, seashell-patterned bathrobe.

This was Mike's first foray into an eBay auction. Up until that point, the grocer had managed to survive reasonably well without feeling the need to bid for other people's tat. But here he was, a newly registered member of the eBay community, bidding for other people's tat. When you've made a bid, Mike pondered, do you become an eBayee? And what was the collective noun for a bunch of eBayers? He imagined BBC newsreaders reporting on a 'pride of eBayers' being fined for incorrectly bidding on a limited-edition copy of *Frampton Comes Alive* in orange vinyl.

As the pride or brood or flange of early timewasters melted away, the battle for the acoustic came down to a straight fight between Mike and fellow eBayee, m**b8. The thrill of the chase was all-consuming as Mike and m**b8 traded five-pound blows across the ether. As the price increased, so did the tension. Mike ditched the bathrobe for fear of heat stroke. £195. £200. The grocer's adrenaline was in full flood – what had he been missing all this time? £220. £225. This was such a buzz, Mike decided, and briefly considered buying everything this way from now on.

Mike placed a bid of £245 at 5.15am with only a minute left on the auction clock. At which point his opponent went strangely quiet. The northerner watched the last sixty seconds tick away on screen. Done. Auction over. His bid had been enough, and he'd made short shrift of m**b8. As the eBay algorithm dispatched a congratulatory email plus the standard "pay now, or else" note, Mike shot both arms into the air. He had prevailed and announced to nobody in particular that this auction malarkey was a piece of piss: the victory, and the guitar, belonged to him. Unbeknownst to Mike, however, was the fact m**b8 had spotted a *Buy Now* advert on the site offering the same guitar – only new – for just £165 with free delivery.

The now-previous owner of Mike's guitar promptly dispatched it with an additional cost of £20 for postage and packaging. He used the locally renowned Gravesend-based courier company, *Promptish Parcels* (*Never Knowingly Over-delivered*), and it pitched up on Mike's doorstep three weeks later.

On arrival, Mike pulled open the parcel like a boy wild with Christmas anticipation and – once he'd finally managed to get the courier representative out of his daughter's bedroom – proudly stood his new trophy up against an armchair. It was indeed a handsome beast. The machine heads gleamed like rappers' teeth and its slim, dark, voluptuous neck seemed to go on forever. The curves of its beautiful body took him all the way back to school – and Mrs. Micklethwaite, the science lab technician. (At the age of thirteen, Mike found Mrs. M's method of transporting volumetric flasks by pressing them against her bosom more than a little alluring).

Mike held the guitar and squeezed it into him, forming his body around the instrument like a teenage boy spooning a mature woman for the first time.

Electricity buzzed the tips of his fingers as the wannabe guitarist ran his hand across the frets and strings. EADGBE. Six notes of perfection. Something magical would come from this union, Mike said softly. The guitar whisperer. Something true was back in his life.

Mike Grimshaw was finally in love again.

GRAEME

"Nice going, Grocer Man!" cried The Peasant's resident open mic host, Graeme Nash, with an unnerving amount of gusto.

"Oh…sure. Thanks, Graeme."

The condescending pat on the shopkeeper's back that followed was in keeping with the MC's usual appreciation of 'lesser talent' on the bill – a term that Graeme himself had used when sat with a bunch of conspiratorial school friends who'd swung by some months before. Experiencing open mic night for the first time, his old classmates had ribbed Graeme about the woefulness of some of the acts. Rather than loyally defend his line up, Graeme chose to demean their efforts further by labelling the performers as nothing more than necessary fillers. Mike happened to be in earshot of the conversation.

While Mike had little time for Graeme, he had to admit a grudging respect for anyone who could put on an amateur music night on a wet and windy Thursday night in rural Suffolk and still draw a decent crowd. Regardless of how many showed up, Graeme, with the looks and suavity of the enduring crooner, Bryan Ferry, would always work the lounge bar like a pro. He pressed scaling flesh, air-kissed farm labourers and warmly consoled anyone over sixty or the under-privileged. In return, there were only kind words for the guy who put his utmost into giving everyone a night of entertainment in the land that time forgot.

As open mic host, Graeme represented a breed of resident MC's responsible for the midweek concoction of amateur entertainment across Suffolk's music venues. Galvanized by local brews, and often swathed in the regalia of local charity outlets, the evening hosts stepped up to microphones of varying reliability to get proceedings underway. In doing so, they would unleash a maelstrom of untold pleasures and unforgettable tortures upon their audiences.

As tradition dictated, the host would open with a self-penned tune, a lament of privilege that would serve as a stimulant, fortifying the upcoming acts and helping to empty any over-anxious stomachs. The opening song – typically of love, heartache or the unearthing of root crops – would fill spaces already choking on a heady mix of nostalgia and stale *Old Spice*. The night's acts then followed. Songs wrenched from the agonised souls of basil growers, gallery owners and discount store checkout assistants would bounce off medieval beams and sherry-stained cribbage boards like Southwold pebbles skimming on the surface of a shit-brown North Sea.

"Another good turnout," said Graeme with a smugness that grated at Mike's soul.

"They're certainly out in force tonight," Mike conceded reluctantly, resisting the temptation to say what he was really thinking, that these people simply had nothing better to do. Although that would be a petty own goal because, after all, what was he doing there?

"Mike." Graeme's sincerity deepened. "Is this the real life? Is this just fantasy?"

And there it was: Graeme's adopted, self-indulgent catchphrase that he passed around like an award-winning marrow whenever a sizeable and expectant crowd turned out. What made it particularly nauseating for Mike was when those who had Graeme on a rustic pedestal felt it necessary to complete the second half of Queen's enduring enquiry. It was a sycophancy worthy of a good beating, in Mike's opinion.

If the overused, cringeworthy catchphrases weren't enough, Graeme was also a committed wearer of holiday-themed jumpers. Christmas, Easter, Passover, Pongal and Eid had all featured in his collection of knitted garments over the years. He chaired the local traffic calming committee, was a hobbying cryptologist and enjoyed local notoriety through his marriage to the very lovely – and very wealthy – Penny Nash (nee Spatula) who was both a guest chef and the weather girl on *BBC Radio Suffolk* on alternate weekdays.

The fact that Graeme was a kept man was irritation enough for Mike, but it was the host's personification of middle England that formed an abhorrence that would never grow old for a lad from deepest Lancashire.

And yet, Graeme always made sure Mike got his five minutes of fame every Thursday, inviting him up as one of the early slots on the mic – a necessary decision predicated on the fact Mike was a nervous performer. Going on any later gave the northerner a window sufficiently large enough to administer a hefty dollop of Dutch courage from the bar; a strategy that typically ended in disaster for both audience and entertainer alike. Graeme would also warmly encourage the best possible reception for Mike as he stepped up to play.

In truth, loathing Graeme's middle-class pompousness was more red herring than red socialism. It was how the man made fronting an audience look so easy that really irked Mike. While his debilitating on-stage nerves would make Mike shake like a shitting dog, Graeme could bash out tunes about divorcing sheep and ironing cabbage without so much as a twitch.

"Should've practiced tonight's songs a little more." Mike self-consciously stared at his feet.

"Nonsense!" dismissed Graeme. "You just need to find some songs that suit your voice, Mike. And your fingers. Besides, you've, what, been learning guitar for a year now?"

"Yeah. About that."

"Well then, don't beat yourself up! You're coming along nicely!"

More unsolicited niceness from mister bloody perfect, thought Mike.

"Maybe." Mike's voice sounded like the dull twang of a bottom E. "But I don't think my second song went down particularly well."

Graeme scratched through the heavy cable knit of his Eid Al-Adha-inspired sweater as he struggled to recall the song. "Remind me."

"Message in a Bottle. By The Police."

"Oh yeah," Graeme winced at the memory. "And you cunningly tried to update the song by bringing it into the digital age."

Mike shrugged his shoulders. "I thought it would add a fresh dimension people could relate to."

"But this is Suffolk." Graeme grinned and began quietly singing *Sending out an SMS* in a mocking refrain of Mike's efforts.

"Yeah." Mike sighed. "Guess I didn't think it through."

"Well," said Graeme, his eyes desperately searching the room for a reason to depart the conversation. "The good thing is you performed it with real spunk, my friend!"

The pair stared silently at a giant pair of ceramic wellington boots that stood in one corner of the pub.

"I heard Penny's forecast this afternoon in the shop," said Mike, eventually. "Amazing. I wasn't aware rain could actually do that."

"D'you know, I think I just saw Penny go out for a Marlboro." Graeme cleared his throat and headed for one of The Peasant's seven entrances.

THE WHIPPED PEASANT

The Whipped Peasant was a classic Suffolk pub nestling in the small village of Peasenhall (pronounced locally as Peas'naal).

The grade-two listed inn had stood on the same site since 1798 and famously lured First Viscount Nelson from his local, *The Pale Sailor* in Norfolk, within only its first six months of trading. The pub's reputation continued to thrive through a number of licensing trade landmarks. In 1887, it became the first licensed premises to open its doors at the earlier time of 11am, prompting the popular phrase, *no time like the peasant*; in 1905, it banned the indoor smoking of Meerschaum pipes long before any nationwide veto; and in 1976 it famously broke the world record for the longest ever 'lock-in'. (Three staff members and fifteen Peasenhall regulars kept the bar propped up for a solid three days and four hours, beating the previous record, held by *The Hog Toaster* in Leicester, by eleven minutes. Sadly, two of the regulars paid the ultimate price for this extraordinary feat and their ashes were scattered over the pub car park one week after formal ratification of the record.)

'The Peasant', as it came to be known, established an early reputation for its excellent ginger ale. It was served to the men folk in wonderfully ornate tureens with jewel-encrusted handles, while women had to forego its delights due to a local by-law. The pub's hospitality was equally well regarded, and the business hadn't been going three years before the property required extending to cover increasing demand for accommodation by wandering stonemasons in the area. A further extension was necessary in 1865 following the General Election victory by Lord Palmerston's Liberal Party, and again in 1972 when the building was clearly suffering from a lack of charm.

As The Peasant's standing flourished, so did its list of salacious patrons.

When not stealing horses in Lincolnshire, the notorious highwayman, Dick Turpin, regularly enjoyed a warm glass of merlot at the inn while the double agent, Kim Philby, was rumoured to have regular clandestine meetings there with his future wife, Rufina Ivanovna Pukhova, before his defection to the Soviet Union. Ex-Prime Minister, John Major, would also pop in for the odd slice of tart on occasion.

In 1983, The Whipped Peasant gained what was probably its greatest accolade when the pub's famous sloping facade was featured on the front cover of *The Lady* magazine.

The inn's interior reflected many similar establishments of its age. Long, low-running beams supported sagging ceilings; powdery walls now yellow with time were festooned with an ensemble of horse brasses and other farm ephemera; and a crotchety flagstone floor ebbed and flowed like a blustery spring tide. A robust, L-shaped bar fed off from the kitchen on the west side of the building – its oak veneer variegated from years of blackening ales on the bottom of tall glasses – and the pub's footprint was neatly divided into separate drinking and dining areas.

Outside, the inn boasted a small beer garden to the rear with a smattering of wooden picnic benches that injected fine splinters into those who braved a seat. A similarly sized patio to the front of the property dropped down onto the village's main thoroughfare. In the warmer months, a mix of hanging baskets and flower bed troughs added a touch of colour to the front while a well-appointed fire pit in the garden would raise spirits in the winter.

The pub's sign had creaked merrily below the first-floor toilet window for over a century and was a local curiosity. It featured a local landowner with a length of birch gripped tightly in his hand bearing down on a farmhand. The landowner's expression was of contorted rage and he was clearly intent on giving his employee a damn good thrashing. The serf lay prostrate at his lord's feet and had the fear of a Chihuahua on heat etched across his face. The scene had been skilfully produced by a local artist cooperative, and its unveiling at the time was greeted with raucous applause from the assembled bigots and village oppressors. Indeed, so raw were the emotions depicted, that it produced the most terrible nightmares in schoolchildren waiting at the village bus stop opposite.

There was something of a hue and cry over the sign several years back. The

Suffolk branch of the *Rambler's Association* was enjoying lunch at the inn after a morning's perambulation and had taken offence at the sign, demanding its immediate removal. With the request flatly refused by the incumbent landlord, the ramblers took their cause to the likes of *Amnesty International, Friends Reunited* and *Knit for Suffolk*, with which they were well connected.

One of the walking party also happened to be father to the editor of the *East Anglian Daily Times*, and the group's demands produced a smattering of unfortunate headlines in the local press: *Un-Peas-C in Peasenhall, Are You Being Serfed?* and so on. The whole shebang proved a storm in a teacup, however. As soon as then Tory MP, Terry Toffee, asked his constituents how else they were supposed to keep the immigrant rural workforce in check, any outrage behind the issue quickly and quietly evaporated.

Besides the legendary pub sign, it was the somewhat unexpected plethora of entrances to the premises that also piqued patrons' interest on their initial visit; the result of a long-running cock-up by Suffolk County Council staff in the mid-80's.

The landlord at the time, Sven Eriksson, applied for an all-day licence extension for the upcoming *Live Aid* concert, which he planned to show on a number of televisions. A local planning manager came out accordingly and confirmed that the council would only approve said licence if Sven added an extra doorway to the property. Public access was, in his opinion: "clearly restricted and unsuitable for such a major event." Sven hastily pointed out that he was only showing the concert on telly and not proposing to host the historic, trans-global music event in a tiny, rural boozer. The council representative was having none of it, however, and mandated Sven to add the extra doorway.

Having duly complied with the council's wishes, Sven had still received no word of his licence extension a full week after the installation of the new northeast doorway. A further call to the offices prompted the arrival of a second planning manager.

"It says here you need to add another doorway," said the equally inept council officer whilst pointing to a yellow, carbon-copy sheet on an oversized clipboard. Sven's protestations regarding his obvious compliance failed to register with the council man and, subsequently, the landlord was forced to install the south-by-south-west door. This act of gross mismanagement by Suffolk Council was to occur on three more occasions prior to Mr. Geldof's charitable extravaganza, and resulted in a total of seven ways to leave or enter the small village pub.

In all, six punters turned up to watch *Live Aid* on the day. To add further insult to injury, the property required significant and costly under-pinning soon after the event as its lower walls had effectively turned into fresh air.

But it was *moosic* that was the spiritual heart of The Peasant.

Over the centuries, the inn played host to an eclectic mix of instrumental and lyrical performers. The Peasant's standing as one of the nation's finest impromptu venues for budding artists became legendary. From The Great Orlando's much lauded set on harpsichord in the autumn of 1822 to David Jones' first road test of *Starman* in the spring of '65 – a song he originally penned about working the fields of Suffolk.

There's a farm...hand... waiting in the sty!

In fact, any musician who hadn't gigged at The Peasant on the road to notoriety would have their credibility open to the utmost scrutiny back in the day. A performance at this rural inn was a rite of passage for songwriters and no CV was complete without it. For the attending collection of largely impoverished locals, the words they sang, and the tunes they played, were indeed the riches of the poor.

HECTOR & CHLOE

Mike leaned on the bar with an oily five pound note clenched in his fist – change from the eighty pounds he'd given to the *Kwik-Fit* mechanic who'd replaced the flat battery on his ailing *Vauxhall Corsa* earlier that morning.

"Getcha motor running?" asked Hector Bramwell, The Peasant's landlord.

"Yeah, finally," sighed Mike. "Bloody money pit. Battery cost more than the car's worth."

"Well if it's any consolation, Mikey, I thought your set tonight was a huge improvement on last week." Hector ushered across his daughter and chief barmaid, Chloe, so she could serve him.

"Thanks, Hector," said Mike. "Pint of *Incontinent Badger*, please, Chloe."

Chloe smiled and began pouring a glass of Guinness. "I thought you were great too, Mike," Chloe offered as she set about trying to draw a pig's face in the magnolia-coloured froth.

"I think that's supposed to be a shamrock, Chloe," said Mike as the young bar hand finished the snout nostrils with a poorly lacquered fingernail.

"Good turn out tonight." Hector ambled along behind the bar, grabbed a bag of salt and vinegar *Hula Hoops* and put them next to Mike's pint. "On the house," he said.

Mike smiled his thanks, always comfortable in the company of his favourite pub landlord.

Hector had been in the pub trade most of his working life, but it had been at some personal cost. He'd been bankrupt twice and had lost three wives to cirrhosis, kidney failure and Lyme disease respectively. The years hadn't been kind to the licensee, and Hector had gradually fostered the appearance of a classic landlord: florid, rotund, bald, knock-kneed and with a keen eye for reclaimed wood. The Peasant was his fourth establishment to date, having cut his teeth on *The Shaved Goat* in St. Albans, honed his craft at *The Awkward Samaritan* in Braintree and developed mild Crohn's disease at *The Stabbed Officer* in Colchester.

It was a career that hadn't gone unnoticed. The publican had been nominated for Landlord of the Year by CAMRA eight times between 1982 and 1992 but missed out on each occasion. A final nomination in 1994 saw him capture this most cherished of awards. Sadly, Hector was unable to be on stage to receive his gong from the Duchess of Gloucester due to an urgent need to evacuate his bowels when his victory was announced.

Hector took over management of The Peasant in 2004 when the previous owners had fallen foul of new legislation on canine hygiene. Roger and Rosemary D'Orange ran a tight ship when they owned the place, and their reputation was built on a thrifty approach. Water was added to the Gordon's, all the lights would go off at ten and their dog, Bogus, would lick clean every soiled plate retrieved from the restaurant diners at the end of their meals. It was this final act of margin enhancement that finally did for ol' Rog and Rose, and it resulted in their incarceration in Hollesley Bay Prison for the remainder of their natural lives.

Although Hector was eyed suspiciously by the Peasenhall community at first, they soon warmed to this seasoned publican and his charming yet decidedly curious daughter.

"What are you doing, love?" Hector spotted Chloe carefully rearranging all the spirit bottles lined up on the back of the bar.

"Oh," she replied, her face arrowed in furious concentration. "I read a section in *Bar Management for Dummies* that said if you sort drinks into alphabetical order, it helps customers choose what they want to drink more easily."

"Does it?" Hector's astonished look matched that of Mike's. "Well I never!"

"May have dreamt it though," suggested Chloe as she moved the whisky to the left of the vodka.

"Okay, darling." Hector shrugged.

"Er, I think the vodka probably comes before the whisky, Chloe," Mike offered. "If you want your system to be right."

Chloe, with her back to the pair, suddenly brought her reshuffle to a halt and sighed audibly. "Don't be silly, Mikey!" she snapped.

At 28, Chloe knew nothing outside of pub life. Slim and sleepy-eyed, with tightly permed, brunette locks that resolutely stayed put regardless of the strength of the prevailing wind, Chloe resembled a bad-hair day for Petula Clark. With thin, gelatinous arms that only shifted from her sides when absolutely necessary, Chloe was a 'catch' in as much as hooking a crab off Bawdsey Quay was a catch.

Questioned by a local about his daughter's general lack of appeal, Hector was rumoured to have replied, "S'fair to say she ain't pretty. She got her mother's looks."

"Loike a magnet oi'd say," chanced the local. "Attractive from the rear… repulsive at the front."

It was a chance that got the local a fat lip and permanent removal from the premises.

Chloe only ever had one boyfriend, Trevor Gibb, the son of a pigman. The relationship was strewn with problems and deep-seated emotional issues and didn't last the length of the school biology field trip they were on together. Ever the optimist, Chloe maintained their break up was 'a good thing' because she could focus on her GCSE's which were imminent. She promptly went on to fail all three.

While arguably not the sharpest pencil in the pot, the absence of any reasonable intelligence would not keep Chloe from her dreams. She was nothing if not tenacious. She wholly devoted herself to her dad, her role behind the bar and the overriding ambition to the get the proportions of a vodka and tonic the right way around at some point in her career.

Chloe was Hector's eldest daughter, whom he'd had with his first wife. Two other children from the landlord's second marriage, Barry and Pretzel, had immigrated to Azerbaijan after the death of their mother and the donation of her kidneys to the local butchers. (Donor cards work a little differently in Suffolk.) The pair made the effort to keep in touch from their newly adopted home as often as possible, with postcards of local landmarks and cheese-based recipe cards. Hector visited them in Baku after the pair had been out there a year but was forced to leave the country almost immediately due to an intense dislike of the Azerbaijani national dish, *bozbash*. His rejection of the mildly herbed lamb soup caused an unexpected rift between him and his younger children, and the frequency of park pictures and dairy recipes quickly faded away.

Chloe, on the other hand, was Hector's rock and the pair worked tirelessly to keep the traditions of The Peasant going, and to provide the good people of Peasenhall with a pub they could be proud of.

"Bit disappointed I only got to play two songs." Mike wiped a Guinness moustache off Chloe's upper lip and asked her to stop drinking his pint.

"I think Graeme's running a little short on time tonight, Mike." Hector's remark was a weak deflection, well aware the plug had been pulled on Mike before he could subject the crowd to a third song.

"Maybe," said Mike, watching Chloe intently as she made a glove out of his *Hula Hoops* for her left hand. "But even Jules got to play three and she was moaning about her fingers being too sore and swollen for banjo."

"She pulled the Bonham's quads out last night, didn't she?" Carl Fleming, owner of the village ironmongers and editor of *The Peasenhall Quandary*, had pitched up at the bar all thirsty and caught the gist of the conversation. "Pint of *Runt* please, Chloe."

"Yeah. Packed in real tight apparently." Mike drained his glass.

"Dad's got a quad. Haven't you, dad?" remarked Chloe in between long licks of her new salt and vinegar finger protectors.

"Maybe she should have had a break from playing tonight," said Hector, ignoring Chloe's remark. "Or just sung instead. Hey, she coulda done a duet with you, Mikey!"

"Yeah, right," Carl scoffed. "Let's all go to the land of obscurity, shall we?"

"Ouch!" Hector pointed an admonishing finger at the purveyor of alarmingly priced hinges and brackets. "You don't sing obscure shit, do you, Mikey?"

Mike shrugged. He was tempted to remind the pair that *Message in a Bottle* had been a number one in the UK, Ireland and possibly Spain, but he didn't rise to the bait. Instead, he scanned the pub for the subject of their discussion. He clocked Jules sat at a table with Shelley Parkinson, who was silently watching the midwife remove fluff from her navel.

"You know what she's like," Mike said after a deep, reflective sigh. "Once she's all fired up, she's desperate to get up there and play."

"Look at her though," said Carl. "The village's latest additions have all but done her in!"

"Well, to be fair," Hector said as he snapped up a wine glass from the bar top dishwasher and began a furious polish. "I hear Mrs. Bonham stayed in the non-recumbent birthing position the whole time and refused to budge. That's a bastard if you're trying to get four out. You ask ol' Trevor Gibb. He tried it with his pigs last year. Said it was a nightmare. You just ask Trevor. Or his son...Trevor."

"I miss Trevor *sooo* much!" The unexpected mention of her ex saddened Chloe to the extent she put her hands on top of her head and pouted like a four-year-old.

"No, you don't, darling," her father said flatly. "That was thirteen years ago."

Mike got a fresh pint of *Arrogant Walrus* (the *Incontinent Badger* barrel needed changing) and went back across the bar to watch the last act of the night. He sat down next to Jules as Alan Hedgeworthy smashed his hands down onto the keys of his Hammond organ and propelled himself into a cover of Olivia Newton-John's *Xanadu*.

"Good set tonight, Jules," Mike said raising his glass to his fellow contributor.

"Cheers, Mike. You too," said Jules, and she offered him a small blue ball of stomach lint from her large, painful-looking sausage fingers.

MIKE

For many rural communities, a local shop is its lifeline. While the produce it stocks is an essential convenience, the shop itself goes beyond all practical facets by serving as a hub for a united bonhomie. From the first step across its threshold, to the genial welcome from its owner, there is an entrenched assurance that the local store will be happy to help and nothing is too much trouble. Whether Napoleon uttered it or not, Britain is way more than a nation of shopkeepers; it is a collective of therapists, care workers, philosophers and general do-gooders. But on certain days, the country's shopkeepers just wished the general public would just be the fuck away from their premises.

"It was an intriguing conundrum, I can tell you."

"Eh?" the shopkeeper looked wearily at Doctor O'Flanagan, his head heavy with the previous evening's indulgences.

"The tapeworm," the village doctor explained.

"Think my cerebral cortex is melting," said Mike, squinting in the flood of fluorescent lighting.

"It had been in the poor girl for going on two weeks." O'Flanagan carried on regardless. "The bugger was deep-rooted."

"That's fascinating," said the un-fascinated and deeply hungover grocer.

"Of course, I didn't have access to the range of medicines I've got these days, so it called for some creative thinking on my part."

"Really? What d'you do?" Mike asked through an uncovered yawn.

"I starved her!"

"What?" Mike winced, his headache agitating him further.

"Oh, only for forty-eight hours," explained O'Flanagan. "She wasn't a terrorist."

"Oh, good."

O'Flanagan explained how straightforward the process had been. How he'd kept the girl off solids for two days, knowing that the slightest whiff of food was going to have her salivating like one of Pavlov's dog. He placed a plate of mince and onions in front of her, she drooled like a pro, and his 'little friend' popped its head up at the back of the girl's throat. He then simply placed a thermometer into the back of her mouth, which the critter happily latched onto, and reeled it in like linguine on a fork.

"Goodness." Mike was impressed. "How long was it?"

"About fifteen feet."

"Oh, I think I'm going to be ill." Mike threw a disparaging glance at the aging GP – who happened to be a doppelganger for Tom Baker, another doctor. For a moment, Mike considered whether the old boy was actually still fit to be running a practice.

O'Flanagan cast an accusatory finger at the store owner. "You know, Michael, you should drink less," he blurted out. "You'd be a lot more affable to your clientele if you didn't spend all night in that pub over the road. Lord knows what it's doing to your insides."

Can't be as bad as having a giant parasitic worm in you, thought Mike, retching slightly.

"D'you know we used to use over seven and a half billion carrier bags in this country before we started charging for them?"

"Don't try and change the subject."

"But, doctor, I only go out now and then…and mainly for the music." The grocer's embarrassment put him on the defensive.

"Uh-huh?" The GP's voice was rich in sarcasm. "Well don't be coming to me when your liver decides to give up the ghost!" He grabbed his wallet out from his coat pocket and pulled two twenties out. "Now, I'll take a bottle of Jameson's off you and be on my way."

"What?" squeaked Mike, humiliation swiftly switching to bewilderment at his doctor's double standards.

"C'mon! I haven't got all day!"

The shopkeeper reached up and removed a bottle from the top shelf of his spirits section. He dropped it into one of the aforementioned carrier bags and exchanged it for the quack's forty pounds.

"To be honest," said Mike in an attempt to placate the man who'd prescribed some excellent cream for his fungal nail infection only the week before. "I have to charge way more than the supermarkets for booze. You'd be much better off buying that from Tesco's."

"Michael, when I want your advice, I'll be sure I give it to you!" O'Flanagan grabbed his whiskey, bid Mike a pleasant day and departed.

Peasenhall's local shopkeeper, Mike Grimshaw, was somewhere in the middle of a fairly spectacular mid-life crisis.

Born and raised in Darwen, Lancashire, where reasonable property still cost less than a fish supper for two, Mike moved to the south 'on the first available train' as he would often tell folk. He was seventeen at the time and despite his mother's protestations, he didn't take his younger brother with him. School had held no magic for Mike and surprised no one by only managing two O-level passes: Home Economics and German. Disillusioned by teachers constantly haranguing him about his lack of application – and that he was capable of so much more than a perfect Apfelstrudel, Mike dropped out of sixth-form college before he'd finished a term. Aware that he was a little different from most lads his age, Mike sought a life away from Darwen and its brooding Pennine moors. He'd had his fill of flash floods, Hetty Wainthropp's continuing investigations, Crown's non-drip emulsions and Samuel Crompton's spinning fucking mule.

News of his intentions to leave the family home sparked a wicked reaction from his father, earning Mike bruises bigger than dinner plates. Alfred Grimshaw, a prominent Anglican and needle-pointer in the area, considered his son's decision a huge betrayal. The family business, *Moor Crochet Vicar?* was to be Mike's inheritance, but the boy clearly wanted no part of it. Mike's mother – an unremarkable woman whose singular enjoyment in life was creating stick figures from pipe cleaners – urged her husband to appreciate their eldest's desire to make his own way in the world.

It took a while, but Alfred eventually came round after talking more rationally with his son, and completing a series of floral pillow designs for the local Women's Institute. Despite his deep-seated reservations, Alfred also ended up pulling a few strings to secure some part-time work for his son in a Northampton shoe factory prior to his departure.

With ninety pounds of his mum's savings tucked into the back pocket of his beige stretch *Farahs*, and a full book of Green Shield stamps, Mike kissed his parents goodbye, flicked V's at his brother and set off down south. As the family waved furiously from the platform, they had no idea Mike had boarded the wrong train and it sailed straight through the famous town of cobblers. Drawing into the bright lights of Watford Junction instead, Mike took the decision to hop off and soon landed himself a job working as a waitress in a cocktail bar.

Le Petit Champignon was situated close to the station, and it served happy hour drinks to those returning from The City after a hard day's bonus counting. For a first job, it wasn't too bad. It taught Mike the rudiments of good customer service, it paid him a reasonable hourly rate and, most pleasingly, afforded the young northerner an opportunity to dabble in his occasional desire to cross-dress.

Mike's proclivity for women's clothes had never been an issue with the older generation in Darwen – the town's male mill workers had always taken advantage of cheap clothing on sale in their factory shops, which was almost exclusively female. But times were changing and the Darwen youth tended to give Mike a hard time when he waited at bus stops or queued for bread. However, given the free-spirited attitudes of the south he'd heard so much about, Mike felt assured his alternative wardrobe wouldn't be as big an issue as it was at home.

The thing Mike didn't foresee, however, was how pernickety the bar's clientele could be. They would taunt their waiter about how his rear zip was askew or that the pleats in his skirt had clearly been ironed on the wool setting. Unable to deal with this sudden attention to detail, Mike tossed his pinny at the bar owner and walked away from his 'perfect job' after only nine months' service.

With his waitressing career in tatters, Mike's future became defined by his inability to do two things. The first was holding down a job as a succession of disagreeable career choices followed the relative joy of *Le Petit Champignon*. Perhaps the most notable of these was his time with the *Destructor Debt Collection Agency*, where he was subjected to an intense six-week training course on doorstep harassment, only to leave after three days of making hostile visits to the homes of widowers. The second was keeping his marriage together.

Mike had just left *Destructor* and secured a job at Radlett Post Office when he and Cecilia first met. Cecilia was still living with her parents at the time and she had a steady job working as a PA for a man known simply to the police as Heath Hatchett. The couple were only six months into their relationship when their world was suddenly turned upside down. Mike got promoted at the Post Office – he was now in charge of posting out *all* the first day covers – and Cecilia got up the duff.

Their daughter, Holly, was due in May but as Hatchett refused to pay for any maternity leave, Cecilia had no choice but to take annual leave to give birth. (Mercifully, one of the days was a Bank Holiday, so she didn't have to sacrifice her entire allocation.) Things settled down when the family found a small, affordable flat in Rickmansworth. Everything was ticking over nicely until Major Sir James St. John Stevens made a formal complaint to the Postmaster General. It concerned the 'tranny' in the local branch sending his boy newly issued stamps.

"Have you lost your moral compass, Sir, allowing these poofters to influence vulnerable boys via the medium of postal communications?" the Major's letter had stated.

As Holly grew, so did the list of Mike's failures at keeping a job. If it wasn't his 'incomprehensible' Lancashire accent, then it would be an ill-judged combination of blouse and skirt. After the Post Office dispensed with his services, Mike had spells of employment of varying length with several companies, including a mushroom farm in Bushey, a pet crematorium in Ware and an outdoor karting track in overalls. Mike's CV started to look like it had been torn straight from the *Yellow Pages*.

As the rejections grew, so did Cecilia's realisation that she may have picked a wrong 'un. While Mike's career floundered, hers flourished as *Hatchett Enterprises* began overseas expansion in the Belgian Congo, and she began to oversee the company's import and export operations. The job was going well, Holly was now into secondary school and far more independent, but her husband was stuck in a rut. His inability to hang on to continuous employment prevented them moving to a nicer, bigger flat, or even owning their own home. For Cecilia, the main breadwinner, life at home was dour, drab and painfully unfulfilling.

"I want choice cuts, not offal!" was how she unwittingly verbalised her dreams to the future retailer. And sure enough, she took a man who matched her ambitions, and she took her leave of Mike Grimshaw.

Following the end of his fourteen-year marriage to Cecilia, Mike decided to remove himself from London's commuter belt entirely by answering the call from Peasenhall and the opportunity to run its curious village shop. First impressions of the coma-induced community didn't sit well with its newest resident, however, and Mike was unsure how long he might stay.

That was six years ago. Six years of selling withering local produce to withering local people. It would have tested the patience of Job, but for reasons only known to the cross-dressing northerner, Mike had stayed.

APE

"Morning!" The doorbell clanged and the ever-chirpy Janice Muffler negotiated her twin buggy into the shop.

"Morning, Janice," replied Mike, his head still a little foggy from too much *Badger*.

"Oi 'eard yer rocked da house last noight!" Janice smiled and placed four packets of *Paxo* stuffing into a wire hand basket.

"Really?" Mike was genuinely surprised. "Who told you that?"

"Jules," said Janice with a knowing wink. She grabbed a handful of *Jus-Rol* pastry.

Mike had more than a passing resemblance for Michael Bublé (albeit a little taller and with closer ear/skull adjacencies). It was a likeness that made the grocer very easy on the eye, and it hadn't gone unnoticed by the small number of Peasenhall mothers. Many, however, were disappointed that, given his musical bent, he didn't have the voice to match.

"You making stuffing pie again, Janice?"

"Hey! Don't go changen the subject!" Janice swung the buggy sharply back round towards the counter, promptly dismantling a floor display of *Maltesers* in her wake and ejecting Clive, her youngest twin boy by nine minutes, out of his seat and onto the fading linoleum. "Yer know she 'as a soft spot for yer."

Mike considered the prospect for a moment while Janice told Clive that, since he was on his feet, he could offer to be 'mummy's little helper' and tidy up the mess he'd just made.

"You think so?" said Mike modestly.

"Uh-huh."

Mike pondered the notion and shook his head. "But it's still too soon for me, Janice."

Mike's divorce had hit him like an express train (an expression that Suffolk folk could never quite get their heads around). His ex-wife, Cecilia, had eventually left Mike for the Baboon Consultant at Whipsnade Zoo, someone she had reconnected with on Facebook after several years of being out of touch.

It was a situation borne of huge irony given that Mike and Cecilia had met after a screening of *Planet of the Apes* at the Odeon cinema in St. Albans. Both had taken the advertisement's advice to visit the Viceroy Tandoori Restaurant ('just around the corner from this theatre') where, due to the sheer weight of other filmgoers seduced by the provocative messaging, they were forced to share a table. As the pair argued over the power of Charlton Heston's portrayal of supreme astronaut, George Taylor, versus the gravitas Roddy McDowell brought to the role of monkey archaeologist, Cornelius, it became clear they would spend the rest of their lives together.

That was, of course, if they'd only managed to live another fifteen years.

Mike's suspicions of misadventure were first aroused when he spotted a number of old tyres covered in fragments of grass and antelope skin in the back of Cecilia's Land Rover. Cecilia initially refuted any suggestion she was seeing someone behind Mike's back; a stringent denial made easier by the fact Mike had assumed she was actually having an affair with a baboon. It wasn't long, however, before Mike discovered a baseball cap in the car's rear foot well that had the word 'BABOONOLOGIST' in gold type across the front. Confronted with this new evidence, Cecilia crumbled and confessed to intimate liaisons with her primate-obsessed lover.

Despite her tearful affirmation, Cecilia was certainly not about to relinquish a man who earned good money and was hung like the beasts he cared for. Mike tried to toss the adulteress out of the house, but Cecilia candidly reminded him she'd paid the mortgage pretty much single-handedly for the best part of a decade and was going nowhere.

Mike had no choice but to walk away, leaving Cecilia and his daughter, Holly, to continue family life without him.

That was six years ago. Six years starved of love. In all that time, Mike had been propositioned just twice; once by a cougar from Ipswich and the second time by a pig from Newmarket. The cougar had come on to Mike while he was shopping for underwear in *Next*. The fact the woman was dressed as an extra from one of Pitbull's music videos, made the offer of an afternoon of sex round at her place an easy one to agree to. It was, however, on the proviso Mike was gone by four because her husband was due back from the allotment then.

Needless to say, Mike's experience of marriage, and his painfully shy demeanour, meant that any effort on his part to pursue a new love was virtually out of the question.

"Come on, Mike," said Janice, re-aligning the tower of *Maltesers* boxes fractionally while throwing a thunderous look at her two-year-old. "Yer bin on yer own far too long. It's toime to get back in the game."

Mike shook his head. "I dunno, Janice."

"And it's the loneliness that's the killer, roight?"

"Maybe, but I'm not sure how Holly would react to me having another woman in my life. She's still too sensitive, too young to deal with something like that."

"She's twenty, Mike." Janice handed over an oily ten pound note from her purse.

"You been to *Kwik-Fit* recently?" enquired Mike.

"Yarp!" said Janice, putting her change in her coat pocket. "Now yer think about what oi just said, okay? Resign yourself to this lovely village and the great people in it, once and for all!" She smiled encouragingly at Mike and exited the shop as chirpily as she arrived.

She was back half an hour later to pick up Clive.

PEASENHALL

The village of Peasenhall dates way back to before decimalisation.

Details of the village's true origins were thought to have been lost following a minor clerical error in the snow of '46. However, an unsubstantiated entry regarding the original settlement was posted onto Wikipedia a decade ago, and due to the hopeless broadband signal available to locals who might have been in a position to question the entry, it remained unchallenged.

The post claimed the village was formed at the turn of the 17th century by a travelling amateur dramatic society. The members of the society had stopped at the site to re-enact some of Shakespeare's plays that were still a work in progress: *The Urging of the Goat, Richard IX, The Light Breeze* and so on. A later addendum to the Wiki-entry even suggested The Bard himself attended a number of performances but this was hastily redacted when the Chairman of Peasenhall Lawn Tennis Club, Terry Toffee MP, confirmed the playwright was in London buying a new ruff at the time.

Given they were rather taken with the spot, the ensemble decided to dwell awhile. Within eighteen months, the filthy thespians had established a crop of small dwellings, a bingo hall, a set of stocks for public floggings and the Church of the Poison Mind. A watermill was also erected on the elegant banks of the River Yox, where minors carried out the painstaking production of bagels and scones.

Steeped in infamy, Peasenhall's most notable addition to the history books was the notorious murder of Rose Harsent, a local servant girl who was stabbed to death when she was 'with child'. Detectives initially thought Rose had taken her own life, but as the only weapon available to her was a recently harvested onion, the notion was soon dismissed as nonsense.

After several minutes of investigation, suspicion fell on the village's sole immigrant, a Chinese campanologist called Tony Yip. Tony was on a sponsored bell-ringing marathon in Asbhy-de-la-Zouch when the murderous act occurred and his alibi was, therefore, irrefutable (but he was still lashed to a milk yoke and stoned away from the village).

The rather arthritic finger of misgiving soon pointed towards Peasenhall's Methodist Preacher, William Gardiner, who was arrested and ended up standing trial twice for the girl's murder. Most local nosey fuckers were well aware of Gardiner's liaisons with Rose and it seemed likely the girl's unborn child was his. However, two trial juries could not return a majority verdict and the Preacher walked free. The judge who presided over the trials was so furious with their inability to come to a unanimous decision that he had each juror flogged with pigs' entrails.

Further examination of the case in later years suggested Gardiner's insanely jealous wife was more likely to have been the true assailant; either her or the family horse, Sugar.

This sudden notoriety made Peasenhall *the* place to move to and set up a small firm of inept solicitors. Subsequently, the number of village residents rocketed to over 400 by the late 1900's. This explosion in population size was augmented by the Saxmundham Tandoori's decision to extend its moped delivery radius by four miles for orders over £17 (not including pickles or raita). There was literally no room on the pavement as the village began to fill with prams, space hoppers and other working-class amenities.

In spite of this exponential growth however, the village didn't physically appear on Ordinance Survey maps until 1991. The reason, as historians continue to laboriously point out, was because its residents steadfastly believed cartography to be the work of Lucifer.

The turn of the millennium proved a prosperous time for Peasenhall. Accolades for its upkeep and floral displays came rolling in, and it secured the much-lauded title of 'most attractive village with working gallows and a Blockbuster' in 2001.

Suddenly on the map, the village began to attract scousers and other tourists from countries outside of the G20. The locals responded magnificently and revived many traditional crafts that were considered lost to earlier generations. The making of cement purses and lamb grooming had been skills deemed essential to the village's economy, and their reintroduction was a hoot. This surge of interest in the community also prompted outside investment which led to the construction of Peasenhall's stunning fountain. It provided a spot where visitors could meditate, find peace and sell their young to passing stationery reps.

In spite of gathering interest around the village, royalty saw fit to grace the fair streets of Peasenhall only once; an event precipitated by an electrical transgression rather than any monarchical desire to visit the underclass.

Princess Michael of Kent was broken down on the A12 near to neighbouring Yoxford, the alternator of her Austin Allegro having packed up. The young princess was duly pointed in the direction of Peasenhall, and the county's only Norwegian motor spares shop: *Halffords*. After a three-mile walk, the 127th in line to the throne found the shop shut, it being a Wednesday and, therefore, half-day closing. It took several minutes of beating on the shop window and howling like a banshee before the Nordstraum family finally heard the princess' cries over their lunchtime preparations, and descended from the upstairs accommodation to let her in.

Local passer-by, Barry Noblett, maintained he overheard the conversation between the princess and the immigrant shopkeeper, and reported the intercourse to the *Peasenhall Quandary*, which ran the story under the glorious headline: *The Princess and the Part*.

"I'm a-sorry but vee are closed," said Mr. Nordstraum.

"But all one needs is a new alternator for one's Allegro. You see, one's broken down and one appears to be in an awful fix." Princess MOK pointed vaguely in the direction of the county's main arterial trunk road.

"But vee vere just about to eat 'erring," whined Mr. Nordstraum.

"I'm so frightfully sorry for the inconvenience," said the princess. "One wouldn't normally be so desperate, but the guys are all expecting one to be at Sandringham at six for gin."

The parts man eventually relented, instructed his wife to turn down the fish and reached for his vehicular spares' manual. "Year?" he asked, rather indignantly.

"1968."

"No, I'm out of stock, I'm a-sorry," said the Norwegian after a quick check in the vast array of steel drawers in the shop's rear storeroom.

"Does one have one for a Morris Marina…or an Austin Maxi, perhaps?" said the princess with a piqued urgency in her voice. "They're all 43-amp models. One's sure one'll be able to squeeze it past the sub-frame, even if the size is a tad off."

Nordstraum huffed and puffed in a way only Scandinavians seem to know how, but finally agreed to check the dimly lit stock room a second time. "You're in a-luck!" the parts man cried as he came back into the shop triumphantly holding the new part high in the air.

Princess Michael of Kent wrote a cheque out for £22.75, placed the new alternator into a Harrods bag she produced from her duffle coat pocket, and asked if the parts man would kindly drop her back to her car.

"My wife is about to serve Daim bar. I'm a-sorry," replied Norwegian.

"Oh," said the bejewelled royal. "One could have sworn it was the Swedish who enjoyed the delicate caramel and chocolate combination, no?"

And that was Peasenhall's one and only brush with the nation's monarchy.

One sad footnote to the episode was that the family of Norwegian car part specialists departed the village soon after the princess' visit under a cloud. Their eldest son was arrested and deported for poaching bream from the Yox. Back in the day, any fish taken from that particular river had to be grilled or steamed. The *Halfjords* name was in tatters, so the shop was taken over by a couple of barristers, who converted it into a beauty parlour called *The Face is Altered*. An abattoir soon followed when the salon failed, only to return twelve years later with additional tanning facilities and a contemporary nail bar.

The premises were finally turned into the general village stores following the terrifying 'UV lamp' incident and Peasenhall finally had a place to purchase peas and all. The original shopkeeper was the daughter of a zealous crop farmer named Maddocks, a man who simply refused to grow anything that couldn't be cooked in lard. However, a life away from ploughing filth – to sell tinned mince to anxious dog-owners – was a life more ordinary for his young daughter and she soon vacated the position to return to the farm; a position that was filled thereafter by one, Mike Grimshaw.

JEFF & SHIRLEY

Jeff Timberlake bolted the doors of *The Startled Goose* a good half hour early.

"Another crazy night!" came the ironic quip from his wife, Shirley, as she pulled the cover over the reptile tank.

"This is ridiculous!" Jeff dragged their conjoined Labradors, Spanner & Cloak, away from their cosy domination of the open coal fire. "Why aren't we pulling in more customers?"

Shirley rung open the till and sighed at the absence of any paper money. "Another evening doomed to utter predictably. What did we manage to sell tonight?"

"Two pints of lager, half a cider, a diet Coke and two bags of dry roasted." The co-landlord of 'The Goose' finished wiping down the bar and walked over to the pub's 'sports area' to wake up his chef.

"You can get off now, Damien," said Jeff as he shook the WKD-saturated cook awake and put the lid on a compendium of games.

"He drinks more in one night than we make in a week," Shirley sniped under her breath.

"But oi'm the best in the county at reheaten veg lasagne!" said the roused idiot. Damien Cartwright sat up in his chair and wiped sweet, neon-blue-coloured saliva off his chin and onto the black t-shirt he was wearing. A large McDonald's logo with the words 'Oi'm Loven It' was emblazoned across the top. The tee was part of Damien's uniform when he had been an intern at the fast food chain's Ipswich store. He lasted just three days. It wasn't the fact he'd crashed out in the ladies' toilet twice that got him the sack, or that he'd managed to scrape tiny shards of metal from the grill top and into half a dozen

Big Macs. It was the pocketing of the cash float from his till station that earned him his marching orders.

"Go home, Chef!"

"Oi'm gorn, coppa!" said Damien, taking Suffolk's glottal stop to new heights.

The owner of an NVQ in Sauce Stirring got up groggily and departed with Shirley's eyes burning holes into the back of his *Hello Kitty* rucksack: he'd hit a nerve.

Jeff and Shirley Timberlake had left Suffolk Traffic Police after fifty years' service between them so they could toss-away their pension trying to turnaround Peasenhall's second public house. It was a decision that had been met with derision by many locals. Such was the fury at their arrival that Carl Fleming was compelled to note in his editorial column in the *Peasenhall Quandary*, that: "having two members of the filth run The Goose was akin to allowing your children visitation rights from a select band of retired Radio One DJ's."

The issue was a simple one. The Timberlake's had been two very effective coppers and, across the years, had systematically ticketed and fined most of the drivers in the area. The fact this couple now wanted to take more cash off the locals through the sale of beer and nuts did not sit well with the village's aggrieved motorists. These same motorists, however, quickly realised the Timberlake's decision to take over The Goose was an opportunity for payback.

Many took the eminently sensible route of simply boycotting the premises and its new owners, but some, including John Bowcroft, Peasenhall's former library van driver, had other ideas.

Latterly, John had been stopped twice by the Timberlake's. He received points on his license, plus a sizeable fine, for driving without securing the van doors properly – an oversight that left a local vicar physically assaulted by both Jeffrey Archer and Sidney Sheldon – and being in charge of a public vehicle with defective hearing. The council 'retired' the old boy after the second incident – unfairly in his opinion – so serving up a cold dish of revenge was the least he could do to welcome the new couple.

Despite his aging years, the octogenarian chose to target the temporary sign positioned high up on the front face of The Goose announcing the establishment was 'Under New Management'. Under the cover of dark, his face masked with an oversized balaclava and carrying his Uncle Ray's stepladders, John scaled the building and set about defacing the sign in a way that would spell out the feelings of the community loud and clear. Employing several bottles of *Tippex*, John proceeded to whiteout key letters on the banner message so it read: "U r a gement". John's bold act of courage had the twin effect of drawing further derision onto the Timberlakes and the establishment of a new word in the Oxford English Dictionary.

"You know, you really shouldn't shout at him," said Jeff, draping a bar towel over the font handles. "He's our third chef in a month…and we really need to hang onto one for longer than a fortnight if possible."

Shirley glared at her husband. She thought how silly he looked, stood there in cycle shorts and a Madonna Vogue Tour t-shirt, but he had a point. "You're right," she conceded. "I'll ring him first thing tomorrow and apologise."

"If he doesn't screen your call," Jeff mused, and grabbed a bottle of Benedictine from behind a hefty brass statue of the Olympic sprint champion, Wilma Rudolph. "Think I'll take a nightcap to bed." As he went to pour a glass of golden spirit from the sticky-necked bottle, there was a tremendous knocking on the bolted door.

"Shit!" hissed Shirley. "That'll be Sammy."

Jeff hung his head. "I thought he was playing *Risk* at The King's Python?"

"I thought he said *Ker-Plunk*?"

"Well, either way, he must have lost."

Sammy Grossefinger, The Goose's only true regular, frequented the pub every night, except when there was a retro board game tournament at some other venue. Married with three children – each of whom suffered from elastic jaw – Sammy was instantly recognisable around the village by virtue of being unrecognisable. The man's countenance was almost completely concealed by hair. A wild and unkempt mane on his head was well supported by an imposing combination of beard and eyebrows, and the whole looked was finished off with the uncontrolled sprouting of hair from his nose and ears.

Sammy ran a blindingly unsuccessful roadside grocery van on the weekdays, while his wife, Pammy, worked at Budgen's Supermarket in the neighbouring town of Eye. Sammy's business seemed to materialise out of nothing given he had neither an allotment to source produce from nor any member affiliation to the Uggeshall Cash and Carry Club. His wife, on the other hand, was Interim Produce Assistant in the fruit and vegetable department at the supermarket, so Sammy's unerring ability to replenish his van stock with six runner beans one day and three broccoli heads the next, allowed most villagers to draw their own, inevitable conclusions.

It was effectively Peasenhall's worst kept secret. The coincidence of Sammy's increased stock inventory in cold weather at the same time his wife starting wearing a bigger coat to work was both smirked at and frowned upon in equal measure. And while Sammy extolled the virtues of 'buy local', the prospect of being charged with receiving stolen goods was enough to deter most decent folk and the reason the veggie enterprise was an abject failure.

Alas, he wouldn't be told, and anyone bold enough to question the eighteen-stone man's business ethics was suitably subjected to Sammy in a full-phlegm rage.

"Open the door, coppa!" Sammy had clearly taken a drink or two. "What toime d'yer call this shutten up shop?"

"We're closed, Sammy!" Shirley bawled back. "We're both ill. We've come down with...H1N1!"

"H1N1?" Jeff looked askew at his wife and then shrugged his shoulders at Spanner & Cloak.

Silence.

"What's that then?" asked Sammy.

"Oh, it's a really bad strain of flu!" shouted Shirley who then proceeded to do a fake sneeze. "It came across in birds or pigs from China. Or Korea."

"What the...?" started Jeff but was furiously hushed by his wife.

Silence. "Oh," Sammy said eventually. "Oi'll get off then!"

Shirley audibly sighed. "Great, thanks, Sammy! Get home safe!" She smiled, picturing herself diving into bed early with James Patterson, the electric blanket full on and a jar of pickled eggs on the nightstand.

"Yeah, roight!" Sammy hollered. "Yer think oi just got off the last banana train? Get this fucken door open!"

Shirley physically withered, and her head slumped forward with such force that her hair formed a perfect teepee. "Go on," she said wearily from beneath a wave of *Herbal Essence*. "Let him in."

Jeff loosened the last bolt and Sammy staggered in.

"I think you mean banana boat, Sammy," suggested The Goose's landlord.

"Gorn and get beoind that bar, pig."

Sammy belched and staggered over to the bar. He was sporting his usual attire of second-hand *Fat Face* clothing from the previous year's Autumn/Winter collection.

A regular in the Saxmundham *Sue Ryder* charity shop, Sammy's wife would seize upon any recent clothing contributions made by the wives of chartered professionals who couldn't bear the touch of anything on their skin that wasn't tweed or manufactured by *Barbour*. If there was a freshly rejected fleece or pair of camo pants on the rack, Pammy would heave toddlers and elderly women to the ground in an effort to claim them.

As he climbed onto his favourite bar stool — a feat that resembled Brian Blessed struggling up the Hillary Step — Sammy looked less than fetching in a cerise gilet and coordinating corduroy trousers. The ensemble was finished off with a pair of black wellington boots that he was never seen without.

"Usual, Sammy?" Jeff said as he began to pour a pint of beetroot cider.

"Yarp! And oi'll be 'aven sausage and mash for me tea."

Shirley flopped the copy of *Police Life* she had just picked up back onto the bar. "Chef's gone, Sammy. Kitchen's closed," she said flatly.

Sammy turned on his stool (which was never a pleasant sight), narrowed his eyes and tried to focus on the landlady. "Oo are yer?" he demanded.

Jeff placed the pint of insipid-looking cider onto a drip mat. "That's Shirley, Sammy. My wife, and the pub's landlady. And the person you've been introduced to everyday for the last three months."

Sammy grunted and swallowed half the pint. "That useless dog Damien smashed again?"

Jeff shrugged.

"Okay," Sammy conceded, "Oi'll 'ave a simple salad niscoise then on account a there bein' no chef."

Shirley dropped a chin of bewilderment while Jeff massaged Spanner & Cloak's temples in sheer frustration. "Food is finished, Sammy!" Shirley growled through bared teeth. "All you can have now is what we've got behind the bar."

Sammy tried to focus on the packets of snacks stashed under the bar top. "Such as?" he asked, realising he was ale-blind.

"For goodness sake," huffed Shirley. "Either Fairtrade, ethically sourced, organic, environmentally sustainable macadamia nuts or...a shitty bag of crisps."

The roadside entrepreneur-cum-fence swayed as he considered his options. "What flavour crisps yer got, boi?"

"The usual," replied Jeff. "Mature cheddar, smoky bacon or trout and custard."

"Oi'll 'ave the trout," said Sammy, and fell head first off his stool.

"This pub has got to get busier, Jeff."

Shirley stared out of the pub's bay window and watched Sammy picking a fight with a wheelie bin that was stood harmlessly on Doctor O'Flanagan's drive before finally drawing the cauliflower-patterned curtains on another unsuccessful evening. "We've got to get more people in here or you're going to have to find another income."

Jeff stood stock-still. "No way!"

"Well, we're losing money hand over fist. What do you suggest?"

"I'm nearly fifty-eight, Shirl!" Jeff protested. "My knees are shot, as are my eyesight and hearing, and all I know is how to nick someone! Exactly what do you suggest?" The landlord was suddenly all flustered and accidentally put the fire guard in front of Spanner & Cloak, who had snuck back in front of the warm coals.

"Oh, I don't know," said his despondent wife.

"Look," said Jeff, conscious of Shirley's sudden dip in mood. "We'll get this going eventually. Rome wasn't built in a day, babe, and we knew this wasn't going to be easy."

"Well," said Shirley, suddenly more resolute. "I suggest you come up with something quick, mister, or you can forget buying any more accessories for that bloody train set of yours!"

Jeff's eyes shot upwards in the direction of the spare room where *Le Grande Network* (as he dramatically referred to it) was taking shape and then grimaced at the prospect of not being able to add an additional passenger footbridge or an un-coupling ramp. His cheeks flushed as Jeff suddenly remembered the order he'd placed with *Sad Hobbies!* A pack of new 00 Gauge track sections was likely to hit the doormat in the morning. Note to self, Jeff thought, keep an eye out for the postman.

"Sure thing, darling," Jeff said to pacify Shirley. He flicked off the remaining light in the saloon bar and followed his wife to bed.

JULES

Mike crashed through the front door carrying a small box.

"I just thought I'd drop off a steak slice or two," he said and stared at the congregation of expectant mothers, each red-faced, flustered and constantly shifting their extended midriffs into more comfortable positions.

"Looks like the enemy has just arrived," one of the pregnant mothers said abrasively.

Jules stood silently staring at Mike.

"This is supposed to be my speciality…this is what I do…bring groceries."

A few women huffed derisively at the comment. Jules just stood.

"Look," Mike said, "I've had a very big day in the shop…a very big day. And I just wanted to share it with my best girl. I miss my best girl." Jules looked puzzled, unsure. "You complete me," said Mike. Jules didn't blink. "I've sold a boat load of bread and tuna and whipped cream and I just wanted you…"

"Shut up!" Jules suddenly cut Mike off. "Just shut up," she said. "You had me at steak slice."

Jules woke from the deepest slumber and decided today was moving day.

Mike Grimshaw was so engrossed in his Jodi Picoult novel that he didn't notice Jules enter the shop.

She drifted around the pasty section of the chiller cabinet, quietly whistling the tune to the latest *Santander* commercial, glancing across every few seconds to see if she could catch Mike's eye. The shopkeeper finished the chapter he was reading then looked up just as Jules disappeared behind an aisle end of locally produced flapjack. He took a moment to scratch under his left armpit and returned to Zoe Baxter's blossoming lesbian romance.

"What are you reading, Mike?"

Mike's head snapped back up again, suddenly startled by the voice. The question appeared to have originated from a batch of marginally out-of-date Piri-Piri Chicken *Pot Noodle*. "It's called…er…Sing You Home," he replied, holding up the book's front cover towards the dehydrated snack.

"Ooh, yeah, that's great," said the *Pot Noodle*. "I've read lots of hers."

"Have you now? Good for you." Mike straightened up from his hunched position over the counter and tried to remember what he'd eaten for breakfast. He wondered if any part of his chocolate brioche was mildly hallucinogenic. He certainly didn't recall seeing any advisory notes on the packet. The Lancashire man pressed a palm to his forehead and felt for any discernible elevation in temperature. He mumbled quietly under his breath, "Need a holiday…can't believe I'm talking to the produce."

"It's me, silly!" Jules laughed as she popped her head around the aisle corner and blew a draught of air up from an extended bottom lip to remove a few strands of excessive fringe out of her eyes.

"Oh, hi, Jules!" said Mike, visibly relieved that his sanity was still intact. "What's up?" he said, furtively tucking his Mr. Greedy bookmark between paused pages.

"Hmm," said Jules wistfully. "I need something for tea, and probably some fruit to keep me going this afternoon."

Julie Wiseman was an independent midwife who ran her own business, *Come-On, Spit-It-Out*, across West Suffolk. For ten years, Julie had provided the vital services of antenatal, labour, and postnatal care to the county's pregnant mothers. It was a vocation Julie had both a natural flair for, and an unusually large pair of hands.

Her original intention had been to study Archaeology at Keele University, but ended up doing a different type of digging on a midwifery course at Stowmarket Tech College after bombing her French A-level and was one UCAS point short of her dream. In the time she'd been qualified to oversee the unrelenting trauma of child birth, Julie had been on hand to deliver tiny men and women in every conceivable location within the county: homes, hospitals, Greggs, beneath a wind turbine and on fairground dodgems to name a few.

A gregarious, flush-faced woman with wild red hair and warm, olive eyes, the unmarried midwife was generous to a fault, and her kindness was mercilessly exploited by local tradesmen and utility companies. Julie was the daughter of Newmarket's very own Champion Steeplechase Rider, Terry Wiseman; a jockey universally feted for his trademark Bruce Forsyth posture as he crossed the race finish line. While Julie – or Jules as she was known to friends – may have inherited her ability to manage large sweating beasts across some tricky hurdles with consummate dexterity from her father, her Amazonian frame most certainly came from her mother.

Born in the German city of Leipzig, Gerta Wiseman (nee Beckenbauer) was a valued and prolific member of the DDR Women's shot-putt team. She missed out going to the 1976 Summer Olympics in Montreal after injuring her hand during a sustained period of domestic violence towards her husband. Violently gifted and violently tempered, Gerta also represented East Germany in the 1979 Eurovision Song Contest, but her banjo-based rendition of Cliff Richard's *We Don't Talk Anymore*, amassed a total of just three points (all from the Swedish judge). After tearing up the green room – and most of the live set after the broadcast was over, Gerta was arrested by Israeli police and ended up serving six months in a Jerusalem jail: the place where Jules was born.

Tragically, both of Jules' parents died in a multi-vehicle pile-up on the A14 when she was only fifteen years old. Leaving Jules at home to finish her weekend homework, the couple were travelling to a model air show in Rougham when their car collided with a milk tanker that had crossed into the outside lane of the dual carriageway without warning. As the Wiseman's car hit the tanker, it forced the vehicle into a *Flour Mills* lorry on its inside, causing it to veer onto the hard shoulder where a van from *Happy Hens Farm* was sat with a flat tyre.

The resulting carnage kept the road closed for over eight hours and created a twenty-mile tail back. No one else was seriously injured in the accident, but the milk tanker driver was subsequently prosecuted and jailed. Surprisingly, neither Terry nor Gerta died from their injuries sustained in the pile-up; instead the coroner's report recorded that the pair had drowned in the ensuing pancake mix.

"Maybe I'll leave the fruit," said Jules wandering over to the sweet counter. "Think I'll take a Double Decker instead. Gonna need a full sugar rush to get through what looks like a busy afternoon."

Mike gave her an old-fashioned look and promptly followed that up with a contemporary look of his own design. "Your sweet tooth will be your undoing," he teased.

"Yes, mum," retorted Jules.

"Are you sure I can't convince you to take one of my over-ripe bananas instead?"

Jules blanched.

Then Mike blanched. "Or…or," he flustered and grabbed a health bar from his counter. "Or one of these new…" Mike examined the wrapper of a recent delivery he thought would complement the shop's health credentials. "Dusty Bars?"

Julie stood aghast. "What the hell's that?"

"A delicate combination of protein and organically filtered dust," Mike read from the on-pack description. "Coated in a low-fat, edible PVC…apparently"

"Is it calorie-free?" Jules queried.

"Pretty much."

"Well, that's shit all use to me then! I've got a twat of an afternoon ahead of me."

Mike blanched for a second time at Jules' colourful language; his head now closely resembling a two-bar electric fire. The midwife's poor selection of vocabulary was a mild form of Tourette's and Jules couldn't help herself. If ever scolded over it, she would merely put her swearing down to being raised by two dedicated, but flawed, athletes.

"Mrs. Horowitz has got twins imminent," Jules continued, "and there's more than a fair chance that Rosie Bradshaw's gonna drop something greasy and hairy today as well." Then her mouth did its usual job of engaging before her brain. "So, in fact, I've actually got two twats of an afternoon coming up!"

Mike laughed weakly and grabbed the chunky bar of confectionery. "Okay," he conceded. "Chocolate it is for Ms. Wiseman. How many do you want?"

"No Dusty Bars?" teased Jules.

"No Dusty Bars," nodded Mike.

"Better take two, I reckon," said Jules, fingering her purse for change. "The Horowitz twins are going to need a bit of encouragement. I may even need to pick up a ball of bailing twine on my way over."

Mike shuddered at the thought and stuck Jules' payment in the till.

"I don't know, Mr. Grimshaw," said Jules. "If everyone came into this store and doubled their purchase after a slice of your smooth sales technique…you'd be retiring to the Med in no time."

Mike laughed and held crossed fingers up in front of his most regular customer. Jules reminded him of a young, buxom (and breathing) Cilla Black with a vibrant singing voice to match (albeit dispensed through a more easy-going set of teeth). She had been a constant in Mike's life since his arrival in the village, and he had to admit that he'd grown fond of her kooky ways and untold number of allergies. Jules' adverse reaction to everyday things was legendary. She was dairy, latex, gluten and lactose intolerant, and highly allergic to zinc plasters. She would slump into immediate anaphylactic shock from bee stings or whale bites, reacted violently to any cat, dog or caged bird lurking within a hundred-metre radius, and blow up like a balloon at the mere sight of a scallop.

On any given day, Jules would be slathered in vitamin E lotion in an effort to arrest her vicious bouts of psoriasis and would carry several tubes of Canesten in her handbag should she fall victim to a rapid onslaught of jock itch. She sneezed over a hundred times a day and hiccupped non-stop between the hours of 4 and 5pm.

Her package of allergies may well have been largely ignored in any other line of work, but as a midwife, there were many mothers-to-be in her care who would grow anxious at the site of Jules rolling up her sleeves and scrubbing large, rash-covered hands and forearms with proprietary bathroom cleaner prior to checking on their degree of dilation.

The whole process was compounded if the psoriasis was particularly bad. Jules' cries of tortured pain would regularly surpass those of any recently delivered child. Many mothers requested a replacement for Jules during the postpartum period, concerned that the constant barrage of flaked skin and projectile sputum over their new born would prove detrimental in the long term. But as she was the only midwife in the district offering postnatal support, it was pretty much Jules or the pig vet from Woolpit Green.

Suffolk's most dermatologically challenged midwife lived in a small thatched cottage on the outskirts of Peasenhall. The dwelling was previously occupied by a local suet wholesaler and was appropriately named *Atora Corner*. Jules enjoyed few hobbies but had a real passion for IKEA furniture.

Such was her obsession that literally nothing in the property could be pronounced coherently. From dombås and förvara to bekväm and ektorp, the minimalist, livid-coloured furnishing spilled out across the cottage like a burst bag of *Skittles*.

When she wasn't searching Gumtree for the next inarticulately named foot stool, Jules spent her spare time listening to downloaded audiobooks, learning Esperanto and making random lists. The midwife was a serial cataloguer, creating two or three lists a day and posting them onto her Facebook page in the hope friends and family would engage and comment on her efforts. She'd posted a list with a musical theme before heading to see Mike at the village store.

Got some hybrid Beatles songs for you guys today. LOL! Which would attract the most downloads d'ya think? As always, vote for your faves!

Eleanor Walrus

Only a Northern Taxman

Got to get you into my Raccoon

A Hard Day's Wood

Norwegian Help

And your Strawberry Can Sing

Lucy in the Sky with Michelle

Tomorrow Never Yesterday

Yellow Mystery Tour

The Long and Winding Blackbird

The post was 'liked' by two people: her old school friend, Nigella, who ran a tapestry collective in Walberswick, and someone called Hannah Lovejuice. Another friend from Tech College, who was now assistant handler at an owl sanctuary in Dunwich, added the only comment: "Nice one, Jules! BTW, how about Killer Rhapsody?! xx".

"Did you see my latest list?" Jules asked Mike as she migrated back towards the aisles and considered the selection of *Frey Bentos* pies on display.

"Er, no," said Mike. "Not yet."

"Come on," she berated him mildly as her considerations transferred to the selection of canned chilli con carne.

"Sorry, Jules." The shopkeeper held his book aloft in a *mea culpa* gesture.

Mike always tried to make the effort to comment on one of Jules' infamous lists every day, but noticed they had got a little darker recently. One of her lists already that week had contained references to medieval torture devices, while another was entitled, 'my favourite satanic ceremony'.

"Ooh, it's a corker this morning," Jules smiled. "It's right up your street, Mr. Moosic!"

Mike liked Jules' smile. It revealed two pointed eyeeteeth that originally started life growing out in front of her upper gum but were encouraged into position by a dental brace. These 'fangs' sat snugly on her lower lip when she smiled, which made her look like a vampire on absinthe. The smile quickly dissipated however, as her face screwed up into a ball of confusion.

"What's up?" asked Mike.

"Well I may as well pick up something for tea while I'm here, but I can't decide what I fancy."

"Well, what did you have last night?"

"Seafood pasta."

Mike was taken aback. He had an intimate knowledge of the food Jules bought and certainly didn't recall her ever buying anything quite so exotic. He found himself suddenly irked: maybe she was shopping elsewhere.

"Seafood pasta?" he probed.

"Yeah," said Jules and deposited a tin of barbeque beans with sausages into the crook of her arm alongside a squidged white loaf. "It was quite tasty, to be fair."

A dark cloud appeared over Mike's head. "Wow, sounds nice. Was it easy to prepare?"

Jules looked at Mike as if he was stupid. "I just grilled the fish fingers and poured the spaghetti hoops over the top, you ninny."

Mike's relief was palpable. "Yes, of course. Sorry, I was being a bit thick."

"You're as fucking daft as a brush!" Jules said teasing the northerner once more before sliding her items onto the counter top. "But I still think you're lovely."

"Behave!" Mike felt two bars go to three.

"You know," said Jules, as she paid for her groceries. "Isn't it about time you got yourself a new girlfriend, Mike?" Go on, ask me out, Jules wanted to scream.

"Oh, don't you start." Mike handed Jules her change. "I've had Janice Muffler giving me all sorts of grief about that."

"Well, she's right, you…"

"Are you kidding? Who in their right mind would have anything to do with me?" Mike's predilection for self-deprecation rapidly came to the fore. "I'm damaged goods." He passed a red and white striped carrier bag across to Jules while holding up his novel. "Jodi is all I need to keep me company!"

Jules' smile had gone. "Oh," she simply said; her obvious deflation impossible to miss.

But somehow Mike missed it.

SUNDAY LUNCH

The weekend in East Anglia was grey and damp.

Heating in The Whipped Peasant was turned on for the first time since late May while a hand-written note in the bay window of The Startled Goose advised its patrons of the benefits of an extra layer or two when frequenting the premises.

As Sunday presented its dour face, lunchtime crowds across the county traded oilskins and white coats for knitted sweaters and maxi dresses, and descended on their favourite Suffolk pubs to indulge in the traditional Sabbath meal of meat with all the necessary accoutrements. Hundreds of A-frame blackboards conveyed a gamut of roasted offerings in an array of handwriting styles designed to entice both regulars and those passing in untaxed motor vehicles into these carnivorous weekend retreats.

Hector had built a fine reputation for Sunday lunch at The Peasant, alongside his trusted head chef, Patrice le Clef, whose wonders in the kitchen meant there was barely any room for elbows around The Peasant's busy dining tables.

Born in the Dordogne, Patrice came to Peasenhall with his parents before his eleventh birthday. Away from the delights of Alsatian Bacon and horse, the boy was raised on British fayre which included the great Sunday roast. It was a tradition he quickly grew to love and Patrice would spend the entire school week craving the weekend's arrival. Rising early on Sundays, he would join his parents in selecting a new destination from their dog-eared copy of the *Greene King Guide to Suffolk Pubs,* and then climb into the family's Vauxhall Cavalier with his stomach growling in wild anticipation. Each trip was a delight. His parents would beam proudly as Patrice devoured every slice of pork shoulder or fork full of mashed swede. And the boy filled pub lounges with cries of "Mon Dieu!" and "Zis is wonderful!" as his future vocation was forged. From the earliest age, Patrice le Clef knew he was destined to be the head chef of a classic English pub.

The price of Sunday lunch at The Peasant was £11.95 a head for two courses. Pensioners got their dessert free and children under the age of nine could eat for half price. Patrice would prepare a choice of pork or beef each week, with lamb on offer every other Sunday. His potato selection would include roast (always) and the regular variants of dauphinoise, farls or tartiflettes. Yorkshire puddings were always from a batter batch made on the day and his seasonal vegetables were assuredly fresh as they would have been stolen from a neighbouring field that very morning.

Patrice's most ardent admirers weren't confined to Peasenhall village, his lunch had been reviewed and critically acclaimed by local writers and national journalists, and one notable tribute to The Peasant's Sunday lunch was a review by the late Michael Winner in his regular *Sunday Times* column.

"While out for a short stroll in Constable Country this weekend, I remarked to Prince Charles – who, mercifully, was accompanying me without that dreadful wife of his – how the local pub food in Suffolk had taken a turn for the worse in recent years. But, stop the intelligent press! What a find we made! Just when I thought we were resigned to another of his appalling homemade efforts, Gordon Ramsey spotted 'The Whipped Peasant' in Peasenhall and got Nigel Mansell to pull the Bentley into the pub's swollen car park.

"In truth, dear old Dicky Attenborough almost vomited when he tasted the unfathomable Rams Buttock, a bitter that should be avoided at all costs, but when it came to the food...well both Roger Moore and I swore we'd never tasted better. The PM's beef melted in the mouth, Stevie G's lamb was a triumph and oh! how we laughed at Bill Gates as he tried to figure out how to eat the sweetest, lightest Yorkshire pudding within miles.

"Hat's off to you, Monsieur Le Clef! You have shown an old man and his unassuming friends what true pub dining can really be in this county of woebegone nomads. I'll be returning...but not with that wanker George Clooney. He wouldn't even try the poor fellow's spotted dick!

Adieu, my darlings! MW"

Hector ran a tight schedule on covers because he always had live music waiting in the wings and the last diners were required to drain their espresso no later than 2.45pm. With the Sunday roast put to bed, the tables were cleared to the side of the pub as the invited artistes tuned their instruments, checked their levels and made a final review of their playlists.

This Sunday was no exception. At 3 o'clock sharp, *Dog-Filled Pantry* cranked up the volume and flew into their set of jazz-folk wizardry. Fuelled by great food and brooding ales, The Peasant crowd howled with delight. With the band's set barely a minute old, the *Peas'naal Hop* was once again in evidence as sporadic dancing broke out on the flagstones of the village's charmed hostelry. A sea of bodies pulsated under ancient beams: it was a traditional Sunday and da house was rockin'!

Over at The Goose, Damien spooned a portion of processed peas onto a plate of gravy-warmed chicken breast slices. The boiled Maris Pipers were overcooked and crumbled into several pieces when they landed on the cold china.

The pub's only lunch order of the day was for Jimmy Jammz, Peasenhall's professional online spammer.

Jimmy had been reintroduced to The Goose by his old friend Sammy Grossefinger and decided to wander over for a bite to eat around four o'clock after finishing a blanket email campaign. (He'd hacked into an email database of teenage girls who'd recently signed up for a monthly newsletter from a popular online music blog. He spammed over twelve hundred registered addresses offering their youthful owners the chance to meet Lady Gaga in person at Felixstowe Docks on Tuesday after school. But unbeknownst to the teenage respondents, the email competition contained a virus that when they clicked on the "Enter Me Now" button, turned all their Instagram posts into Welsh).

"Is that ready yet?" Shirley had come into the kitchen to find out why Jimmy was still waiting for something to eat forty minutes after ordering it. Damien looked up at her with eyes half closed and a stupid grin on his face.

"For fuck's sake!" Shirley screamed furiously as Damien dumped a second spoonful of peas over a bowl of reheated treacle sponge pudding. "Jeff! Get in here now!"

Jeff placed Jimmy's lunch in front of him. "Sorry about that," he said.

"No matter." Jimmy grabbed a knife and fork wrapped in a paper napkin. "Where's Damien goen?" The chef and his Hello Kitty rucksack were swerving out of the pub car park.

"Just had to sack him. He's been at the wacky baccy again."

"Prob'ly why yer board outside says '£19,999 for Sunday lunch'." Jimmy grimaced at the taste of the peas.

"You're joking?" Jeff exclaimed, craning his neck to see into the front car park.

"Yarp! And apparently yer got 'Roast Fuck' on the menu today."

"Oh, for crying out loud!" Jeff grabbed a damp cloth from the bar and headed outside to make the necessary changes.

"Sorry to have kept you waiting so long, Jimmy." Shirley had returned from the kitchen and leant against the doorframe, a picture of dejection.

"Ah, fret not," Jimmy said brightly. "It'll all come good, you'll see."

The ex-policewoman made the effort to acknowledge Sammy's kind words with a graceful nod of her head. She looked out of the pub's bay window at the pathetic sight of her husband furiously wiping down their A-board while shouting a stream of obscenities at it. A tirade that was mercifully suppressed by the day's grey stupor. Beyond him, his cloth, and his stick of chalk, just a short stroll down the high street was The Whipped Peasant. Shirley could almost hear the songs, the laughter, and the fun oozing out of its many doors. She could feel the warmth generated by so many who revelled in the warm glow of a much-loved community boozer; the perfect tonic for the stresses and strains of daily life. But most of all she imagined the satisfaction of the landlord's face and how it continually reflected in the surface of his till; a till he would visit repeatedly across the afternoon session.

"Is that okay, Sammy?" Shirley said trying to shake off the funk she was in.

"Er," Sammy pointed at his plate. "Yer int got a spoon oi could 'ave to pick up these spuds by any chance?"

MIKE

Mike Grimshaw wandered over to the young couple as they packed their instruments away.

"Nice set, guys." Mike offered out a hand to the pony-tailed musician who was bent over a stubborn clamp of his weather-beaten violin case. "My name's Mike Grimshaw. I run the local shop."

"Sounds to me like there's a bit o'Lancasheer in that accent o'yours," said *Dog-Filled Pantry*'s violinist – who could easily pass as Iggy Pop with the right stage lighting. He stood upright to meet Mike's eye and engage in a warm handshake. "I'd say, Blackburn or maybe Chorley, if I were a bettin' man."

"Which you're not," his attractive blonde partner offered in perfect received pronunciation.

"Darwen, actually." Mike was genuinely thrilled at finding a fellow county-man in a place that was actually less fashionable than where they hailed from.

The musician smiled broadly. "Close enough. There's poverty…"

"And then there's Darwen!" Mike finished the sentence and the pair guffawed together.

"Good grief!" winced the girl and locked away her saxophone.

"Ah-reet, Mike. I'm Steve and this 'ere's Maddy!" He introduced his partner with a broad sweep of an arm as if she was about to come on stage at the O₂ arena.

"It's Madeleine," the girl said flatly and gave Mike a pinched smile.

"Hi," replied Mike, consciously omitting her name, as there was clearly some debate as to which version was acceptable. "You guys local?" he enquired.

"We're down from Norwich," said Steve.

"Norwich! Crikey! That's one hell of a schlep." Peasenhall's shopkeeper was impressed.

"Well, this is *The* Peasant," said Steve. "There's many that 'ave travelled further than us to play 'ere!" The performer closed his eyes and breathed deeply through what was an exceptionally large nose. "You can just smell the 'istory in 'ere."

"Well, you can't miss it with that!" sniped Madeleine as she pointed at her partner's extensive olfactory system.

Mike choked on the Marmite mini cheddar he'd just popped into his mouth. "A little harsh," he said.

"Ah, she's just pullin' me plonker." Steve dismissed the put down and gave Mike a nudge on the arm. "Still, know what they say about a big nose, eh?"

"Yeah," said Madeleine, her eyes rolling. "A massive susceptibility to the common cold."

"Hah! She's reet, mind! I do get me fair share o'flu!" Steve grabbed his pint and drained the last mouthful of The Peasant's guest beer, *Spurious Weasel*. "Ugh!" he said, unimpressed at the taste. "Shite southern ale!" Steve placed the empty glass on top of the pub's tired piano. "Does tha play, lad?" he asked Mike.

"I dabble," Mike offered with little conviction. "Play guitar a bit."

"Guitar?" Steve shouted way too loudly. "You'll do for me!" He gave Mike an over-zealous slap on the back and headed towards the bar for further refreshment. "Reet! Two pints of this southern bilge water to remind us what we're missin' back 'ome! Same again, Maddy?"

"If I must." The girl's less-than-enthusiastic reply suggested another moment in the pub was anathema to her.

With Steve suddenly away at the bar, an awkward silence fell between the shopkeeper and the young saxophonist. She couldn't have been more than five stone dripping wet, Mike thought, and had an uncanny resemblance to Kate Bush in her *Wuthering Heights* video. She was sporting a rather tight t-shirt with the message, *Ta-Dah!* written across the chest and Mike was struggling to keep his eyes pointing in an appropriate direction; respectfully away from where the vast majority of that five stone appeared to be stored.

"You both play really well," Mike said finally, making a close examination of the ceiling. "Have you recorded any of your stuff?"

Madeleine shrugged. "I only play these gigs because Steve likes to. He's wasted doing this, though. He's capable of so much more."

"He is very talented, for sure," said Mike. "You know I could speak to Mickey Koblenz and get you guys some studio time if…"

"That girl's going to knock both of those pints over."

"I'm sorry?" Madeleine's random comment caught Mike by surprise.

Madeleine sighed impatiently. "I said, that girl, Chloe I think her name is, is going to knock those drinks over when she gives the change back to her customer."

"I'm sorry…Madeleine. I'm not with you."

The girl twirled her auburn hair into a loose coil and tucked it up into a blue NY baseball cap. "Look!" she said, nodding in the direction of the bar where, sure enough, Chloe handed some change to a customer and promptly dispatched two full pints of *Spurious Weasel* over his rust-coloured chinos.

"What?" Mike went ice cold. "Was that just a lucky guess?"

"And now she's going to mix up the landlord's…Hector's…jumper that he took off earlier for a tea towel and mop up the mess with it." Madeleine pulled on her denim jacket. "Which is likely to draw an unlikely religious comparison."

Hector's cry rang out across the pub. "Chloe?! Jesus Christ!"

Mike's feet turned to clay.

"Oh, I'm so sorry." Madeleine noticed the colour drain from Mike's face and put the lightest touch of her hand onto his trembling forearm. "I forget myself sometimes. I'm psychic. And a pretty good one at that!" Feeling decidedly perkier, Madeleine left Mike with this little head fuck and went to give Steve a hand.

Mike was a non-believer. He wasn't, however, an active non-believer. He didn't go around demanding cold, hard facts from people who put their trust in god, or the stars, or fate – he simply didn't buy into it on a personal level. His life had ticked along reasonably enough to date and he'd never felt the need to seek guidance from a higher spiritual being or discover the shape of his future from a spurious hag under a B&Q pop-up marquee on Felixstowe pier.

That was, until he did.

When Mike was at a particularly low ebb after his divorce, he decided to seek some help from Madame Florin, an Egyptian-born clairvoyant who worked from her flat in Little Bealings during the off-season.

He booked a thirty-minute reading and arrived promptly only to find a Post-It note on her front door that said: "Back in ten minutes." Madame Florin turned up shortly after, carrying a pint of milk and a bag of easy-peel satsumas. With her straggly white hair, faint outline of a goatee beard and thickset eyebrows, the psychic looked like Crosby, Stills and Nash all rolled into one. She unlocked the dead bolt and invited Mike in.

The clairvoyant led Mike down a gloomy hall, his eyes suddenly itchy from scent and pollen streaming off a vase of lilies perched on a narrow table halfway along the vestibule. "Funeral flowers," Mike mumbled, and sneezed into the crook of his arm. At the end of the hall was a door that had patently received just a single undercoat of orange paint. Madame Florin opened it, and walked into the room where her readings were conducted. It was surprisingly plain. Mike had expected exotic drapes, lava lamps and stylish Moorish antiquities dotted hither and tither. But there was only a bland table, two chairs, a bookcase filled largely with James Patterson co-author-novels, a futon covered in dog hair and a Jack Vettriano print on the wall. Why would anyone dance on a beach in the pissing rain, Mike thought?

The psychic flicked on a standard lamp that stood in the corner of the room like a naughty pupil, a dark maroon cloth draped over its flower-patterned shade. "You have beautiful eyes," the woman said as light from the eco-bulb slowly began to take over the room's gloom. "You really don't have to enhance them with eye liner.

Great, thought Mike, I've come here to see what life has in store for me and I get make-up advice.

The clairvoyant then lit a small candle on the table that gave off a smell akin to the application of *Toilet Duck* in a men's urinal. "Before we start," said Madame Florin, "you need to cross my palm with silver."

Mike quickly pointed out that he had already been directed to the fortune teller's online PayPal portal when booking the appointment. The woman scratched at something underneath her filthy bandana and informed Mike she wasn't up to speed with modern technology. With no further expansion from the psychic on said point, Mike assumed the issue of payment was now settled and the reading could progress. The woman stretched out a grizzled hand and took Mike's in it. She stared deeply into the candle's flame.

"I sense that a man might be sick or in trouble physically."

"That's probably me," Mike offered. "I've not been on top of…"

"Don't speak!" The mystic cut across the shopkeeper.

Mike blanched.

"I feel pain," the woman continued. "But it's short lived."

Mike brightened.

"I see another man. David, I believe. Yes, David is his name."

David? Mike thought. He didn't know any David. Unless she was talking about David Sampson, whom he'd given a wedgy at school when he was eleven.

"David is a new man in your life."

"Eh?"

"Yes. David. David will come. David will ease the pain."

"What are you talking about?" The pitch in Mike's voice went up a notch.

"You're not supposed to be talking!" The clairvoyant's gaze held steadfastly onto the flame which began emitting plumes of thick, dark smoke.

"But who's David?"

"You lost Cecilia. There were reasons. But as the clouds of despair break up and disperse, David will walk through the mist."

"But," Mike suddenly realised where the woman was going with this. "I'm not gay!"

"What?" The psychic flicked her eyes sharply at Mike.

"I'm not gay!" Mike retrieved his hand from hers. "If a David did come through the mists, he'd get short bloody shrift!"

"But!" The old woman gestured at Mike's attire.

"Oh, for crying out loud!" Mike picked up his keys and wallet from the table and stood up. "Just because I wear women's clothing every now and then, doesn't automatically make me a homosexual!"

"But!" the woman continued to protest. "That's a twin set!"

"What?" exclaimed a disgusted Mike. "This," the grocer waved a hand over his outfit, "is a Kate Spade two piece! And we need to log back in to your PayPal account!"

"What's up, cocker?" Steve handed Mike a fresh pint. "Looks like tha's seen a ghost!"

"No. No. It's alright," Mike stuttered. "I've just been talking to Madeleine."

"Great, int she?" Steve waved across at Madeleine as she collected their appearance money from Hector.

"Yeah, you could say that." The shopkeeper swallowed a mouthful of ale. He looked up and across the bar to see Jules and Patrice le Clef talking in a very intimate fashion; the chef actually playing with a strand of her hair at one point in the conversation. Mike felt an unexpectedly disconsolate twang at his heartstrings.

"Look!" Madeleine beamed as she returned waving a wad of cash at her boyfriend and planted a well-earned kiss on his lips. "Hector liked us so much, he gave us an extra fifty quid!"

Steve leant across and gave the crest-fallen Mike a little nudge, a knowing look on his face. "She already told me that were goin' to 'appen."

THE STARTLED GOOSE

The Startled Goose always struggled as Peasenhall's second pub, ever since the Chairman of the Dallinghoo branch of the Rita Chakrabarti Appreciation Society opened it in 1977.

The Goose was the first new building in the village for over a century and consequently stuck out like a sore thumb. Amid a sea of rat-infested thatch and Suffolk pink, The Goose's pointy gables and pitiful bay windows was straight out of a Barratt's Homes catalogue, and sat like a marzipan jelly in a box of praline whirls.

Designed and built by local firm, *Owmuch & Sons*, the construction site was the target of regular and pointed protests from local residents. They bemoaned the impact of the vulgar, modern design on their picture book village and questioned the need for a second public house. The Ukrainian workforce employed by *Owmuch* was continually subjected to verbal abuse and the workers regularly found the site skips full of homemade jam when they returned to work in the mornings.

Why Too Pubs? asked the front page of the grammatically challenged *Peasenhall Quandary*. Was the UK's impending entry to the Common Market at the heart of this scandalous decision? Or were planning committee members simply in the pocket of *Owmuch*'s inscrutable owner, Harry Owmuch? The paper continued to challenge the ongoing build before reporting on the exorbitant price of shoelaces in neighbouring Chillesford. Despite the outcry – that included an all-night vigil that local-born actress and *Eastenders* soap opera superstar, June Brown, nearly attended – The Goose was completed and ready for business in six months. (And with only six deaths on site across the entire build, it was a company record for *Owmuch & Sons* at the time).

The Goose was divided into two functional sections. On entering the pub through a set of plain double doors, the main lounge was off to the right. It contained a bar that was described in popular online forums as basic, but intrinsically useful. In fact, it was ideally suited for the sale and consumption of drinks. Should the rather bland but user-friendly stools at the bar all become occupied, then an assortment of practical table and chairs provided alternative seating options for patrons.

Off to the left was the uniquely dull but eminently serviceable restaurant that, while offering no standard bar, did have an assortment of no-nonsense tables and chairs that proved invaluable for positioning diners at the correct height for effective dining. The high ceilings in both areas ensured that any atmosphere in the place evaporated like high-octane fuel and the overall blandness of the interior suggested that the inspiration for its construction could only have come from examining the inside of a cereal box.

Paint, carpet, curtain, pictures, plastic sheeting, moose heads…nothing currently in existence would add any semblance of character to The Goose: it was a pub bereft of life.

Once open, The Goose suffered a series of incidents that, in hindsight, were unfortunate and largely preventable in equal measure. These early portents hinted towards a business that was going to prove a little testy for those who would own and manage it in years to come.

The pub's inaugural week was at the end of March 1977, around the same time Pink Floyd's *Animals* album was released. As part of the opening festivities, the newly installed owners decided to float a giant, helium-filled pig from the roof of the pub. It was hoped this would both endear the swine-loving locals and create some well-timed publicity. The pig had barely been afloat for an hour when Suffolk County Council officers were on the scene decrying the absence of any appropriate airspace permission for the flying pig.

"What's the cubic volume of that pig?" asked one of the council officers.

"I beg yer pardon," said The Goose's suspicious landlord. "Can oi see some ID, please?"

The council officer flourished a plastic wallet under the licensee's nose. "There yer go!"

"Isn't that a season ticket for Ipswich Town?" the eagle-eyed landlord noted.

"Look," the officer was insistent. "That pig is over 20 cubic feet and yer need an approved ASP-30 form!" he said brandishing an odd-looking, yellow leaflet.

"Dave," said the landlord's wife, pointing at the document. "Oi think that's a photocopy of *The Golden Panda's* Sunday buffet menu."

"Yer need to 'ave that pig down in the next six minutes, and if yer don't concur we 'ave the authority to close these premises indefinitely." The officer was proving a terrible liar. "And to demolish it, probably."

"Yer not kiddin' anyone, mate," said the landlord. "That's not even a proper beard!"

"Foine. If yer not gorn to get that pig down, then we're sendin' the bulldozers in today!"

"No, yer fuckin' not!"

As strong words descended into strong fists in the car park, there was a terrific crash as the pig ripped away from its mooring atop the pub, taking half the roof with it.

Further angst for the pub's new owners that year was the result of planned celebrations for the Queen's Silver Jubilee. A strong commonwealth theme had been set in motion and The Goose promised a party that would bring together nations the ruling classes had shat all over like never before.

The planning for the event was meticulous. The food was to be a barbeque of shrimp (Australia) and lamb (New Zealand); vegetarian food would be dhal (India); music would be an all-day mix of Neil Young and Leonard Cohen (Canada); drink would be a rum punch (Jamaica); and a group of Swahili dancers (East Africa) would provide a jig or two. However, on the morning of Tuesday 7th of June – a one-off public holiday – the dance troupe legged it with the cash from the pub's till, most of the pre-prepared grub and the owner's top-of-the-range Sharp GFx radio-cassette player. Due to a mix up on the delivery dates, the rum punch was also missing a vital ingredient: rum.

The Goose's misfortune paved the way for The Peasant to enjoy a full house the entire day and helped coin the popular phrase: *what's good for the goose, is good for Uganda.*

The catalogue of calamities was relentless. This seemingly cursed boozer suffered nine floods, three lightning strikes, four major fires (the second a genuine accident by all accounts), partial bulldozing, dry rot, foot and mouth, and it even suffered the ignominy of being selected as a location venue for an episode of *Doc Martin*. The pub's ownership changed hands twenty-nine times in forty years, during which it had been a tied house, a free house, a house-house and generally regarded as an out-and-out shithouse.

Over time, the locals started to believe that it was actually bad luck to drink in The Goose, and the place soon became a commercial pariah. Indeed, one long-standing joke was the competition between the county's various painting and decorating companies to see which one could claim to have refurbished the pub the most times. (Unofficially, *Glosster United*, a firm of brothers from Sutton Hoo, held the record at six.) Each new owner was full of blind optimism, confident they could turn the pub around. Sadly, The Goose was just a money pit, and its tenants invariably crawled away from the challenge with their tail between their legs.

For whatever reason, the respective pub owners had never cottoned on to the village's deep passion for *moosic*. One of the more forward-thinking landlords did install a jukebox during the early eighties, but the fact it only offered tunes from Curiosity Killed the Cat, Phil Collins, Men at Work and Billy Joel, meant its fate was quickly sealed.

Local: "What's that then, boi?"

Incumbent landlord: "It's our new jukebox!"

Local: "What's that noise comen out of it, boi?"

Incumbent landlord: "It's Billy Jo-el's wonderful, Uptown Girl!"

Local: (long pause): "Yer turnen that machine off now, or oi'm gorn medieval on this pub."

Incumbent landlord: "Righto!"

Despite all its woes in its relatively short history, The Startled Goose had only ever been officially closed for one weekend in August 1996 – and that was just to ensure that the victim's body hadn't contaminated the water tank. And now, *le defi de l'oie* – as the latest crop of Rita Chakrabarti acolytes would say – lay at the feet of the Timberlakes... and they were already struggling.

JEFF AND SHIRLEY

Nick Crabbs was readjusting the focus on his projector as Jeff walked into the bar carrying a gnarled crate filled with slimline tonics.

The landlord put down the bottles, glanced at his watch and seeing it was only ten o'clock promptly squawked, "We're not open yet, pal!"

"Calm down," said Shirley as she came into the lounge bar behind her husband. "This is Nick from Crabby Marketing."

Nick put up a hand to say hello and walked over to realign the rather large projection screen that he'd erected over the pub's fireplace and the slumbering Spanner & Cloak.

Listed at #86 of the East Anglian Daily Times' list of Top Suffolk Marketing Gurus (in the 18- to 35-year-old category with a degree in Environmental Science), Crabbs considered himself a tour de force when it came to 'mindshare', 'holistic campaigns' and 'thinking outside the envelope'. If there was an opportunity to use an egregious marketing comment when plain English would suffice, Crabbs was your man. He could see 'the big idea', he would take 'the low-hanging fruit' and he knew, beyond any doubt, that 'content was king'. This was a man who could comfortably out-tweet a twat.

"Well, what's he doing here?" Jeff said rather indignantly.

"I told you he was coming," Shirley hissed back. "Honestly! Your bloody memory!"

Jeff had absolutely no recall of that conversation whatsoever and it was written all over his face.

"He's here to give us some ideas of how we can promote ourselves and get some long overdue business into this pub of ours." Shirley donned a pair of rimless reading glasses, sat down and gazed up at the screen boldly radiating the *Crabby Marketing* logo and a shot of Nick Crabbs. The image was clearly from an earlier epoch, given the difference in hair and weight between the guy in the picture and the person in front of them now.

"But I've got to re-stock this bar," Jeff protested. "I can't be sat round listening to some idiot…"

Both Shirley and Nick turned quickly and looked sharply at him.

"Er, no offence, mate," said Jeff awkwardly. "But I've got to get on."

Shirley crossed her legs and cleared her throat in a manner that assumed full authority. "Of course, darling," her tone was beyond condescending. "You take the time to replace the single bottle of tonic water we sold alongside three pints of *Buggered Wizard* last night and, when that infinitesimally tiny fraction of time is over…come and sit the fuck down!"

"Okay," he sighed. "Whatever." Realising there was no merit in getting his wife's gander up so early in the day, Jeff left the crate on the bar, grabbed his mug of tea – which had *NOICE COPPA TEA!* emblazoned on the side – and moseyed over to a spot next to Shirley.

Her time in the force hadn't been kind to Shirley. The long shifts, the constant haranguing from whinging drivers who'd been stopped 'for no reason', the never-ending calibration of speed guns: they'd all taken a toll on the woman. As the years went by the weight piled on. Her face took on the appearance of a worn cushion and her hair became totally unmanageable.

Jeff on the other hand thrived in the role and went at it with a positive enthusiasm that was bordering on the psychotic. He was always in the station gym, dedicating any spare time to the weights and machines. Jeff's inability to bulk up, however, meant that he just looked permanently gaunt rather than toned. It was a look that incited banter from his colleagues along the lines of "more meat on a sparrow's knees". Indeed, such was the contrast between the couple that when they were together in the squad car they resembled a uniformed version of Richard and Judy.

"Oh, oi've just bought that book yer recommended in Smiths," was a regular comment from pissed farmers they pulled over and who wouldn't be making the following morning's milking.

The decision to take over The Goose, however, had given Shirley a new lease of life. She'd thrown herself into its refurbishment and the work needed to get the place ready for reopening with renewed zest. In six weeks, she'd gone from a size 16 to a 12 and looked fabulous. High on energy, and with a huge desire for success, Shirley was the driving force behind the next stage of the Timberlake's journey. And she wasn't going down without a fight.

"Sit down." Shirley gestured to the tub chair next to her.

"Well, how long's he gonna take?" Jeff whined.

"Sit! Down!"

Nick Crabbs pulled up his own chair and waved a finger over the mouse of his laptop to get the now dormant opening slide back up on the screen.

"Many thanks for your time today, guys," the marketer started brightly. "I really appreciate you inviting me in to talk through some of your business issues."

Jeff snorted, squirmed uncomfortably in his seat, took a black look from his wife and wished he had something heavy and blunt to propel at this intruder. Nick clicked on his mouse and a new slide was revealed, accompanied by an unnecessary whooshing sound. It read: Our Clients.

"You're shitting me!" cried Jeff, almost choking on a mouthful of tea.

The slide revealed a wide array of household names from Amazon and Rolls-Royce to Coca-Cola and Tesco's; it appeared Crabby Marketing was in bed with most of the nation's finest blue-chip corporations.

"Impressive!" Shirley remarked, nodding sagely.

"What?" Jeff stared at his wife in disbelief. "Why on earth is he wasting time talking to lowlife like us if he's got this lot lining his pockets?"

Shirley slowly turned her attention on her husband and spoke very deliberately. "If you say another word, that thing you asked for in bed this morning will never, ever happen again."

Jeff went deathly silent. Nick went deathly pale.

"Right," said Crabbs as he endeavoured to eradicate a rather unfortunate mental image that had just popped into his head. "First off, I'd like to share some thoughts from Steve Jobs, which I think are very relevant here."

Jeff frowned. "Relevant? Are you for real? Steve Jobs, the dead guy who single-handedly gave Apple a business turnover equivalent to the GDP of Poland? How's that relevant to us?"

"What did I just say?" his wife barked. "Give Nick a chance!"

"Sorry." Jeff slumped back in his chair. He was done and wouldn't say another word.

"Apologies, Nick," Shirley invited the marketing agency owner to continue with an elegant wave of an increasingly liver-spotted hand.

Crabbs smiled smugly at his hostess, emboldened by her apparent belief in him. "Thank you, Shirley. This, I think, sums your situation up nicely." He then swished a finger and the next slide illuminated the dim lounge.

> "You've baked a really lovely cake, but then you've used dog shit for frosting."
>
> - Steve Jobs

Shirley shuffled uneasily in her chair, while Jeff stifled an enormous grin. The landlord knew, to the exact penny, how much of their life savings they'd thrown at this pub to get it into its present condition. They'd splashed out on new electrics, complete redecoration across two floors, reclaimed the flooded cellar, retarmacked the car park, fitted new external signage and negotiated the removal of Benny the tramp from the front door well. (This complex feat ended up involving Suffolk social services, four local magistrates and, eventually, a trail of beef jerky carefully laid out one piece at a time towards the village pond). Crabbs' eloquent summary of their efforts to date was, to say the least, a little insensitive...and Jeff couldn't wait for his wife's reaction. To her credit, Shirley kept her counsel and merely raised her chin defiantly, awaiting the marketing man's next words.

"When I look around," the suave executive smoothed his tie, "I see a place bursting with opportunity." Jeff slunk a little lower in his chair. The fireworks weren't far away now. "This pub is a good space. A great space, in fact. But the previous owners' choice of lighting and décor...their inability to eradicate the constant smell of damp in the place...the poor fascia and external communication...plus this misguided idea that freak show animals would be a suitable attraction for customers...well, frankly..."

"Can I just stop you there?" Shirley was done.

"By all means, Shirley." Nick's expansive bodily language indicated an enthusiasm for client comments.

Jeff immediately recognised the stupid look on Crabbs' face as a clear indication that he'd no idea what he'd done or, more importantly, what was coming. His wife fixed the marketer with what they used to call at Ipswich nick, *The Shirl Stare.*

"What you see around you, Mr. Crabbs, is not a legacy."

'Mr. Crabbs?' thought Mr. Crabbs.

"What you see around you, Mr. Crabbs, is the result of the investment of hard-earned life savings in order to expedite these particular choices of internal renovation, lighting, décor and exterior signage…choices that my husband and I made personally after much careful and deliberate consideration."

Suddenly aware of his extraordinary faux pas, Nick started nodding furiously in agreement. "Um, forgive me, Shirley, I just assumed…" Crabbs was folding like a warm Cadbury's Ripple.

"Have you got any *fucking* idea how hard it's been to make this place even marginally habitable for my family, let alone open the doors to the public?!" Mrs. Timberlake was at around gas mark eight at this point.

At that point, Crabbs did an insanely stupid thing. In an effort to deflect the mounting suffocation of his host's threatening stare, Crabby Marketing's otherwise unflappable owner pointed to the main bay window and said, "So, when are you going to get round to the curtains then?"

On later reflection, Jeff put the marketer's reaction down to a pressure meltdown, pure and simple. As he restocked the bar, he smiled as the morning's enduring scene came back to him for the umpteenth time. The image of Spanner & Cloak chewing on the finest Hugo Boss material while his good lady forced cries of mercy from Ipswich's finest communicator with a perfectly executed half nelson would stay with him for some time.

Come in, number 86, your time is up, he thought.

OPEN MIC

It was Thursday night: open mic night! And yet another parade of local talent with no obvious filter.

The ever-busy Hector was in full flow before the start of the night's performances; endlessly corralling used and fresh glasses, preparing rounds of egg, cress and marmite sandwiches for all the scroungers at the halfway point and helping Chloe decide on some suitable headwear for the evening. She couldn't decide between a sombrero and a fez. As he busied himself and threw welcoming waves each time the door opened, he noticed Greg and Gaynor Bradley sat over by the speakers engaged in a rather enthusiastic kiss.

"You two alright?" he enquired as he ambled over.

Greg was a local barrister and Gaynor held down the manager's role at the Herringfleet Daycare Centre, and they had rather a bawdy reputation. Despite being married for over thirty years, they remained unable to keep their hands off each other, to the point where they would regularly be seen groping and attempting to swallow each other whole in various public locations. Unsurprisingly, it was a sight that did not sit well with most and, indeed, many of her fellow crèche colleagues would object to Gaynor violently tonsil-hockeying her husband each time he collected her from the nursery.

Such behavioural extremes initially became apparent to those attending the couple's wedding day at the Peasenhall Assembly Rooms. As horrified guests looked on, the pair declared their vows and promptly consummated their marriage directly on the registrar's table. Gasps and anguished cries went up as the registrar pronounced Greg and Gaynor man and wife, and they set upon each other like a couple of crazed wildebeest. The assembled entourage of family and friends could barely watch (but did have the presence of mind to leave business cards and contact details with the video production team). To her credit, the resident registrar kept a stoic air of detached serenity on her face and only became flustered when her request for guests to move outside for official photographs was drowned out by Greg's cries on his vinegar stroke. Few could stomach the wedding breakfast as Greg and Gaynor spent the afternoon smearing the various luncheon courses over one another, and there was a noticeable exodus when Greg licked a whole bowlful of Eton mess off Gaynor's lower back. How the wedding cake was dispatched is still part of Peasenhall folk law.

"We're fine thanks, Hector," said Gaynor, finally coming up for air.

"Oh well, that's good," said the sardonic Hector as the unabashed pair went back at each other. "Enjoy the show! If you don't ingest each other first." Hector slung the bar towel he was carrying over his shoulder and headed back towards the bar.

"Oh, Hector," said Greg. The swift detachment from his fifty-eight-year-old wife was akin to a rubber bath mat being ripped off the tub's surface. "Do you have some lip balm by any chance?"

Music and song on open mic night at the Peasant would often throw up a surprising and disturbing array of voice and instrumental variations. Guitars and squeeze boxes would regularly feature, as would the piercing shrill of a fucking penny whistle.

Less expected, however, were the quirky acts that would arrive in from as far afield as Snape and Fornham St Genevieve. One of the strangest acts included a chorus of vuvuzela players who thrashed out the theme tunes to long-forgotten BBC sport programmes such as *Sportsnight*, *Pot Black* and *Grandstand*. On the scarier side, an exceptionally well-trained gaggle of geese from Great Wrattling honked their way through some favourite West End musical hits that caused much consternation and anxious plucking of ear hair. But even music and song sometimes had to give way to some other alternative modes of shite entertainment.

Roger Barnett was a retired care worker turned radio show presenter on the local station, *PeasePlease FM*. The station was tucked away high on the medium wave dial and could only be fully appreciated if there was a decent following wind. Roger's increasingly substantial frame was attributable to a diet consisting principally of *Ambrosia Creamed Rice*, which, as he regularly pointed out to unsuspecting listeners, had a consistency he could 'relate to'. With lips that disappeared when he smiled, rouged hamster cheeks, wide eyes and the seamless transition of head into torso, Roger had all the aesthetic appeal of a London double-decker bus.

Roger was someone clearly at odds with himself. He was a dedicated pansexual and had recently been reclassified into a gender category all of his own, such were his physiological and psychological attributes.

As the open mic community's only open LGBT representative, Roger's acceptance into a society that was more accustomed to buggering creatures that were unable to wipe their own arse, had been hard fought. To gain the respect from the county's eclectic mix of betweeded accountants and surveyors and pig murderers, Roger had offered a number of eminent traders in the area 'outside'. They included the Butcher of Aldeburgh and the Tailor of Walberswick, and when the soft-spoken, flaxen-haired radio ham wrestled the under-13 Woodbridge Rugby Team into submission, only then did the locals finally accept Roger and his bizarre concoction of genitalia.

A regular feature of Roger's daily show, *A Raucous Roger*, was the broadcaster's poems. Each day Barnett would discourse the several foolscaps of verse he'd poured over the previous night, enlightening his audience with unexpectedly graphic insights into his life. Over the air, Roger would expunge himself cathartically with descriptions of his adventures with brown packing tape, bleat tearily over love lost via the use of non-organic yoghurt, and despair for those with a tendency to stay too long in hotel lifts. The poems were a central feature of his show that essentially kept any chance of an audience at arm's length.

Given his failure to accrue any empathy over the airwaves, Roger decided on a different tack and, for the first time, brought his soul-wrenching missives to open mic night at The Peasant.

The acts on this particular Thursday were being handsomely rewarded by generous applause from the locals – even Dave Neal, the village butcher, received a great reception for his version of *I'm a Barbie Girl in a Barbie World* on his Bodhran drum. The timing appeared ideal for Roger's debut foray onto the amateur circuit. Graeme Nash welcomed the radio poet onto the stage. As he took his place in front of the mic, Roger looked across the sea of faces which, to a man, seemed to be saying, "Poetry?"

Roger cleared his throat.

"Insignificant now. That time passed.

We stand but we don't care.

Once one, now two.

Your silence says nothing. Your actions say less.

And yet, see…it's all there.

Juxtaposed to the painless, your heart firmly closed…

My penis dark and cold."

It was the last line of prose that made Shelley Parkinson snort a whole mouthful of Slow Comfortable Screw through her nostrils, down her top and onto the flagstone tiles beneath her.

Roger stopped.

Shelley, a forty-eight-year-old dance teacher with goitre, quickly stood up and headed to the toilets to clean herself up, but was so discombobulated by Roger's recital that she stepped into the gents by mistake and stumbled on Steve Naysmith investing in a vibrating love ring from the vending machine. Flustered even further, Shelley dashed out of the toilet and knocked herself clean out on the 'Mind Your Head' sign on the low beam in front of the door to the ladies.

"My wrath is unabated," Roger carried on bravely as Shelley's prostrate body was dragged into the kitchen area. "My love is gone. And now all I have is your space to fill again."

The Peasant was silent. A stillness that was eventually broken by Shelley coming to in the kitchen and releasing a rasping shot of gas from her over-relaxed bowels.

"Oh, someone let Polly out the cage!" Chloe announced over the silence.

Roger swiftly declined Graeme Nash's offer to deliver a second poem and quickly disappeared off stage.

"Many thanks to Roger there, folks. A ripper of a poem," said Graeme, forcing more than a few guffaws from the assembled crowd. "And now give a warm Peasant welcome to your very own Paul Pickering!" crowed Graeme as a bewildered-looking Shelley Parkinson was helped back into her seat.

Paul Pickering was a classic open micer; a constant presence at amateur nights across the county with the same three self-penned compositions in hand. There were no surprises, no mistakes, and very little entertainment. His songs were known verbatim and the crowd would sing along, not necessarily because they liked the tunes, but because the words had been fried into the subconscious like small vignettes a mother would regularly hum to a child.

Paul's songs were 'nice' and the creation of a man who spent many hours beheading used matches and aggregating them to form historic UK landmarks like St Paul's or the Angel of the North or Oldham bus station. The sweet-faced man with Brylcreemed silver hair, thick-rimmed glasses and upcycled clothes, was the sort of bloke many imagined being on *Blue Peter* at least twice in his youth, and almost certainly a curious guest on some daytime farming show demonstrating a disturbing contraption capable of disembowelling ferrets. His regular renditions of *Meat in the Freezer, My Heart Yearns for Barry Island* and *The Shepherds' Stomp* were CD replications of the previous gig... and the clapometer recorded exactly the same result.

"Awesome as always, Paul." Graeme Nash thanked the secondary school teacher for his triumvirate. "Now," he continued after stifling a wide yawn, "on The Peasant's passable piano...please give it up for Sally Womber!"

Observing it all from a corner of the pub, away from the attentions of the crowd, sat a middle-aged man nursing a half pint of *Beguiled Salamander* – a guest IPA from a microbrewery in Clopton. A baseball cap sporting a logo of the local chamber of commerce was pulled low over the stranger's dark sunglasses.

From his seat he absorbed the events of the evening; his face never altering from its stoic grimace. The only emotion the man displayed was when a sip of *Salamander* dislodged one poorly adhered half of the fake moustache he was wearing. A slight panic ensued, but the agent provocateur was able to fish the slug-like hairpiece out of his glass and reattach it without attracting any unnecessary attention. With only two acts left on the bill, the stranger finished a last inch of ale and got up to leave.

The sultry-looking Sally Womber enraptured the crowd with her slight adjustment to Paul Simon's *You Can Call Me Sal*. "Thank you. Good night," the stranger mumbled to no one in particular, head bowed and collar up in order to protect his identity.

"Yeah, thanks for popping in, Jeff!" Hector called out above the wailing kinesiologist. "Love to Shirley!"

The evening finished without any further drama. Plates of sandwiches and oven chips were inhaled, barrels of thin beer were changed, and the cup of cheer was full to the brim.

All the usual suspects completed their turns competently enough; even Sally Womber managed her set without the obligatory nosebleed between tracks. Mike had played. Jules had played. Much to Mike's disappointment, however, their paths hadn't crossed. This was largely due to the attentions of a chef called le Clef who'd been charming her all night with newspaper clippings featuring reviews of his perfect suet dumplings and his prodigious use of local chutneys. Jules was being spoon-fed and she appeared to be savouring every mouthful.

Exhibitionists and voyeurs alike stumbled home happy and The Peasant had enjoyed another profitable evening, a result that was in deep contrast to its sad neighbour, which needed a plan, and needed one soon.

SATURDAY MARKET

Originally part of *The Pork Road* – an ancient network of vital trading routes that connected pig breeders based in northern parts of Suffolk with markets located in the south – Peasenhall High Street had retained many of its unique features over the decades. At less than a quarter of a mile, walking the length of the street to take in its historic nuances didn't take long.

The ancient almshouses greeted visitors travelling through the village on the right of the main thoroughfare if heading west towards Stowmarket. Originally built as one house in the 16th century, it was converted into a home for the aged around 1900. Like so many buildings in Peasenhall, its visible timber frame, red herringbone brickwork and extravagant light casements provided onlookers with a glimpse back to a time when begging was a cottage industry.

An original red telephone box stood outside the almshouses, which to many people's surprise, had been registered as a listed building in 1999. The phone box had been sold recently by *Spore & Mouser Estate Agents* for £25,000 and was now home to a local speech therapist.

Following the small brook, which ran the entire length of the street, Neal's Butcher was the first commercial property on the left, and once the turning towards the village of Halesworth had been negotiated, Mike's village stores and Carl Fleming's ironmongers could be found on the right. The shops were part of a two-hundred-yard run of medieval properties sloping viscously towards the road. Over the crossroads that took motorists to either Saxmundham or Heveningham, The Whipped Peasant, The Startled Goose and the Peasenhall Assembly Rooms could all be located within a hundred yards of each other. Opposite the crop of community buildings sat Peasenhall's primary school and its much-cherished parish church; a large grey construction with some stones out front that had dead people underneath them.

A small, unmade road led up to the church, and at its entrance stood the village sign. The sign carried a large ironwork crest; an elaborate lattice within which sat the village name in bold letters and the outline of a peculiar agricultural machine.

James Smyth's seed drill had been invented in 1800 and it was the first that allowed farmers to adjust the rate of sowing. Its vastly superior manure box made it immeasurably better than any shitty apparatus before it. In fact, many generations of Peasenhallians considered Smyth the true father of the seed drill – a claim that was refuted vehemently by fans and followers of Jethro Tull, the 18th century agriculturist and prog rock guitarist. Legend has it that Smyth and Tull had a full-on scrap outside *Oxborrow's Tea Rooms* in Sibton to finally put to bed who was the true inventor of this contraption, but as forty years separated their lives it seemed unlikely that ever happened.

"Mm, that's delicious!" Sammy Grossefinger stood in front of the *Peasenhall Pies* stall sampling some chopped up slices of its crusty fayre.

The stall was one of six set up on the School Meadow car park – a pay-and-display site complete with recycling banks for bottles, weak cardboard and annoying pets – that constituted Peasenhall's Saturday Market. It was a weekly affair that ran from eight in the morning to sometime later and was managed by the village hall committee. The other five stalls offered such delights as ladies' hats, bread and cakes, flowers, cheese and Japanese war prints. A seventh stall, which sold a wide variety of bird boxes, was absent. The owner, a woodwork teacher at Leiston High School, got his pupils to make the boxes in their lessons, which he'd then sell at the weekly market. As it was only the beginning of term, his stock was low and he wouldn't be back in situ for another couple of weeks.

"Oi added a little drop o'tabasco into the pastry just to give it a bit of a kick," said the pie stall owner.

Sammy rarely purchased anything from the market. He typically scoured it for free tasters that would usually last him until lunchtime. "'Ow much?" he asked.

"Two fifty," said Jenny.

Sammy pinned his ears back. "Goo on then, oi'll take one!" He rooted for change in his padded gilet that had been the property of a local accountant not three days ago. "But don't bother wrappen it," Sammy urged. "Oi'm eaten it now!"

The way Sammy devoured a pork pie was both cruel and unusual; within seconds, it was gone.

"Looks tasty." Jimmy Jammz had been perusing a framed print, which depicted sea and land battles in the Russo-Japanese war, when he noticed his friend and decided to join him.

"Ha, Himmy!" Sammy's mouth was full of pastry.

Jimmy acknowledged his friend's welcome and stared menacingly at the produce on the market stall. "Where d'yer get the pig meat from?" Jimmy almost spat the question at the stall owner.

"Er...Jarmin's," the woman replied, somewhat baffled by the inquiry.

"Pah!" Jimmy launched a dismissive wave of the hand. "Rubbish!"

"What? Why?" said the ruffled stall owner, conscious of anyone in earshot of this unwarranted slight on her products.

"Wrong sun cream."

"What?" the stall owner spluttered.

"Jarmin's," said Jimmy. "They use the wrong sun cream."

The pie maker demanded an explanation from this peculiar-looking man whose effect on trade was akin to a drop of detergent on the surface of greasy water. Jimmy was happy to enlighten her and explained how local pig farmers had to protect the animals from the sun across the summer months and, naturally, would use a proprietary sun cream. However, the quality of sun cream employed normally matched the standard of breeding and, subsequently, the meat, which would then determine where the pork finally ended up.

"So," Jimmy continued. "If yer buyen a Tesco Foinest pork pie, chances are that pig were slathered in Ambrey Solar." Sammy nodded shrewdly at this awesome insight. "And if yer buyen similar in, say, Budgen's...well then, that pig's probably only 'ad a cheap generic lotion from Superdrug slapped on its back."

"So, what's that got to do with my pies?" said the stall owner, indignantly.

"Well, it's Jarmin's!" Jimmy cried as if that said it all. "They 'ardly use P20 do they, love?"

While scuffles broke out around the pie stall and the village's famous roaming peacocks meandered untroubled between the legs of the early shoppers, Patrice le Clef was sniffing around the cheese stall, eager to find something a little different for his board selection for the forthcoming christening party.

As he whiffed at some beech wood cheddars and cognac-infused stilton, the Frenchman clocked Jules trying on some hats on the stall opposite.

"I sink zat hat is perfect for a christening!" Patrice had crept up behind Jules and spun her round by her waist.

"Patrice!" Jules exclaimed. "You shit the life out of me!"

"Ah, your beautiful, foul mouth." Patrice's expression was similar to his savouring the smell of a fine Burgundy. "'Ow I love it so!"

"Now you're taking the piss," snapped Jules, placing a red fascinator back on the stall table.

"Never!" Patrice looked wounded.

"I'm sorry," Jules offered up a small smile. "I'm just a little cranky this morning. A woman over in Martlesham took six hours to spit one out yesterday and I'm pooped!"

"Well, I know ze perfect rem-erdy for zis." Patrice fetched the hat back off the table and positioned it perfectly on Jules' head. He positioned her in front of the stall's small mirror. "Voilà!"

"I *will* take it," said Jules after a moment's consideration. "Thanks, Patrice. That was very kind of you."

"Mon plaisir," Patrice replied. "Now, I sink we should do somefing today."

"Oh, Patrice, I can't…"

"Listen." He pressed a large, single finger on her protesting lips. "You are tired and 'ungry and you could come over to mine…"

"But honestly…" Patrice's finger squashed her lips further.

"And maybe I could prepare somefing to, 'ow we say, amuse your bouche?"

Jules let out a small, slightly terrified squeak; the Frenchman was really pushing his luck.

"I'm sorry, Patrice." Jules managed to wriggle out from under his massive digit. "But I have a lot of paperwork that I've got to get done this afternoon. I'm afraid it's tea, toast and the accounts for me right through to bedtime."

"Maybe, anuzzer time zen?" Patrice knew he had to let this battle go if he was to win the war.

"Of course, Patrice," said Jules. "Maybe another time."

As Jules headed home, Dan Naysmith set up his small battery amp and microphone stand, plugged in his *Martin & Co* guitar and began his set.

Dan was an unemployed graduate and an accomplished busker; street playing was his only source of cash until he either 'broke through' or got an honest job. His father, Steve Naysmith, was the owner of Peasenhall Farm and, being Dan's biggest fan, had bought him an instrument that demanded to be played well and positively encouraged his son to follow his dreams.

"Inheritance of the farm can wait," Steve would say. "Let's get yer on Top of the Pops first."

Like Dan, many open micers supplemented their earnings by busking and their common occurrence on the county's streets and pavements added to the cultural mix of the region. So, while the great unwashed circled the Peasenhall village car park spending their weekend budgets on whatever took their fancy, Dan's presence was a constant joy as he accompanied their prevarications with some fantastic guitar playing. His set included stuff he'd written himself and some well-chosen covers that fitted in perfectly with the slow, unfettered pace of a rural Suffolk market.

JULES

Despite the poor weather, there was a healthy turnout for the christening of the Bonham's quads. Rain had arrived early on the Sunday morning and low, ominous clouds suggested it wasn't going away anytime soon.

Father Mackenzie's warm welcome to each member of his flock as they arrived at Peasenhall's modest parish church quickly cast away the oppressiveness of the grey skies, and folk blissfully sauntered in to their humble place of worship. As ten o'clock approached, it looked like the priest would have a full house on his hands. The added bonus of a christening on top of the normal Sunday service was clearly sufficient incentive for the village's crop of passive believers. Moreover, it was also a chance for the locals to once again witness the famous 'Mackenzie Dip' which silenced even the hardiest of ballers at the baptismal font.

"I'm looking forward to your sermon this morning, Father," said Mrs. Winterburn as she popped her umbrella down.

"Ah, to be sure, it's a feckin' cracker, Mrs. Winterburn," the priest confirmed in his familiar Irish brogue.

"Where can I put my brolly?" the ancient woman asked.

"Ah, just trow dat piece of shite down in the vestibule."

Jules found a pew about half way down on the left-hand side of the church by the east wall. Inside was gloomy, cool, and smelled of a well-seated dampness that wrinkled noses until they were acclimatised. The midwife glanced up and saw the stained-glass window above her that depicted a crucifixion scene. Cheerful little spot, she thought.

Jules had been asked by the Bonhams to attend the service, as well as the christening party back at The Peasant immediately after the church ceremony (a decision the family hadn't come to lightly given their indisposition towards people with primary immunodeficiency diseases). Jules happily agreed as she always did: going to a christening was an occupational hazard. It wasn't that she loathed them, it was just she'd prefer to be back in bed having a toasty Sunday morning lie-in – lots of tea and marmite-covered crumpets while Andrew Marr ripped various MPs to pieces. Divine.

"'Allo, Jules." It was Patrice. Again. He was preparing the christening breakfast but had taken a few minutes to pop over to the church and see if he could find the object of his desire.

"Patrice?" she said, startled by the fact the vehemently passionate atheist was in church.

The chef eyed her up and down rather creepily. "You look fabulous," he said as the large church doors clanged shut.

"Oh, you know," Jules said dismissively, wondering what Patrice was up to. "A girl loves to put on her Sunday best every now and then."

The midwife was wearing a little above-the-knee black number and a pair of killer heels that she saved for such occasions. She loved to squeeze into the dress and it amused her that people barely recognised her out of her workaday navy brigade uniform.

"What time will you be at ze function?"

"Um, straight after this I guess."

"I sought maybe me and you could go somewhere else together for a drink after ze lunch crowd has been and gone?"

"Boy, you really are on a mission!" Jules exchanged slightly embarrassed glances with the people sat around her, who clearly thought the church was probably not the most appropriate place for a Frenchman to hit on a girl. (Or more probably not the most appropriate place for a Frenchman.) "Well, I wasn't planning on staying long. I didn't get much of that paperwork done, there's all the housework to do, plus I've got two, possibly three, drops tomorrow."

"Pff!" Patrice wasn't taking no for an answer this time. "You can leave zis for anuzzer day. Let's just get away for a few hours, eh? What do you say?"

Jules was completely flustered. "I don't know, Patrice. Let me have a think about it."

"Oi! Frenchy!" boomed the village priest now stationed in his pulpit.

Patrice looked up, snarling at the way he'd been addressed. "Oui?" he replied through gritted, vin-rouge-stained teeth.

"Are ye stayin' or goin'?"

"No, I 'ave food to cook for all zese people."

The congregation smiled in unison at the prospect of fine, free grub.

"Right, well, would ye kindly feck off cuz we need to get started."

"I will see you later zen," Patrice said to Jules and marched out and back to his own church.

"Now, how about we crack on wid the Lord's Prayer? Everyone okay wi'dat?" asked the cleric. A few nods of agreement and Mackenzie was underway. "Our Farder…"

As the *Pater Noster* descended on to the faithful, Jules spied Janice Muffler and the twins perched on a pew further back down the aisle. Clive appeared to be colouring in one of the carved characters on the misericord next to him with a green *Sharpie*. Janice pinged a finger at her son's ear and threatened his existence before noticing Jules' looking over. Janice flicked her head in a come-over-here gesture. The midwife picked up her handbag as quietly as she could so as to not disturb those in prayer and moved stealth-like to sit with Janice…her five-inch heels clacking monstrously on the stone floor in the process.

"Hey, how's things?" Janice whispered above the murmurings of the congregation.

Give us this day our daily bread…

"Good," replied Jules, still wincing from the racket her shoes had made.

"Getten a lot of attention there from our resident chef, oi see," Shelley teased.

"Don't," said Jules.

Janice was the nearest Jules had got to being a best mate. The pair would get together periodically to share a couple of bottles of Chardonnay whenever Jules was lonely and in need of some company, or when Janice's husband, Alan, was away on business and she needed a reward for managing the kids all day on her own. Alan Muffler was the CEO of a local skip hire company and would regularly travel abroad to catch up on the latest international skip developments or attend seminars on how he could make his lorries more dangerous on public highways.

"Is Alan back tonight?" asked Jules as the prayer finished with what sounded to her more like, "A-hem!"

"'Amara," replied Janice. "'E's stayen overnight in Bruges to see some noo skip desoigns."

Coughs and groans filled the church as those who chose to kneel in prayer clambered back onto their seats. A task that was clearly becoming more troublesome to some of the elder generation.

"'Tis grand to see so many of yuz in here today." Father Mackenzie began his oration once everyone was settled again. "And I'd particularly like to welcome the four new members of our flock to our humble parish."

Nods and agreeable whispers all round.

"Welcome, Gary, Barry, Harry and Belinda."

Mrs. Bonham nodded her thanks to the priest, blew a kiss to each of her beautifully behaved children, and smiled genially to the assembled group of family members, friends and those with nothing better to do.

"I have to say, tis rather unusual to be conductin' a christenin' when de bairns are only ten days old," confessed the priest. "But what de feck?"

Father Mackenzie glanced down at the pages of his sermon sat on the angled top of the church's ornate pulpit. He briefly smoothed them with the back of his hand, closed his eyes, straightened his back and commenced his homily.

"What!" he bellowed. "If God was one of us?"

Powerful start, Jules thought.

"Just a slob like one of us?" the priest continued. "Just a stranger on de bus, tryin' to make His way home?"

Jules glanced over at Janice. "Is he just reciting the words to that Joan Osborne song?"

"Don't ask me, darlen," replied Janice. "The only song oi know at the moment is the wheels on the bastard bus."

"And yeah, yeah, God is great," Mackenzie warbled on. "Yeah, yeah, God is good."

"I think Mike played a version of that a couple of weeks ago," Jules mused. "But changed God for dog, as a tribute to those who suffer from dyslexia."

"What's 'appenen with you two?" Janice asked, still unsettled by the close attentions of the garlic-breathed Patrice earlier.

Jules shook her head. "I think I've got into a bit of a tangled mess somehow, Janice."

"Yer duplicitous cow!" Janice winked at her friend.

The priest came to the end of his sermon. Jules looked up at the church's vaulted ceiling. I need to sort my life out, she pondered.

The Bonhams and their babies were invited to the font. The four were sweetly dressed in brilliant white gowns and each crop of hair had a kiss curl put in it by an auntie who stood proudly around the scene with the rest of the family.

Father Mackenzie used oil to sign each child with the cross and then blessed them in turn with his trademark dunking of the head into the christening water, accompanied by the familiar cry of "Wa-hey!" as they were immersed. Mrs. Bonham and her husband, Mr. Bonham, lit candles and, along with the newly appointed Godparents, made promises on behalf of the children. The babies didn't batter an eyelid, taking everything the priest could throw at them and keeping the broadest smiles on their faces the whole time.

"Dese children are truly blessed," Father Mackenzie told the Bonhams after finishing the prayers he'd offered to them.

"Thank you, Father," said Mrs. Bonham, and the ceremony was complete.

As they stepped back outside the church, it looked for one second as if the cloud would break and bathe this glorious group in warm September sunshine.

But it didn't.

Hector had raced ahead of the christening party to get the pub open and make sure Chloe had the fires going. To his astonishment, everything was as it should be. The bar had been fully prepped, the lounge was warming nicely from the open fires, Patrice's handsome buffet was laid out to perfection in the dining area and the 'Sunday lunch' playlist on Hector's iPod was floating gently in the background.

"Chloe!" Hector called out. "Thank you, darling! It looks great down here!"

Patrice stuck his head out from the kitchen. "Um, Chloe is still upstairs trying to fill 'elium balloons that spell out ze children's names." He nodded with some annoyance at the preparations. "I 'ad to do all zis myself."

Hector apologised, thanked Patrice profusely for his efforts, and ran up to his daughter's bedroom. As he knocked and walked in, Hector was accosted by a sea of inflated letters as they seized the opportunity to escape the confines of the cramped room. Chloe was slumped on her bed in tears.

"What's wrong, darling?" asked Hector, swatting a B away from his face.

"This is just too difficult!" she wailed.

"Is it the helium canister?" Hector was at a loss as to what could be causing so much distress.

"I didn't buy enough A's and Y's!" she sobbed.

"Right."

"And I can't figure out how to spell Belinda!"

"Oh, I see."

Chloe sat up and stared blankly at her father. "OIC? Even I know you don't spell Belinda like that!"

The Peasant swelled as the christening party arrived and set upon the food and drink that had been generously provided and paid for by the deliriously happy parents. The children's four-seater buggy was manoeuvred into position beneath the forest of balloons that spelled out their newly christened names: GARY, BARR, HRRY and BLINDER.

"Nice sermon, Father." Jules toasted the man in black.

"Now for someone who brings the Lord's children into dis world, I find yer rejection of de church feckin' contemptible!" Father Mackenzie slammed a mouthful of Jameson's down his throat.

Jules smiled. It was the same old blarney and she knew he was just fucking with her. "Four more sheep to patronise," she nodded over to the ever-cheerful babies. "And they look like good listeners, too."

"Don't dose feckers ever scream?" The priest had been mildly unsettled by the fact the babies were *so* well behaved. "D'ey must have the divil in 'em."

"Oh, Father!" Jules gave the priest a gentle slap on the wrist. She was about to say something else but caught Patrice looking for her over the crowd of partygoers. "Listen," she said to the cleric. "I need to disappear and could do with someone covering for me."

The Irishman followed the direction of her gaze and got her drift. "Now," he said. "I tink God's love has taken its toll on ye dis marnin'. I'd be gettin' some rest, if I was ye."

"You got it," smirked Jules. "Thanks, Father!"

"No problem, my child," the priest smiled as Jules slipped away unnoticed.

MIKE

Sunday without The Peasant's regular musical treat was a drab affair for Mike.

With so little Sunday business to be had, it was never worthwhile wasting the energy needed to heat and light the shop. By nature, Mike was an early riser, so even the lure of an extended stay in a warm bed wasn't something he'd do to use up a few hours on this seemingly endless day.

There was never a shortage of things he could be doing in the shop while it was closed, but Mike craved other distractions on his day off. He always woke with the best intentions, the whole day ahead of him. But by the time he'd poured a second cup of coffee, his enthusiasm waned and he was finding reasons not to do the things that may have crossed his mind.

The morning rain had ruled out going on his bike; he was strictly a fair-weather cyclist. The lack of a gym in the village ruled that out. He could ring his daughter, Holly, for a catch up, but she *would* be enjoying a lie in. He could practice his guitar, but he did that the night before in the absence of having any fun on a Saturday night. A day out with his camera capturing the romance of Suffolk's untamed coastline was an option, but the memory card was already full with umpteen shots like that.

Of course, he could always go out, find a woman, get to know her, make passionate love with her, marry her and spend Sundays together eating warm teacakes and reading *The Times* weekend supplements, but... But.

In the end, as more often than not, Mike trotted down the stairs of the property and started doing stuff in the shop...on his day off.

The awning above Peasenhall's general stores still carried the original owner's name; the washed-out letters of MADDOCKS' PROVISIONS were just visible across a grill of pale red stripes on greying fabric.

Beneath the awning's weathered canvas, a flimsy array of fruit and vegetables sat in open crates on a disconsolate wooden bench. On the wall above it, a thin selection of daily newspapers perched on a tarnished metal rack would oscillate wildly in anything approaching a light gust. To the left of the door, a couple of bins offered logs, kindling and a few bags of smokeless fuel to those who needed it.

Customers entering the shop would find the till and main counter, which was home to a display of assorted confectionery, immediately on the left. Mike had steadfastly refused to follow the lead of oh-so-altruistic supermarkets removing chocolate, sweets and temptation from their checkout areas. On the contrary, Mike actively encouraged children to peruse his sugary selection leisurely, while their parents paid for groceries.

On the wall facing the front door, wooden shelving held a range of beers and red wines. The white wines cooled in the chiller that fronted the centre aisle. The cabinet also offered soft drinks, milk and a small collection of takeaway sandwiches supplied daily by a local company in Hasketon. *Fantastic Baps* was run and aptly named by Andrea Rattle, a woman who hadn't seen her toes since the age of twelve. Each morning, Andrea would bring fresh supplies of tuna, beef and chicken sarnies and replace any out of date items. (She would then remove the labels and sell these on to the unassuming office workers of Friston Business Park.)

The produce aisles ran the length of the shop – about thirty feet, give or take – and steered customers to a broad freezer on the back wall. The chest offered the usual suspects of fish fingers, beef burgers, chips, ice cream and loosely packaged offal. Mike's agreement with the village butcher, Dave Neal, prohibited him selling any fresh meat. As part of the quid pro quo, Dave graciously agreed to forego the sale of catnip and stationery.

A door to the left of the freezer accessed a small storage area; a room which backed onto arable land directly behind the shop. It was awash with mousetraps. Mike was plagued by field mice that would constantly get in and wreck his supplies. The mice were particularly fond of the bags of cheese puffs he got from the cash and carry. Mike would set the traps every day with small morsels of Mars Bar and he'd catch at least one a week. Each snap of the trap was always a little victory for Mike, but as they typically 'went off' when he had a customer in the shop, he quickly learned his celebrations needed careful management.

Mousetrap: *Crack!*

Mike: "Yes!"

Customer: "What was that? It sounded like a mousetrap. You haven't got mice in the shop, have you? Full of disease, those buggers."

Mike: "Nooo!"

Customer: "So what was that noise?"

Mike: "That would be the arthritis in my fingers…it's the damp weather, you know."

Customer: "Well, get it treated."

Mike: "Naturally."

The door to the right of the main counter opened onto a set of stairs which led up to the property's modest accommodation. A lounge-diner, kitchen, two modestly sized bedrooms, a bathroom with a hand-held shower attachment on the bath, and a cloakroom literally only wide enough for a vacuum cleaner, made up the upper floor space. And all contained beneath ceiling beams that were a perfect height for medieval midgets.

Most of the furniture had been acquired from the village auction rooms in Campsea Ashe. Every *Toosdi*, people across the county would flock to a collection of condemned farm buildings and begin haggling on a host of filthy items cleared from the houses of dead people. It was bargain central. Whole suites of furniture plus any resident mites could be snapped up for a tenner. Overly wary on his first visit to an auction, Mike struggled to get in the swing of things. I'm going to embarrass myself by bidding for something at a ridiculous price, he thought.

The rapid-fire auctioneer who took the Suffolk dialect down to incomprehensibly new lows didn't help his apprehension.

"'Ow much doo oi 'ear for this 'ere lengtha roop? Ool gi'me too? Too? Too? Oi got too! Ool gi'me foive? Foive? C'marn! Buy noo or it's gorn amara! Ool gi'me noine?"

But once Mike bid and won a picture of some dogs playing a game of pool for only a pound, his inhibitions melted away and he was suddenly an auction aficionado.

Armed with Dave Neal's meat wagon for his second foray, Mike picked up all the chairs, tables, beds and mattresses he needed for the flat for less than fifty quid (although he had to discard one of the mattresses due to the blood). He also picked up a washing machine, a CD-player, an old Polaroid camera, a picture of some dogs playing poker, and his beloved bike. The total for the day was £120. Once the van was packed up, he went and grabbed a valedictory cup of tea and a sausage roll from the on-site canteen, which he promptly threw up on the way home.

"Nice stuff, Dad," Holly had said when she visited his newly furnished flat. "What's with the beige PVC settee?"

"Yeah, sorry. It's a bit retro. It'll do for me, though."

"And what is a *Bendix* washing machine? I've never even heard of that."

"I think they finished production in '83. So, built to last, right?"

The settee and the washing machine were moved on in the intervening years and Mike finally put a fresh mattress on the guest bed. There was still plenty he'd wanted to do with the place; carpet the stairs, re-do the bathroom, get central heating…

Mike's phone woke him up on in the chair he kept behind counter. Maybe he should have had that lie in, he thought, as he slowly dragged himself up to answer it.

"Hello?" Mike said, his face contorting in confusion at all the packets of cigarettes on the floor. Ah, yes, he'd been trying to alphabetize them – Chloe's idea when she came in for a pair of leg warmers earlier in the week. She was genuinely surprised he didn't stock leg warmers.

"Hi! My name's Sunil. How are you today?"

Mike huffed. "It's Sunday. I don't want whatever it is. Please, fuck off!"

JEFF & SHIRLEY

"What's that sign yer got there then, boi?"

Jimmy Jammz pointed to an orange piece of A4 paper taped to the inside of The Goose's large bay window. It read: 'Amateur Music Evening, Thursday Night, 8pm. All Welcome. Free Drink for Performers'. It also had pictures of guitars, microphones, and a few geese in silhouette around its perimeter.

"Sorry?" said Jeff, coming back up from the cellar with a fresh crate of mango and swede J2O (a limited-edition flavour exclusively for the Suffolk market). "What d'you say, Jimmy?"

"What's that sign yer got there then, boi?" Jimmy repeated word for word.

"Oh! We're having our own open mic night."

"What's all that about then, boi?" said Jimmy, before encouraging a whole slice of gala pie into his mouth.

With all the charm of an Ipswich hen night, Jimmy Jammz was probably Peasenhall's most unsavoury character.

Born on a container ship transporting espadrilles to the Greek Aegean Islands, Jimmy was deserted by his parents before he was ten-months-old and had been adopted and raised by the owners of an under-performing tiramisu factory in Athens. After the infamous Marsala wine incident in August 1983, the factory fell into receivership and, with no prospect of taking over of his adoptive parents' business, Jimmy headed to Britain a bitter man. The authorities washed their hands of the asylum seeker as soon as legally possible and deposited the young man in Peasenhall with nothing more than the clothes on his back and a holdall full of mascarpone cheese.

With no immediate support from the welfare system – and now the son and heir of nothing in particular, Jimmy lurched from one job to the next over a period of ten years. He earned a wage wherever he could, a journeyman labourer erecting fences here and bailing hay there. As time passed, his sultry Greek accent slowly evolved into the largely incoherent Suffolk dialect: drink soon became *bibble*, five was suddenly *foive,* and Tuesday quickly turned into *Toosdi*.

A directionless loner, Jimmy inevitably fell into bad company and his life took a fateful turn following a chance encounter with an IT specialist working for Network Rail. For a year, *Luncheon Meat*, as he was known on internet forums, trained and nurtured Jimmy in the much-maligned craft of email spamming. The former trainee soft cheese spreader was soon versed in every devious strategy to get unnecessary, pointless and often harmful content into people's email boxes. When *Luncheon* moved on in the spring of '06, Jimmy was a competent spammer and emblematic of a contagion that was to enrage the digital world. He had a world of frustration tucked up his sleeve and was ready to foist it upon an unassuming public.

"Well," said Jeff, replacing the Lambrini optic. "Shirley and I thought it…"

"Me and Shirley," Jimmy chipped in.

Jeff was irked by Jimmy's interruption. "What?"

"It's not Shirley and Oi. It's me and Shirley. Yer grammatically incorrect."

"No, I'm not!" Jeff's voice cracked into a girly squeak.

"Int yer?"

"No!"

"Oh," said Jimmy and pondered momentarily on how he'd got that hypercorrection so dreadfully wrong.

"So," continued Jeff cautiously, "Shirley and…I…thought it would be a good idea to have an open mic night. They seem to be popular around here."

Jimmy stopped stewing on his grammatical gaffe and nodded knowingly. "Yer mean singen with guitars and flutes and all that malarkey?" The a in malarkey seemed to go on for days.

"Yeah," Jeff nodded, suddenly excited. "You see, Shirl and me thought it would be a good…"

"A-ha!" cried the one-man email crime wave. "Shirl and me, eh?"

"Fuck!" Jeff whispered sharply under his breath; he hated getting caught out by *these people*, as his wife referred to them.

"What 'appened to Shirl and Oi, then? Hah!" Gala piecrust fragments filled the air.

"Yes alright!" Jeff conceded, while simultaneously giving Jimmy the finger out of sight below the bar. "Anyway, we thought we'd try and do some simple things to get more punters in." Jeff folded the tea towel he was holding and absent-mindedly put it over Spanner's face. (Or was it Cloak's?) "We had some nonce of a marketing guy come round the other day telling us how we needed to invest in this and spend on that to make a go of this place."

"That'll be ol' Crabbsy then," Jimmy said without looking up from the remainder of his ploughman's lunch.

"You know him?"

"Everyone knows Crabbsy. Claims 'e does all them promotions and wot-not for big companies like Ford and Bovril and the loike, but in truth 'e couldn't sell an 'orse to a glue factory."

Jeff's interest was piqued further. "Have you done business with him then?"

"Oi int. But I know FW dealt wiv 'im when 'e started up 'is business."

"Who the hell is FW?" Jeff tried to mimic Jimmy's pronunciation, *eff-dub-ya*.

Jimmy pushed an unwanted piece of cos lettuce to the edge of his plate. "Bill Fearnley-Whittingstall. FW. 'E sells wills for a liven."

Jimmy told Jeff how Nick Crabbs had persuaded FW to let him run the will writer's 'corporate communications' on his behalf. With his services retained, Crabbs started a public relations charm offensive by putting up a marquee in Mildenhall crematorium. Decked out in bright colours to grab the attention of families bringing their loved ones to be burned, the marquee was also furnished with a PA system and stark images of coffins, flames and graves on large posters that carried a call to action: 'Get a Wake. Get a Will.'

"FW 'ad to pull the plug on Crabbsy. 'E 'ad *Disco Inferno* blasten out over the speakers as some poor woman was bin wheeled into the furnace. Shocken it were!"

"Hm." Jeff stroked Spanner & Cloak's chins thoughtfully. "A little late to be selling wills. Hadn't that particular ship sailed?"

"S'what oi said!"

"Sounds like FW got taken up the garden path."

"And Crabbsy charged 'im over two grand for it!"

"Shit! That's daylight robbery!"

Jimmy jabbed his butter-covered knife towards the landlord. "Sounds like yer saw through 'im though and 'ung on to yer cash. Good man!"

"Absolutely." Jeff was almost in a cold sweat.

"But now yer got a noo master plan, roight?" Jimmy was keen to hear more.

"Well, thought we'd give it a go...our own open mic night. We don't need any fancy marketing or bloody expensive gimmicks, just a good old sing-song!"

"But, don't The Peasant 'ave them open mic nights on a Thursday?"

"Er...can't say I've noticed, Jimmy," Jeff said with less conviction than a nun politely agreeing to an evening of naked *Twister*.

A broad, knowing smile – which unfortunately revealed a mouth full of mashed pig and onion – came over Jimmy's face. "'Ere, I know what yer up to! You gorn into competition against The Peasant!" The odious man laughed hoarsely and a sliver of gelatine flew from his mouth and pitched up on Jeff's left cheek just below his eye.

"Don't be ridiculous, Jimmy!" Jeff wiped his face and retched softly. "And don't you be spreading any malicious gossip to that effect!"

The internet pest scooped a handful of Branston pickle out of its jar and transported it directly to his churning jaws. "Don't moind me," he said. "Oi loikes a bit of 'ealthy local rivalry!"

He was just about to grab the jar of piccalilli when a thought struck him. "'Ere, why don't oi do a bit a spammen for yer? Git word out on yer be'alf?" Jimmy actually belched the word 'be'alf' and his face quickly contorted. "Ooh, oi were a lil' bit sick just then."

"Absolutely not, Jimmy!" Jeff pointed a twizzle stick at the evening's only customer. "I don't want your grubby little fingers anywhere near this!"

Jimmy looked hurt. "Grubby lil' fingers?"

Jimmy's spamming had started off innocently enough.

Innocuous emails asked recipients if they wanted any fat-burning pills or to acknowledge receipt of a Nigerian lottery win. It was annoying, but effectively harmless nonsense. But after *Luncheon*'s departure, Jimmy's mails took on a more malevolent purpose as they became laced with corruption. His targets were snared with messaging like, *"the attached eviction notice requires your urgent attention"* or *"your bank account has been suspended due to suspicious activity, click here to reset"* and so on. A single click on the appropriate link and the mail's disguised infection would rampage through his victim's machine with devastating effect.

Jimmy got paid well for his malicious activities. There were no anger issues behind his involvement and he wasn't doing it just for kicks. Equally, he was never concerned by his actions from a moral point of view. All Jimmy cared about was that he was on the payroll of some political agitation group and the work was better than twelve backbreaking hours in a field pulling vegetables out of the ground.

He was breaking the law, however, and Suffolk C.I.D. had raided his home on several occasions. But each time they burst in ready to seize his equipment and shut the operation down, Jimmy always managed to deflect their suspicions with the carefully placed distractions of whiskey and faggots. Locals were furious every time the enforcement teams left Jimmy's house and staggered to their cars empty handed. The community was well aware of his sordid practices and wanted the man banged up.

"Look, Jimmy," Jeff felt he'd been a bit harsh. "No offence, mate, but you as our PR manager would be like hiring Josef Fritzl to baby sit the kids."

Jimmy was injured further. "But…yer int got any kids."

Jeff looked down at Spanner & Cloak, who had snuck behind the bar and were working their way through a couple of bags of trout and custard-flavoured crisps. "You know what I mean, Jimmy."

Jimmy drained the last drop of his cosmopolitan. "Well, if yer can't beat 'em, join 'em," he announced sprightly.

Jeff suddenly looked worried. "What does that mean, exactly?"

"Oi'm gorn to come along an' play, boi!"

"Play what?"

"Moi ennanga."

Jeff stood silent; the only noise was the dogs' destruction of a fish-inspired potato snack. "You're what?" he finally asked.

"My ennanga," Jimmy repeated. "It's a wooden zither, boi. It's from Uganda, so it seems appropriate to play it 'ere, eh?"

"Eh?"

"Long story."

Jeff looked around the new planet he clearly had just landed on. "Sorry, Jimmy. *What?*"

"It's an eight-stringed instrument," he continued. "The strings sit over a wooden trough, see, and run parallel to the resonator." Jimmy noticed this addendum had done nothing to arrest Jeff's impression of a fifteen-year-old lad stood over the contents of a sock drawer.

"Oi learnt to play it – in Belmarsh."

JULES

"Please take a seat, Julie."

Jules slipped her coat over the back of a red, faux-leather padded chair and sat down.

"Just give me a moment while I pull your details up." The co-founder of the dating agency tapped a sequence of letters and numbers adroitly onto the detachable pad of her mobile tablet and hit the return key with gusto. "Can I get you a drink?"

RuralMatch.com was a dating website with a tiny, second floor office in a block of professional service companies near to Ipswich's town centre. It was run by two friends, Clare and Harriett, who had met at Suffolk College. The pair made the decision to surrender the psychology degree they were doing together and set up Suffolk's pre-eminent relationship site for adults who reside at least a half hour's drive from any reasonable public amenity.

Jules had stumbled across *RuralMatch.com* after typing, 'haystack frolic needed ASAP' into Google search. The company logo on the home page – a silhouetted man and woman kissing – sprung out at her when she clicked on the link. At its heart was a message, *Continue for Your Love Map,* which glowed and pulsated alluringly.

At first, Jules thought the logo was a man kissing a pig but on second glance, the woman's silhouette was clearly distorted by the hat or helmet she was wearing. As she ventured deeper into the site, Jules was intrigued by the site's promise of matching her with a man of equivalent looks, intelligence and socio-economic background. "Colin Firth look-alikes pull onions for a living too!" the headline crowed.

"No thank you, Clare," Jules refused the offer of a drink and returned

Harriet's smile, who was also sat on the other side of the single desk next to her colleague.

"Sure." Clare scanned the screen in front of her. "Okay. Right. Well, we've completed your profiling based on the information you kindly supplied." The twenty-three-year-old delicately scratched the tip of her petite nose with a painted fingernail. "So, let me print that off and we'll take a look!" The girl sprang off her chair as if twenty thousand volts had just been shot through it.

Jules nodded as a palpable wave of discomfort washed over her. Was being at a dating agency merely a cry for help, she thought? She was aware of her strong feelings towards Mike, but his indifference – and Patrice's recent close attentions – had confused her. Her decision to look for love away from the familiar quarters of Peasenhall – to keep things uncomplicated – seemed the right thing to do after events in the church. But now she wasn't so sure. What good could possibly come of revealing her personal data and, worst of all, her vision of a 'perfect man' to total strangers?

Still a spinster well into her thirties, Jules hadn't worried about how long it was taking for love to come calling. She'd only had one serious relationship in her life; a six-year liaison with Colin Beecroft, a care worker at the *Yew Tree Nursing Home* in Felixstowe. They'd been close, but it was never love. Jules had actually panicked when she thought Colin was going to say 'those three words' one night in his flat while they were sat watching repeats of the *Call the Midwife* on iPlayer.

"I…I…lo…lo…lo…" He was building up to something, but it transpired it was merely the start of a sneeze.

The pair had met at *Yew Tree* when Jules was required to manage the post-natal care of a resident octogenarian with advanced Alzheimer's. The old lady's illness meant she couldn't recall who'd seeded her and, given the new-born's bald and wrinkled appearance, there were no further clues as to the father's identity after the birth. The woman flatly refused to agree to a DNA test, insisting that she had never been good at maths. Therefore, the child was given a placeholder, and duly dispatched to a foster home as soon as Jules declared it fit to do so.

He's the spit of Marc Almond, Jules thought, when she saw Colin the first time (an unnecessarily salty comparison, by all accounts). The care worker took an immediate shine to the quirky midwife holding *Baby X* in her large hands, and he wasted no time in asking Jules out for a drink. Nine pints of *Worry* later in the public bar of *The Sailor's Crotch,* and the two of them were an item.

The unspectacular relationship ticked along, appearing to suit Colin's lack of ambition far more than Jules'. He supplemented his paltry pay at the care home by selling Nazi memorabilia at weekend car boot sales. Every Saturday and Sunday Colin would trawl the county selling copies of *Heinrick's Henchmen*, pieces of Third Reich dinnerware, and swastika branded ear muffs. He'd happily wax lyrical to filthy time wasters about the fact he would – with no sense of irony – give his left bollock to have just one item of Hitler's affects from 'the bunker' on his trestle table.

But chatty, stall browsers were a dying breed, and Colin grew increasingly agitated with the swelling numbers of local immigrants 'taking over the events'. Equally, he tired of telling them repeatedly that, no, he wouldn't take ten pence for this or twenty pence for that.

"They come over," he'd moan to Jules over a Sunday afternoon KFC. "With their SportsDirect.com bag for life and their t-shirts that say 'Oi'm with stoopid', and their over-padded body warmers, and they just expect stuff for nothen'!"

"Well, it is a car boot sale, Col," Jules would reply. "It's generally full of crap that people are trying to get rid of for next to nothing."

"Yeah, but next to nothen' int nothen'!"

In a show of support, Jules agreed to help Colin with a boot sale over in Wickham Market one Sunday morning. Hindsight suggests the day didn't go to plan for two reasons.

Firstly, selling books such as *Don't Hassle the Hoffmann* – a semi-autobiographical account of Ernst-Wilhelm Hoffmann, the last commander of the fourth Panzer Tank Division and passionate hater of door-to-door salesmen – didn't sit well with the midwife. Secondly, on Colin's invitation to take a scoot around the site during a lull in sales, Jules managed to fritter away the small amount of money they'd made that morning on a fondue set, a cuddly toy, a set of champagne glasses and his-and-hers matching bathrobes. While occupants of the adjacent cars remarked on how well Jules had done,

Colin had a total sense of humour failure. So incensed was he with her 'irresponsible attitude to cash', that he slumped into his pop-up camping chair and refused to utter another word all morning.

In fact, the next conversation that did finally pass between them was Jules telling the care worker, "I think we're done."

The midwife shifted uneasily in her chair, and the motion produced a noise from the seat's fabric that strictly belonged under a duvet. Jules' cheeks bristled with embarrassment, but the agency's owners didn't react. They must have missed it, Jules thought. That or they'd been rendered insensitive to abrupt bodily emissions from years of dealing with a public collective predisposed to unrestricted flatulence.

The heat in the room was suddenly overpowering. Jules felt the walls of the claustrophobic office closing in on her, her vision blurred and tunnelled. Harriett's fixed smile twisted eerily…

"Here we go!" chirped Clare as she carried Jules' future over from the printer. "Now…" Clare moved her chair round so her and Jules could go through the results together. "Let's see what we've come up for you."

"Okay." Jules breathed again as a mild buzz of anticipation managed to claw its way above her stifling attack of anxiety.

"So." Clare slipped on a pair of reading glasses that had been nesting in a swathe of blonde hair. "Suffolk has a population of just over 720,000, of which 41 percent reside in rural areas. Which is where we specialise." Clare quickly pumped her fist and silently mouthed the word 'yes' as if to underline the uniqueness of the company's market position. "So, that leaves us with a little under 300,000 to have a go at."

Impressive, Jules thought, with those numbers there's bound to be someone out there besides a non-committal shopkeeper or an over-cloying chef.

"To begin with, you said you wanted a man."

"You go, girl!" said the grinning Harriett.

Jules' eyes widened a little; how was she supposed to respond to *that*?

"Which brings us down to 144,000 possibilities," Clare confirmed.

"Oh, the pain of the skewed gender split," said Harriett, who placed the back of her hand to her forehead in mock distress. "More girl folk than men folk in these parts…'tis so unfair!"

Harriett's descent into medieval dialect drew a sharp look from her business partner.

"You also requested a match aged between thirty and thirty-eight." Clare's eyes narrowed as she studied Jules' report intently. "Which limits us to just four per cent of the male demographic."

"Oh," remarked Jules, suddenly feeling less positive. "How many does that leave?"

"5,780." Clare confirmed the rapidly diminishing number. "Then you said you wanted to avoid anyone with a history of sexual impropriety."

An audible tut emanated from behind Harriett's fixed grin and she muttered something Jules was convinced was along the lines of "beggars can't be choosers".

"And that takes us down to 2,300."

"What?!" said Jules incredulously." More than half the men in Suffolk in their early thirties are sex offenders?"

"According to our records," replied Harriett in contemporary English.

"And then," Clare continued, "you said he had to be straight."

Another tut from Harriett.

"Which leaves us with 980."

"And then over half again are gay!" Jules folded her arms and sat back in her chair. "That's nonsense!" She felt toyed with.

"Seriously, Julie," Harriett went on the defensive. "We've built this database over four years. It's an absolute peach!"

"No golfers." Clare charged down the list. "That leaves 660."

"We even won an award for it at the Suffolk Chamber of Commerce Database Innovation Forum last year," said Harriett. "What a night that was!"

"No BMW owners. 285."

"They fully appreciated the beauty of a well-crafted spreadsheet."

"No visible injuries below the waist from farm machinery or livestock. 133."

"You have to agree, Julie," Harriett enthused. "Producing the perfect neurological match from nothing but raw data is kinda sexy, right?"

"No religious fanatics. 132."

"It's how we start the mating process here, baby!"

"And the fact you wanted to be dated with guys free from any neurological complaints…"

"Not a big fan of the nervous ones, eh?" Harriett winked and nudged her elbow. "Don't blame ya!"

"Brings us down to..." Clare double-checked the bottom of the document. "Ten."

"Ten?" Jules sat bewildered. "Are you for real?"

"Now the clever part!" snorted Harriett.

"Given your own personal profile and the fact that, statistically, members are only ever attracted to ten per cent of the dates they meet," Clare was finishing with a flourish. "We're down to a choice of one...and we've been able to select your perfect man!"

Clare passed the document across the desk to Jules who stared at the name at the bottom of the sheet.

"Do you know him?" enquired the grinning Harriett.

It read: Mike Grimshaw.

EFF-DUB-YA

Wednesday aside, weekday lunchtimes were typically a hit-and-miss affair in The Peasant.

Stuck some way off the beaten track, The Peasant didn't benefit from a passing trade. The few stragglers that occasionally made it through the door were familiar faces desperate to escape mundane tasks in the fields, the workshops or the organic delicatessens. A successful lunchtime in the working week was largely weather dependent and Hector would curse his luck if storm clouds were overhead as they would typically dampen the day's takings.

"In for another quiet session today, methinks," griped Hector as he flicked on the lights to lift the gloom in the dining area.

Chloe looked across at her father from the tables where she had been laying out mats, cutlery, and condiments for those who might drop in for a spot of lunch. "Well, Mr. Grumpy. I heard Penny's forecast and she said it was going to be fine all afternoon," the gauche girl said with some aplomb.

"Sorry, darling, what was that?" Hector replied. "I can't hear you over the violent clattering of rain on the kitchen's metal roof."

"Oh, it doesn't matter," shouted Chloe. "Just take that sour look off your face, you old sponge cake!"

Hector smiled at his hopelessly witted daughter. "Darling?"

"Yes, daddy?"

"Do you think you could put the napkins *on top* of the placemats instead?"

Hector unbolted The Peasant's door bang on the stroke of noon and in barged a very damp FW.

"William," said Hector, much to FW's further annoyance. It was either FW or Bill. "You're drenched!"

"Bloody car window decided to get stuck just as I was leaving an appointment in Foxhall," said FW, his glasses steaming up from the heat in the pub. "I only wound the bloody thing down to spit my gum out and then it jammed. I've been pissed on for sixteen miles!"

Hector took the will writer's coat and sat him on a table next to the smokeless coal fire which had just taken a hold. "Let me get you a drink. On the house."

"Cheers, Hector." The landlord's hospitality had the effect of instantly vaporizing FW's bad karma and he relaxed back in his chair, the fire's heat slowly warming the small of his back.

Bill Fearnley-Whittingstall was a rounded character in every sense. Piggy features on a moon face sat atop a frame derived from a lifetime as a sales rep. FW drove and sold. Anything. Pencils, pharmaceuticals, household cleaning products, cheap Bulgarian wine and, latterly, last wills and testaments. Life on the road and three square meals a day (the food truck on the A1152 for breakfast, a pub of his choosing for lunch, Melton chippy for tea) had compressed FW into a homogenous blob. Years of being cramped in saloon cars packed with sales samples had left his legs contorted in such a way that he was only able to kick the left side of a football.

His appearance was compounded by an inability to shake the weight of the world off his shoulders: at heart, FW was the eternal pessimist.

"It's such an awful day," said Hector, "I think I'll join you." The landlord poured himself a jolt of Islay malt and took a pint of *Swine Fever* – a dark, perspiring mild – across to FW.

"What's the special?" asked the will writer.

Hector squinted at the chalk scrawl on a blackboard above the fire to see what Patrice was conjuring up. "Tuna pasta bake by the look of it."

"Okay. Sold."

"He wants a word with you by the way," said Hector as he swiftly replaced the spoons Chloe had put on the tables with knives and forks.

FW was puzzled. "Who does?"

"Patrice."

"What about?"

"A will, I suppose," said Hector flatly. He drained his glass and took FW's order to the kitchen.

FW had been selling wills for nearly a year.

He was self-employed, but affiliated to a small will marketing agency, *Death Becomes You*. It provided FW with a combination of pointless training and fruitless sales leads via its call-centre located in an old fish warehouse near Grundisburgh. Given the agency's paltry supply of lukewarm appointments, FW endeavoured to drum up some of his own business. The salesman would often be found lurking in the hat and scarf department of Bury St Edmunds' *Marks and Spencer* with a handful of business cards. A target-rich environment, in FW's opinion, particularly in the summer months. He figured that if old folk were purchasing knitted accessories in July then their inability to warm up during the hottest months could only mean they were knocking on death's door.

"Do you know," FW's opening gambit would startle even the most unflappable pensioner. "For the same price of those woollen garments you have in your basket, I can ensure it's your loved ones that get their filthy hands on your estate and not the probate office?"

Most accosted veterans would simply wave his advances away but others, especially elderly women, would often go into shock, cry out for a nurse or simply wet themselves on the spot. In this event, FW would quickly extract himself from the scene and wait in another part of the store until the clean-up team had dealt with any spillages. After three months assaulting the vulnerable and the confused in *M&S*, and some four hundred unsolicited representations, FW had only managed to convince two people to agree to a home appointment.

The first call, to a trigger-happy farmer with vascular dementia didn't end well. The farmer tried to explain to the arresting officer that the reason he'd offloaded two rounds into the side of FW's Toyota Corolla was because he assumed the man in the suit was from the Inland Revenue. The other thing he neglected to mention, however, was that he'd been on the *Stoli* since dawn. FW's second lead was marginally less life-threatening, but still proved as shocking nonetheless.

Jayne McDermott lived in an ex-council house in the village of Hollesey, about half a mile away from the open prison of the same name. She was a spinster but, as FW quickly discovered, she certainly wasn't short of company.

Jayne motioned for FW to come in via the rear of the property after he'd announced his arrival with a knock at the front door. She warmly welcomed the will writer, thanked him for keeping the appointment, and beckoned him in through the kitchen.

She must have nieces around to visit, thought FW, as he spied a collection of 'naked' dolls lying on the sink draining board.

"Come into the parlour," Jayne said.

Parlour? FW gave the unmarried woman a half smile and squeezed past her into the lounge.

"Can I get you something to drink? Tea? Coffee? Cocoa, perhaps?"

The spinster's words barely registered with FW as the room's contents struck him dumb. His briefcase slipped out of his grasp and landed with a dull thud onto one of the few remaining clear spaces on the lounge carpet; every other available inch was taken up by a sea of toy dolls. Dozens of pairs of black, lifeless, glass eyes rooted him to the spot.

"Um... a glass of water's fine, thank you," FW said finally, his composure momentarily beyond him. "And maybe a valium?"

"Water and...what, sorry?" said Jayne, straining to pick out the second request.

FW forced his gaze away from the soulless dummies. "Er, just some water please, Jayne."

"I've got gin if you'd like something stronger. It's one of those awful discount store brands, but it does the job!" she shouted as she returned to the kitchen.

"God, no!" FW blurted out, forgetting himself for a second.

"Sorry, was that a yes?" Jayne cried.

"No. Thank you!" FW loudly reaffirmed. "I'm driving!"

The will writer examined the room again. Dolls occupied every possible nook and cranny. Small ones on the mantelpiece and bookshelves, big ones on sofas and sideboards, some stood on their own two feet in front of the fireplace, spilling out across the carpet like an invading army of zombie girls. FW looked over at the front door, barricaded by two Silver Cross prams in mint condition, their occupants sat upright and staring across at him.

That's the reason she needed me to come in through the back, FW figured.

The other thing that struck him was the clothes the dolls were wearing. They were all dressed the same. Victorian chintz-patterned dresses with delicate lacy collars, knee-length lace socks and the ensemble finished off with a pair of patent black buckle shoes.

"Oh dear," FW suddenly realised to his horror, that was exactly what Jayne had on.

FW retrieved his case from the floor and thought momentarily about legging it, but he had to stay; the dying trade was, well, dying. This situation, he bitterly complained to anyone who'd listen, was down to the increasing availability of DIY wills on the internet – an issue that could have been significantly more desperate had Suffolk's broadband been anything more than hopeless since the inception of the World Wide Web.

But where would he sit? The only seat in this doll-infested hell was a pine rocking chair with a tartan throw over the back of it. FW agonised over whether he should sit down as things began to turn all Hitchcock-esque.

"You'll have to make yourself comfortable on the carpet I'm afraid!" Jayne barked from the kitchen. "As you can see, me and the girls are a bit tight for space!"

Me and the girls? FW suddenly felt ill.

"Just plonk yourself down. I'll be in in a second."

Seriously? On the carpet? FW mused. "But this suit has just been dry cleaned," he muttered.

FW sat down in a clear spot next to one of the prams and began pulling a raft of documents out of his briefcase. He selected a biro from the collection in his jacket pocket and mentally prepared his schpeel. The 'girls' watched his every move. What's keeping her, he thought presently, how long does it take to fetch a glass of water? Then he heard the kettle switch off; she was obviously making herself a hot drink.

"There you go." Jayne came back into the lounge carrying the sort of pale blue cup and saucer you would typically find in a mental institute. "A nice, piping-hot cup of water."

The appointment lasted three and a half hours, the bulk of the time taken up by FW constantly having to advise Jayne it wasn't a good idea to leave her estate to the dolls.

"But Hannah's such a good girl," she would plead. "I have to leave her something…!"

With no friends to speak of, and no living relations to name in her will, the estate was finally divided up between the *Aldeburgh Cheese Sanctuary*, her local boy scout chapter (whose activities she would watch every Friday evening from the sanctuary of the playing field's toilet block) and Kendrick Lamar's online fan club. With tears in her eyes, Jayne eventually conceded to a more reasonable fate for the dolls. She could not imagine how they would cope if she was gone and, at one point, even mooted the suggestion of a Waco-style suicide pact so they could all 'meet their maker together'. Finally, Jayne agreed they should go to the children's hospital on her death, on the basis they each might find a child to love them and provide a new home. FW put the final detail into the draft will.

It was dark when FW left Jayne's house and he wished her a pleasant evening.

"Thank you for all your help," said Jayne as she shook FW's hand. "I'm sorry I kept you so late."

At last, a modicum of sanity, FW thought. "It's okay," he said. "It was important to get your will right."

"I know," Jane nodded appreciatively. "But now I'm running late too and those girls will be waiting for their tea. 112 helpings of Heinz ravioli won't cook themselves, you know."

FW ran to his car.

Patrice came over from the kitchen, shook hands with FW and sat down opposite him.

"Blimey," said FW. "It's like shaking hands with a JCB."

Patrice stared at the man across the table. "The tuna bake." The chef ignored the salesman's comment and gestured at his empty plate. "I put caramelised shallots in zis time. Did you like zem?"

People often found it difficult to say no to Patrice le Clef. At six-foot-four and with the build of a swarthy, French rugby prop, he was nothing if not intimidating. "Yes. Yes, I did," said FW, wiping away remnants of his lunch from his damp chin. "They gave it a certain…" FW searched for the right word. "Zing!"

"Zing?" The word left le Clef's mouth with sinister intent. "What is zing?"

FW went to take another swig of *Swine Fever*, but his glass was empty.

"Um…" The chef was starting to look increasingly menacing so FW thought it best to get down to business. "So, Hector says you need a will?"

Le Clef twisted the tea towel he held so tightly that it began squeaking. For a moment, FW wondered if the Frenchman had a small kitten inside it. "I 'ave found someone zat truly deserves my life's chattels once I am gone."

"Well, that's excellent." FW couldn't help thinking that, despite his imposing frame and somewhat alarming outward persona, the chef was a total drama queen.

Patrice scratched at his dark, two o'clock shadow. "I love zis person deeply, passionately. She 'as to 'ave my life, my soul, my very existence. Once I know that my commitment to 'er is down 'ere in black and white," he tapped FW's draft will document with a bulbous, heavily garlicked finger, "I can continue my quest for 'er undying love."

"Right, well." FW reached for a pen from his wet jacket. "Let's get some details down."

The chef reached fretfully for the will writer's arm. "You know I love 'er so much?"

"Well, of course," said an unnerved FW, the power of Patrice's hold preventing his access to the paperwork. "So, best we get your instructions down post-haste!"

The chef tightened his grip. "'Ow much will eet cost?"

"Excuse me?" said FW.

"Writing ze will. 'Ow much do you charge for eet?"

FW had to think for a moment. Why was the chef, who seemed so utterly determined to leave, not just his chattels, but his very existence to someone, suddenly concerned about the price? "Um. Well, the basic cost of the will with no exemptions or trusts is a hundred and twenty pounds."

"Pff! Forget eet!" said le Clef, waving a massive hand at the salesman.

"What?" said FW, now concerned he was about to lose the only sale of his week so far.

"Zis is too much."

"But I thought you had to leave her your soul, your existence and wot-not so you could go and quest her undying love or something?"

"Yes, but, zis," he prodded the draft deed again. "Zis I should be able to do for ten or fifteen pounds max-ee-mum!"

"You having a laugh! Ten, fifteen pounds…" FW laughed nervously.

Patrice got up to return to his kitchen. "And if you say my lunch has zing again, I will cut your fucking balls off!"

The Peasant's chef and landlord crossed paths as Patrice retreated to the sanctuary of his kitchen and Hector came over to clear FW's plate away.

"Chin up, William!" said Hector. "You know what these Gallic, alpha-males can be like."

"Sure," said the stunned salesman.

Hector collected the unused bottles of brown sauce and homemade jam his daughter had put out. "He'll come round in a while. Besides," The Peasant's landlord said buoyantly, "you've got your open mic debut to look forward tomorrow night."

MIKE

Half-day closing on a Wednesday was a tradition lost within a generation, precipitated by the public's need to keep shopping at all costs.

A once subservient nation happily accepted the retailer's prerogative to refuse entry to his emporium after noon on hump day. It was a privilege they were afforded given no one had ever starved or was left wanting for a new pair of socks because of Wednesday's shortened trading hours.

Distressed Customer: "What are you doing?"

Workshy Retailer: "I'm shutting up shop."

Distressed Customer: "But it's only midday!"

Workshy Retailer: "It's Wednesday, mate. Half day closing."

Distressed Customer: "But I urgently need a new lawn mower, my grass is nearly a foot high!"

Workshy Retailer: "Well, I'm afraid you'll have to wait 'til Thursday to cut it."

Distressed Customer: "But you don't understand!"

Workshy Retailer: "Look, I've had a busy two and a half days in this place and I'm shattered. Moreover, I am obliged by the Shop Hours Act of 1904 to close these premises at lunchtime. If I don't comply, representatives of Suffolk County Council who regulate this may pay me a pointless visit."

Distressed Customer: "This leaves me in a very difficult situation regarding my lawn."

Workshy Retailer: "Well, there you go. I mean, what next? Opening on a Sunday?"

The actions of a minority of egomaniacal shopaholics, however, forced a review of the law, which was repealed in 1994. While shops across the land took full advantage of the opportunity to keep their lights, heating and staff on for the additional six hours just to service one customer's need of a rubber band, Mike resolutely stayed with tradition and closed his store on a Wednesday pm.

Wednesday lunch in The Peasant was a thing of beauty.

Open mic nights provided a perfectly reasonable platform for performers of varying ability to try out a new song or roll out an old favourite. But there was a select band of aging musicians who steadfastly refused to participate, often citing the event and its prevalence of preening fops as vulgar.

This collective – formed by locals from Peasenhall and its denizens – did, however, like a jam, and The Peasant on a Wednesday lunch was their time. With Mickey Koblenz on piano, Charlie 'Flatbed' Pickup on double bass, Hans Holgate on guitar, Tommy Scroatle on harmonica and Steve 'Tiger' Kipling on box drum, this motley crew would congregate, chew the fat over a few pints and finally pick up their instruments and play. There was never a planned set, one of the players could just start a tune and the rest would simply follow. It was a magical formula and anyone who happened to be in the pub at the time would be in for a treat as the boys rolled from song to song. Guest players were occasionally invited to join the motley crew if they were passing through and could lend additional quality to the impromptu set. Like one of Patrice's mushroom risottos, all the ingredients came together beautifully.

"What key's that in, Mickey?"

"That'll be A-sharp, Flatbed."

"Okay, lads. Let's go!"

Mike sat on a table by the pub's north-by-southwest door with Carl Fleming. The two of them were discussing the possible merits of an additional half-day closing on Tuesdays when Mike noticed a child sat alone next to the assembled players in full flow. The boy, of Asian descent, could have been no more than eight or nine years old and was engrossed in a game he was playing on his phone.

"Whose kid is that?" asked Mike but turned to see his fellow retailer disappearing into the gents.

After a minute or so, Mike's preoccupation with the unaccompanied boy got the better of him and he strolled over to where the youngster was sat. "Hello," the grocer said.

The boy looked up from his game briefly and Mike was taken aback as long dark curls of hair unravelled and tumbled over the shoulders of the child's Metallica t-shirt.

"Oh, I'm sorry!" Mike said awkwardly. "I thought you were a boy."

"I am." The boy returned to his game.

"Oh, I'm sorry," Mike began to sound like a scratched record. He looked around for any signs of a guardian. "So…" Mike struggled for something to say. "So, when are you going to get that mop cut?" he mocked gently.

The boy was on an advanced level of *Candy Crush*. "My dad cuts my hair," he said on the completion of another stage. "And I think he likes it as it is right now."

"Get out of it!" Mike continued to tease. "That's girl's hair!"

The boy sighed, paused his game and was about to throw a well-honed scowl at the adult and his unwarranted opinions when he noticed the grocer was wearing a vest top with a soft, plunging neckline. "Girl's hair, eh?" said the boy with an irony beyond his years. He promptly emitted a short snigger and returned to the screen.

"You okay, Tom?" The boy's mother was sitting over at the bar finishing off her drink when she noticed the attentions of Mike and came over to ensure all was above board.

"Yep," replied Tom.

"Hello," said the tall, elegant Asian lady to Mike, the tone more enquiry than salutation.

"Hi." Mike was immediately captivated by this stylish woman suddenly at his side and was more than mildly enthralled by the way she made a simple jeans and t-shirt outfit look super chic. Mike regularly struggled to make conversation with new faces, but in the presence of such beauty, he was prone to out and out stupidity.

"Shouldn't Goldilocks over here be in school?" He nodded in the direction of her son.

"Sorry, who are you?" said the boy's mother, suddenly alarmed by the opinions of a total stranger.

"Oh, I'm Mike Grimshaw." His offer of a handshake was declined. "I run the local shop over the road." The shopkeeper's credentials did little to placate the unnerved woman. "I was just concerned the little fella was on his own and...well..."

The woman's body language suggested this conversation wasn't going particularly well, so Mike decided on a different tack. "I haven't seen you in here before, are you from the village?"

"My husband and I live over in Bruisyard," said the woman, defrosting slightly. "He runs the hairdressing salon over there, *Tony and Gee*."

"Ah! You must be Saj Ghafoor's wife! I get my hair cut up there all the time!" Mike was thrilled he'd probably just clawed his way out of a deeply dug hole. "So, you're the one!"

"Excuse me?" the woman could not have been more offended.

"Oh, that came out all wrong," Mike tried to explain. "I meant to say, you're the one he's always talking about...Yolande, right?"

"Right," Yolande replied, her eyes filled with suspicion. "Come on, Tom. It's time to go."

"Oh, look, please don't go on my account. Just ignore me. I'm an idiot at the best of times."

Yolande forced a half smile. "It's fine. I've got to get Tom back to lessons."

"Oh, so you *do* go to school!" said Mike, a tad perplexed.

The boy turned off his phone. "Nope."

"We home-school," explained his mother, lightly touching his delicate locks.

"Hah! Home-schooled?" Mike scoffed and looked around to see if anyone else was listening to this nonsense.

"Look, what *is* your problem?" Yolande hissed aggressively at Mike and stepped in front of her son by way of protection.

Saj and Yolande were raising three children and each was home-schooled. They had agreed the local schools were unable to provide their kids with appropriate moral and spiritual needs and therefore took full responsibility for their education. The tutoring took place in a permanent classroom set up in a summerhouse situated at the bottom of their garden and was kitted out with old-style desks (complete with inkwells), a blackboard, a bookshelf full of books and a cane. Each child was tested regularly to ensure they were on track for the standard examinations that were now looming large for their eldest.

Aware that many parents had openly criticized the Ghafoor's on their decision, they made sure all three of their children had a strong social interaction program with their peers. To that end, the kids enjoyed scouts, chess, and badminton clubs, Tom played for the local under-nine football team and all three actively engaged on *Tinder*.

"So…who's your favourite teacher?" Mike asked the boy, still grinning from the idea the lad was getting a home education.

"Mum and Grandpa teach me."

"Can you please just stop talking to my child?" Yolande was becoming hysterical.

Mike looked askance at Yolande. "Don't you have a job then?"

The question proved to be the final straw. Yolande grabbed her son's things and threw on her coat. "You're a pest!" she screamed. "Just stay away from us!"

Mike was dumbfounded. "What? I thought it was a reasonable question!"

"Grandpa teaches me in the morning and then Mum takes over when she comes in after her morning shift is done!" the boy cried as he was dragged off towards one of the many exits. "Tomorrow, we're making shoes out of fennel!"

Mike headed back over to the table where his drink was waiting. "What the hell was all that about?" he asked the recently relieved ironmonger.

Carl patted Mike's shoulder as he sat down. "So, you think that his schooling is phoney?"

"I guess it's hard not to agree," replied Mike. "And what makes them qualified to take on such a responsibility?" Mike protested. "He cuts hair and she does a morning shift doing…what exactly? Modelling on daytime TV by the look of her?"

"Hmm." Carl pushed the grocer's drink back across to him. "The rather lovely Yolande takes the morning physics lectures at Suffolk College and good old grandpa, aka Professor Akrim, was one of the original members of the project team on the Hadron Collider."

Mike put his drink down; his world had suddenly got a tad fuzzier.

"You really should try engaging that brain of yours before speaking every now and then, Mikey." Carl stood up; it was his round. "It helps enormously with public relations."

As the ironmonger/editor chuckled and headed for the bar, Mike sat quietly, cursing his inability to keep his thoughts to himself. He looked over at Greg and Gaynor Bradley, who had begun a lost afternoon of drinking, snogging and playing *Top Trumps* – a Suffolk version that pitched John Deere's tractors against those of Massey Ferguson's and turnips against sugar beet. The sumptuous notes cascading from The Peasant's impromptu band intermingled with the pair's exultations of horsepower and carbohydrate content.

Mike looked down at his feet and saw they had magically grown into a size eighteen, and he wondered if he was having a stroke.

CLOAK & SPANNER

As far as dogs go, Cloak & Spanner were unique.

Their uniqueness wasn't, however, derived from the fact they happened to be conjoined Labradors, a predicament which left the pair with the standard quota of heads and tails, but only a single body containing the shared organs.

As soon as he clapped eyes on the newborn pups, the vet at *Martlesham Mutts* suggested they should be destroyed. The dogs were unlikely to survive the first few days or weeks and the most humane thing to do, in the vet's opinion, was put them to sleep. The family whose bitch had given birth to the litter of seven pups, which included Cloak & Spanner, discussed their options in the vet's waiting room before deciding to take the canine anomaly home so it could spend what short life it had left with its brothers and sisters. (The family's eldest son also wanted to make a short film on his phone about Cerebus planning his retirement from Hades and trying to recruit a suitable replacement.)

As it transpired, Cloak & Spanner proved the veterinary surgeons wrong, and rather than simply laying down and dying, they grew stronger with each passing day. The dogs' ability to cling to life was remarkable but it didn't make them any more attractive to families looking to give a pup a home. Any attempt by the family to offload Cloak & Spanner in a bizarre BOGOF deal was promptly pissed on from a great height by prospective buyers. So, one by one, they watched as their siblings were sold off to new owners until only they remained.

They were good-natured pups, but like all twins, they squabbled over life's details; what food they ate, when they went to sleep, which direction they should wag their respective tails in and so on. Walking them was the equivalent of trying to ride a tandem in opposite directions. Cloak would always want to sniff out the kids' playground tucked away behind the village Assembly Rooms while Spanner would demand a dig for bones in the church graveyard. The ensuing tug-o-dog would often leave the walker requiring a shoulder to be popped back in.

Clearly encumbered with the unusual pairing, the family did grow to love them over the years, despite having the words "DOG FREAK SHOW" sprayed on their garage doors on a regular basis. But as they grew older and much bigger, Cloak & Spanner's two heads became an insurmountable issue as the pair began to eat their owners out of house and home. The family simply could not afford to keep them and had no choice but to deposit the much-loved pet with the staff at the *Ipswich Home for Unseemly Pets* (Tagline: *Who wants a pug with an ugly mug?*).

The challenge for Cloak & Spanner was now the six-week window to win someone's charitable heart and bag a ride home: get an owner or a lethal injection, simple as. With only two days remaining on their stay chart, Shirley Timberlake had popped into the home on the day of her retirement from the police. She was there to say a final farewell to a retired police dog that was knackered and on its last legs. Shirley had mulled over whether to take it home or not, but it was pointless; the dog couldn't walk and had no control over its bowel movements. Just as Shirley scratched a last goodbye on its chin, she spotted the conjoined labs.

Jeff was furious with her when he came home to find that a mythical beast had eaten his dinner, slippers, and most of the pages in of his copy of *The Train Modeller*. "If we're going to get this pub, that thing's just going scare punters off!" Jeff had reasonably argued as the dogs started eating lumps of coal.

"Suffolk people love pets," countered Shirley. "And the quirkier the better. They have an affinity towards them." She was in no mood for budging.

And so it was that Cloak & Spanner were installed as the resident dogs at The Startled Goose. Any initial shock customers experienced from their appearance soon mellowed as the dogs' sweet personalities were quickly revealed and, if lucky enough, punters would be treated to the thing that made Cloak and Spanner truly unique: give them a plate of spaghetti and meatballs and they could re-enact the scene form *Lady and the Tramp* down to a tee.

JULES

She spied him through the shop front window.

There he was, Mike Grimshaw, punching in another collection of grocery prices into his till. Poor lad, she thought, as his image intertwined with hers in the reflection of the glass, he so needs looking after.

Jules now believed she was the one to do it.

The quaint shop bell rang as Jules stepped in off Peasenhall's main street. "What's occurring, Mr. Grimshaw?" Jules asked cheerily as Mike was handing a small carrier bag back across to the ever-frail looking Mrs. Winterburn.

"Oh, hi, Jules," Mike said with slightly more restraint and nodded solemnly towards the old lady.

The eighty-six-year-old's hunched and petite frame draped in a heavy, dark overcoat – which got an inch closer to the ground each year – was a familiar sight in the village. Many would throw her a wave as she made the daily trek from her small terraced cottage to either Neal's Butcher or Mike's shop for provisions. It was no more than 150 yards each way, but her average walking speed ensured each leg of the journey was on a par with one of Sir Ranulph Fiennes' expeditions.

Jules frowned. "What's up?" she mouthed.

"There you go, Mrs. Winterburn," said Mike, making sure she had a tight hold of her groceries before pointing over her shoulder. "Look who's here. It's Jules!"

The woman turned stiffly to face the midwife, tears rolling down her face.

"Oh, Mrs. Winterburn!" Jules rushed over full of concern. "What the devil's the matter? Why are you so upset?"

The old lady shuddered as she tried to compose herself, but the grief was too great and she descended into more tears. Jules' sorrowful eyes narrowed and she looked at Mike as if to say 'poor thing'.

"Come on," she said, placing a comforting arm around the pensioner. "Tell me all about it."

"It's my father," the old woman said through heavy sobs.

Jules' frown returned. "What about your dad?"

"If he were alive…he'd be 126 today," she said and crashed her sobbing face into Jules' shoulder.

"Oh, it's his birthday!" Jules used a stretched-out finger on her free hand to make circles by the side of her head.

"She wanted to make him a special tea," Mike interjected, stifling a grin. "But I persuaded her to keep it to her usual tin of pilchards for a Thursday. Isn't that right, Mrs. Winterburn?"

"The Lord takes them at such a precious age," bemoaned the tearful woman.

"But your dad died when he was ninety-eight, I remember the funeral." Jules gently eased the woman's frail body away from her chest. "He has the village record for Peasenhall's oldest ever resident."

With that, the pensioner dissolved into a convulsive fit of inconsolability. "Come on," Jules said, fearing a losing battle. "Let's get you in the car, I'll run you home."

"You shouldn't laugh. If nothing else, she's a regular customer." Jules gently scolded Mike after settling Mrs. Winterburn in her car.

"What?" Mike snorted flippantly. "She barely buys sufficient calories required to keep an Ethiopian mouse on the go."

"You won't be saying that when Aldi opens up next to the Assembly Rooms, will you?" quipped the baby grabber. "You'll be desperate for customers like Mrs. Winterburn when they decide they're happier buying four hundredweight of lard for the same price as one of your little packets."

Jules had hit a nerve. Mike's trade had been steadily falling for some time and the number of familiar faces visiting the shop regularly was noticeably on the slide. Popping in for a quick pint of milk wasn't so crucial when you had a nine-gallon keg from a superstore in your fridge.

"So, how's your day been?" Mike wanted to change the subject.

"Trafficky," said Jules.

"Yer got a leave yesterdi if yer wan a get there 'amara'" was a popular Suffolk phrase used by locals when city types enquired on the approximate time required to go from A to B. Alongside vitamin deficiencies and a crazed aversion to immigration, Suffolk suffered from one other serious affliction: slow traffic.

After the previous day's cooling rain, the Indian summer had kicked back in and the warm September sunshine put a smile on everybody's face. Unfortunately, one other by-product of 'a bit of currant' was the abrupt materialization of pensioners on every rural by-way.

Emerging from homely burrows and relaxed straightjackets, thousands of aging drivers – who couldn't normally be trusted with a fish knife, would hit the county's roads. Smelling mildly off urine and biscuits, pensioners would set off at speeds synonymous with the Stone Age: 19 in a 30, 26 in a 40, and 28 in a 60. Mile after aching mile of pent-up motorists would boil and frazzle behind these road sloths as they ambled along tight lanes on the lookout for knitting clubs or garden centres advertising seasonal offers of free tea and scones with every purchase of an herbaceous border.

They added countless unnecessary hours onto people's journey times that they would never get back. Efforts to hurry them up through the flashing of headlights or the beeping of horns were all to no avail. The elderly occupants of these cars were either oblivious to it or simply remarked, "You won't get there any faster!" Most had given up looking in a mirror, either at home or in the car, some years earlier, and as the number of overtaking opportunities in the entire county totalled thirty-seven, once one of these accelerator-shy seniors was in front of you…you were doomed!

Jules had begun her morning round by pointing her Fiat 500 east towards Framlingham and its impressive castle. As expected, she encountered the usual sticky, rush hour traffic into the quaint market town. The small jams were made more bearable by the sun's warm rays and the unexpected airtime of a couple of her favourite tunes on Radio 2.

Like a cat in a bag, waiting to drown, this time I'm coming round!

Her first appointment at nine was at the Hampton's residence. The growth curve of Billie Hampton's four-month-old son was way above the average, and

Jules had to insist on Billie returning to formula and keep her infant off *Birds Eye* potato waffles for now. Back in the car after an hour, the midwife's next call was in Saxmundham – a drive of 15 to 20 minutes at most in any other part of the world with a reasonable road traffic system – but she got caught behind a loaded tractor soon after leaving the Hampton's.

No Farming, No Food. Please be Patient.

The message adorned the back of many Suffolk farm trailers as they galumphed their way along the highways at harvest time. The farm vehicle Jules was stuck behind was pulling a crop of recently harvested onions and as she dropped down into third gear, she realised she could actually smell its cargo from her car seat.

"Shit sticks," Jules mouthed, noticing her speed had dropped to around 15 mph. The day was already getting away from her and the intense smell of onions from the trailer was making her tummy rumble; she suddenly craved a bag of *Walker's* crisps.

The tractor's bulk occupied most of the road's width which, regardless of any oncoming traffic, made overtaking impossible. The load height was also substantial and the midwife regarded the precariously balanced onion mountain high above the sides of the trailer with some trepidation.

Please be Patient.

The words were being scorched on Jules' soul as the minutes behind this lumbering wagon ticked by and her patience wore onion-skin-thin. A second later, she was travelling noticeably slower.

"What the...?" Jules huffed as her speedo dropped to 13mph. The tractor had caught up with a couple of cyclists clad in bright lime green spandex, riding two abreast and merrily chatting away. Jules reached across for her mobile. She thought it best to tell Mrs. Hynard to cross her legs; sampling her urine would be a little later than expected. But before she could dial a number the tractor slowed further.

"Seriously?" Jules shook her head as the needle in front of her flirted with the 10mph mark. The cyclists had caught up with a red Nissan Micra, the occupants of which were clad in *Edinburgh Woollen Mill* and also merrily chatting away.

This is ridiculous, Jules thought. She edged the Fiat out to the right in a determined effort to find a way past. As Jules craned her neck to see beyond the Nissan, there was a violent *thunk!* The tractor had hit a pothole and a precariously balanced onion was projected from its trailer and onto the Fiat's windscreen.

"Whoa!" Jules cried as the pulped vegetable slithered across the glass. She was just about to turn the wipers on to dislodge the mess when the tractor smashed into another, much deeper pothole. This collision dealt a catastrophic blow to the onion mountain. In an instant, dozens of light brown missiles began raining down on Jules' car. The midwife slammed on the brakes, but it was too little too late; she didn't stand a chance as the Fiat was struck repeatedly by a viscous vegetable onslaught.

Dazed and confused, Jules stumbled out of her car and watched as the tractor took an immediate right turn into a field entrance, the cyclists paused in a passing place to take on some water from their bottles, and the Nissan turned left into the driveway of a garden centre (or a knitting club). The road ahead was clear. A sign at the roadside said: *Saxmundham Welcomes Careful Drivers*.

"Monkey knobs!" was what Jules thought of that, and the midwife turned to climb back into her car. Her jaw immediately slackened and her knees softened as the damage to her beloved Fiat by the onion storm was fully revealed; it had been bhaji-ed.

"No point getting all bent out of shape, Jules," Mike said as he checked the sell-by dates on his doughnuts. "You more than anyone should know you've got more chance of seeing the Queen's backside than getting anywhere in a hurry round here."

"You're right, Mike," conceded Jules as she looked out of the shop window at the onion-coated Fiat containing Mrs. Winterburn, who sat furiously wrinkling her nose.

"Not allergic to onions by any chance?" Mike smiled.

"No, I'm not as it happens, Mister Funny Bollocks."

Mike blushed again at Jules' unerring ability to bring the coarsest language into any everyday conversation.

"Hey!" said Jules, starting what was the beginning of a conversation she'd been going over and over in her head for a couple of days. "Did you see The Goose is advertising its own open mic night this evening?"

"What?" said Mike, genuinely surprised. "Open mic at The Goose? They don't seriously think they're going to prise regulars away from The Peasant, do they?"

Jules shrugged.

"Hang on." Mike eyed her cautiously. "You're not thinking of going, are you?" The shopkeeper was clearly troubled by the prospect.

"No, don't be daft!" said Jules, her vampire/rabbit teeth brightly resonating on her lower lip. "I'm only winding you up!"

"Good job too," snorted Mike.

"But," Jules said coyly. "I was rather hoping that after we're done at The Peasant, maybe we could go get a curry or something after?"

"It wouldn't exactly be fair on Hector if we just jumped ship at the first opportunity to go and play somewhere else..."

"Although, I think I'll probably pass on the bhajis," Jules afforded herself a giggle.

"And while Graeme can be a bit of a tool sometimes, you can't fault his efforts..."

"You're not actually listening to me, are you, Mike?"

"And The Peasant does get a great turn out each week..."

"MIKE!" Jules slammed a large foetus-grappling hand onto the counter top. "Are we going for a curry after the gig tonight or fucking what?!"

The pair walked outside to Jules' car after agreeing that Mike would book a late table for two at *Pappa Dum Preach* in Woodbridge.

"Well...see you tonight, then." Mike sounded like a fourteen-year-old.

"See you tonight...then." Jules mimicked his rather sweet line and the pair laughed together.

"Aah, look at Mrs. Winterburn," said Mike turning to the car. "She's dozed off."

"Nope," replied Jules with a slightly anxious look on her face. "I forgot to leave a window open. I think she's in a heat coma."

OPEN MIC

It was Thursday night once more. Once more, open mic night in Peasenhall.

This particular Thursday night, however, represented a sea change in the availability of live *moosic* in the village of Peasenhall as both its public houses welcomed amateur performers through their respective doors. Separated by just a couple of terraced houses and the School Meadow car park, the village people had, for the first time ever, a straightforward choice: *moosic* at either The Whipped Peasant or The Startled Goose.

At 8.30pm in The Peasant, Graeme Nash calmed his cronies, stepped up to the microphone and commenced proceedings. At precisely the same time in The Goose, Jeff Timberlake, stepped up to the mic stand and suddenly realised he was short of a bit of kit, and in doing so set a familiar pattern for the rest of the night.

The running order for the evening across the two establishments was set earlier in the day and each had been publicised a little differently. Graeme had posted The Peasant's smorgasbord of precocious local talent on his popular Facebook page, which had 832 'likes' and was the go-to social media site for the highly regarded event. The line-up for the evening looked strong.

8.30 – Graeme Nash, Host: Marzipan Junction (own composition)

8.40 – Mike Grimshaw, Guitar: The Coward of the County; Ebony and Irony

9.00 – Jules Wiseman, Banjo: Push Baby Push (own composition including powerpoint presentation); Lust for Life

9.20 – Alan Hedgeworthy, Keyboard: Flashdance (What a Feeling!)

9.30 – Paul Pickering, Guitar: Meat in the Freezer; My Heart Yearns for Barry Island; The Shepherds' Stomp

10.00 –Mrs. Dorothy Wellman, Acapella: Ziggy Stardust; When Doves Cry

10.10 – Dan Naysmith, Guitar: Bound to Love (own composition); High & Dry

10.20 – Roger Barnett, Poetry: Help me, Mother; Soil on my Face (own compositions)

10.30 – George Raft, Jew's Harp: Mashed Potato, Grilled Tomato (own composition)

10.40 – FW, Guitar: tbc

10.45 – Sally Womber, Piano: Papa's got a brand-new pig bladder (trad); Crystal Healing (own composition)

10.55 – Herbert Nash, Guitar: The Dinghy Song (own composition)

11.00 – Time.

Meanwhile, Jeff posted The Goose's line-up on an A4 sheet, a copy of which was left on every table in the pub. (An ex-colleague from Ipswich nick had promised Jeff some publicity through a trendy local events magazine, *Hippnen!* which he was now editor of, but had to pull it when an ad for a fundraiser for a new badger underpass needed inserting.) On paper, The Goose's first foray into open mic territory appeared to lack the variety and depth of its renowned neighbour.

8.30 – Jeff Timberlake, Host: Health & Safety Statement (own composition)

8.40 – Shirley Timberlake, Co-host: Request for consideration of local residents when leaving the premises (trad)

9.00 – Jimmy Jammz, Ennanga: Nigerian Inheritance; Mr. Virus Man (own compositions)

9.20 – Sammy Grossefinger, Wooden Pallet: Green Onions; Help!

9.30 – Roxanne Leathers, Guitar: I Want Your Sex

9.40 – Pammy Grossefinger, Acapella: Shouting Popular Public Announcements from Ipswich Train Station

10.00 – Tammy Grossefinger, Assorted Empty Jars: Do the Shake and Vac! (trad) (extended remix)

10.20 – Jimmy Jammz & The Grossefingers, Musical Ensemble: Do They Know it's Christmas Time?

10.30 – Time

With all the talent lined up and raring to go, the moment of truth had arrived. Bragging rights were up for grabs for the first time in this otherwise sleepy little Suffolk hamlet. An audience of sixty odd crammed into The Peasant for its regular feast of *moosical* highlights while The Goose had nine in attendance (including staff and animals) for its initial harmonious outing. History was about to be rewritten as the two pubs went head to head; both determined to make *folk stuff* happen in Suffolk.

Hector wasn't taking anything for granted.

The Peasant's landlord laid on the usual welcoming snacks for performers and audience alike but had gone the extra mile given the introduction of some nearby competition. Plates of brie-covered chips and trays of coronation goose sandwiches (an ironic gesture on Hector's part) circulated the tables to triumphant acclaim.

Over at The Goose, Jeff and Shirley both forgot it was Damien's night off. In the absence of any suitable kitchen support, the landlady hastily prepared a few bowls of roast potatoes but, with her back turned momentarily, they were instantly snarfed by Cloak & Spanner. The only other choice she had to offer the clientele was a spit roast, but that would take hours to defrost, and the prospect of the inevitable double-entendres was unthinkable. Shirley was therefore resigned to ordering a couple of large pepperonis from *Speedy Pizza* in Rendlesham. When these still hadn't been delivered after an hour – despite the constant haranguing of the takeaway's Lithuanian staff, she slung a bag of trout and custard crisps at anyone who wanted one.

The evening line up in The Peasant produced some unusually fine *moosical* performances. Hector sensed that word had got round about The Goose trying to muscle in on the scene and this had fuelled a desire by the performers to turn on the style in a display of open defiance and allegiance.

"Bit of a rum do, The Goose putting on its own gig," Dan Naysmith told Hector.

"It's okay." The publican remained philosophical. "Just means I have to try a bit harder. No bad thing really."

"Well I'm going play my heart out for you," Dan said to the very humbled landlord.

Each act went down a storm, but one notable performance was a fine rendition of *Mashed Potato, Grilled Tomato* by George Raft on the Jew's harp. The tune was a variation on Johann Albrechtsberger's concerti for the instrument in E-flat that the Austrian composer had penned in 1770. The crowd was totally enthralled by the enigmatic piece right up until the moment when George's tongue started bleeding rather badly. The other main highlight in the free house was, of course, the debut of Mr. Bill Fearnley-Whittingstall. As a newbie to open mic, FW had just two songs committed to memory that he was comfortable playing to the assembled patrons. The first had a familiar ring to it and was his own take on a lonely American farm labourer who longed to be released from the evil clutches of his tyrannical master. His second ditty was a cover of Paul and Michael's *Matchstalk Men and Matchstalk Cats and Dogs* that he did in a high falsetto.

"Ladies and gentlemen!" Graeme Nash gave a thumbs-up over the heads of the audience to George Raft, who had trudged back to his table and dropped his still bloody tongue into a glass of salt water. "Please give a warm, Peasant welcome to Peasenhall's very own merchant of death...FW!" As the crowd clapped with wild abandonment, FW took a large gulp of *Incontinent Badger* to steel his nerves, gave a final adjustment to the strap of his guitar and smashed down on the first chord of *Serf in the USA*.

Mike and Jules sat together, cheered on their fellow contributors, and enthusiastically celebrated each other's performance. With Patrice ensconced in his kitchen as a result of the constant supply of free and paid-for food, Mike had Jules' attention for the whole evening with no pony-tailed, French foodie cramping his style.

It was all going exceptionally well; an evening in stark contrast to events over at The Goose.

After a delay of forty minutes (while Jeff fetched the microphone his step brother used for his troubling clown act at children's birthday parties), the opening announcements by the Timberlakes regarding health, safety and noise abatement were met with derision from the thin and tiresome crowd. As Jeff pointed out the need for caution when using the hot tap in the ladies' toilet, he actually received one of Jimmy Jammz's loafers to the side of his head.

"That's a farewell from the Iraqi people, yer dog!" cried Jimmy. The patent leather slip-on bounced off Jeff's pate and onto an overcrowded table of magazines, leaflets and several unwanted copies of the *Peasenhall Quandary*, spilling pointless literature all over the pub floor. As the

Grossefingers wiped away tears of laughter, Jimmy grabbed his ennanga and headed to the stage.

The internet spammer mixed the quirky sound of the gnarled, Ugandan zither with words sung straight from the body copy of one of his illicit emails.

An urgent business transaction, oi must solicit yer strictest con-fi-dence!
The source of this fund be com-pli-cated, but it's lyen here just doen nothen!
All oi need's Yer Name and Address! Yer Bank Details! Yer Postal Code!
And we need a retainer, boi...to get things goen!

The song was made even more remarkable by the fact Sammy and Pammy Grossefinger got up and began dancing to the cruel noise emanating from the bizarre on-stage act. As they gyrated around the tight bar space, Pammy's sister, Tammy, took to her pipe.

"Er, you can't smoke in here, Tammy!" Shirley shouted above the tuneless twanging.

"Uh-huh," said Tammy, ignoring her.

With Jimmy done, Sammy's efforts to illicit the notes of Booker T and the MG's classic instrumental, *Green Onions,* out of a wooden pallet were brought to a sharp (and gratifying) end when he managed to stick several large splinters in his forearms, and pain forced his early retirement from the show. Roxanne Leather's maiden performance was then held in abeyance when the dry-ice machine Jeff had hired malfunctioned and the pub had to be cleared, adding a further delay to proceedings. Roxanne was Sammy's cousin, and a thirty-two-year-old masseuse who advertised her 'services' in the classifieds section of the *Peasenhall Quandary.*

"Not got a bad voice, 'as she?" said Sammy proudly.

"Yer roight there, boi," agreed Jimmy, picking shards of pine out his skin. "By the way, is she still liven off the fat of the gland?"

While Roxanne managed a passable rendition of *I Want Your Sex* – although singing through a slaughterhouse window would have been a generous review, it only represented a very small light at the end of a very long tunnel. Pammy Grossefinger's recital of train station announcements soon followed that offered much to support the call for the wholesale castration of the lower classes.

"The next train to leave platform three will be the six-fifty fast service to Low'starf!" wailed Pammy, as her adoring fans clapped and cheered the sequence of train departures and arrivals from every conceivable corner of the county.

Then, as incredible as it seemed, the evening took a turn for the worse.

As Tammy Grossefinger popped her pint of rum and coke at her feet and steadied herself and her collection of poorly rinsed pasta sauce jars for the performance of the popular TV commercial tune, *Do the Shake and Vac*, a furious row erupted across the bar between Jimmy and Shirley.

"The poster most clearly states 'free drinks for performers'!" The deplorable emailer taunted his host by waving an empty pint pot in her face.

The ex-traffic officer stood her ground. "No, Jimmy. It reads 'a free drink for performers' and that means 'one free drink per performer'. You've had that. Now anything else has to be paid for."

"Look!" Jimmy was adamant. "Yer been 'appy to exploit all this free moosical talent in order to git some punters into this shit pub o'yers." The spammer looked around. "And oi'd say this is by far the busiest yer bin since yer opened. So, in fairness, oi fink yer 'ave to give only those performen free drinks all noight."

"Don't be daft, Jimmy," Jeff stepped into the argument in an attempt to calm an escalating situation. "All the punters in tonight *are* performers, so that would mean free drinks all night for everyone."

Jimmy launched his arms into the air. "Yay! Jeff 'ere just said free drinks all noight!"

"No, Jimmy! My point was…" Jeff desperately tried to backtrack.

Shirley fixed her husband with a look of raw hatred as the band of Grossefingers headed towards the bar. "Are you fucking insane?"

"Shirley, you know, and more importantly, he knows, what I was trying to say," maintained Jeff as the evening's patrons descended like a tropical storm. "It's just this bunch of freeloaders are taking the piss."

At which point, a dreadful hush fell.

And then the fists started flying.

MIKE & JULES

Mike and Jules were shown to a square, white-linen-covered table for two alongside the bar-cum-takeaway-counter and were offered the traditional appetizers that had been the mainstay of the sub-continental dining experience in the UK for decades: lager, poppadum and assorted pickles.

Mike grabbed the PVC menu from the waiter and feverishly examined its contents. "So, what's good here?" he said, smacking his lips.

"Well they've done a decent job of retiling the ladies' toilets," said Jules, eyeing the starters.

"No," said Mike, nodding at the menu. "What do you recommend to eat?"

"Oh, I see," said Jules, taking a glug of lager. "Well I normally have the lamb pasanda, but I've noticed lately they been buying lamb taken from the neck. So, you know, it's quite sinewy. Can't go wrong with good old chicken tikka masala…I think I'll have that."

"But it's got nuts in it."

"Yeah, so?" Jules was puzzled by the grocer's need to state the bleeding obvious.

"Aren't you allergic to them?"

Jules shook her head. "Me? Nuts? No!"

"Hmm," said Mike, clearly unconvinced.

"For God's sake, Mike, I'm not allergic to *everything*!"

"Sure. Sorry." Mike apologised. "Well, tikka masala sounds like a good shout, but I think I'll have me a chicken saag."

He closed his menu and quickly glanced around at the only other couple in the curry house, who were now freshening their faces with the hot towels supplied with the bill and the obligatory three gold-wrapped, chocolate mints.

Why do they always do that, the thought struck him, give couples an odd number of chocolates?

When he turned to face Jules again, he saw that she'd quickly dipped into her handbag, pulled out a small tube, and was applying a dab of cream under her eyes.

"Is that…haemorrhoid cream?" Mike squinted at the information on the tube.

"Yup, great for tired eyes, particularly when you spend all day focused on one spot, if you know what I mean?"

"I guess so," Mike said, taking a sip of lager that suddenly didn't taste quite right.

"So, did you like my new song tonight, Mike?" Jules' olive eyes twinkled in the glare from the soon-to-be-exhausted tea light on their table. *Push Baby Push* had been well received by The Peasant faithful but, in truth, Mike had found the content a little harrowing at times. He'd never admit it, but the verse about the afterbirth and the accompanying pictures on the PowerPoint slides were, in his opinion, a bit extreme to say the least.

"It was…amazing," Mike lied.

"I wrote that in Ipswich maternity ward. The tune popped into my head when I had both hands…"

"I thought the slide show was an inspired idea," Mike quickly interjected. "It really added to your set. You know, very visual, like a U2 show…except with more blood."

"Naaw! Thanks, Mike!" Jules pouted with pride. "Hector also enjoyed that part. Said everyone should try to up their game with something similar. But Graeme shouted him down, saying that was nonsense. He got quite irate about it actually."

"Oh," remarked Mike, fully condoning the response from the man he loathed.

Jules held up a hand. "Enough about me! You were great too, grocer man!" The broad smile she beamed over to her date faltered as she tried to remember something. "What was your second song again?"

Mike cleared his throat. "It was a version of the McCartney and Jackson's song which deals with the contradictions of dealing in outlawed elephant remains."

"Oh yeah," said Jules as the rendition came flooding back to her. "Ebony and Irony." She'd never admit it, but it was shocking. "It was…amazing!" she lied.

"So," Mike shuffled forward eagerly in his chair and asked playfully in a faux-teenager manner, "tell me a little bit about yourself."

Jules pondered Mike's request for a second. "My epiglottis!" she finally barked and snorted loudly.

"That's actually a bit within yourself," said the pedant as the midwife struggled to gain some composure. "But I like what you did with that," he added. "It's actually one of my most favourite words. Epi…glottis!" Mike articulated the word in a style he imagined Rowan Atkinson would say it and, in doing so, made himself look like a bit of a twat.

"Ooh, don't do that," said Jules. "It makes you look like a bit of a twat."

"Fair enough," Mike felt a little crestfallen and dunked a piece of poppadum about the size of Wales into the mango chutney.

"So," said Jules leaning in towards Mike a little seductively. "Tell me a little bit about yourself, Mr. Grimshaw."

"Okay," said Mike also leaning in, but managing to look far less seductive. "My right testicle"

"Whoa!" Jules recoiled as if she'd accidentally taken a mouthful of lime pickle. "That's a bit frisky for a first date!"

Mike flushed with embarrassment. "No! Sorry, Jules. I was just trying to repeat your funny answer with something that wasn't…that…funny."

There was an awkward silence.

"Good evening. Welcome to Pappa Dom Preach. Are sir and madam ready to order?" The advancing headwaiter eased the tension. Mike looked up and noticed the man bore a striking resemblance to the game show host in the film, *Slumdog Millionaire*.

Mike pointed a finger at him. "Aren't you…?"

"No sir," the waiter said, anticipating the shopkeeper's question. He then dispensed his stock answer that was cleverly correlated to the film's director. "The only Boyle I am familiar with is the one at the base of my lulli."

The waiter smiled genially as the pair silently guessed at what that could possibly mean, and then ordered rapidly before their appetites were completely destroyed. With the dishes noted, Jules stood up. "Must pop to the loo," she said.

As she disappeared down a flight of stairs, which made the Cresta Run look like the ball slide in a Wacky Warehouse, Mike glanced back across at the other couple. They had begun an argument over who was going to have the remaining chocolate mint that sat shining brightly between them. With neither party prepared to concede, the scene quickly turned ugly as the remaining chapattis and then the dregs of lager were launched across the table. With nothing left to throw, the pair went at each other with such force they ended up wrestling on the carpet as the argument descended into a full-on battle.

"Isn't that the vicar from Felixstowe and his wife?" asked Jules, returning to the table just as their order of curry, rice, Bombay potato and a side of tarka dhal arrived.

Mike shrugged and spun back round to focus on the delights laid out before them. Jules sat and inhaled the piquancy of her spiced chicken, her eyes closing as the warm delicate vapours enveloped her.

"Good?" Mike asked.

"Yeah, simple cut and paste job," Jules said nonchalantly. "Barely a mark on the paper."

Mike's eyes widened a little. "I meant...the curry. Does the curry smell good?"

"Oh, I see," said Jules. "Yeah, it smells divine."

To Mike's astonishment, Jules then proceeded to eat her meal using her fingers.

"Ahem!" The midwife's unusual dining approach unsettled Mike. "I didn't know you were such a traditionalist, Jules," he said.

"Hm?" Jules was distracted by a river of dhal that was running off the back of her hand and onto her lower forearm.

Mike swiftly glanced round to see if anyone else was watching this, and was equally disturbed by it. Fortunately, the two waiters in the restaurant were both preoccupied with clearing up after the vicar and his wife's removal into a waiting black mariah, so Mike was spared the exchange of any quizzical looks.

"Traditionalist? What are you talking about?" Jules flicked a cardamom seed off her index finger and it pinged off a light fitting above them. "Oops!" she giggled, cowering like a five-year-old.

"Um. You're eating with your fingers?"

Jules stopped her assault on the orangey chicken and studied the brightly coloured fusion of rice and sauce decorating her fingers. "Well, I can't exactly use this, Mike." Jules gestured towards her powerful left hand. "That's my *toilet hand*." Jules only mouthed the words 'toilet hand' so as not cause offence. This struck Mike as rather strange given she'd happily shout 'bollocks!' at the drop of a hat.

Mike edged his chicken saag away from him. "Why don't you just use your fork?"

Jules paused and stared hard at her dinner date and then down at her unused cutlery. "Oh!" she said more brightly. "I'm allergic to cheap metal."

"Two more pint Kingfisher." The waiter seamlessly switched the couple's empty glasses for fresh pints.

"Better make this my last," said Mike. "Don't want the old bill on my case again."

Mike explained how he'd been pulled over twice in the last month and breathalysed each time. He had been drinking on the second occasion and, as the police dragged him out of his car and tore the bottle of Listerine away from his mouth, they could smell the fear, if not the beer, on him. The officers informed Mike that they had stopped him because his tail light was a slightly deeper shade of red than normal. They asked him for his driver's licence and his full name, but Mike couldn't speak on account of the large number of two pence pieces in his mouth – a pointless trick an old colleague from Radlett Post Office had told him would 'disguise any amount of alcohol intake from the filth'. After spitting out £1.20's worth of copper into the lay-by, Mike dutifully blew into the analyser. When the test finally proved negative, a huge wave of relief washed over Mike and he collapsed gratefully to the ground while the traffic cops reeled away in bitter disappointment. It had been a close call.

"Talking of the old bill, I wonder how The Goose went on tonight," Jules mused.

"Not sure," Mike replied. "But it didn't look good as we drove past, did it?"

"Was that Jimmy Jammz being frog-marched out of the pub by the Timberlake woman?"

"It looked like it."

Jules grinned. "Early teething problems for their open mic night."

"Yeah, they've got no chance. Look how good it was tonight at Hector's.

The Timberlake's should cut their losses. Any attempt at a musical evening over there has got to be doomed, right?"

"You sound very sure of yourself there, Mr. Shopkeeper," Jules nibbled at a piece of naan bread seductively. "I hope you're right," she smiled.

As the evening drew on the pair chatted about their favourite music genres, whether Benedict Cumberbatch would ever win a major acting award, how Brexit would impact the price of pork pies, the natural birth options available to expectant mothers under the NHS, and Mike's choice of blouse for the evening. They picked at their exotic dishes until the small hours, enjoying each other's company, and sharing the assortment of spiced treats by either traditional implement-based strategies or shovelling it in by the palm load. The restaurant waiters waited patiently by the exit, continually flipping the open/closed sign loudly against the glass door until the pair finally finished their meal.

"I really thought you played well tonight, Mike," Jules said with true affection. "Your playing's coming on great."

"Thanks, Jules," said Mike, sheepishly glancing down at a half-empty bowl of Bombay Potato. "I thought your set was terrific too."

"Get a room!" came a voice from the kitchen.

The couple left just after one in the morning, their orange-stained fingers gently entwined.

HECTOR

Hector carefully finished polishing the silver-framed *Best Pork Product of the Year Award,* which sat proudly on a glass shelf next to an optic of lime cordial.

The Peasant's infamous sausage roll had won a merit in last year's PBEX competition: a bi-annual celebration of all the things you can do with various parts of a pig. Hector had missed the presentation because he was holed-up in the gents, but was thrilled when he returned to his table to see that his efforts wrapping seasoned swine in elegant puff pastry hadn't all been for nothing. As he blew the final speck of dust from the frame, he turned and found Alan Hedgeworthy propping up the bar.

"Oh!" Hector said, somewhat surprised. "Hello, Alan. Don't normally see you in here at lunchtime. You revelling in your fine performance from last night still?"

"It is rather inclement weather in Moscow for this time of year, don't you think?"

Hector reached for a pint glass. "Usual, mate?"

"I see the bluebells are out early in Budapest," came the reply.

Alan Hedgeworthy possessed the peculiar tendency of starting every conversation in spy-mode, a self-developed affliction that he insisted on maintaining during his working day as a sales assistant at Bennett's Electrical Stores. For instance, when customers asked about the energy efficiency rating of a fridge or the output wattage of an mp3 docking station he would normally remark on how warm it was in Leningrad or urgently request the whereabouts of 'the microfilm'. Alan's statements were affected by an accent, the origin of which most folk were unable to pin down. For those stupid enough to enquire as to its provenance, Alan would allude to a Ukrainian lilt, formed in the suburbs of Odessa during his 'orientation'. To everyone else, however, he just sounded like a scouse Pakistani.

"There you go." Hector plonked Alan's drink onto the drip tray. "One foaming pint of *Squealing Weasel*. I enjoyed your rendition of the Flashdance theme last night. Very...energetic."

"Well, the spawning salmon often sings in colder climes."

"Hey, have you guys taken in any stock of those new liquidisers yet?" Hector said, ignoring the clandestine comments from one of his more insane customers. "My one's on its last legs and I'm thinking about doing a push on smoothies this month."

"Yeah, they're in." Sanity at last. "Shall I hold one for you?"

"If you could, Alan. I'll be over Saturday morning to pick it up."

Alan took a slug of *Weasel*. "What type of smoothies?"

"Oh...strawberry, banana. Nothing too technical."

"My missus does a wonderful roasted beetroot smoothie. Fills it full of starch. Like drinking red cement. Shall I get you the recipe?"

Hector smiled and told Alan, in the politest terms, to fuck off.

As the deluded organ player trotted off to recruit other potential Stasi officers, The Peasant's landlord glanced anxiously at the vintage-style wall clock above the fireplace. It was gone midday, and if the pub's chef wasn't in soon, the meagre amount of lunchtime food trade Hector did have could well go down the swanny.

"Where the hell is he?" Hector whispered to himself.

Chloe came into the bar with a large chocolate cake covered in flaming candles and looked ready to burst into song.

"Darling!" Hector urgently called over to his daughter. "His birthday isn't until next week, lovely. Save it 'til then."

"Oh, I was only doing a practice run, daddy," lied the young barmaid.

"Okay," Hector acknowledged. "Have you seen Patrice by any chance, sweetie?"

"Yes, he's a tall Frenchman, dad...with massive hands. He works for you, silly!" Chloe shook her head at her father's peculiar question and disappeared back into the kitchen, furiously blowing candle wax and large swathes of chocolate icing onto the floor.

Hector sighed, counted to ten and thanked his good luck he was only running a pub with his daughter and not the Bank of England or NASA. He sidled over to Carl Fleming, who was glaring at his smartphone.

"Bloody thing!" Carl muttered before casting a sizeable handful of Bombay Mix into his mouth.

"What's up? Got no signal?" said Hector, noticing how perplexed the ironmonger appeared.

"Nah!" Carl blurted as he chomped. "Predictive bloody text! It's a total pain in the arse."

Hector nodded. "I know. I sent Chloe a text last week while I was at the cash and carry. I wanted her to clean the bar before I got back, but what my text actually said was 'could you clean the bat, please, love?' When I got back, she was actually brushing a winged mammal." The landlord glanced back over at his daughter – who was back in the bar rearranging slices of lemon and lime into her favourite scene from the Bayeux Tapestry, and gave her a wistful look.

"What have you just sent?" said Hector, focusing back on Peasenhall's part-time-disher of mediocre gossip.

"Well," said Carl, sharply tapping the screen on his phone in an unorthodox effort to correct the mistake he'd just made. "I was sending the wife a text to say that I'd just dropped in here for a quick pint, I'd be home soon, and that I was looking forward to seeing her."

"And what did you send instead?"

"You've ruined my life, you turgid witch."

Hector puffed his cheeks in a way that said, "You're screwed", left Carl to ponder on his fate once home, and set his mind to clearing up Chloe's citrus tapestry, which had now extended along the length of the bar. As he moved away, Alan Hedgeworthy quickly replaced the vacant spot next to Carl.

"I hear Rotterdam's tulips are crimson this season."

Carl threw an irritated glance at Alan as he continued his efforts to recall the offending text on his phone, so the shop assistant decided on a more appropriate line of conversation. "I hear you're going global," he said.

Word was out that Carl was planning a hostile takeover of *Robert Dyas*, the national chain of ironmonger stores. "Yeah, my financial team's running the numbers as we speak," confirmed Carl.

Carl's 'financial team' was his best friend from school, Larry Sullen Jr., who ran his own low-key accountancy business in Sweffenham. Aside from

Carl, Larry's other clients currently included *Rugs n Snugs* in Eye and *Fast Clips (A haircut in under four minutes...or your money back!)* in Waldringfield. Larry's experience of hostile takeovers was limited at best and when asked about his experience with the Sage package he would invariably confirm that he was more of a basil man.

Carl had opened *Screw Ewe* nine years ago, with grand plans for the future. His timing, however, could not have been worse as the global recession soon followed effectively pouring cold water over any lofty ambitions he had. The business barely clung on as the bottom fell out of the companion set market. An employer of a shop crew of sixteen initially, Carl had to let his staff go one by one. His personal 'Black Monday' was March 12th 2011, when he laid off a total of eight employees (including the voluptuous Finnegan sisters and Zippy the Tooled-Up Lion, the shop mascot). The only reason *Screw Ewe* didn't fold was the fact that, as editor, he could make every other advert in the *Peasenhall Quandary* one for his business – which proved just enough to maintain footfall through the door thus securing its survival.

"When do you think you'll hear?" Alan was suitably impressed; The Peasant had a real-life wheeler dealer in its midst.

"Not sure," said Carl, as an incoming text beeped its arrival. "Larry sent an email to info@robertdyas.co.uk on Tuesday and we're just waiting for their legal bods to respond."

"That's amazing!" said the awe-inspired keyboard player. "I expect it'll be champagne all..."

"Fuck!" squealed Carl on opening the text message. "I've gotta go."

It was one in, one out, as Patrice le Clef arrived for work and Carl Fleming headed home for a beating.

"The Danube has swollen somewhat from the early rains, don't you think?" Alan posited as the chef rushed past him.

"Eat shit, you unnecessary electric person!" spat the French cook.

"You're late," said Hector, careful to make it more statement than accusation. "Everything alright?"

Patrice stormed into the kitchen, threw off his *Belstaff* motorbike jacket and pulled on his chef whites.

Hector followed in behind. "You seem a little upset, Patrice." The landlord was in no mood for histrionics; missing the lunchtime crowd was one thing, but Friday night was a big food night and he needed his star turn on song.

"She went out wiz eem, last night." The chef pouted and ran his enormous hands through his black hair, which was untied and bounced loosely on his shoulders.

"Who is 'she'...and who is 'eem'?" enquired Hector.

"'E took 'er for some shit spicy food that I would not even serve up to my dog."

"You've got a dog?" Hector was even more confused.

"No, you fool! I am using artistic licence to make a point...'ow you say, figuratively speaking." Patrice pronounced each syllable of the last two words in the strongest French accent he could muster.

"Sorry. Who *are* we talking about, Patrice?"

"Jules, and zat shopkeeper who wears women's clothes and plays guitar like a cock in oil."

"Mike Grimshaw?"

"I know," said Patrice grimly. "Can you believe zis shit?"

"He's a cross-dresser?" The landlord was toying with his chef. "Who knew?"

The chef stared wide-eyed at his employer. "Yes! But zat is not zee point!"

"Well, there's a turn up for the books." Hector's feigned ignorance continued. "And there's certainly room for improvement in his guitar playing, that's for sure."

"No, you fucking eembecile!" Patrice was taut with rage. "Zat purveyor of processed *merde* has got his filthy eyes and attentions all over the love of my life!"

"Who, Jules?"

"Yes, Jules!"

For a moment, Hector distinctly thought he heard the seams of Patrice's whites start to rip open. He decided to tread carefully. "Sorry," the landlord said gently. "I wasn't aware Jules was...that you two were an item."

Patrice leant his head against the cool metal of the extractor hood. "It's complicated," he said a little calmer.

"Ah," said Hector, suddenly seeing all the signs. "She doesn't actually know this yet."

The chef looked across at his boss with doleful eyes: he was welling up. "You see," the narcissist began to explain. "It's her hands. She has lovely, giant hands that she needs and uses so beautifully in her work."

"She has massive hands. Just like you," observed Hector.

"She is my soul mate…my life."

"And you are a giant hand fetishist, Patrice?"

"Yes."

Hector stepped across and put his own, normal-sized hand on the Frenchman's shoulders, which were now rising and falling in gentle sobs. "I think it's time to put the oven on, Patrice," Hector said. "It's past one o'clock."

JULES

Like the Sword of Damocles, a sizeable chunk of quartz crystal suspended from a brass-coloured chain swung precariously back and forth above Jules' midriff as Sally Womber, East Anglia's pre-eminent kinesiologist, offered words to calm and soothe.

"Let the light, the life force of the stone, fall upon your skin, and may its healing properties enter your body and freely flow through you." Sally's gaze was fixed on Jules' solar plexus. "Succumb to the power of the crystal's energy and abandon yourself to the life force."

I've abandoned myself to losing forty quid to this nonsense, thought Jules, who was ruing agreeing to a session with Sally in the pub last night. Cornered by the kinesiologist after her set, a somewhat squiffy Jules had shown genuine concern that the crystal therapist was struggling on the business front, and foolishly suggested that trade was sure to pick up soon. That was the cue for an intense sales battery from Sally and, before she knew it, the name of Julie Wiseman was being loaded onto the practitioner's iPhone calendar for a lunchtime session the following day.

"Waves of positive energy will be flooding your sinews and neurons." Sally spoke calmly as the milky rock oscillated wildly. Incense filled the room and a CD player perched on a small, reclaimed cabinet tucked away in a corner churned out the strange and unnerving chants of animals that had been crossed off the World Wildlife Fund's endangered list long ago. "Harness this force and let it counteract all the negative energy you have."

Jules was oblivious to her therapist's drivel as she scanned the consultancy walls from her horizontal position on the therapy couch. There was a good smattering of art prints and frames on display, most of which were lewd, black-and-white etchings, and appeared to be the work of the same artist.

"Do you know Mike Grimshaw well?" The question just popped out of Jules' mouth.

Sally seamlessly swapped the quartz for an even bigger piece of amethyst and promptly suspended it over the midwife's crotch. "You really shouldn't talk during realignment," the dark-haired kinesiologist said, a little catch of annoyance in her voice. Duly admonished, Jules returned to silent mode, and lay there wondering why she'd asked the question as Sally and the purple stone bore down on her fanny.

Sally's 'practice' was one of three compact offices on the first floor of a small building halfway up the thoroughfare in the quaint market town of Woodbridge, for which she paid a peppercorn rent to a rather benevolent landlord who owned the whole block. The adjoining office to hers was empty having recently been vacated by an international darts trainer short on match practice. A gay couple ran a chiropody practice from the other room. The floor above was one large office space and had been rented to an up-and-coming social media agency, *Facebark*, which specialized in online communications for dog owners, and the ground floor was home to a busy bakery.

The crystal healer had taken up residency in Woodbridge three years ago having relocated from her Chelmsford consultancy following a disagreement over a misplaced piece of Fluorite. On her website, Sally claimed she could achieve all manner of things with crystals and oils. Testimonials on the site trumpeted great personal goals achieved through the power of sparkly rock: "my depression was successfully cast out forever!", "my arthritic joints are now joyously pain free!", "my husband has finally fucked off!" With diplomas in reiki, pet psychology and bending spoons, Sally found a natural and welcoming home in Suffolk's we'll-take-any-nut-job culture. It was a refreshing change from the aggressive negativity of clients in neighbouring Essex; a county for which, according to Sally, there would never be sufficient tonnage of healing crystals.

Sally's boyfriend was Dutch and he travelled over on the Eurostar to see her and bed her about once every six weeks. Jos was the artist responsible for the etchings that graced Sally's walls; the dozen or so nudes on display clearly revealed his penchant for sketching genitalia of all shapes and sizes. His particular specialty, as Jules keenly observed, was extreme hair, and many of his pictures focused in on the extravagant female bush. Jos was not Sally's sole love interest, however, and her real notoriety was borne not from the application of spurious holistic treatments, but from a voracious appetite for men. She was a cougar, through and through, employing whatever mystical powers she thought she possessed to get men in the sack.

"He's a lovely boy, isn't he?" The answer came out of nowhere.

Jules was on the verge of sleep when Sally spoke and her comment startled her a little. "Yes," she said, trying to shrug off a fuzzy head. "Are you finished?"

Sally stepped over to the couch, placed a drop of jasmine oil on Jules' forehead and began gently rubbing it in. "Yes, your chakras are fully aligned," said Sally, sounding more like someone who'd just rebalanced the tyres on Jules' Fiat rather than a complementary therapist. Then Sally tilted her head and, using an overly suggestive tone, said, "I think someone's ready to face the big, bad world again."

Jules sat up. "Thanks," she said, a little freaked out. She grabbed her purse and handed over two twenty-pound notes. "I think you said forty, right?"

"Lovely. Thank you." Sally took the money and popped it into the reclaimed cabinet's drawer. "So why did you ask about Mike Grimshaw?"

"Oh, nothing." Jules could have kicked herself for even mentioning him.

"Rumour has it you and he had a cosy dinner after the show last night." Sally sat back down, crossed her legs and bit down on the tip of index finger. "Did you have fun?"

What is she doing? Jules thought as the sexual charge in the room went up a notch. "It was really nice," Jules muttered. "Can I get a receipt for that? I can charge it against…"

"I'm quite good friends with Patrice le Clef…"

I bet you are, thought Jules.

"I thought you two were…well, you know," smiled Sally.

A heady mix of crystal nonsense, incense and jasmine oil was clearly having an effect on Jules, as she felt increasingly woozy. She steadied herself against the bed and saw that her hands were massively swollen. Oh dear, Jules thought, and glanced across at the spiritualist, who appeared to licking one of the large stones in a highly suggestive manner. And that's when things really went off piste.

Sally's hair suddenly catapulted upwards, exploding into something that was more suitable for a *Top of the Pops* audience in the 80's than a small, backwater clinic. It was wild, unkempt, brazen and totally T'Pau! Sally pulled the back of her right hand violently across her face, which had the effect of striping thick, bold make-up high onto her cheekbones, like the war paint of a warring banshee. Her clothes rippled and were ripped into shreds by some invisible force, revealing glistening, sculptured muscle that was clearly capable of holding a man down for hours and extracting every possible desire.

Sally's warrior transformation was complete, but the fact that struck Jules the most at that particular moment was not how fantastic or mind-numbingly scary this scene was, but how inappropriate the name Sally was for this incarnation in front of her. Boudicca, of course, Artemisia, by all means, even Diana at a push (but the bullshit connections to a silly princess Jules could never relate to, let alone cry crocodile tears for, meant that was probably a no on reflection). But Sally? No way! But this was no Sally. Now, she was ingénue. She was la traviata. She was the scarlet woman.

"Me and Patrice?" Jules addressed the apparition. "No. We are just…there's nothing between us!"

The banshee stood up and towered high above her prey, storm clouds brewing and forming above her dramatically remodelled head. "I took the Frenchman and I tore him apart," Sally bellowed, her voice unrecognizably deep and raspy. "He was no sexual match for me!"

"No. I'm in no doubt about that." Jules nodded furiously, as she tussled with the notion that she may have descended into an even poorer remake of *Ghostbusters* for girls. She then made a mental note to leave crystal therapy well alone in future.

"And next, I'm going to take your shopkeeper and fuck him until his dick falls off!" Sally's eyes rolled back in their sockets and she tossed her head back, roaring with laughter as a maelstrom of thunder and lightning built to a crescendo around her. She laughed, the thunder crackled and Jules' could do nothing but hold tightly onto her purse: was this the end?

When Jules woke up, Sally had just finished writing a receipt out for her session and was sat sipping gently on a cup of Darjeeling tea. Everything was back to normal.

"How do you feel?" Sally politely asked. "Bless you. You fell asleep just after I took the amethyst out. A lot of clients do."

Jules sat up and looked up at the ceiling: no clouds. She looked at Sally sipping at her tea; *china in your hand*, she thought with a touch of irony. "Wow," Jules said finally. "Powerful stuff this crystal therapy."

"Isn't it, though?" said Sally and smiled broadly.

MIKE

Mike Grimshaw's preoccupation with previous night's events had intensified following the phone call from his daughter, Holly.

"Hey, dad!" Holly's constant upbeat personality was always in stark contrast to her father's regularly dour demeanour.

"Hey, Holls! What's happening?"

"Well, I was going to ask you the same question." Holly's tone had a frost on it. "Haven't heard from you in ages."

"I'm so sorry, sweetie." Mike wordlessly cursed his stupidity. "What with the shop and all, I've…"

"Been busy, daddy?" Holly interjected rather than let him make some feeble excuse. "And here was me thinking you'd gone and got someone more important in your life."

Guilt wrapped around Mike's throat like a dog collar on a pig. "Now, you know there's only ever one girl that means the world to me." He cleared a catch in his voice. "I'm sorry I haven't had a chance…"

"Don't sweat it, dad," Holly said, cutting across him again. "Listen, I'm down your way tomorrow. Got a collection to make for the sanctuary. I thought maybe I could stop at yours for the night and we could grab a bite and catch up."

Mike's heart was fit to burst. "Ah, that would be great, darling! I'll make up the spare room."

"Yeah, but don't be putting *The Little Mermaid* duvet on the bed."

"No, of course not!" scoffed Mike, and then panicked as that was exactly what he intended to use. "You're not bloody nine years old anymore!"

"Exactly!"

Just then, the doorbell rang crisply and Peasenhall's priest walked into the shop and gave Mike a hateful look for being on his mobile phone. "Look, baby, I've got a customer..."

"It's okay, I heard them come in. I'll be done and across by seven. Can't wait to see you, daddy!" And she was gone.

Father Mackenzie picked up some rice from the shelf where a pudding had been. He also grabbed a jar of balti sauce, the other essential ingredient for his traditional Friday night fish curry. It was a well-orchestrated purchase as his wife, Mary, would collect two pieces of fresh pollock from Harvey Rumpole's fish van perched on the grass verge outside Peasenhall Assembly Rooms at the same time.

The priest selected a bottle of cabernet sauvignon from Mike's meagre and wildly over-priced section of alcohol and popped it into his basket. He added a second after a moment's consideration.

"Can't get away from tradition, eh Father?" said Mike, punching in the code for the curry sauce on his till.

"In God's name, what de feck would ye know about it, ye heathen?"

The priest's descent into foul language was never a good sign. Mike went scarlet: the religious put down was bad enough, but did a man of the cloth really need to swear quite so openly?

"I'm not sure the big man upstairs would approve of that language, Father." Mike regretted the words as soon as they'd left his mouth.

"What I do, ye gobshite, represents an abstinence and a sacrifice dat ye have no comprehension of whatsoever!" When he said whatsoever, it sounded like it started with a ph. "And how I go about dat, is my concern and mine alone, are we clear on dat?"

"Crystal," squeaked Mike.

At six-foot-six, Gary Mackenzie made the pulpit in his church resemble a footstool.

Brought up on a small farm in the bleak, isolated fields of Connemara, the priest had known only hardship. Winters would be spent trying to keep the small amount of livestock on the farm alive and summers would be spent trying to raise the money to buy new livestock to replace the ones that had perished the previous winter. He was one of nine siblings crammed into a tight, ground floor bedroom with only a single window for light. The farmhouse was actually a good-sized, five-bedroom property but Gary's parents refused to miss out on the post-war stereotyping of the impoverished Irish. Mealtimes consisted of raw onion broth and the evening's entertainment was provided by the lyrics and melodies of Thomas Moore. More often than not, Gary and his siblings were left alone with *The Minstrel Boy* on constant loop while his parents were upstairs executing their perpetual quest for procreation. Gary was never sure what was worse, the constant eye watering from raw onion, the constant drone of shite Irish prose, or the constant down pouring of plaster from a ceiling rocked by parental fornication.

His calling came after a chance school outing to see the Sacred Spoon of Cong, where the boy happened upon a miracle. Escaping briefly from the house where his media studies teacher was droning on about the fantastical powers of the infamous spoon, the boy stepped out into a downpour. As the rain eased and the storm clouds broke, the sun reappeared. Considerably darker than normal, the sun began to project multi-coloured rays of light across the streets of Cong, its residents and its post-office-cum-bar-cum-store-cum-escort agency. To his astonishment, Gary's clothes were instantly dried, as the sun's sphere appeared to pulse, growing from its regular size to something much bigger. Gary wondered if this was the end of the world but the warmth of the rainbow dancing across his face suggested only peace and love was descending.

A small memory tucked in the deepest recesses of his mind came forth: *the miracle of the sun.* He'd had the reality of miracles beaten into him since he could ingest solid foods and he recalled the miraculous apparition of the sun across Portugal in 1917; he was now witnessing the same vision. It was a seminal moment and Gary made the decision there and then to follow the Lord and do His work from now until eternity. (Unbeknownst to Gary, the mushrooms that his teacher had brought with him and dropped into the school lunch of onion soup to add 'a bit of texture' were of the psilocybin variety. As Gary's one and only encounter with magic mushrooms furnished him with a psychedelic sun dance, his classmates were tripping so badly they built a fire with the sacred spoon and cavorted naked around its ashes until the bus arrived to take them home.)

Mike was deeply troubled by this deeply psychotic pastor. "Sorry." His voice was weak. "I was just trying to make polite conversation."

The priest suddenly reached across the counter and grabbed the shopkeeper's hand, forcing it down onto the counter top. "Look at yer fingers!" balled the priest. "Yer clearly been self-satisfying yerself!"

Mike's hands were visibly shaking as he regarded the orangey-stain on his fingertips, considering them shortly before realising the priest's misinterpretation. "No, no! That...that's sauce or colouring or whatever they use for Bombay potato!" Mike pleaded vehemently. "It's not from my anus!"

"D'ye tink our Lord Jesus Christ would ever have tolerated de likes of John or Ringo toyin' wid demselves in such an abhorrent manner?"

"I think you may have just mixed the disciples up with The Beatles, Father."

The priest stopped in his tracks as Mike slapped a hand over his smart-arse mouth.

"So, help me God!" The priest leaned over the counter until he was right in Mike's face. "If I ever catch ye at your backside with dose fingers again, I'll cut every one of dem off. Do we understand each other?"

The store owner furiously nodded agreement.

Father Mackenzie paid for his shopping and, without taking his eyes off Mike, took his change and headed out the door. The doorbell seemed to have a more profound tone to it as the closing door struck it. As if the hand of God was on it, Mike thought.

Outside, the priest bumped into Janice Muffler.

"Oh, good morning, Father!" she said effusively.

"Ah, good morning back to ye, missus. 'Tis a glorious start. Now, how are yer twins?"

The pair chatted breezily and briefly before Father Mackenzie, wiping some dirt from his hands, walked away from the shop.

GRAEME

Hector planted a pint of *Saturated Goblin*, a light, herby mild from Grundisburgh, in front of Steve Naysmith; the owner of Peasenhall Farm had called time on his day and was in for an early livener.

"Thanks, 'ector!" said Steve, and blew the froth off the top of his pint before taking a first draught. Hector found the farmer's habit of doing so maddening, particularly when it resulted in Chloe receiving a hoppy moisturiser, as it did on this occasion.

"No problem," said Hector, passing his daughter a dry tea towel. "That'll be three-sixty please, Steve."

"Bloody disgusten proice of beer these days!" bemoaned the farmer, and he tossed a screwed-up tenner at the landlord. "Every toime oi come in 'ere seems proices 'ave gorn up!"

"Whatever," replied Hector, motioning to Chloe to stop polishing glasses and use the towel to dry her beer-covered face. He was not in the mood; he had a testy conversation imminent. "Anyway," the landlord chimed. "You can afford it. Rumour has it you earn enough in royalties to buy this place ten times over!"

"Wow!" exclaimed Chloe, her face streaked with mascara. "Is that true, Doctor Naysmith?"

"He's a farmer, darling, not a doctor." Hector set his daughter straight before taunting his regular further. "He's on to a right little earner, aintcha, Steve? Go on," Hector encouraged. "Let Chloe into your little money-making secret."

"Okay, if yer insist," said Steve with false resignation. "I write post-match interview clichés for premiership footballers."

Chloe stared vacantly at the farmer: no element of the last sentence made any sense to her.

"It's simple, Chloe," said her father spotting her utter bewilderment. "If the likes of Jordan Henderson or Harry Kane or Marouane Fellaini say certain things to the TV reporters after a game, Farmer Naysmith here gets a nice little kickback!"

"It's not that much!" protested Steve.

"How much do you get now, then?" barked Hector.

"I get about 60p for any of my lines used on Five Live or Match of the Day and nine quid if they're mentioned in Sky or BT Sport interviews," Steve clarified.

"And which lines are yours?"

Steve had to think for a second. "Er, off the top of my head, 'oi don't want to focus on my performance...what's important is that we got three points today', 'we got a great spirit here and the gaffer has got us playen as a team' and 'we're just taken each game as it comes'."

"Ooh, some popular ones!"

"Yeah, not quite as popular as 'no, oi didn't see the penalty incident, so oi can't comment'."

"Oh, that's a shame," Hector grimaced. "Who owns the rights to that little rascal?"

"A chap from Preston called Frank Coe. He copyroighted those phrases across all formats of football, rugby and cricket back in 1966 and also threw in 'it's a game of two halves', 'Oi'm over the moon, Brian' and 'yer know' for good measure. 'E's worth a fucken fortune."

"Who's Maureen Felony?" said Chloe.

Hector launched his hands skyward in exasperation. "For goodness sake, Chloe! We *saw* him when we were in Greece. D'you remember? We were in that cosy little tavern just along the beach from the hotel and he came in with his great big ball of hair and ordered a cola float. Remember? When he sat down he was mobbed by loads of United fans all after his autograph. You must remember. Big, tall fella."

Chloe reflected for a moment or two. "We've been to Greece?"

Hectors hands came back down onto his hips. "Right. You need to go and put the rubbish out."

"But I want to hear about Doctor Naysmith's cliques."

"Now!"

"You've done well to bring that girl up on yer own, boi." It was a sincere comment from the farmer as the pair watched Chloe stomp off into the kitchen.

"Dan still okay to play this weekend?" asked Hector, eager to move the conversation on.

"What, Suffolk's answer to Ed Sheeran, d'yer mean?" came Steve's cock-sure response. "Course 'e's gorn a play."

Hector scratched the crook of his arm. "You do know, Ed Sheeran's from here, don't you?"

"Never!" Steve looked aghast.

"Raised in Framlingham, my old cocker."

"Oh," said the farmer. "In that case, 'e's Suffolk's answer to P Diddy!"

"Yeah. No." A feeling of helplessness washed over Hector. "That doesn't even begin to make sense." At that moment, The Peasant's north-by-northwest door opened and in strolled Graeme Nash; the imminent conversation had arrived. "I'll leave you to figure out who your firstborn could be Suffolk's answer to," Hector told Steve and wandered over to meet Mister Nash.

Steve rubbed his stubbled chin thoughtfully but before he could dwell on it any further, he caught sight of Paul Pickering having a quiet half before heading back to school. "'Ey, Paul!" the farmer shouted. "You got any work for Dan yet?"

"Um, not yet, Steve," Paul replied. "Leave it with me."

When he wasn't teaching chemistry at the Sir Launcelot C of E Primary School in Copdock, Paul used his spare time offering private guitar tuition. His website, pickingwithpickering.com, advertised hour-long lessons for beginners and intermediate players who wanted an opportunity to extend their repertoire.

"Can we learn something else please, Mr. Pickering?"

"No, we won't be doing that."

"But, Sir, I'm rather tired of playing *Meat in the Freezer, My Heart Yearns for Barry Island* and *The Shepherds' Stomp* every single lesson."

Either his students would take their lesson at Paul's house or – for those parents who couldn't be arsed to drop their kids off, he offered in-home visits.

He was a man seriously in demand six months ago, which was when he'd asked Steve if his son might be available to take a few lessons off his hands and earn a few bob in the process. That was before it became *de rigueur* for parental do-gooders to start asking about appropriate background checks. And before a slight mishap in the recording of the guilty party in a recent sex scandal resulted in business effectively falling off the edge of a cliff.

"Yer know 'e's better than yer at guitar. C'mon! Give the lad a break!"

"I will, Steve. I promise," Paul lied. "Things are just a little slow right now."

Steve nodded knowingly and sipped at his beer. "People still given yer shit 'bout that incident down at Crown Pools?"

"Look!" Paul snapped and was on his feet. "You, along with everyone else, know *that* was my brother, not me."

"Yarp!" Steve's shoulders shook with laughter.

"And besides, it was a total misunderstanding. He was just trying to give the boy a wedgy."

"You can take the boi outta Pickering…!"

"Right, that's it! I'm off!" Paul collected his coat and brown leather suitcase and headed for the nearest exit. Which obviously wasn't far away.

"And another thing, the local residents have been complaining the music goes on way past eleven o'clock." Hector's arms were crossed high across his chest in defiant mode. "I'm in danger of losing my license if that carries on."

Graeme gripped his pint mug and was pointing it at The Peasant's landlord in confrontational style. "Well, the reason why I have to carry on past last orders," a surge of *Cobbler's Bollock* sloshed precariously close to the rim of his glass as Graeme reinforced his argument, "is because I have to give all your precious punters a chance to play."

"They'd all get their go if you actually started the evening on time. As bloody advertised!" protested Hector. "It's supposed to be a seven-thirty kick-off, but you rarely get going before nine. You and Penny seem intent on sharing all your showbiz gossip rather than starting proceedings. I've had dozens of people grumbling about the fact they get on too late."

"That's crap!" retorted Graeme.

This was not going to plan. Graeme had taken a good look at the bustling crowd at the last open mic night and considered himself a tad undervalued by The Peasant's management. He therefore decided he needed to up his rate for putting on this increasingly popular gig and had asked Hector for a meeting. Graeme's ambitious demands of an additional thirty percent on his fee felt like an ambush and Hector promptly told him where he could stick it. Graeme was already down to a reduced plea of ten percent more, but the venue owner was now in no mood to budge: the fee was the fee.

"It's not crap, Graeme," barked Hector. "Gail Frogmarch sat patiently waiting for you to call her up and play last week. It got to eleven and you still hadn't indicated when she was likely to get on, but then she had to leave because she was up early the following morning for goat slaughtering."

Graeme pulled his notorious face of incredulity. "Gail Frogmarch?"

"She plays the harp," explained Hector. "Chunky girl. Looks like Adele in a vacuum."

"I must have missed her."

"She was sat on a table in front of you," Hector eluded further. "She's nineteen stone. With a massive fucking harp between her legs! How could you have possibly missed her?"

"It's not easy, Hector," the househusband protested. "I have to be a little bit selective or we'll be here 'til gone midnight."

"But we are here 'til gone midnight, Graeme. That's the problem!"

"So, you're now saying I'm doing it all wrong." Graeme got all defensive. "That's rich given all the trade I bring in here on a Thursday night. I don't see you moaning too much when you cash up of an evening."

Hector knew his opponent had a point, but the landlord refused to be held to ransom; it was a position he swore he'd never get in after watching Mel Gibson's dramatic film, *Ransom*. "We're not stupid, Graeme. All the regulars know you and Penny put on your brown-nosing cronies…the same old faces who do the same old songs."

"Nonsense."

"Really?" snorted Hector. "So how many more times exactly are we going to have to listen to your cousin, Herbert, play that god-awful song of his? Forever warbling on about him reclaiming and refurbishing a neglected dinghy."

"Everyone loves it!" Hector squealed. "We all sing along to the words."

Hector drew the tea towel from around his neck and considered throttling his chief entertainment officer. "Everyone, Graeme, adds their own words to the song because they're so tired of it."

"What?" Graeme's incredulous face had returned.

"Oh, come on, Graeme, you must have heard! When he sings 'I've sanded the rowlocks and polished the brass', everyone else sings, 'I landed my bollocks right up her arse'."

"No, they don't," Graeme said meekly.

"Yes, they do, Graeme!"

The open mic host's pint glass was finally still, his expression suddenly forlorn. "Next you'll be telling me nobody likes my jumpers," Graeme mumbled pathetically and smoothed a hand over a large yellow daisy pattern on his latest number.

"What's that?" said Hector, nodding towards the flower.

"It's in celebration of the Ethiopian New Year."

"Yeah," sighed Hector. "I'm afraid your jumper themes are a little lost on me if I'm totally honest."

The words stung Graeme and he looked as if he might burst into tears.

"Graeme, look," Hector sensed the conversation was heading nowhere. "Open mic is Thursday night. You run it on schedule from seven thirty to eleven o'clock on the dot and I will pay you the previously arranged fee. We all stay as we are and everyone is happy."

"Okay. I'll make sure the whole thing runs to time and I promise everyone will get a chance to play. No favourites."

"And for the usual fee?" Hector was as suspicious as one of Graeme's jumpers.

"Well how about I take a cut of the evening's food and drink proceedings, instead?" said Graeme brightly and held out his hand for Hector to shake. "Let's say twenty-five percent and not a word to the taxman."

Graeme pinched his nose in an effort to staunch the flow of blood as he walked out of the pub. With his head pointed to the sky, he failed to see Mike coming into The Peasant for an early evening drink and the two collided.

"Oh, sorry, Graeme, I didn't see…" Mike then saw the state the MC was in. "Oh, are you okay?"

Graeme mumbled several expletives that Mike struggled to fully understand and the bloodied ex-open mic host of The Peasant headed across the road to the pub car park. Mike gave him a quick wave as he sped off in his Qashqai and the shop owner walked into the bar. He immediately spotted Chloe and her father stood by the kitchen door; she was engrossed in attending to Hector's right hand and appeared to dabbing it with what looked like a toy dog.

"It's okay, darling, don't fuss," Mike heard Hector tell his daughter. "If you'll leave me alone, I'll get the first aid kit and apply a traditional plaster."

"Hey, guys!" Mike called across to the pair. "I've just seen Graeme leave with a particularly bad nosebleed."

"Ah, Michael," said Hector, looking up from his split knuckles. "Just the person I wanted to speak to!"

ROGER

Roger Barnett leaned closer to the microphone. "Good morning everyone and welcome to Dessert Island Dish."

As the radio ham finished the sentence, the shamelessly plagiarised theme tune of BBC Radio 4's long-running flagship show washed across the airwaves.

"And today's guest," Roger's voice was thick with nostalgia, "is Peasenhall's very own Catherine Bush who, as I'm sure you all know, runs the village fete every year and has been doing so for forty-two years."

"Forty-three, actually," Catherine quickly interjected.

"Oh," sniffed Roger, somewhat irked by an uncharacteristic error in his research. "My apologies."

The elderly lady's exorbitant blue eyes shone brightly and, along with her deliciously enigmatic smile, they rooted the *PeasPlease FM* presenter to the spot; get on with it you fool, they seemed to say.

Roger had dreamt up the idea of Dessert Island Dish twelve months earlier. It replicated the original in that its duration was 45 minutes but differed by inviting local personalities to come into the studio and discuss eight puddings they wished to have with them if ever stranded on an island or in a doctor's surgery. It was one of several radio formats that Roger had 'borrowed' for the benefit of his own broadcasts. They included *Just a Minuet*, a panel game in which players had to speak for one minute about a social dance of French origin; *Whose Lure is it Anyway*, which openly discussed the true ownership of local fishing baits and *The Shitting Forecast*, where the show's callers could discuss their most recent bowel movement.

"Now, Catherine, what have you chosen for your first dish today?" Roger's voice had returned to its most unctuous form and he returned the woman's steely blue gaze with a rigorous stare of his own.

Catherine Bush was a much-valued member of the village community and her debonair looks and mannerisms brought a touch of class to the place. She was often referred to as the Katherine Hepburn of Peasenhall. Catherine was classic Suffolk old money but most of it was now tied up in a draughty, old manor house to the east of the village, her late husband having ripped through most of the available inheritance her father had left to her, pissing it away on three-card brag and vintage port. She had brushed aside many suitors since his death, her charitable work and community support of far more interest to her than being remarried to another red-nosed heir to a pig fortune.

"Well, Paul…"

"Roger."

The woman cleared an irritation in her throat. "Well, Roger, my first dish is Eton Mess!"

Dessert Island Dish had quickly become *Peas Please FM's* most popular show and regularly reached an audience of thirty or more. The show's list of regularly featured favourites included bread and butter pudding, treacle sponge and sherry trifle. (While the puddings were commonly cited castaway favourites, they also featured regularly in many of the listeners' diets given the fact they could be chewed and swallowed relatively easily.)

"What a great choice to kick things off this morning." Roger stifled a yawn. "Tell us what memories you have of Eton mess, Catherine."

"Well, many of your audience may remember my father was master baker in the village during the war," the woman's grainy voice wavered momentarily. "But he could be a hard task master. When he wasn't thrashing my sister and me to sleep with a leather apron, he would taunt us with fresh oven-baked bread and often consume sweet pastries and confectionery right in front of us."

Roger was mildly perturbed. "Did he never offer to share the treats with you or your sister?"

"Never!" came the emotional reply.

"Such cruelty," Roger considered solemnly.

Catherine fetched a tissue to her chin where she had dribbled slightly. "Yes, he was a rotten fucker."

Roger coughed urgently. "I, er, can only apologise to listeners for any offence caused by our guest's vivid description of her father." He threw a bewildered look at the old lady. "If you would like to continue, please Catherine. With slightly less colourful language, maybe?"

"Whatever!" she retorted. "Anyway, one Sunday morning my sister and I stole into the back of the shop where my father usually readied all the sweet cakes and pastries for the following week's trade. They were all finished and laid out on a large steel tray on the worktop as usual. However, on this particular weekend, our father had been fortunate enough to get hold of a rare consignment of blueberries and raspberries from one of his many wartime contacts. So, between the standard fare of custard tarts and iced fingers, sat half a dozen glorious individual Eton mess meringues crammed with cream and topped with the delicious fruit."

"Oh, I think I know what's coming here." Roger feigned further mild interest.

"Of course! Can you blame us?" Catherine's eyes blazed. "We literally lunged at these exotic treats, devouring them in such a fashion you'd have thought we hadn't eaten a thing in weeks. And, oh," the lady closed her eyes at the memory, "how sweet they were! The rich textures of the meringue and cream contrasted with the sharp tang of the fruit…we were never closer to heaven." The fete organizer bit her lower lip in an expression of mischievous guilt. "But it was gone in seconds so, naturally, we had another."

"Oh, you must have been in so much trouble." More flagrant insincerity from the show's host.

"Oh, we didn't care!" Catherine waved a dismissive hand. "It was payback time, so neither my sister nor I thought for second about scoffing up another meringue. But," she smiled wistfully, "because we weren't used to such rich food, we both felt terribly sick suddenly."

"So, you left the remaining two treats, crept out of the bakery and blamed it on a much-loved pet, right?" Roger almost sighed the words as he picked at a hangnail.

"Oh no! We slipped out of our nightdresses and began smearing the final two desserts over our naked, nubile young bodies."

Roger Barnett stopped breathing for a second. "Excuse me?"

"It was simply divine, darling!" the fete organiser chuckled expansively. "You should try it. We had so much fun covering each other in these wondrously ostentatious ingredients."

The mildly panicked voice of his producer came into Roger's earpiece. "I think you need to move on, Roger...she...she should be onto sticky toffee pudding by now." But Roger was suddenly engaged, finally, in nearly a year of doing the show, one of his guests was actually revealing something of interest.

"Go on, Catherine," he encouraged.

"Well, we were slapping cream here and meringue there...but then daddy stormed in, in a frightful temper as it seemed our boisterous frolicking had woken him up from his nap." Catherine paused for a split second. "And then he made us do something really wicked."

"Roger!" the producer screamed.

"Okay, we're going to take a break for some music and we'll be right back for Catherine's second dish shortly." Roger pushed a grey button in front of him and Lionel Ritchie burst into song.

There was a palpable sigh of relief in Roger's headphones from the production booth.

"Sorry to cut you off," he told Catherine with a rueful expression. "We weren't quite sure where you were going with that."

"It's okay." Deflated, the village veteran slumped back into her chair.

"Do you mind me asking what your dad did to you?" Roger saw the hesitation in her blue eyes. "It's okay, we're off air. No one can hear us."

Catherine thought for a second before answering; she had mentioned this to no one since that fateful day. "He made us eat jam doughnuts, one after another, until we were both properly sick," she finally confessed. "A lesson, if you like, to stay away from the cakes."

"Oh," said Roger, somewhat surprised that it lacked the sinister edge he and the producer feared. "Is that why doughnuts aren't on your dessert island list?"

The fete organizer nodded. "Haven't been able to face one in seventy years."

The pair sat quietly while the record played out. "That's a nice song," Catherine said, breaking the short silence. "What is it?"

Hang on, Roger mouthed wordlessly at his guest as the 'on air' light came back on and he leaned forward into the microphone. "That was Lionel Ritchie there, folks, with *I'm Creamy like a Sunday Morning*."

It was a slip of the tongue Roger Barnett would be reminded of for some time to come.

JEFF

Jeff had the final interviewee of the day in front of him; it did not look promising.

The Goose's landlord had managed to squeeze an advert for a 'professional' to host the pub's open mic nights in the Friday evening edition of the *East Anglian Daily Times* just before the closing deadline. Unfortunately, Jeff and the newspaper's ad sales representative got their wires crossed on the call and the rep thought the publican was after someone to manage an 'open bike' night. As part of the confirmation process, the ad rep had duly read the submitted copy back to Jeff. However, at the crucial moment, Cloak & Spanner's bark at the *The Peasenhall Quandary* landing on the pub doormat drowned out the sales guy briefly, and the errant word went unheeded. Consequently, once the ad was uploaded and published on the recruitment section of the paper's website, Jeff had been inundated with calls from local motorcycle enthusiasts trying to get more information about the position and the concept behind such an unusual event.

The ex-policeman quickly got his contact in the sales department to correct the typo and Jeff finally received five calls from more relevant, interested parties. He was able to dismiss two immediately on the basis they were unable to speak a word of English. (He hadn't envisaged a regular night of Ukrainian karaoke to begin with, but kept details of the callers handy – given the numbers of the Eastern Europeans toiling the fields of Suffolk, a night of song for them and their kinfolk wasn't necessarily the worst idea in the world.) The remaining three were invited in for a chat.

"I'm Jeff." The landlord extended a hand.

"'Lo there, boi," the interviewee shook the offered hand vigorously. "Oi's Dave Toosdi."

"Dave Tuesday," Jeff repeated for his own benefit.

"That's it!" Dave then promptly kicked off his boots in an effort to get more comfortable.

"Well, many thanks for coming over at such short notice, Dave," said Jeff as he stared at the man's stockinged feet.

Dave noticed Jeff's puzzled gaze. "Oh, sorry 'bout this," he began to explain. "Oi ran out o'clean sarks this mornen, so oi 'ad to borrow a pair of the woife's toights. Hah!"

"Very resourceful of you," Jeff responded, unnerved by the man's inventiveness and the way he said *woife's toights*.

"Damned if oi could foind a pair that weren't laddered," he grumbled. "More holes than Blackburn, Lancashire!"

The musical reference wasn't lost on Jeff and was actually impressed at how it'd been brought into the conversation. "So, you know your music, then?"

"Oi'll say! Moosic is moi loife!" Dave effused.

There's that accent again, thought Jeff. *Moi loife.*

"Oi've been looken for an opportooniti loike this for ages. But for it to come up in a place like Peas'naal…s'a dream come troo."

This was literally *moosic* to Jeff's ears, as each of the previous candidates across the morning had clearly no inkling of popular music, the local band scene or what, indeed, an open mic night entailed. The first, Joe, a plumber from Alderton, maintained he had contacts with a number of prog rock groups and was sure that, for a small fee, he could persuade them to come out of retirement and do a turn on a regular basis. Their travel from Northampton and an overnight stay at a local Premier Inn, however, would also have to be expensed. The second candidate, Caroline, was a member of an extreme death metal band which had a reputation (Jeff discovered on Google once the girl had left the premises) for carrying out their ablutions on stage mid-tune. It proved unsavoury viewing on YouTube even for an ex-copper.

Jeff settled into his questions. "So, tell me, Dave, how would you go about building a regular, successful open mic night at The Goose?"

Dave thought about the question before politely asking, "Would it be possible for me to 'ave a drink o'water? Only oi'm a lil' bit nervous."

"I'm sorry," Jeff jumped up. "Of course, you can. It was remiss of me not to ask you in the first place."

Dave was puzzled. "Sorry, what was that you did in the first place?"

"I said…oh nothing."

As Jeff fetched the drink from behind the bar, the sound of hoovering filled the pub as Shirley thrust the vacuum cleaner into the lounge bar and across the threadbare carpet (its replacement was on the Timberlake's 'to do list', but as funds had got tight of late, it was a job that would have to wait).

"Er…not now, darling!" Jeff shouted above the din.

Shirley flicked the off switch. "Well, it needs doing before we are swamped by the Saturday lunchtime crowd!" she said, with no effort to mask the sarcasm.

Jeff gestured towards his bootless candidate. "But you can see I'm interviewing."

Shirley tutted, stomped over to the wall socket, removed the plug with an over-zealous heave and began wrapping the cord back around the vacuum cleaner's handle.

"Besides," Jeff told his wife as he presented the drink to his interviewee and sat back down. "I don't think we should be using that since Spanner chewed through the flex. It's an accident waiting to happen."

"For your information, it was actually Cloak who chewed it, and now that you've reminded me how dangerous it is, YOU CAN VAC THE FUCKING PUB YOURSELF!"

As Shirley stormed back upstairs for a soak in the bath, Jeff gave his candidate a knowing smile and raised his eyebrows as if to say, *bloody women!*

"With that dodgy flex, oi'd say she were dicen wi'death," said Dave.

"Ha!" Jeff belly laughed loudly. "Oh, that's very good!"

"Sorry?" said Dave, somewhat puzzled again.

"Dyson with death!" Jeff guffawed some more. "That's brilliant!"

Dave sat blank faced. "Sorry," he said again. "Oi'm afraid oi don't quite foller."

Dave's interview lasted for another twenty minutes. He was no stranger to hard work and gave Jeff a brief outline of his employment experience to date, which included offal packing and hosing down *Hurry Bucket* units (*Best Keep It*

Quick) at *moosic* festivals and other public events. On the point of managing The Goose's open mic nights, Dave's proposal was that, for a fee of £150 a night, he could drum up support from the local Royal Legion club in Orford – which had a handful of old but enthusiastic players and encourage a number of younger musicians along from a photography evening class that his wife attended. On top of that, he was Treasurer of the *Felixstowe Indigestion Society* – a private club whose members met every Monday to discuss their experiences of acid reflux and trapped wind – and was confident of enticing a few of that crowd along. And last but not least, Dave had a number of Cliff Richard songs up his sleeve that he would use to get the evening off to a flyer and all the necessary sound equipment to put on a decent show; all this on the proviso that he could find the key to his lock-up.

It was Hobson's choice for Jeff: Dave Tuesday was looking like Plan A, B and C, so the deal needed to be done. Dave wasn't a bad stick. Okay, he managed his sock draw poorly and was barely understandable given the richness of his Suffolk accent, but he had an audience, equipment and a truly passionate heart, the decision was actually a no-brainer. Jeff stood up from the tub chair ready to shake Dave's hand when a rather forlorn-looking Graeme Nash walked in through The Goose's front door.

CARL

"If you, or anyone else you know, has been affected by this issue, please contact Suffolk County Council, which has operators ready to take your call...between the hours of eleven and twelve am...on a Toosdi. And now let's see what the weather has in store for us with Penny Nash!"

Carl Fleming flicked off the radio so he could focus on the job in hand. "Cool!" he said.

Carl saved the word document carrying the headline story for the forthcoming week's edition of *The Peasenhall Quandary*. He was pleased with his journalistic efforts. The article, in his humble opinion, nicely captured the prevailing mood around the village's biggest scandal since Steve Naysmith's dog, Samsonite, crashed one of his tractors through a hedge and onto the A12 back in 2005. (Steve always maintained he hadn't given the dog permission to drive as he was home 'sick' in bed. Samsonite had made it as far as Stowmarket before being pulled over by a police patrol car – which had Shirley Timberlake at the wheel – and eventually had his dog licence revoked.)

Carl had been PQ's editor for over twelve years, taking on responsibility for its output while he was still doing a diploma in Ironmongery and holding down a part time job at the local Falconry and Hawking Centre (a job made deeply unpleasant due to the number of visiting Chinese tourists). A workaholic, Carl was always busy on one project or another: the shop, the paper, his portfolio of shares, his authorship of a book on how pigs aided the World War 1 effort, an industry blog from the ironmonger's point of view, several hostile takeover bids and so on. He had been married to Judy for eleven years. She was an awkward looking woman whose eyes and teeth were clearly from a larger person's head thus rendering her more cartoon-like than human. Carl's work kept him clear of her for most of the day, and for all the times in between he would take himself off to Yoxford Gym, a state-of-the-art fitness facility that offered one elliptical training machine and a sprout press.

The use of aerobic exercise as a means of wife avoidance on a daily basis had the net effect of making Carl look like a very svelte Piers Morgan which, given the over-riding passion for irresponsible journalism, was a bit weird.

Over the years, Carl had moved the journal on from its basic premise as a village notice board to a no-holds-barred exposé of rural life that would give any Fleet Street rag a run for its money in terms of salacious and scandalous stories. He broke stories that had real personal interest and introduced regular features such as *On Yer Bike!* – an editorial piece which probed the backgrounds of individuals who didn't come up to the standards demanded by such a close-knit community – and *Who Do You Think You Are?* – an editorial piece which put the microscope on individuals who didn't come up to the standards demanded by such a close-knit community. Carl was a hack writer who would dig the dirt, pulp the facts and churn the sensational …and he loved it!

After a final proofread, Carl copy-and-pasted the article into the main layout of the paper, which was about ready to be published, and sat back in an antique leather desk chair admiring his front page.

You're Taking the Mic-hael!
A PQ exclusive by Carl Fleming
A storm is brewing in Peasenhall village following the recent decision by Hector Bramwell, landlord of The Whipped Peasant, to remove Graeme Nash from his position as the pub's popular open mic host and replace him with local shopkeeper and northern outsider, Mike Grimshaw.
Sources close to Mr. Nash have revealed his termination was both unwarranted and prejudicial. Local radio star, Penny Nash said: "Graeme has provided Mr. Bramwell with a quality product over many years now and for the pub landlord to release him simply because he dislikes Graeme's knitted garments is, quite frankly, astonishing." The PQ also understands the

confrontation between the two parties ended in an exchange of blows and that criminal charges may become a feature of this dispute if Suffolk police can be bothered to investigate.

It appears Mr. Bramwell had been plotting the demise of Mr. Nash for some time given news of Mr. Grimshaw's appointment was in the public domain within minutes of Mr. Nash's dismissal. The allegations have been strongly denied by Mr. Bramwell's public relations team which offered the following statement: "Our client has acted in the best interests of the pub and its regular clientele. Any suggestion that Mr. Bramwell is prejudiced towards woollen attire of any ilk is utter bollocks."

The drama is set to rumble on, however, if unconfirmed reports that Mr. Nash has agreed terms with The Startled Goose to run its open mic night prove to be valid. This would represent a great coup (or honk!) for The Goose given its talent nights to date have been completely shite. The northerner was unavailable for comment (typical).

Carl added a quarter page advert for a 24-hour inflatable skip service from Alan Muffler underneath the article and uploaded the whole file to his printers' Dropbox; he couldn't wait to see the finished edition in his hands. The editor closed his laptop and headed downstairs to the busy trading floor that was *Screw Ewe*.

"Has anyone heard anything from Larry or the Robert Dyas team on our proposed takeover?" he asked of no one in particular.

The staff stared blankly back at their boss muttering a series of 'no's' and 'don't think so's'.

"Ooh, yeah!" A Saturday boy with large rings in his earlobes suddenly piped up. "Mister Mullen popped in earlier and mentioned he'd got a reply back from…er…Robert…"

"Robert Dyas! Yes, yes!" Carl hissed impatiently. "Why didn't you call me?"

"Well," the boy hesitated. "Jenny said not to disturb you while you were putting the paper to bed," he said, pointing at a girl in an orange apron who was methodically restocking drill bits.

Carl ground his teeth together. "Okay. What exactly did he say?"

"Um," the boy struggled to remember. "He said the email was something along the lines of 'thanks for getting in touch, we've received your request and our customer service team is working to get back to you with an answer as soon as possible, but please note it can sometimes take up to 72 hours for us to reply.'"

"Ah, great!" said Carl, clearly impressed with his old school chum's efforts. "That sounds like real progress!"

HOLLY

"I use my own frozen sausage-based method of determining the various stages of dilation," Jules explained.

Mike had suggested it would be nice for him, Jules and his daughter to meet up so he could introduce Holly to his 'midwife friend' and they could get to know each other over supper. Once Holly had arrived, dived upstairs to freshen up, grimaced at the *Peppa Pig* matching duvet set on the spare bed and got back down with some slap on, Mike took her across to The Peasant to meet Jules.

"If I can squeeze a chipolata in, I know we're entering the initial stage," Jules continued to outline her technique. "After that, it's then a case of applying sausages of increasing girth to determine where the expectant mother is in the process. It's a saveloy next, then a Lincolnshire and then a Cumberland. As soon as I'm able to get a full liver sausage in there, it's pretty much game on!"

Holly offered Jules a troubled smile and glanced behind her in an effort to find out why her father was taking so long to fetch three drinks. He seemed to be delayed by a young, slightly odd-looking girl at the bar who was struggling with the card payment machine; she distinctly heard her dad say on more than one occasion that *he* needed to put in the PIN number when requested.

"So how are things at the sanctuary?" asked Jules as Holly turned back round. "Mike say's you're happy as a pig in shit!"

Holly, a chip off the old block, blanched at Jules' squaddie language. "Did he?" She said somewhat sceptically.

'Nah!" mocked Jules and gave her a friendly nudge. "I'm just messing with ya!"

Holly had established *Needham Hog Sanctuary* back in the spring; a dream that was finally realised through the generosity of her stepfather and his offer of much-needed capital for the project. (He initially tried to persuade Holly to set up the facility for unwanted baboons but eventually agreed that idea probably had financial ruin written all over it.) The principle aim of the sanctuary was to provide a secure environment for any pig that had been the victim of neglect. Pigs generally received a bad press and could often be found beaten, abandoned, ignored, teased, bullied or subjected to images of applesauce and chestnut stuffing. Holly's cause célèbre was to protect these creatures – and name and shame the dirty swine responsible.

Holly knew this was her vocation from an early age – the seed of her future life quickly germinating as she sat glued to episodes of *Animal Hospital*. She would never admit that to anyone now, of course, because as part of that awakening was her unbridled love for the TV show's presenter, Rolf Harris. Crying and laughing with him in equal measure as the nation's pets and livestock were treated, cured or exterminated, Holly's deep-rooted affection for the man was on a par with any regular parent. Of course, the man's fall from grace left her, like so many other lifelong admirers, in emotional tatters; all innocence lost in the blink of an eye. It hadn't mattered that he'd ruined songs like *Stairway to Heaven* with his wobble board, or that he'd flagrantly tried to tie a kangaroo down – which was clearly at odds with his altruistic work with animal charities later in life – to Holly, he was a God. And now he was just a sad man on the sex offender's register. And she was a disillusioned pig rescuer.

Holly's latest mercy mission involved the collection of a pig called Desmond, now comfortably sat in the horsebox attached to the girl's Jeep parked in the yard behind Mike's shop. Douglas' owner was Swaffham's infamous EuroMillions winner, Richard 'Tricky' Treehouse, who picked up a cool seventy-five mill in a Friday night draw and promptly fucked off to Cannes. The pig the lad had left behind in his haste to find a plastic surgeon and a posse of Russian hookers was popular with many of the Swaffham villagers. He would often be seen accompanying Tricky in the car when he went off to watch his beloved Leiston United FC play their home games. The alarm was raised when Douglas hadn't been seen grunting support for the Eastern Counties football league side for over a month. Holly was contacted by the local RSPCA and she had raced over to secure the release of the oligarch's distressed pig.

The early days of the business suffered from a freak coincidence – a direct result of the company's acronym. When Holly's initial promotional efforts for Needham Hog Sanctuary included her use of an 'NHS' tag on internet search engines to help people find her online, it prompted some rather unusual telephone conversations.

"Hello, Needham Hog Sanctuary!"

"Good Mornen! Oi'm ringen 'bout the appointment wi' the proctologist."

"Oh, I'm sorry. We don't offer those services here. Is it a pre-existing rectal condition your pig has or are you just looking for a regular colonoscopy? I can probably put you in touch with someone."

"Well, oi know 'e doesn't take too much proide in the way 'e looks…but oi think *pig's* a bit 'arsh!"

"I'm sorry, who's this?"

"My 'usband's doo for colorectal surgery 'amara about ten and 'e just wanted to know when 'e needs to stop eaten. Yer know, the antiseptic an' all."

"We are a pig sanctuary."

"Well, oi know the NHS has gorn down the shitter a bit in the last foo months…but *pig sanctuary's* a bit 'arsh!"

"Sorry, it's our mistake. We're not the NHS, we're Needham Hog Sanctuary. There's been a bit of a mix up on Google. I've got the number you need, just let me get it for you."

"Yer wanna get that sorted out else yer gorn a get some roight weirdos callin' yer."

"Here we go!" said Mike as he popped a tray of drinks onto the table. "How are you girls getting on?"

"Fine," said Holly, a tad tersely.

"I was just telling Holly about my ground-breaking sausage technique," Jules smiled proudly at her new beau.

"Oh, I'm sure she doesn't want to hear about all that icky-sticky stuff, Jules," said Mike, detecting the slightly curt response from his daughter.

Jules immediately felt patronised and somewhat embarrassed by the grocer. "Well, Michael." The smile quickly evaporated. "Young Holly may well experience the miracle of birth at some point in the future and if she's on my watch…she'll be subjected to a fucking sausage or two!"

Mike glared at Jules. "You know you don't always have to say whatever comes into your head."

Holly took a swig of her gin and tonic which contained a large pineapple chunk. "I'm popping outside to check on Douglas." The pig rescuer popped her glass down onto the table and disappeared through the pub's east exit.

"What's got into you?" Mike hissed at the midwife.

"Well," said Jules, taking a clove out of her glass of Frascati. "She's a bloody princess, your daughter! Couldn't bear to look at me when I was telling her about my forceps delivery this morning."

"Oh, for pity's sake!" Mike put down his pint of *Athletes Foot*, a cloudy bitter from Campsea Ashe, and chased after his daughter.

"I'm not sure she's right for you, daddy," said Holly over Douglas' gentle grunts. She had given the pig a bag of potato peelings and it was merrily chomping away.

"Jules is…" Mike wanted to say how kind and warm-hearted the local midwife was but it was a tough sell to someone who had just been subjected to a graphic clinical procedure, with a large amount of profanity thrown in. "She's just a friend."

Douglas' shiny snout stuck through the bars of the trailer in search of more peelings and Holly gave it a small stroke. "All gone, Dougy, I'm afraid," she said.

Mike knew what was going through his daughter's head. "I know you've never really forgiven me for not trying to keep the family together, but your mum had baboon boy and…"

"Craig."

"Oh, is that his name?" Mike realised he'd never actually found that out. "Well, she had Craig and I had, well, very little choice." Holly appeared unmoved. "It's been six years, Holls! Am I not entitled to a little company after all that time?"

"I know, dad." There were tears in Holly's eyes. "But you're all I've got. Mum and Craig are either working away or at some ape recognition seminar or other and I'm…" she paused. "It's just not fair."

"You've got the sanctuary," Mike offered some perspective. "That's keeping you busy. It's going brilliantly by the sound of it."

"It is," agreed Holly. "But being the great pig liberator is hardly a recipe for an active social life."

"But you've got," Mike struggled to recall the names of Holly's employees. "Um…"

"Stuart and Josh."

"Yeah, those guys. I bet you guys have a great craic running the place. Don't you?"

"We do," Holly sighed. "And they're great at what they do and really supportive. But they've both got partners and shoot straight off every night to cosy up with a ready meal in front of Emmerdale."

Mike could not think of anything worse. "So, my little girl needs a boyfriend," he finally surmised.

"And your little girl isn't going to attract one spending her days and nights rescuing porkers which get a rough ride." Holly completed the diagnosis.

Dougy grunted as if to say, "How's your luck?"

Mike walked over and took his daughter into his arms. "You've had a hectic six months and you've had no time for yourself. That'll change, I promise."

"Promise?" Holly looked up into her dad's eyes.

"Promise. You know, love tends to strike when you least expect it. You'll see."

"And in the meantime?" Holly pressed.

Mike hugged a fraction harder. "And in the meantime, you've still got me. I'll make more of an effort to stay close and get less…distracted."

At which moment, the southwestern door swung open and Jules popped her head out. "You two shisters want another drink? It's my round."

SUNDAY LUNCH

"Looking forward to this afternoon's band, lads?" Hector passed two pints and two pinot grigio chasers over to the Lewis brothers.

"Oo's playen?" asked Liam.

"Steely Dan Naysmith. The farmer's lad."

"Sweet." Liam nodded and smiled while his elder brother, Joe, pulled a face.

"What's up with you?" snorted Hector.

Joe blinked furiously and took a glug of the chilled wine before answering. "Oi think oi can 'ear me eyeballs movin'."

The Lewis brothers were regular and passionate open mic attendees.

Joe Lewis was a part-time window cleaner with vertigo issues, while the youngest, Liam, worked at the Brendan Matthews' (no relation) turkey processing centre in Spexhall. Liam had been in charge of turkey welfare at the plant for the last six months. It was a job he truly relished and went at with no small amount of enthusiasm and imagination. Such was his dedication to the birds' well-being that he would often be seen walking them along the coast at Aldeburgh taking in the sea air. Liam considered this an important treat prior to the animals' conversion into breaded drummers, kievs or dinosaurs. Both the local community and animal rights groups considered Liam's actions highly laudable and would regularly post praise on his personal blog, *Quirky Turkey,* commenting on how refreshing it was to see this young man escorting the birds atop the seawall, treating them to a 99 Flake or affording them a quick look at the sale rack in Jack Wills.

Turkey welfare was Liam's third position at the firm; the job he was originally appointed for had ended at some personal cost to him. Following five weeks in his role as stock supervisor at the processing centre, the fair-haired, doe-eyed boy from Tunstall lost both his legs.

Liam had been conducting a stock take of *Turkey Mini Kievs* in one of the principal frozen storage units and was accidentally locked inside when a passing colleague closed the freezer door she thought had been carelessly left open. With no one around to hear his cries of help, Liam spent three days at a mean temperature of eleven below zero before his absence was noticed by colleagues, family and avid followers of *Quirky Turkey*. He was eventually found and released from his frozen tomb by the plant director who, on seeing his stricken subordinate, immediately raised the alarm.

By rights, the lad should have perished, but in a valiant effort to survive as long as possible, Liam kept his upper body frost free by building a small ice cave from the inventory of turkey crowns. He managed to hold it together using the pricing labels and a selection of promotional flyers he'd carried in there with him. His legs, however, were fully exposed across the 72-hour ordeal and did not fare so well. Blackened and swollen beyond recognition, Liam's legs had succumbed to deep frostbite. The young man screamed in agony as the plant director lifted him onto the prongs of the factory's only forklift truck so that he could be transported to the first aid room and the waiting paramedics.

Following a month of umming and ahhing over whether Liam's legs could be saved, renowned surgeon and prize-winning cauliflower grower, Mr. Edwin Frost (an irony which was lost on the immediate family), decided to operate. Fourteen hours later, Liam's Cajun-like limbs were in the hospital's recycling bin.

The initial stages of Liam's recuperation were to prove as painful an ordeal as the injury itself. In spite of free access to baby aspirin and *Calpol* from Ipswich Hospital pharmacy, the early pain was intolerable. The food on the lunchtime was often deeply upsetting (turkey leg, leg of lamb etc.) and his prosthetics were a joke. Liam's first artificial limbs were a pair of standard issue hospital crutches, which not only looked ridiculous, but were also totally impractical for any kind of movement. The crutches, however, did have one surprising upside and that was the fact their length could be easily adjusted using the variable height holes along their shaft. Liam could therefore wake up on any given morning and – with the push of a small metal button – decide whether he wanted to be 6'8" or 4'7" for the day. This ability to turn from midget to lanky boy in a heartbeat made him a firm favourite with the ladies on the obstetric ward.

Fortunately, the Brendan Matthews' team was quick to resolve Liam's early issues when they got wind of his hardships following surgery. The company forked-out on the very best pair of hi-tech prosthetics (a set Liam had drooled over while watching archive footage of a shockingly inept murder trial in South Africa); paid for extensive rehabilitation and physical therapy in Yoxford Gym and returned him to the turkey plant with an increase in salary and a new position tending the turkey ovens.

However, Liam returned to the hospital after only four weeks back at work having scorched most of the skin on his forearms (an accident Mr. Frost seized upon, but his eagerness to amputate again and 'complete the set' earned him an indefinite leave of absence). After reviewing his situation for a second time, the turkey farm management team agreed he was best off away from any extremes of temperature and was handed the new corporate social responsibility role of turkey welfare.

"Hey, Hector!" Mike arrived through the main door.

"Hey, Mikey," Hector replied. "Someone's happy!"

Hector's assessment stopped Mike in his tracks. "How did you know?"

"You're wearing a skirt!" Hector nodded at Mike's choice of a black, pencil number. "You always dress up when you're in a good mood. Jules with you?"

"Nah. She went off in a bit of a strop last night after I said Holls and I just wanted to spend the rest of the evening catching up together."

"Has Holls gone?"

"Yeah. She headed off with Douglas about an hour ago."

"Good looken pig, that," Joe Lewis chipped in from his seat behind Mike.

"Oh, hi, Joe. Liam. Any new dark theories this week, gentlemen?"

Hector's eyes rolled at the thought. "Oh, please no!"

Apart from Liam's traumatic recent history and Joe's ingrained fear of heights – an affliction which meant he could only tolerate cleaning the ground floor windows on a property – the only other remarkable thing about the pair was that they were the world's worst serial conspiracy theorists.

With zero evidence to back up any of their claims, they argued that it was the late liberal democrat leader, Charles Kennedy, who had been gunned down in Dallas, the Apollo lunar landings had all been filmed in a cabbage field near Lavenham, both Elvis and Shergar were actually dead and the scooters chasing Princess Diana into the Paris tunnel that fateful evening were being ridden by mutant kung-fu tortoises.

"Yer remember those planes flyen into them twin towers?" Joe said to Hector one quiet spring afternoon in the public bar.

"Terrible business, Joe," Hector conceded.

"Nothen to do wi' them Al Keeda, moind."

"Really?" Hector sighed with painful ambivalence.

Joe took a slug from his pint of *Watchful Magistrate*, a light stout brewed on a boat anchored in Bawdsey Quay estuary. "That were all the government's doen, that were."

"How d'you reckon that then, Joe?" Hector peered in vain over Joe's shoulder praying someone less troubled would make their way into the pub.

"Stands to reason, boi."

"Does it really?"

Joe ignored the landlord's indifference and continued. "Just think about it! 'Ow could Bush's government report the incident in September when the attack clearly dint occur until much later? It's loike they noo it were gorn to 'appen."

"What are you talking about?"

"Noine 'levern?" crowed the vertiginous window wiper. "That's the nointh of November, my friend. Them planes hit fully two months after they reported it. Now that's pure conspiracy in anyone's book."

Joe leaned a little closer to Mike. "Well, sir, I did 'ear a whisper just a day or two ago."

"Go on," encouraged Mike.

Hector could hear Chloe signing the theme to Postman Pat down in the cellar and he had a sudden and overwhelming desire to be in another country – or a maximum-security prison. "I'm going to leave you guys to it. I'll get you a pint, Mike, and then we need to talk Thursday night."

The prospect made Mike's heart stop. "Okay," he whimpered.

"Yer alroight?" asked Liam. "Colour's suddenly gorn from yer face."

"I'm fine," said Mike and put his hosting of the forthcoming open mic out of his mind as best he could. "So, what's this latest conspiracy of yours?"

"It concerns the Rendlesham Forest UFO sighten."

"But that's already a conspiracy!" argued Mike.

"Yeah, so this is conspiracy plus…squared," said Liam with little conviction.

Hector swung by quickly to give Mike his drink. "Fucking idiots!" he said and swung off again.

Back in December of 1980, a number of military personnel reported sightings of unexplained lights near Rendlesham Forest, one of the county's woodiest patches. The events occurred just outside RAF Bentwaters that, at the time, was home to the U.S. Air Force. It was USAF personnel who claimed to witness these strange lights and included one Deputy Base Commander, Lieutenant Colonel Charles Halt, who maintained that what he observed was undoubtedly a UFO sighting. The Ministry of Defence quickly hushed things up, however, stating the event posed no threat to national security and was therefore never investigated as a security matter. A spokesperson for Suffolk County Council also dismissed the likelihood of any alien contact but confirmed they were putting up business rates just in case.

The incident soon became referred to as 'Britain's Roswell' as the sightings were officially explained away as nothing more than a misinterpretation of nocturnal lights.

"Well, there's noo evidence," said Joe in a low, murky voice.

"Hang on." A thought struck Mike. "Yeah, I think I heard something about this on the radio recently. Something about retired radar operators now willing to talk."

"Yeah," Liam said conspiratorially.

"Well, yer know we were there that noight," said Joe.

"No, you weren't," replied Mike flatly.

Joe squirmed. "Well, we were in the vicinity, let's say."

"It was two years before you were born, Joe."

"Yeah, but…"

"Look, the fact is," Liam quickly interjected before his brother made a complete tit of himself. "It weren't a UFO they'd sin. It was the ghost of a mammoth." And in saying this, made a complete tit of himself.

"Utter bobbins!" exclaimed Mike.

"Mike!" Liam protested. "GPS and sat nav surveys 'ave been used to show there's a mammoth preserved in the peat underneath that forest. Them air force bois dint see no UFO, they witnessed a mammoth haunten!"

"A mammoth haunting? How do you boys sleep at night?" enquired Mike and took a slug of *Maiden's Arse*.

Liam looked mortally offended. "It's God's truth. Innit Joe?"

"Yarp!" said Joe beaming with assured confidence.

Hector suddenly appeared beside the band of conspirators. "You wanna talk through Thursday now while I've got a moment between lunch orders?" he said to Mike. "And any more of this abject nonsense from you two," he pointed a gravy-covered finger at the Lewises, "and you're barred!"

SUFFOLK

Mike wheeled his mountain bike into the road, climbed into the saddle and pedalled down a silent Peasenhall High Street.

The first rays of sunshine had just kissed the early morning and the air was sharp on Mike's face as he picked up a bit of momentum. Quickly off the main road and onto the lanes, the horizon in front Mike opened up as a vista of meadows shorn of their hay, corn and barley crops filled his view. Only frosted blue sky above, Mike followed his normal circular route, pushing on past dense hedgerows of rosehip and blackberry and catching the odd glimpse of dew-laden webs carrying their spindly creators.

On he cycled, between acres of constantly changing arable land. From stubbled soil to golden ears, Mike would see the landscape change with the seasons. Watching the transformations over his handlebars with each outing, Mike would often think of his journey as the one taken by the traveller in the film of HG Wells' *The Time Machine* where he observed the ever-changing sequence of fashions on two female mannequins in the clothing shop window.

Mike rode on down flat lanes banked high with hawthorn that gave way to the ups and downs of a host of small river valleys. He always smiled at the general misconception that Suffolk was flat country: low-lying, maybe, but flat, no. Okay, as a Lancashire lad he had to concede there was nothing on a par with Pendle Hill but he'd suffered enough lengthy, oxygen-sapping inclines in his adopted county to know a long ride for the occasional cyclist was no cakewalk. With the wind at his back and the road ahead bathed in sunshine, Mike could just eat up the miles. His carefully planned route kept the shopkeeper away from the main highways as they busied on a Monday morning. Skirting settlements and farms, he was at the mercy of the land and its occupants, constantly on his guard should a grouse or partridge leave the protection of the hedge and dart across the road in front of him. Across the patchwork of arable land, Mike would catch a glimpse of the toy kites – modern-day scarecrows – angling and dipping in the coastal breeze. While the sound of plastic sails rippling through the air zipped across the fields, the sunlight bouncing off repurposed CDs attached along the length of the kite strings dazzled Mike and scared off birds in equal measure.

For this unassuming northern lad, riding was a type of therapy. As soon as he was in the saddle, the big problems in his life would scatter in the headwind. For an hour or two he could stop agonising over whether the shop's sales would pick up, or what more he could do for Holly, or how he was going to manage his stage fright or, as of now, what the future held for his relationship with Jules? On the bike, he could just be at one with the world. He could do nothing but think positive thoughts on his ride: get that first song written, paint the living room the colour he actually wanted it and so on. Snippets of songs of hope and celebration would pop into Mike's head as he rode, ear worms that created a soundtrack to every two-wheeled journey.

Throw those curtains wide…one day like this a year will see me right!

Exercise held no attraction for Mike normally and he would often fight the notion of getting out to ride. However, he always questioned his reticence once he was underway and soaking up Constable Country. It was escape, a chance for a moment of utopia, as this stranger in a strange land rode on.

As he approached the middle of his route, arable turned to heath and the spiky, yellow-flowered gorse added a glorious new texture to the landscape. Beyond the freshly excavated molehills on the damp soil, Mike picked out a dog and its owner navigating their way through the gorse on their own path of discovery. Rendlesham Forest soon loomed large with broad, mixed canopies of evergreen and leaves that were just thinking about turning. Mike could sense the reds, browns and yellows just waiting to burst through. Cutting through the wood, the smell of earth and pine combined as Mike rode through the lungs of a giant primeval beast. A mammoth, maybe? He grinned.

With the morning light obscured by the trees, the air-cooled and Mike pedalled harder until he was out and back in its glow. Onto Iken and the view across the River Alde, the little church balanced precariously but beautifully on the small peninsula that poked out into the estuary, keeping a constant watch on the ebb and flow of the tide. Stable yards, fields of cattle and piggeries, with their swathe of Nissen huts set out like a World War II airfield, all melted into a blur as he sped by.

Not long, thought Mike. A mile up the road and he was at Snape, his usual spot to rest. He dug in for five minutes more and arrived at the gravel drive that led him into the village's famous maltings.

With a coffee in hand from the quaint café, which had just opened its doors, Mike kicked off his trainers, sat down on the river wall and dangled his legs over the water. The sun warmed his face as he looked out across the marshes towards the old sailing barges moored by the side of the quirky concert hall. The stillness in the water reflected a sparrowhawk hovering over its prey perfectly and, given the early hour, all Mike could hear were the shrill cries of distant warblers and the drone of darter dragonflies probably taking one of their last few flights.

Better get going, Mike thought, get that shop of mine open. But he sat there a while longer, enjoying the tranquillity and the fact he'd found something so utterly satisfying without having to look for it.

Serendipity. That was the reason Mike Grimshaw had stayed.

MICKEY

"Bin riden?"

"Yeah."

"See any road kill?"

"Yeah. A fair bit."

"Oi came across some over the weekend. Oi thought it were a unicorn at first, but when oi got out the car, I saw it were just a pony that 'ad bin knocked down and the bastards 'ad gorn and stuck a Cornetto on its for'ead."

Mickey Koblenz was generally Mike's first customer of a morning. Same thing every day: twenty Benson and Hedges and a pint of milk. Mickey was a recovering alcoholic – recovering nicely thanks to eight pints of *Fruli* every night down at *The Fading Obelisk* in Ashbocking. He swore by the strawberry flavour because, as he would explain to onlookers concerned about his health, it represented eight of his five a day.

"Big noight Thursdi." Mickey winked.

"Don't," moaned Mike. "You will be there?"

"Wouldn't miss it for the world, pal."

Mickey appeared harmless enough, but his tattooed neck and a reckless attitude towards drinking unfiltered water suggested a darker past. He was a rare sufferer of SHD – Seasonal Hair Disorder – one of only nine cases in the Western Hemisphere (eight of which were in Suffolk). The disorder meant the man was totally bald across the duration of the winter months. This perennial shedding of hair was not a pretty sight, and 'airmaggedon' – as it was locally referred to – would often offend passers-by to such an extent, that they complained directly to the personal grooming watchdog, OfHair.

Villagers who'd grown blind to Mickey's follicle affliction merely knew him as the 'bloke oo 'ad the stoodio'. What they didn't know about Mickey, however, was the fact he had a full-time career as a mortuary technician; something he kept a closely guarded secret. Like the rest of Peasenhall, Mike was blissfully unaware that the character who welcomes wannabee recording artists into his home to lay down some tracks of an afternoon, spent most of the morning eviscerating bodies in Ipswich morgue; a job which effectively drove the man to drink.

"The worst thing is getting a couple of songs together for the top of the show," Mike nibbled at a fingernail. "I'm terrified."

"You'll be foine," Mickey assured the grocer. "Hey, oi've been practicen an old number over the last couple o'days. Torn Between Two Lovers."

"Oh, yeah. That's a great track. Mary MacGregor, wasn't it?"

"Yarp," confirmed Mickey. "Saw somethen last week that inspired me to find the moosic."

"Yeah? What was that?"

Mickey coughed and randomly pointed to the sweet counter. "'Ow much are yer wine gums?"

Mickey was a great pianist and, while he didn't always join in on open mic night, everyone loved it when he showed up at The Peasant, put his amateur night prejudices away and took himself over to the piano to tinkle the ivories.

Mike had only witnessed this twice on a Thursday night, but it was pure magic. Always modest about his undeniable talent, Mickey would never dance to anyone's tune. If he was in the mood – and only then – would he immerse himself in a melody or two and play blues, jazz, swing...basically anything that came into his head. He'd add lyrics to a few of the songs and, for a man who looked more like one of Dian Fossey's studies, his voice could charm the birds from the trees.

"Got anyone booked into the studio this week, Mickey?" said Mike, replacing the wine gums that the mortician seemingly didn't want now.

"A couple a groups." Mickey scratched between some remaining strands of hair. "I got a boi band from Stowmarket in on Toosdi called...let me think…The Hashtag Lads. And Superaten Wound on Wednesdi, who are a death metal outfit."

"Superating Wound, eh? They sound…charming."

While Mickey's playing may have been something truly special, his ability as a producer was decidedly shaky. His 'stoodio' consisted of a laptop, a microphone, a set of headphones and a DAW/Audio interface combo – nothing more than an app that mixed the music. It was basic to say the least, and the results weren't spectacular either. While Mickey was painfully unassuming about his own talents, he would enthuse wildly about anyone he'd had in the studio and literally demanded everyone, on pain of death, to listen to the most recent CD he'd just cut. Long in the memory will stay the night Mickey brought his recording of *Zumba Wumba*, a dance-reggae hybrid band from Shimplingthorne, over to The Peasant and stuck it through Hector's Bose speaker. The quality of the sound was so bad it reminded everyone of Amy Winehouse live on stage.

"Will you play on Thursday?" Mike's request sounded more like begging.

"Dunno, Mike. I'll see," said Mickey, as non-committal as ever. Truth was, Mickey was a big fan of Graeme and Penny who'd introduced him to a lot of contacts, and had helped get his little side line away from the daily disembowelments up and running.

"It's okay, Mickey." Mike tried to put on a brave face. "I'll manage."

Over at The Goose, Graeme and Jeff were sharing an early morning coffee and planning their Thursday evening.

"If those four decide to sing together then that's going to look like a troop of slightly geriatric Spice Girls," Graeme explained.

"Yes, sorry, Graeme, that's a terrible idea. Scrub that," conceded Jeff.

"It wasn't down anywhere, Jeff. Where do you want me to scrub it from?"

Jeff got the message. "Look. Best I just leave it to you, right? After all, you're the open mic guru."

"That's why you're paying me two hundred and fifty quid. Cuz I'm the guru."

Fuck me, Jeff thought, I really do have to make sure Shirley doesn't get wind of his fee.

"Jeffrey!" screamed Shirley from the restaurant.

"Mm, better go." Jeff upped and disappeared next door.

Graeme looked at his options for Thursday and it was looking bleak. Most of 'his talent' that he'd spoken to were still torn between him and Hector and hadn't decided where their loyalties lay and where they would play. There was also the added dilemma that they still considered The Goose an utter shithole. Graeme knew though that if he didn't deliver the goods, that two hundred and fifty quid wouldn't be on the table for long.

"Two hundred and fifty quid?" Shirley was screaming and whispering simultaneously. "Are you FUCKING INSANE?"

Jeff had a hold of both of Shirley's forearms, wise in the knowledge that she was probably going to use them on him forcibly in the very near future. "It's okay, listen."

"We haven't got two ha'pennys to rub together and you're giving a man dressed in a scarlet jumper with a massive dove on the front...TWO HUNDRED AND FIFTY QUID?"

"Yes, it's International Day of Peace...apparently."

The couple stared at each other in silence for a minute.

"Can you let go of my arms now, please? I need to hit you."

"Look," said Jeff, clinging on for dear life. "The Peasant clears a grand, easy, on open mic nights, with booze and food. And that's because they've had Graeme and his oh-so-popular missus to pull that crowd in." Jeff released his grip and Shirley didn't immediately swing. Result, Jeff thought. "Now, I know we won't get that from day one, but it won't be long before Graeme builds the acts and gets the crowds coming in." Still no swing. Brilliant!

"How many has he confirmed so far?" Shirley's tone was cold.

"Including himself, um, two!"

Graeme thought he heard the sound of a car backfiring and looked up to see Cloak & Spanner coming through the adjoining door with all four ears pinned back. Then stillness. Jeff must have dropped something in the cellar, he thought. He gave the piece of paper in front of him a hard stare but the list wasn't getting any longer. His phone was also quiet, which meant Penny was having no luck either, and she would soon be starting the weather forecast.

"Great balls of fire!" Graeme cried, just as Mickey Koblenz mooched through the door.

JULES

Jules smashed down the lid of her laptop. "What's the point of having this technology if it doesn't bloody work?!" the midwife shrieked aloud.

While negotiating the county's über-challenging travel network was one thing, trawling Suffolk's cyberspace was most definitely another. Despite the continued promise of astonishing download speeds from over-paid actors during ad breaks, the supply of broadband in the eastern province remained, for the most part, resolutely narrow. 'Limited Service' and 'Emergency Calls Only' were common messages on mobile phones across the region, and the modern phenomenon of 'buffer face' was now so popular among Suffolk's smartphone users that its ubiquity as a countenance was only second to the 'could-you-repeat-that?' face.

Jules had been trying to Skype one of her mums-to-be. Heavy with child in the third trimester of her second pregnancy, the woman in question had a nasty yeast infection and Jules wanted to check on the progress of the cream she'd recommended without having to drive an arduous forty miles to Lowestoft.

"Okay, so can you try again and pop your daughter's iPad between your thighs please?" This was the fourth attempt; the call had dropped on the previous three.

"She'd kill me if she noo oi were usen it for this," said the mum-to-be.

"Yes, I know. But Daisy's only four, I'm sure she won't mind," said Jules shaking her head. "Now remember you need to flip the direction of the camera...all I can see is your feet at the moment."

"'Ang on," groaned the woman as she reached over her bump. "Not easy with Sherlock in the bloomen way."

Sherlock?

It was all Jules' could do not to burst out laughing. "Aah, sweet name," she said, choosing a more professional approach. "I didn't know you'd been told it was a boy."

"What?" said the puzzled woman. "Oh! No! Sherlock's the fucken dog! 'E won't leave me alone when oi'm on the couch." Another groan as she stretched further forward. "Roight. Oi'm gorn a press this camera thing now. Yer ready?"

The Skype call promptly dropped again, leaving the midwife with a message box asking: "How would you rate this call?" Almost apoplectic with surf rage, Jules smashed out a note in the instant message box on the woman's Skype page.

"Damn internet! Couldn't see on the camera. Has the inflammation gone down?"

She considered putting an emoji with a troubled expression on the end of the message but simply pressed enter to send. Nothing happened. The woman was now offline according to the status button and, after waiting another ten minutes to see if it would go green again, Jules knew she would have to make the trip.

While the business community would rail against Suffolk's lack of any reasonable broadband service, many locals thought it added an extra layer of quirkiness to the area and was in keeping with the county's slow-paced lifestyle. The fact that the internet was simply incapable of keeping itself 'up' was actually viewed positively by locals who desired change about as much as they desired a dose of the squirts. By happy coincidence, it also meant local councillors and politicians could deflect the issue with some aplomb.

In a recent constituency meeting, Tory MP, Terry Toffee, was quizzed and harangued by frustrated business representatives over the poor performance of broadband and the impact it was having on progressive trade in the region. Mr. Toffee listened closely to the arguments in front of him, nodding sagely and sympathetically before taking a straw poll of those who were more than content with the current service. As well over half the hands went up in the audience, Mr. Toffee nodded in appreciation and said, "Okay. Agenda point number four. The proposed introduction of *Hurry Bucket* portable toilets alongside Orford Keep."

Jules' mobile rang. (The ringtone was a download of Stereo MC's *Connected*. Oh, the irony!)

"Come on, Spit it out! Julie Wiseman speaking."

"Jules." It was Mike.

"Hey."

"You got a minute?"

Jules hesitated. "I'm kind of in a rush, Mike. I've got to get up to Lowestoft."

"Sure." Mike hesitated. "Look, can we get together later?"

If Jules had been hands free, they'd both be on her hips. "Oh, so after two days of silence you now want to talk to me?"

"I know," kowtowed Mike. "I'm sorry. It's just that I got a bit wrapped up with stuff with Holly and then yesterday was…"

Just then, the signal dropped on either Mike or Julie's phone (probably both) and the conversation came to an abrupt end.

"She hung up on me." Mike stared at the mobile device in utter astonishment.

Jules nearly threw her phone through her open conservatory door such was her anger. She decided against it as it was basically her whole life, and quickly tried to call Mike back. No signal.

"Mother…Hubbard!" she mouthed.

The midwife grabbed her car keys and her bag, muttering how lucky it was for the cat or dog she didn't have as it would have been getting a proper kicking right now, charged through her front door, got into the car and headed off to review personally what technology failed to.

MIKE

"Dettol?" Mike called over to the teenager sifting through the collection of items in the 'reduced price' basket.

"Yarp!" replied Dettol.

"Why does everyone call you that?"

"Cuz o'moi name," he said, grabbing a three-day-old loaf of bread.

"And what's your name?" pressed Mike.

"Anthony Septook."

"Antiseptic."

"Roight," confirmed the youth, digging in the pockets of his decorating overalls for a 50p.

Mike swallowed a mouthful of coffee. "That's a bit harsh."

"Oi dunno," said Dettol, brightly. "It was Parazone to start with and then Domestos."

"But they're bleach brands, not antiseptics."

"Oi know."

"So, why did they settle on Dettol?" Mike smiled inwardly at his impromptu rhyming couplet.

"Easier," Dettol said without hesitation. "Less syllables."

Dettol paid for his bread and left, crossing paths with Catherine Bush in the doorway as she came into the shop.

"Hello, Mike," she said in a dreamy Hollywood voice that everyone loved.

"Oh, hi, Catherine." Mike's welcome didn't exactly match his usual effusive standard.

"Sorry, Mike. Have I caught you at a bad time?" asked Catherine, registering an air of dejection in the shop.

"It's fine," Mike dismissed her concerns. "I've just got a bit het up with doing this open mic gig tomorrow night, that's all."

"I heard," smiled Catherine. "Don't worry. You'll be great. Everyone's rooting for you."

"Everyone except Graeme Nash," Mike was quick to point out.

"Oh, don't worry about, Graeme. He'll get over himself soon enough. Besides, he's a pedant. I bet he keeps his tomatoes in a fruit bowl."

Mike kept quiet.

"Anyway! This is *your* time to shine! *Carpe diem*!"

"Sorry?" Mike's Latin was shite.

"Seize the day, Michael!"

God, you're posh, Mike thought. He then thought what a smashing looking woman she probably was back in her heyday. Posh totty. "Anyway…" Mike pushed inappropriate images from his mind. "What can I be doing you for, Mrs. Bush?"

"Well, I do need some moist toilet wipes." Catherine removed a pair of long, black gloves as she spoke. "But first I want to know if you would be interested in supporting the Peasenhall Pea Festival for next year?"

"But that was disbanded a couple of years ago?" queried Mike. "Lack of volunteers to help organise it or something, wasn't it?"

"Correct. But I've come up with a plan."

The Peasenhall Pea Festival was a village occasion that had been held each summer in the Assembly Rooms for seven years on the trot. It had grown from a small local event, which raised money for the nearby Almshouses, into a nationally recognised festival that attracted pea fans from each corner of the nation. The farmland around Peasenhall was a major pea-growing area and the festival reflected its importance to the locals who could not get enough of this pointless vegetable.

While Peasenhall's unique festival was advertised as a fun day out for all the family and a 'celebration of all things peasy', it was not an event to be taken lightly. Numerous pea-themed events added an intense competitive edge to the day. They included the World Pea Podding Championships and the National Pea Throwing title, among other popular tournaments. Teams from as far afield as Lithuania and Poland would enter, looking to claim the major honours on offer. Competition was fierce and teams would go all out for victory. Few would forget when Bosnia and Herzegovina entered a team of ringers in 2010 that included the internationally acclaimed podder, Branko 'The Pea' Pozderac. They cleaned up, winning all bar the Pea Eating Open title which, given competitors had to use chopsticks, was nailed by a squad from Beijing. Sadly, the peashooter competition was banned by the Suffolk County Council administration in 2011 when Johnny Naysmith – Steve Naysmith's youngest lad – lost an eye in an unfortunate crosswind.

One of the highlights of the festival was the pea parade which started outside Neal's Butcher and would circle the town before arriving to a muted welcome at the large car park on School Meadow. Peasenhall's primary school children would spend all year making huge paper mâché peas that would form a guard of honour for the hordes of festival visitors walking the route. The peas were ceremoniously tossed into the River Yox after the parade, creating a spectacular vegetable flotilla and ensuring heavy localised flooding for weeks after. A marching band would lead the parade and bash out pea-themed songs such as The Stones' *Peas to Meet You*, Coldplay's *Pod put a Smile on My Face* and Xzibit's *Bird's Eye View*. As festival goers congregated at the car park, they were invited to dine on Patrice le Clef's infamous *Suffolk Risotto aux Petit Pois*, a heart-warming dish that the day's hungry competitors from many Eastern European countries would guzzle down and the remaining abstemious visitors would avoid and get a burger on the way home.

The success of this proud festival and the level of organisation required to actually get it off the ground did, however, finally take its toll on the small number of dedicated volunteers from the village, and the decision was made not to run it for an eighth year. A number of sponsors offered to come in and support the festival – including *Hurry Bucket*, which offered cash to support a new competition idea that involved their portable toilets, and was a play on the word 'pea'. But it was too little, too late.

"So, what's your plan?" Mike asked

"Well, first of all," Catherine begun. "I'm going to raise a teensy-weensy amount of cash from all the local businesses in order to get the project up and running again. That's where you come in."

"Okay," said Mike suspiciously, somewhat doubtful that his definition of 'teensy-weensy' was the same as Catherine's.

"And then I'm going to sell the TV rights to BT Sport," Catherine boldly announced. "They're paying out huge amounts of money for all kinds of sporting nonsense these days."

The first point concerned Mike, but he concurred with the second. "Go on," he urged.

"Simple, Mike," she shrugged. "The money raised will allow me to fund a new organising committee that can be employed full-time to arrange the event, promote the whole occasion better, get overseas investors, yada, yada, yada! Basically, put together a robust business plan that'll keep the festival as a permanent fixture in the villages for decades!"

"And you're sure BT Sport is going to go for this?"

"No question."

Doubt smothered Mike's face like cheap vanity cream.

"Look, son." Catherine wagged the finger of reproach at the grocer's obvious opinion of her plan. "I'm fucking Peasenhall royalty! That bunch of jumped up telephone engineers are going to march my tune, let me tell ya!"

With Catherine and her batty ideas gone, Mike was left to rue the day past and the day ahead.

He had tried calling Jules a few times on her mobile, but it was just going to voicemail. Was she screening his calls, he wondered? Mike hated leaving messages, he always ummed and ahhed so much that the resulting communication was just a garbled mess. He would try once or twice more but then he'd have to focus on tomorrow's open mic night. He needed to practice his opening numbers and get his head sorted out because, at that moment, it was all over the shop.

OPEN MIC

Thursday night. More of the same shite.

Mike tapped his microphone. "One, choo! One, choo!"

Hector put a thumbs-up from behind the bar. "Sounds good!"

As Mike tinkered with his levels, Alan Hedgeworthy came up with his organ.

"Oh, hi, Alan," said Mike, genuinely delighted that his keyboard player had decided to come. "Just pop it over there next to the piano."

"The Kremlin towers look majestic in the evening sun," came the shop assistant's response.

Mike was busy. Nervous. And he could do without Alan's bullshit. But he'd shown up and that meant he deserved some respect. "Of course," replied Mike. "I've put the microfiche in the fish," he said trying to play along with, what he thought, was a pretty good line given the stress he was under.

However, the effect on Alan was catastrophic. "Christ! You must tell no one of this development!" Alan screamed, literally full of terror. "It's not safe! You're not safe! We must get back to Carla!" And with that he spun round, keyboard case in hand and disappeared out of the east-by-north-east door.

Everyone in the pub had stopped and was looking at Mike: still half an hour to go and he'd already upset one of the performers, they thought. That didn't bode well.

"Everything alright?" Hector came over with a pint of *Thatcher's MILF*, a lively, heady number from Rumburgh.

"I've got absolutely no idea what just happened," said Mike, suddenly at odds with this whole idea.

"You'll be fine." The landlord put a reassuring hand on Mike's shoulder.

"Sally, Paul and George are already here and ready to go, so…just relax and own this! It's yours!"

By eight o'clock, The Peasant was pretty much full as usual and Mike had caught the eye of most of the regular performers, making a mental note of the running order so no one would get left out.

But there was no sign of Jules.

Graeme lit Penny's Marlboro.

They were both stood outside The Goose, taking a moment before heading inside to meet, greet and generally crawl up the arse of anyone who had turned up.

"Mickey's done us proud," said Graeme.

Penny nodded. "We'll show that Hector Bramwell."

Over three years of helping out bands and singers to get their tracks onto an MP3 file – albeit a slightly distorted one – meant Mickey Koblenz could call in a few favours. He'd put word out that he was helping a friend pull an open mic night together and would they come over and perform for one or two weeks while the thing got going. If they could bring friends and family along too, then so much the better.

"Think we're about ready to go," said Mickey, sticking his head out the pub's front door.

"Ready?" Graeme asked his wife.

"Ready," she said and escorted her husband inside.

The Goose was already jumping!

"Hello, you!"

Mike was busy trying to tune his guitar when he heard Jules' voice. "Hello," he said without looking up.

That's awkward, thought Jules. "Just come over to wish you luck."

"Sure. Thanks." He twanged a flat G string and twisted the machine head until the digital display on his tuner signalled all was well.

"Have I done something wrong?" Jules huffed when it was clear Mike didn't want to meet her eye.

This time Mike looked up. "You hung up on me."

"What?" Jules was confused. "I didn't." The penny dropped. "Oh! No! I lost the signal when we were talking and then I had to drive to Lowestoft so I couldn't use the…"

"And then you ignored me for two days."

"No!" Jules was getting cross. "I told you I had to go to that training seminar on bacterial vaginosis, which was up in Groton, where there is absolutely no signal whatsoever, and I've just arrived back from there now. I had to drive super fast to get here on time!"

"You couldn't call me on a pay phone?"

"What's a pay phone?" asked Jules in all seriousness.

"Whatever." Mike went back to his tuning. "I've got a show to do."

No one had ever seen Julie Wiseman use those large hands of hers in anger until she fetched Mike Grimshaw what was best described later in the *Peasenhall Quandary* as: 'A Slap to End Them All'. The audience had gone deathly quiet for a second time as Jules pushed through the crowd, her eyes puffy and her face streaked with tears. When Mike finally got to his feet, the accusatory faces bore down on him; he had shamed one of Suffolk's most warm-hearted and loveable individuals in public. A couple of tables finished up their drinks and got up to leave, while others grumbled and went back to their conversations.

"Okay. D'you wanna get things going, maybe?" Hector had come over and was now rather eager for Mike to get the mood back.

"Yeah, I was just about to start," said Mike. "Hey, Hector!" Mike noticed something wasn't as it should be.

"What?" said a decidedly grumpy landlord.

"Where's the food?"

Hector sighed. "Patrice is off."

"What, is he sick?" Mike pressed.

Hector considered there was no point in lying; it was a small community. "He refused to work tonight while you were running open mic. Says he's got an issue with you and Jules."

Mike was somewhat dazed. "Oh,"

"But it's pork scratchings all round!" said Hector, encouraging his host rather than throttling him. "So, play, Orsino, play!"

Fuck, Mike thought.

Mike stepped up to the mic. "Good evening, everyone!" Silence. When Graeme said that, he was usually met with huge applause. As Mike looked at the mix of expectant, angry and purulent eyes in front of him, he had an urgent need to be somewhere else. FEAR. His legs began to shake and his mouth went bone dry; a small bead of sweat trickled off the small of his back and into the crack of his arse. He needed to pull it together. And quickly.

"Get on with it!" someone shouted.

"Okay, tonight," Mike found some saliva and, thankfully, words followed. "I'm going to start with…"

"Where's Graeme?!" shouted Chloe.

Hector shot his daughter what was best described later in the *Peasenhall Quandary* as: 'A Look to End Them All'. A few grumbles of 'for fuck's sake' echoed around the pub.

"So, I'm going start with," Mike battled on, "a song about a woman who just needs a small amount of herbs to finish the family meal she's cooking. Ladies and gentlemen, may I present, *Give Me Just a Little More Thyme*."

With a clear throat and a poised plectrum, Mike was ready to begin his career as an open mic host and, in doing so, open up a completely new chapter in his life. As he crashed down on the first chord of his newly rehearsed song, the speaker fizzed, his guitar buzzed and his amplifier exploded, sending sparks, smoke and the internal workings of the box against the back wall of The Peasant.

Mike stared at the smouldering debris and then back at a stunned audience, then a large crack in the earth opened up and dragged him in screaming.

Jeff and Shirley were behind the bar with their arms around each other. In the corner of their pub *Zumba Wumba* were rocking the audience.

"I don't you give enough credit most of the time, Jeff," Shirley shouted above the *moosic*. "But I have to say on this occasion…well done, my husband!"

Jeff squeezed her a little tighter. They had cleared over five hundred pounds and it wasn't even ten o'clock yet. He sent a wave over to Graeme and Penny who both smiled back. He looked at Shirley and was about to ask her something when a sweaty punter came to the bar eager for a top up.

"Go on and serve him," said Shirley, playfully pushing her husband away. "It's okay," she said, noticing he looked a little crestfallen. "I know what's on your mind, Mr. Timberlake." Shirley smiled. "And you'll be rewarded soon enough."

MIKE

"Afternoon Janice."

"Oh, Mike!" Janice parked the twins' buggy next to a floor display full of *Haribo* sweets. "What did yer do?"

"Don't!" Mike really wasn't in the mood.

"Yer the talk of the village," she told him. "You and Jules!"

"It was a mistake. I was all wrapped up with doing the gig...and I've been worried about Holly and...it all just got away from me."

Janice produced *The Peasenhall Quandary* from her bag. "'Ave you seen today's *PQ*? Only Carl's gorn and put it on the front page. Chapter and verse."

"You're joking?" squeaked Mike and snatched the copy Janice had just picked up off a table in the Assembly Rooms where she'd been doing Pilates.

"Noice picture of yer on the front, moind," said Janice as Mike scanned the article. "How old are yer there?"

"Thirteen."

"Just forget it, Mike," urged Janice. "Nobody reads the damn thing anyway. Only thing it's good for is today's chimps."

"D'you mean tomorrow's chips?"

Janice paused for a moment. "Possibly."

"Yeah, well, Mister Fleming can bloody well get his Nutella from somewhere else now. I won't be serving him. In fact, I don't think I'll be serving anyone anymore."

"Ooh, Mike, yer don't mean that!" said Janice, venturing down the stuffing aisle.

"I don't know, Janice." Mike pointed to where he'd relocated the pastry. "It felt like I was going to be lynched last night. Something's gone badly wrong."

"But what will yer do? Yer can't leave." Janice went to grab some fruit juice but thought better of it. "What about Jules?"

Good question, he thought. "I think I need to give Jules a bit of space right now. I hurt her."

"Storm in a tea cup," said Janice dismissively. "Everyone knows that."

Everyone knows. Yeah that's the damn problem round this village, mused Mike. "You know, I've never really belonged here, Janice. Always an outsider."

"Now, don't start, mister, with the whole the-world's-against-me thingy."

"My name's never been above the door and I don't think it ever will be," Mike confessed, giving his kookiest customer the saddest smile.

Janice shrugged. There was only one man in charge of what the bloody awning had on it. "What do yer want me to say?" she asked.

Mike shook his head and looked over at her two charming children. "Shit!" he suddenly cried. "I think Clive's on his sixth bag of Haribo!"

While Janice forced her eldest son to spit out a mouth full of eggs and cola bottles and gathered up the empty sweet bags that had been happily discarded over the side of the buggy, Mike considered the alternatives open to him should he decide to leave.

He could return to work for the Post Office. Its policies on equal opportunities had moved on since his dismissal all those years back, and he remembered reading an article on *The Huffington Post* about the new CEO being in an open relationship with an investment banker called Peregrine. Stamps, however, weren't as popular these days, so the first day cover business would probably be in free fall, he figured. And when was the last time he, or anyone else he knew, had posted a proper letter? His own stock of stamp books didn't exactly define the normal conventions of an FMCG item. The only shopper who had been in for stamps recently was Joe Lewis. He was sending some 'newly unearthed evidence' on Jesus and Mary Magdalene to the Archbishop of Canterbury.

No, stamps were now part of a bygone era, Mike decided, so a Post Office job was no longer a viable career option. He could go back to waitressing. There were a few central London bars seeking experienced staff where cross-dressing was actively encouraged. A return to the pet crematorium was also a possibility.

He didn't get much of a kick out of turning dogs to dust, but the pay was okay and there was the added bonus of consoling all those grieving children.

But did he really want to give up being his own boss? That was the one thing he loved about his role as a village grocer – it was a livelihood based on his terms. If Mike wanted to stock deep-filled steak and ale pies, then he bloody well could. If he decided to move the tuna chunks onto the top shelf next to the Devon custard, then the locals would just have to suck it up. The Lancashire boy could make merchandising decisions with impunity, and there was nothing anyone could say.

"How about yer start by getten yer own name over that door, Mr. Grimshaw?" said Janice almost reading the shopkeeper's mind. "Let folk round here know yer still mean business."

"Oh, don't go all motivational on me, Janice," whined Mike.

"Foine," she huffed. "Then just accept defeat, move on and do it all again for another six years somewhere else." Janice was clearly in no mood for Mike's histrionics, she had another friend who was hurting too. "Now oi have to take Clive outside to be sick."

She had a point, Mike thought, as the door closed on Mrs. Muffler and the strains of her son retching next to the fruit and veg bench. After all, it's not like he'd murdered a child or anything (although the fact that he could now see Janice holding Clive in the Heimlich Manoeuvre could quickly change that).

He needed to think clearly; get some perspective. His current predicament was the result of a mix up (shite internet), stress (nervous host) and a genuine accident (explosive amp) – hardly an irredeemable set of circumstances, he concluded.

A positive mind set was needed. He would order that new awning in the morning for starters. As Janice said, something with his name on that told these people he was here…and here to stay! Even if he did screw up their Thursday night.

Mike picked up his mobile and tapped out a text.

Hi Hector. Really sorry for last night. Getting new amp and my shit together TODAY. Will see you Thursday for a proper show. Mike.

The text beeped as it flew into the ether. "I'm getting my name over that door," he said.

JEFF

Jimmy Jammz was propped up against the bar.

"What's this then, boi?" he asked, pointing at a garish new plaque attached to one of The Goose's fonts.

"*Iron Fist*," said Jeff, quietly delighted his latest introduction to the inventory had finally produced some interest.

Jimmy was back in favour with the Timberlakes after the rumpus of the first open mic night. They kissed and made up after Jeff decided he didn't have the heart to press charges. After all, Jimmy was right, he, Sammy and his family had literally kept the ex-coppers afloat in their new venture. If their luck was about to change after a successful open mic night, now was not the time to start making a new set of enemies. Besides, Jimmy was their loveable rogue and the days would be long ones without his nonsense to keep them going.

"What's that then, boi?"

"It's a new IPA. It's from Milwaukee in the good ol' US of A!" replied Jeff, his attempted Yankee accent sounding more like something from the suburbs of Karachi.

"Gorn then, oi'll try a point," said Jimmy with an unprecedented slice of gay abandon.

Jeff pulled the bright, tawny fluid into a straight glass, its foamed head building steadily like a light soufflé. Jeff carefully navigated the glass over the tall font spindles and placed it confidently in front of his adventurous punter. Jimmy raised the pint to his lips and took a steady glug of the cool beer.

"Mm," he enthused after gulping the ale. "That's alroight. S'got a fresh taste to it."

"Yeah, a lot of the IPA's coming out of the states have got a strong citrus element to them."

Jimmy nodded approvingly. "Well, it's better than the normal pish yer get from 'em. Oi could get used to this," the boorish spammer suggested and started on his second mouthful.

"That'll be six-fifty, please, Jimmy."

Jimmy choked and promptly shot a stream of lemony IPA across the bar, showering Spanner & Cloak.

"Six-fifty?" croaked Jimmy between gasps and coughs. "What? Did yer gorn over and fetch it yerself?" exclaimed Jimmy wiping a film of *Iron Fist* from his chin.

"It's one of these new craft beers," said Jeff, suddenly trying to justify the exorbitant price. "They're all the rage right now."

"Maybe, boi," Jimmy pushed the reminder of his drink back towards the landlord. "But oi int payen that much for a beer…no matter where the fuck it's from!"

"For crying out loud, Jimmy!" Jeff protested. He pointed at the specials board above the fireplace and the numerous printed A4 photocopies in the bay window announcing the arrival of the international ale. "It's not like I was trying to keep the price a secret."

Jimmy glanced over at the various notices the landlord alluded to and the fantastic price adorned across each sign. "Oi thought that were the ABV, not the bloody proice. Yer off yer 'ead if yer think people are gorn a pay those sort o'proices round 'ere."

Jeff sighed. Jimmy was right. That was the first pint of *Iron Fist* he'd sold in a week. "Look," he conceded. "Just give me four quid and we'll call it quits."

"Make it three and oi'll 'ave another," said Jimmy and dragged his glass back with a smile.

It was early on Friday night and Jimmy Jammz was once again the sole customer in The Goose.

The dramatic success of last night's open mic night hadn't proved to be the watershed moment Jeff and Shirley hoped it would. As they'd merrily stumbled up the stairs after closing time on Thursday, all Shirley could talk about was how the night's success would change things, and that The Startled Goose would now be seen in a new light. All Jeff could talk about was if Shirley wanted to go on top.

"Hi, Jimmy." Melancholy filled Shirley's voice as she stepped into the bar.

"Ooh, Oi'd say there's someone wi' the blues," Jimmy remarked.

"D'you know. I sometimes think this was just one huge mistake."

Jeff sidled over to her. "Come on, Shirl. It's still only eight. It may pick up yet."

"Who are we kidding?" Shirley toyed with a solitary peanut on the bar. "Without a crowd for hire, we're just the same old pub everyone loves to hate."

"The only sure way to avoid maken mistakes is to 'ave no noo ideas. Don't sound loike much of a loife to me."

"That was very prophetic, Jimmy."

"Einstein. Was on a meme. So, oi guess oi can't claim it."

"No, you can't." Shirley thought how, every now and then, Jimmy had a habit of revealing a small piece of his true inner self, and it pleased her to think that maybe he was redeemable at some point down the line.

"But yer praably roight," chirped Jimmy. "Yer can't polish a turd!"

"You're not helping, Jimmy," snarled Jeff.

"Besoides," continued the malicious hacker. "Why dint me and Sammy and the girls get a look in last noight? After all our efforts last week, yer not involven us really 'urt."

"Ah, sorry, Jimmy." Jeff stuck out his bottom lip, mocking the spammer's less than sincere concern. "We love you, but no. You lot are terrible and you weren't getting anywhere near that mic last night."

"Fair enough, oi s'pose," conceded Jimmy. "Well, give us a bag o'them new stoat an' turnip flavour crisps, Shirl, and let's git this Froiday noight party started!" Jimmy rubbed his hands together as he set himself for the full session ahead.

As Shirley trudged over to the snack shelf, Cloak & Spanner began to bark furiously and a blast of pulsating blue light from the car park flooded the pub lounge. Seconds later, the front door sprang open and the police walked in for Jimmy Jammz.

The tallest of three officers headed over to where Jimmy was sat. "Mr. Jimmy Jammz?"

"Yarp!" said Jimmy.

"I'm arresting you on suspicion of theft, the intent to defraud and illegal trafficking. You do not have to say anything, but it may harm your defence if you do not mention when questioned something which you later rely on in court. Anything you do say may be given in evidence."

"Hello, Freddie!" said Jeff.

The arresting officer looked across the bar. "Bloody hell! Hello, Jeff," he said, recognising his old colleague. "Hello Shirl! I had no idea this was your boozer."

Sergeant Freddie Stevens had been with Suffolk Police since he left school. He reported directly to Jeff and Shirley when he first joined traffic and the pair had taught him the ropes (which included all the shitty little tricks they had up their sleeves). Traffic wasn't for Freddie though, CID was what he yearned for, and as soon as got his chance he jumped. Five years ago. The last time he had seen the Timberlakes.

"You haven't changed much," noted Jeff. "Apart from your barnet."

Freddie smoothed a hand over his bald pate. "The dreds went long ago, man."

"So, what's our Jimmy been up to, Freddie?" said Shirley, suddenly anxious by the sudden turn in the night's proceedings.

The officer waved a finger. "Now you know I can't tell you, Shirl. Even if you are ex-Babylon."

"Oi think oi can," said Jimmy.

"Mr. Jammz," said Freddie. "You really don't have to…"

"Is it cuz oi sent the wife out, to gorn sell the Big Issue?"

Jeff and Shirley were dumbstruck.

"We didn't know you were married, Jimmy," said Shirley after collecting her thoughts.

"It's an internet thing," Jimmy explained. "Oi got an email sayen there were a foo women comen over on the 'Arwich ferry in the back of a lorry and oi was invited to 'ave one."

Shirley's hand covered her mouth. "Oh, Jimmy, no!"

"Oh, but oi've treated her roight, moind. Put a roof over 'er 'ead, you know. More than she 'ad in the country she were runnen from. She's not wanted for nothen and oi've never kept 'er against her will. We just needed a bit more money comen in, so we agreed she'd go out and try and git some."

Freddie explained how Jimmy's wife had been reported stealing copies of the magazine from another seller. "As soon as we got her down the nick and found out who she was, the fact she is illegally in the country and assuming married status with no legal documentation...well, the rest you now know." Freddie's summation finished with him slapping handcuffs on Jimmy and the two junior officers led him outside to the car.

"Him and that bloody internet!" cried Shirley, unable to hold back the tears. "I knew it would be his undoing."

"Catch you around, guys," said Freddie as he put his cap back on.

"Yeah, see you, Freddie," said a stunned Jeff.

A crowd of onlookers had come out from their houses and walked over to the car park to see what the fuss was about. They were stunned as they watched Jimmy being put into the police car and driven away. (But not quite as stunned as they were by the appearance of a black man in Suffolk.)

"May as well have a pint while we're here," said someone in the crowd.

"Not a bad idea," said another.

And so it was, on the night of the arrest of one of Peasenhall's most notorious characters – and The Goose's most likeable regular – that the pub enjoyed its second most profitable evening under the management of the Timberlakes.

O'FLANAGAN

"I'm afraid it's the big C, Sammy," O'Flanagan announced sombrely.

Sammy buried his head in his hands; it was the worst possible news. "No!" he cried. "Oi'm so sorry, old girl."

"Yeah, a short course of antibiotics should do the trick though," the doctor added.

Sammy didn't understand. "Yer sayen antibionics can cure it now?"

"Of course! But remember, I am just a GP. You should really have a vet come and have a proper look at her."

"But don't she need radiation therapy and all that malarkey."

"Whatever for?" The doctor looked quizzically at the man with a demonstrably low-IQ.

"To burn the cancer out of 'er!"

"Oh, I see!"

"Yer gorn to lose all yer beautiful hair!" Sammy wailed.

"Sorry, no, please don't cry." The doctor stood awkwardly over his patient. "I was talking about canker."

Sammy put the Pitbull terrier back down on the carpet. "Canker?"

"Yes, this…" O'Flanagan pointed to the dog's ears. "All this disgusting gunk around your dog's ears…"

"Lady."

"Yes. All this infection around…Lady's ears is canker. Soon get it cleared up," the quack said trying to lift the dark mood he'd inadvertently created.

"What's caused it?"

"I dunno," O'Flanagan said flatly. "Let me think. Does she…Lady go in the water much?"

"Oi take 'er down to the River Yox every mornen. Lady likes to fetch the poisoned moorhens."

"Ah, well, there you go!"

James O'Flanagan had been Peasenhall's village doctor for what seemed like forever.

His tiny surgery was three doors down from The Goose and he worked Monday to Friday mornings between eight thirty to ten and four to six on the evenings. Any emergency consultations were covered after six and the doctor enjoyed one weekend off in three. The whole village population was on his books – around five hundred souls – and he loathed every one of them. He never thought of his patients as 'bad people' he just despised their constant need to come and see him whenever they were ill.

"What the fuck?" he would say to his peers while enjoying a golf weekend paid for by the fawning pharmaceutical companies desperate for increased drug sales. "If they've got something wrong with them, fucking stay away! I don't want to catch their shit!"

House calls were the things he hated most. He would invariably get stuck behind some piece of farm equipment and then be unable to inform the patient he was running late because there'd be no phone signal. And then, nine times out of ten, the emergency was for a pet. There was no vet in the village so the locals simply called O'Flanagan, assuming he would know what to do – medicine is medicine, right? More importantly, of course, he came courtesy of the NHS. In the last six months alone, O'Flanagan had diagnosed two cases of blue tongue, nine cases of canker, seventeen cases of classical swine fever, an outbreak of skin fluke infestation and eight cases of BSE. O'Flanagan was able to treat most of the issues but one case that troubled him was a weasel with horrific sinus problems that he ended up referring to Ipswich hospital's ear, nose and stoat department.

The other ten percent of house calls were for petty complaints like a bad cold or an upset tummy. Jimmy Jammz had actually called him out once with a hoax complaint of HTML.

The doctor was born and bred in Peasenhall but was farmed out to a boarding school long before the Suffolk dialect could enter his body and restrict his career options. Schooling in Hertfordshire and a medical degree at

Kings ensured his accent was as bland as packet soup. He had actively sought a rural practice and going back to his roots seemed the right and proper thing to do at the time. By the end of his first week in his compact consulting room, O'Flanagan was already regretting the decision. He was a young man. He wanted adventure, daring cases of outlandish diseases, wild romances with nurses who were up for anything: sex and drugs and rock and roll! Instead, he got line dancing at the Assembly Rooms, rheumatoid arthritis and a county full of females who adored walking their dogs far more than the prospect of fellatio.

Rather than throw himself into the jobs market, O'Flanagan threw himself into drink. *Jameson's* Irish whiskey became his poison of choice and he'd faced each new day, each new case, in a whiskey haze since the age of twenty-eight. As the years rolled by the doctor somehow managed to keep things ticking over, but his celebrated alcoholic denial would manifest itself into O'Flanagan berating many of those around him for drinking to excess.

"You know those children of yours deserve a mother who was just sober every once and a while," would often be the advice he gave women coming into his surgery for a repeat prescription for Prozac.

The chance of a better life did fleetingly pass the doctor a few years back. Attending an AA meeting late one Thursday evening in far-off Oulton Broad, he found himself sat next to a young woman who couldn't keep her hands off the peach schnapps. As they got to know each other over the following weeks, it transpired Joan, as she was known, suffered from the rare genetic disorder, congenital analgesia. Her inability to feel any pain was, O'Flanagan thought, a godsend. If they ever became an item, he would never have this woman mithering him about a pain here or an unusual lump there or insist on his professional opinion.

The quack had only ever bedded working girls but, for the first time, he was staring at love head on. However, before he committed himself to the full-blown romance that was clearly within the couple's reach, O'Flanagan decided he needed absolute empirical proof that Joan was truly pain free. After being tossed down the stairs eight times, stabbed with a fire poker, garrotted with a cheese wire and slapped in the face with several breeds of fish, Joan could take no more and sadly walked away.

In the end, his situation was a vicious circle he couldn't remove himself from: the more he wished for a better practice, the more he drank. He dreamed about buying some land but he'd have to give up the booze and the one-night stands. That clearly was never going to happen.

So many plans, but so little progress; such were the troubles of Dr. James O'Flanagan.

PATRICE

With the lunches all happily consumed, the dishwasher on its final cycle, *Dog-Filled Pantry* halfway through another pulsating set, and his part in Sunday at The Peasant all but done, Patrice le Clef sat enjoying a cigarette outside on the inn's front patio.

He glanced over at Greg and Gaynor Bradley who had joined him out front for a smoke. In between drags on their shared L&B, they would kiss passionately and fondle each other shamelessly. Patrice sighed and stared at a large, black ox stood motionless in the field across from the pub. Fucking ox, he thought, and lit another cigarette.

Despite decades of government-funded health campaigns and pointless efforts to cover up cigarettes in shops, Peasenhall remained the nation's only village where the number of residents who smoked actually increased over the last five years.

According to the last census, smoking in this Suffolk ghetto had risen from eighty-five to ninety-two per cent of the population. On an average night in The Peasant, more than half the pub's clientele would be found outside smoking at any given moment (source: YouGov).

Hector had responded to this startling statistic by erecting one of the finest outdoor fag areas in the far east. Giant halogen heaters were suspended from a gyroscope system, which tracked across the front of the pub, automatically seeking out the smokers and keeping them comfortably warm. Two large, sturdy pergolas marked the boundaries of the smoking area and it was covered with a unique membrane capable of converting the rising smoke into a granular ash that could be safely recycled into a nourishing plant supplement. There were zippo lighters on retractable wires on the pergola poles and the ashtrays were made of 18-carat gold. So revolutionary was The Peasant's "smokearium", that it had been internationally recognised with an award from *SmokeMag.com*. Hector had attended the awards evening, but missed the presentation of his prize, as he was, once again, toilet-bound.

At the time of the smokearium's erection, the newly established phenomenon of smirtin' (smoking and flirting) was as popular in The Peasant as Patrice's 'batta puddens'. Indeed, a number of marriages were the direct result of Peasant smirtin', most notably Barry Noblett and his wife, Horse, who tied the knot two years after he'd offered to roll her a snout and she'd licked his face in return. Most patrons however, just enjoyed the tranquillity of strolling out onto the pub's front patio and letting doctor nicotine do his job as they watched a cherry sun dip below the horizon.

"Thought I'd find you out here," said Hector, closing the west-by-east-west door on the sounds of rampant fiddle and sax. "Another great lunch, thank you, Patrice."

Patrice had worked for Hector for ten years. He had been instrumental in building the landlord a strong and profitable business, which was no mean feat given the shocking demise of a nation's proud pub trade. But Patrice had been thinking of a fresh challenge for some time; he'd tired of the same old faces and recently felt like the needle was just stuck in a groove.

"I re-zine," the chef said flatly.

"What?" spluttered Hector. "What are you talking about? You can't resign!"

"I can. I 'ave." The French-born parsnip wizard flicked his cigarette butt into the road.

"But – why?" Hector's perfect Sunday had just disintegrated into mush. "What are you going to do? What am *I* going to do?!"

"Zis is not my probleme," said Patrice, ignorant of the fact he'd just turned Hector's world upside down. "I sense zat sings are changing 'ere," the chef continued. "And not for ze best." He handed Hector a tea towel and eased himself out of one of the smokearium's sumptuous massage chairs.

"What? You're leaving *right now*?" Hector was in a blind panic.

"I can. I am."

Sensing the end of days, Hector decided to go on the offensive. "Look, you owe me, you semi-Gallic twat! I was the one who gave you a break in this poxy village, letting you loose on a group of carrot-crunching losers who wouldn't know a soufflé from a…souff…b!" Hector's finger jabbed at the chef's chest. "It was me who believed in you! It was me who supported you all these years! None of these inbred, shit-chuckers would have given you the time of day if you'd gone to them with your noncey culinary aspirations. What?" Hector sneered. "You think whatever you do next, these fucking peasants are actually going to follow you? Hah!"

It had gone very quiet. Where's the music? Hector suddenly thought.

Patrice flicked his thick, dark eyebrows up, gesturing to Hector to turn around. It was the interval and *Dog-Filled Pantry* had taken a break. As The Peasant's landlord turned on his heels he faced thirty or more punters all stood silently in the smokearium; they'd heard every word of his rant.

Patrice drained a last mouthful of red wine and set the empty glass down on the patio table. "I start work at The Goose on Wednesday."

Deep murmuring accompanied Patrice going back inside the pub to collect his things. Outside, Hector felt exposed. Naked. He searched the faces of his most loyal and (supposedly) loved regulars for a sign of understanding; just one look from someone among them that showed they knew where he was coming from on this. When even the sweet organiser of all things bazaar, Catherine Bush, shook and dropped her head in shame, Hector knew this was bad.

Inside, Patrice picked up his whites and his motorcycle jacket. "Bye, Chloe," he said, as he came back through the bar.

"Oh, bye, Patrice," replied Chloe. "See you at seven! Oh, by the way, if you see dad on your way out can you tell him I've got my hand stuck in the sink?"

Patrice nodded with a smile, and turning to leave, walked straight into Maddy's path.

"'Allo," said the chef, making no effort to avert his eyes from Maddy's chest.

"In your dreams," said the musical psychic.

Patrice was irked by the instant rebuff. "Can I 'elp you?"

"Go to her."

"What?" Patrice leaned back as if offended by the woman.

"Go to her," Maddy repeated. "You can be together."

"Ah!" The chef suddenly got the drift. "I know you. You are ze witch oo fucks wiz people's 'eads."

Maddy gently laughed the cynicism away. "Seriously. Go to her. I see a good life and a rewarding future for you both. You should not deny each other such an opportunity."

"You talking about Jules?" asked the man with *Ronseal* skin.

"No, Edith Piaf." Maddy sardonically retorted.

Patrice eyed Maddy carefully. He had considered meeting and speaking with Jules, declaring his love in the hope she might dump the fop that had wormed his way in and then humiliated her so tragically. He thought he might persuade her that they could have a future together; two lovers large-hand-in-large-hand forever. He wanted to tell her everything would be okay with him.

"Yes. You should do all that," said Maddy.

An irritable Jules was repacking part of the delivery she had received from Ikea while away in Gorton – there was a single dowel missing from the fixing kit for the new beside table rendering it useless – when there was a knock at the front door.

"Oh, hello, Patrice," she said to a giant silhouetted frame stood on her new green Bjergby (doormat).

Patrice headed straight to *Atora Corner* as soon as he'd left the pub. Driving out The Peasant's car park, he noticed he wasn't the only one leaving the afternoon's entertainment prematurely. Perplexed couples and distraught families fled in their droves following Hector's disastrous comments. As they poured out and away from the pub, many chose to make their feelings know and the landlord, standing prostrate in the smokearium, suffered the slings and arrows of his outraged locals. Of the few remaining in the bar, the departing chef could see Steve was clearly remonstrating with Maddy, their gig clearly over. His wagging finger could only point to one thing: Maddy hadn't seen this coming.

"Wow," said Jules, passing Patrice a cup of chamomile tea. "You're actually serious. Working at The Goose."

"Oui," he shrugged nonchalantly. "I can turn zat restaurant of theirs into somezing really special."

"But it's got previous," argued Jules. "*And*, you'll be following Damien Cartwright!"

"Trust me," said Patrice. "After what went on at ze Peasant zis afternoon, ze people round 'ere are going to need somewhere new to drink and eat. You see."

Jules frowned. Patrice had explained, what he called, Hector's meltdown in front of the villagers. She loved Hector and could not bear to think he might be suffering right now. Equally, she couldn't quite believe he'd said all those terrible things. Carrot-crunchers, she thought, but I'm allergic to carrots.

Patrice leant nearer to Jules and took her large mitt in his. "Listen, Jules," he said. "I need to tell you somezing."

"Whoa, hang on, big fella!" Jules tried to pull her hand away but the Frenchman held firm.

"Look, you know I have ze deepest feelings for you and I know I can make you 'appy given ze schance."

"Ze schance?" Jules repeated.

"Yes, ze schance," Patrice said again quizzically. "Ze schance. Ze…er…opportunity."

"Oh, I see," said Jules.

"I know you are probably all messed up in zat pretty 'ead of yours wiz everyfing right now. But I want to give you time. Because in time, I know zat you will truly love me."

It was a good call, Jules thought, she was in a total head fuck right now. She knew she over reacted on Thursday night, but no word from Mike since, was both unexpected and hurtful. Jules had agonised over whether it was her who should apologise first, but she thought, sod it, the guy was in the wrong and 'sorry' was written on a ball in his court right now. But 'no word' meant 'no interest' in her book and here was a man right in front of her ready to commit, with no distractions and a voice that was a bloody aphrodisiac. She knew she was intrigued; but love?

"Wiz you by my side, I can do great zings wiz ze pub and we can plan a future together. I fink zis has been, ow you say, written in ze stars," said Patrice with a flourish and the image of Maddy's tight T-shirt in his head.

Powerful stuff, Jules mused. "I need some time, Patrice, but I hear you." The midwife paused. "So how about this? No promises, but let's just take things slowly and see how we go, okay?"

Patrice was overjoyed. "I swear," he said, taking Jules' other hand in his. "I'll do zis at your pace. I will be led by you alone."

"Cool," nodded Jules, smiling.

JEFF

"So, loike oi say," Sammy Grossefinger was more than a little drunk. "Oi know the secret to a good marriage."

"What's that then, Sammy?" asked Jeff.

"Trust."

"Is that so?" Jeff was impressed and surprised in equal measure by the man's candour.

"Well, accorden to the woife's diary it is."

Jeff pulled a face, passed a pint of *Quilt* – a new wheaty lager from a serious town in Belgium – to Sammy and suggested his playing partners were waiting for him.

The Grossefinger's were playing a game of *insert the vegetable* and today's theme was films.

The premise of *insert* was a simple one. Each player around the pub table took it in turns to say the title of a film and replace one of the words in the title with a popular vegetable. Other themes that the group had previously employed included place names, chocolate-based sweets, electrical goods, famous archaeologists and types of foreign soft cheese. Players had thirty seconds to come up with a title. If they ran out of time, or came up with a spurious title, they had to pay a forfeit by drinking one of the many shots of tequila purchased specifically for the game.

As it was a Wednesday – and therefore half day closing – the Grossefingers had been joined by Dave Neal, the village butcher. It was the first time Dave had drunk in The Goose, having been forced to move on from his usual drinking hole after being labelled an 'inbred shit-chucker' by its landlord. The game had been going for about half hour and the four players were all as pissed as arseholes.

"Roight!" Sammy bellowed at the top of his voice. "Tammy! Yer go!"

Tammy's eyes crossed when she was thinking, which made a woman you thought couldn't get any more unattractive, more unattractive. "Er...er..." she said, scratching around her brain for inspiration.

"Ten seconds," said Dave, the nominated timekeeper.

"Ooh, fuck!" cried Tammy. "Um...er...ooh! Silence of the yams!"

"Brilliant!" cried Dave, who hadn't had as much fun in a boozer for years.

"That's actually very good," conceded Jeff from over behind the bar.

"Well done, Tam," barked Sammy. "Now yer go, princess!"

Sammy's constant reference to his wife as 'princess' amused and baffled Jeff in equal measure. Was it a reference to the appalling car from the 70's? The only other princess he could possibly be referring to was Princess Fiona...after sunset.

"Roight, yer fuckers," said Princess Pammy, steeling herself for the challenge. "Lord of the Onion Rings!" she offered up swiftly.

"Wow!" Dave was seriously impressed.

"Ah, oi reckon yer 'ad that one up yer sleeve," Sammy accused his princess.

"Pure genius!" his wife retorted and tried to blow Sammy a drunken kiss, but her hand missed her mouth and she poked herself in the eye.

Dave bounced in his chair like an over-excited four-year-old. "You now, Sammy!"

"Okay. Start yer watch, Dave." Sammy bit his bottom lip as he considered the vast array of stolen goods he'd received from his wife over the last few months and if any would fit into a film title. "Err...Barley and Me!" he shouted.

"Noice one!" shouted Dave.

"Oh, oi love that film," said Tammy. "'Specially when the dog gorn and doies."

"Hang on," Jeff couldn't help making a point of order. "Surely barley is a cereal, not a vegetable!"

"Oo asked yer?" said an indignant Sammy.

"Oh, 'e's roight tho, Sam," said the princess.

"Pah!" Sammy flapped a hand at his wife. "Barley and me. Perfectly alroight."

"No," Dave chimed in. "Actually, oi think that earnt yer a shot."

"Alroight! Alroight! Sprout of Africa! There. That's a fucken vegetable for yer!"

"Good shout," said Tammy, raising her glass to her brother-in-law while sticking two fingers up at the landlord.

"Well, excuse me!" said Jeff. "I was only trying to make a point of order."

"Oi'll 'ave a point of order, if there's one gorn," said Dave with a huge, inebriated smile on his meaty face.

A few seconds later, the whole table roared with laughter.

"Point of order!" said Sammy with tears running down his face. "That's brilliant!"

"Honestly," said Jeff and headed down to the cellar, leaving the fools to it. He had to get ready for the dray.

"Roight, c'mon!" said Pammy, done with the schoolgirl giggles. "Let's go! Dave – yer turn! Oi'll be toimekeeper."

Dave picked himself off the floor, dabbed his eyes and got into game mode. "Okay. Er…" Dave had come up with nothing so far and had been forced to down nine tequilas so far. The early stages of his tenth round did not bode well. "Um…"

"Ten seconds," said Pammy.

"Um…a-hah!"

"Go on, then," said Sammy, desperate for Dave to land one.

"The Lambshank Redemption!" announced Dave proudly.

The three other contestants looked at each other in silence for a couple of seconds and then in complete unison shouted, "DRINK!"

Jeff came back up from the cellar after checking everything was ready for the delivery and, as he resurfaced from the cool basement, the dray pulled up round the rear of the property.

"You guys alright for a minute?" he asked the Wednesday afternoon mess in a corner of the lounge. No coherent response other than a garbled cry from Dave: "Full Metal Jacket Spud!"

As Jeff got outside, he found Greene King's dray woman already busy dragging the new kegs off her truck and positioning them next to the cellar drop.

"Hi, Suzie!" called Jeff.

"What's gorn on 'ere then?" said the ruddy-faced Suzie Few, one of the beer company's youngest qualified dray drivers.

"What d'you mean?" asked Jeff, shielding the bright autumn sunshine from his eyes.

"Foive barrels in a single delivery? You launderen ale some 'ow?"

Jeff smiled. Clientele were up, sales were up, so he needed volume. "We seem to have hit a bit of a purple patch." By purple patch, Jeff meant the offended folk of Peasenhall needed a place to drink.

"Well good for you!" said Suzie with a profusion of hearty cheer. "Now, let's get these barrels on the pig!"

The pig Suzie'd referred to, was the name given to the heavy-duty, cork-filled sack positioned at the bottom of the metal ramp – the skids – that connected the cellar floor with ground level. The pig cushioned the barrels as they rolled down the skids, preventing any serious damage during the drop. The provenance of the drop mat's name is lost to the mists of time, but Sammy always had a theory that it was because they used real pigs in the 14th century. But then Sammy was clinically insane.

"Roight!" said the busy dray woman. "Oi got one *Abbot*, one *IPA*, one *Hen*, one *Inverted Flycatcher* and one *Leafy Spasm*…our new autumn ale."

"Spot on," confirmed Jeff.

"Lovely. Soign there please, Mr. Timberlake. Now leave the rest to us," said Suzie as she motioned to her dray assistant to pull open the cellar drop doors. "We'll see yer next week."

Jeff took the copy of his delivery note off Suzie and disappeared back into the pub. Inside he saw two things that made a good day even better. Firstly, Dave and the Grossefingers were all sparko, and secondly, there was a gathering of people waiting to be served.

"I'm so sorry to have kept you," said Jeff, dashing back to get back behind the bar. "Now, what'll you have?"

"Do you do food by any chance?" one of the customers enquired.

"D'you know," said Jeff. "We do."

JULES

"He did about twenty covers yesterday. Best day in the restaurant they've ever had!"

"Crikey. Jeff and Shirley must be thrilled."

"That's in the entire history of the The Goose, mind you."

Jules had bumped into Sally Womber in a coffee shop in Saxmunham; the midwife often popped into *The Grinder* to grab a mid-morning brew to have on her rounds. She'd just paid and got a final stamp on her loyalty card – yay, a free turnip muffin next time! – when Sally caught her eye from the window seat she was sat in. Jules didn't particularly want to engage given Sally's friendship with Patrice and the recent developments between Jules and the chef, but the crystal vixen was insistent she sit down for two minutes for a quick natter. Jules already knew that Patrice had enjoyed a good first day at The Goose. They had met for a quick drink in the pub last night and he'd enthused at how well his beef bourguignon had gone down with the first lunchtime crowd. Word then seemed to get out around the village and a few more hungry souls made the journey into 'that pub' across the day.

"So," Sally said, sliding down the leatherette chair with a wicked look about her. "Patrice tells me you and he are taking things…how did he put it…one step at a time?"

"Did he now?" replied Jules, quietly fuming that the big lump had felt the need to share that intimate detail with her. "He appears to be keeping you well informed what with news of his triumphant first day at the pub and…us."

"Well, who can blame you, darling? It's not like that bloody grocer's got much of a look in now after humiliating you like that in front of everyone."

"To be honest, Sally, he was the one on the floor with a slapped face. If anyone did any humiliating, it was me and not *that bloody grocer!*" Jules picked up her coffee and got back on her feet. "Or, as other decent people might refer to him, Mike!"

"Oh, darling, it was never my intention to offend," pleaded Sally. "Please, sit down, Jules, I'm dreadfully sorry."

Jules stared at the kinesiologist and wondered if any part of that crazy hallucination in her consulting room a week ago was true. Had she had Patrice? Was she out to snare Mike? She was so confused. Still no word from Mike in a week and, while everything was cool with Patrice and they were up to nothing more than holding big hands on occasion, she still didn't feel like there was closure on their relationship. She'd driven past the shop once, on Tuesday afternoon, when she saw Mike arguing with a couple of guys putting up a new awning. She obviously didn't stop to see what the fuss was about but was quite surprised to see "GRIMEY STORES" emblazoned across a new front awning. Suddenly drained of energy, she plonked herself back down beside Sally.

"Oh, poor Jules," said Sally. "You look absolutely terrible, darling."

"Boy, you're just on fire today," the midwife said and dropped her head in her hands.

Carl finished briefing the *Screw Ewe* staff on what he required of them over the next fifteen minutes and headed upstairs to his 'editing suite' where Hector was waiting patiently.

"You'll have to make this quick, Hector," the ironmonger said, turning on his iMac Air. "I'm just about to go to print."

"Thanks, Carl. Appreciate it." Hector watched as Carl pulled up the latest file and opened it up as a full screen on his Mac. The headline read: 'Jammz Preserves the Right to Remain Silent'. Hector was appalled. "Come on, Carl, give the guy a break!"

"'E's a wrong-un, Hector," was Carl's final word on the matter.

"I notice you stuck it to Mike Grimshaw as well, last week. I thought you two were mates?"

"Mike will understand there's no room for sentiment in journalism. It's nothing personal." Carl held out a hand. "Now. You got that memory stick?"

Hector handed over a black USB. "The file title is *Sorry*."

Carl plugged the device into his laptop's port and opened up the document.

"Nice work, Hector!" said Carl as he copied the text and transferred it directly into the space he'd cleared on page two of *PQ* specifically for this exclusive *mea culpa*. Gold dust!

"There," said the well-satisfied editor. "You're good to go."

"How much do I owe you?" the words burned on Hector's tongue.

"Just put something on the slate for me at the pub. I'll leave it up to you."

"Oh, so you're not deserting me like everyone else, then?" Hector's words were filled with a mix of bitterness and regret.

"I've been called worse." Carl smiled, uploaded his paper to Dropbox, signed out and escorted Hector downstairs. "See you tonight, landlord," he winked.

PQ presents, An Apology.

Dear PQ Readers,

As some of you may be aware, last Sunday afternoon at The Whipped Peasant public house, I made some ill-judged remarks concerning the good people of Peasenhall.

I have been a faithful servant to this community for over ten years now and I have only the utmost respect for all those who have visited my establishment over that time, and who have supported me and my family unconditionally. With that in mind, there is no possible excuse for the remarks I made last weekend and I would like to make a full and unreserved apology for my comments, and the way they may have come across. I have never thought of members of this fine community as "carrot-crunchers", "inbred" or, indeed, "peasants". The fact that I used those words in, what I thought was, a private conversation with a third party was both stupid and crass of me, and I hereby humbly apologise.

As a show of good faith to those who stood by me all these years, I would like to welcome you to our Quiz Night tonight (Thursday) when I will put on a free bar, free food and reveal the pub password for the Wi-Fi between 7 and 10.30pm. (NB – this will only be honoured to those I know as regulars or Peasenhall residents with a valid utility bill).

It is my deep hope that this olive branch will begin to heal any wounds opened by my foolishness and, if you'll please allow me to reiterate, my opinion of this village as a proud, strong and wonderfully creative community will never falter.

I believe there is a way forward. After all, it's not like Gordon Brown lost a general election after calling some dizzy, old bird a 'bigot', now is it?

Sincere apologies again. See you all tonight.

Hector Bramwell, Landlord of The Whipped Peasant.

Copies of the Peasenhall Quandary were on the Assembly Rooms' table by noon and Hector's plea for clemency was for all to see. Alongside the landlord's statement was a half-page paid-for advertisement announcing a new, Suffolk-wide competition: The Battle of the Pubs.

OPEN MIC

It was Thursday night in The Peasant. Again!

"Doctor Who star David Tennant's surname is made up because his real one clashes with another established actor. What is his actual surname?"

Cries of "Broadchurch!" and "Scots git!" circled the room as teams ventured to put off their opponents with bogus suggestions.

"Ooh, I think it's McDonald." Table 5's Shelley Parkinson carelessly said aloud. Further cries of "Cheers, Shell!" and "Yeah, knew that!" came from the other teams as they quickly hunkered over their quiz sheets to add the gifted answer.

"For fuck's sake, Shelley!" said temporary host FW, revelling in the limelight of the role of official quizmaster for the evening. "Keep your answers to yourself. Not much point in having a Quiz night if you give each other the answers."

Hector's press release had worked, to a point, and The Peasant had a healthy turnout for the impromptu pub quiz and night of free food and drink. A small crop of locals had seen the published apology in *PQ* – and Chloe's hastily advertised 'Pub Quince Night' on The Peasant's Facebook page – and decided to give the old boy a second chance. Hector had welcomed everyone personally at the north-by-south-west door, offered them a further apology and invited them to get a drink from his daughter at the bar and help themselves to the modest buffet in the dining area.

With no chef, Hector had required the assistance of outside caterers. With a perfectly good kitchen out back, it was a necessity that stuck in his throat. He contacted *Fantastic Baps,* which did a number of 'party packages', and ordered just enough to look like he wasn't penny pinching. Andrea Rattle was poorly and away from the business, but the delivery was made promptly by her able assistant and part-time manager of Peasenhall's under-11's girls' football team, James Seville.

"Right," said FW with continued gusto. "Here's question number nine on Film and TV. Let's hope *The Shaved Goblins* can keep their traps shut on this one." Shelley Parkinson bowed her head, not sure if she was more embarrassed by her uncontrollable desire to shout out the answers or the really inappropriate name Carl Fleming had chosen on the team's behalf. "What's the connection between The Magic Roundabout and Saving Mr. Banks?" roared FW.

As the teams huddled in consultation across their tables – and Shelley Parkinson cupped both hands over her mouth – a cool draft of air filled the pub as Mike Grimshaw burst in fully laden with guitar, leads, stands and an impressively shiny new amplifier. The sight of his audience feverishly scribbling answers on a quiz sheet rather than sat eagerly awaiting the arrival of the *moosic* man stopped Mike in his tracks. A slight mizzle outside had dampened Mike's hair down which, as he stood in the doorway with his mouth open, made him look a bit school boyish.

"Oops! Looks like someone's been out the loop for a few days," came a comment from someone in the hushed crowd.

"What's going on?" asked Mike, carefully placing his equipment on the flagstones. "Hector?"

"It's okay," said FW, encouraging Mike in. "You can join team 3, *The Flat Defibrillators*. They're a man short."

"But, it's open mic night!" Mike protested.

"What are you singing tonight, Mike?" shouted Chloe, who was pouring *Ipswich Throttler* into a cocktail glass for Liam Lewis.

Hector popped a tray of cheese and pineapple sticks on to a table and came quietly over to see Mike.

"What's going on, Hector?" The shopkeeper's forehead glistened with the mizzle.

"Mike," began Hector. "We've had a trying few days, lad. Did you not see my piece in the *Quandary*?"

"The Quandary?" Mike was baffled. "No. What's up? Didn't you get my text?"

"I did. But… it's a long story. Come over and I'll get you a drink and explain."

As the rest of the pub returned to the question of how many teeth the shark in Jaws 3 had, Mike and Hector sat in the restaurant away from any distractions. Hector brought the grocer up to speed with Patrice's resignation, his own faux pas, and the need to make amends sharpish. He was honest with Mike when he told him he didn't think the grocer would be welcome back in The Peasant after the previous week's debacle, but he knew it was just an unfortunate mishap and that what went on in his personal life was his own business. At the end of the day, Mike was a valued customer and friend and Hector was pleased to see him.

"Have you seen or heard from Jules?" Mike enquired of Hector.

"No. Nothing."

"Me neither. I thought I would give her a few days to cool off then try and see how the land lied. But I've just been so busy with stuff I needed to do around the shop."

Hector grinned. "Yeah, I saw the new awning up yesterday. Why "GRUMPY STORES"?"

"Oh, that's the fucking sign-writers! They just cannot get it right. They've got an intern from Ipswich in at the minute."

Hector laughed out loud; his friend's misfortune was a bright spot in a very dark week. "I don't mean to laugh," the landlord apologised.

"S'okay," said Mike, who was also smiling now. "But I've really sorted the shop out, Hector, you won't recognise the place. I've got some new chillers and feature aisle ends. And I've changed a few suppliers so I can get some really strong pricing offers together. I'm telling you. Tesco, Schmesco."

"That's great, Mike," Hector was pleased for him. "Really great. Now best I crack on with rebuilding my reputation."

"So, where's this apology of yours?" Mike kept the landlord from wandering off momentarily.

Hector handed Mike a copy of *PQ* opened up on the relevant page. Mike scanned the article and then the advert next to it caught his eye.

"Hey, look!" Mike said turning the page back towards Hector. "There's an open mic competition for Suffolk pubs. Top prize five grand."

Hector snatched the paper back. "So there is!" Hector studied the ad a second longer and then looked up at Mike. "D'you fancy our chances?"

"And my heart yearns for…Barry Island!" Paul Pickering faultlessly strummed the final D on his second song and thanked the crowd for their appreciation.

Mickey, Graeme, Patrice and Jeff were all stood conspiratorially over a copy of *PQ*, the latter with his finger firmly pressed on a certain advertisement.

"Why didn't we see this earlier?" queried Jeff. "Entries have to be in tomorrow and judging starts in a week?"

"What's up guys?" Shirley had just finished serving the lead singer of *Superating Wound* a glass of Chilean merlot.

"Listen up, babe," said Jeff, slipping on his reading glasses. "Do you host the best open mic night in Suffolk? If so, then The Battle of the Pubs is for you! Winner takes all, five thousand pounds first prize. Pubs will be judged independently across October with the winner announced on the 5th of November. All entries to be in by eob on Friday 25th September. Cost of entry three hundred pounds per pub. Contact Pete at pete@pete.com."

"No chance," said Shirley, immediately dismissing the idea.

"But…!" Jeff went to protest.

"Oo's eob?" said Mickey.

Graeme tutted. "It means end of business. The entry has to be in by 5pm tomorrow."

"What I could do to zis restaurant wiz five thousand of your eenglish pounds," Patrice's enormous hands came together in prayer.

"Yeah, and I could go on a cruise to the Bahamas. It ain't happening," dismissed Shirley.

"But…!" Jeff went to protest again.

"We won't win and we'll be three hundred quid lighter." Shirley was adamant. "Now somebody serve Jules while I take this flaming Sambuca over to Mrs. Winterburn."

Jules had snuck in while *Superating Wound* was tearing up the stage (and most of The Goose's furniture by the look of things). She gave Patrice a little wave – not easy with such large hands – and Graeme a warm smile as he came over.

"Jules," he said, giving the midwife a peck on the cheek. "Lovely to see you, kiddo."

Graeme was a father figure to Jules.

Penny Nash had been friends with her parents having met Gerta Wiseman many times at the BBC Radio Suffolk studios in Ipswich. The German was a regular session musician on *Banjovi!* – an hour of soft-rock covers played on banjo and ukulele. Even when the popular show fell out of favour with the listening public after a fortnight, Penny kept in touch and both she and Graeme shared the joy of watching the Wiseman's vivacious daughter grow up. Graeme was particularly fond of Jules; the child he and Penny could never have. He was a Jaffa, and Penny was as barren as Needham Market. They took Jules in after the accident and it was Graeme who convinced the young lady to carry on with her banjo playing after her mother's influence died with her. The Nash's got Jules through her A-levels before she left for the midwifery course in Stowmarket. Jules always wished there was a way to pay back the huge debt of kindness she owed Penny and Graeme Nash.

"Hey, you!" said Jules, pinching an errant piece of cotton off Graeme's jumper. In celebration of the harvest festival, he was sporting a golden number with black ears of corn dotted all over it. "Where's that lovely wife of yours."

"She's decided to stay in to catch *Crimewatch*. She thinks she might know who did the job on that helmet factory last month." Graeme noticed she didn't have her banjo with her. "Hey, you not playing for us tonight?"

"No, I'm taking a break for a bit."

Graeme nodded his understanding. "It's been a funny old week, hasn't it?"

Jules warmly rubbed the side of Graeme's arm. (Her hand would come out in a vicious rash later after reacting to whatever material was in the man's jumper). "And some," she agreed, and looked over to see what Patrice was up to.

"So, if Graeme agrees, we're on?" Jeff rubbed his hands.

"'E will," stated Patrice, a little too menacingly.

While the open mic MC was keeping Jules company, his three cohorts had come up with a strategy around The Battle of the Pubs. Mickey, Graeme and Patrice would stump up a ton each to cover the cost of entry, while Jeff would invest in a decent spread on the night that would keep both punters and judges happy.

"Oi'll work with Graeme and Penny to sort the bands," offered Mickey. "We may even be able to get a few ringers in!"

"Wow, that sounds amazing, Mickey," gushed Jeff. "Who've you got in mind?"

"Sting," said Mickey without blinking.

"Sting!" bellowed Jeff. "You're fucking kidding me?"

"Shh!" urged Mickey. "Let's just keep our genies firmly in the bottle for now."

Shirley breezed past the conspirators carrying a tray of empties. She eyed each of them suspiciously; they were up to no good.

"Hi, babe," said Jeff. "This lad's good, isn't he?"

On show was Finbarr Ashton, a wool comber from Minsmere. His act was all the more special given he suffered from acute asthma and was prone to regular epileptic fits. But tonight, he had the crowd eating out of his hand: "I got 99 problems but the twitch ain't one!"

Jules came over to say hello to the resident chef.

"'Allo," he said, gently touching Jules' hair.

Her mobile buzzed in her pocket and she retrieved it. It was a text from Mike.

Hi Jules. Hope u ok. Sorry been busy with shop. Would love a catch up soon. Miss u. Mike x

"Anyone we know?" said Patrice as the signal dropped on Jules' phone.

"No," she replied.

SUFFOLK

For those with no access to their own means of transport – be that car, unicycle or a ramshackle cart pulled by a family pet – getting around Suffolk has proved a sizeable challenge for its citizens over the years. While many held the belief they were living in the twenty-first century, the prevalence of buses, trains and taxis was utterly at the mercy of rural life.

Arriving into the county by train from the nation's capital was straightforward enough. Commuters and visitors enjoyed a regular train service out of the city's Liverpool Street station that delivered them across the county boundary in a little over an hour. The *Six Finger Express*, to give it its affectionate handle, had seen better days, however; the rolling stock pre-dated nationalisation of the railways as did much of the on-board catering. For instance, a tin of warm ale plus a slice of locally sourced flapjack offered the seasoned traveller a curious mix of refreshment and emergency tiling material.

While the train would creak, groan and disseminate vast quantities of 'brake stink', the service was typically reliable and would mercifully speed through Essex with little, or no, fuss. That is, unless it snowed, rained, blew a gale or was unseasonably mild. In such circumstances – or during the never-ending series of weekend and holiday engineering works – customers would be availed of a bus replacement service. This sub-human alternative to a perfectly adequate mode of transport gave passengers a fully extended tour of the villages and hamlets in the region and delivered them back safely to their loved ones upwards of nine days after leaving London's east end.

But if all was well, then the journey to the county town of Ipswich could be a relative joy. Should the need arise to travel further east, however, the picture of how one was to complete the trip became much less predictable.

The East Suffolk Line, which runs from Ipswich to the UK's most easterly town, Lowestoft, was one of the UK's earliest established rail tracks. The first short section of track opened triumphantly in 1854 and was shut down again in 1859 when local ombudsmen realised nothing had been invented to travel on it at that point. As soon as the first train arrived, however, the limitless possibilities it offered quickly became apparent. Passengers flocked in their thousands to ride on the single gauge line from Beccles to Bungay, waving at those under feudal restraint toiling in the fields and shouting profanities at the county's livestock.

And all at the heady average speed of nearly 11mph.

Tourist areas were soon connected by the track's growing infrastructure, thereby creating the dawn of 'the weekender'. Families were now able to reach the attractive seaside towns of Aldeburgh and Walberswick in twice the time it took them to walk it. They spent Saturdays and Sundays drinking bootleg whisky and taking pinhole-camera photographs of their relatives taking a shit underneath the numerous, recently erected piers, which added a whole new dimension to the 'age of steam'.

The East Suffolk Line brought prosperity to wherever its steely tentacle extended, and communities across the breadth of the county's hinterland demanded to be part of what the coastal track infrastructure could offer. An opportunity which, at the time, was not lost on the hurriedly assembled Peasenhall Railway Society (PRS). Its members issued an urgent 'manifesto of discontent' stating the village was losing money 'by the shed load' each day and insisting on the immediate construction of a line branch so that 'the people of Peasenhall might exploit this newly developed enterprise like a bastard'. The PRS proposal was reviewed by a series of rail sub-committees based both in London and a signal box in Saxmundham. After nine months' prevarication, a decision was finally afforded to the PRS and was told in no uncertain terms to: 'fuck right off'.

As a consequence, accessing Peasenhall by train has always required a certain type of tenacity not normally found in intelligent life. Without a car or a helpful lift from a close aunt, getting to the village required an additional means of public transport once travellers had alighted at its nearest station, Darsham. Darsham station was to modern-day travel what *Spearmint Rhino* was to modern dance. The single railway line skirted a solitary platform upon which both north and southbound passengers were obliged to congregate. The small waiting room had been boarded up since 1972 and the Old Station Café – which used to be a busy, thriving Victorian establishment selling teas, cake and an assortment of pig offal – was now a storage facility for *Screwfix*.

While the station had fallen into disrepair over the years, the one thing that made passing through Darsham station not a wholly unpleasant experience was the ever-present array of well-tended hanging baskets. From April to September, the *Darsham Guild of Floral Perspicuity* would ensure a most agreeable display of fuchsia, snapdragons and clematis from the platform's ornate canopy. Their efforts were regularly rewarded with awards of increasingly obscure designation, the latest being 'Most Flowery Display at a Crap Commuter Destination' bestowed upon the guild by *Vogue* magazine.

While the guild's sterling efforts were a joy to behold, they could never make up for the appalling randomness of the train times. The publication of the summer or winter timetables would always feature in the next available episode of *The World's Greatest Hoaxes* on UK Gold. The underlying problem was the fact that the trains suffered from Suffolk's own version of 'leaves on the line'. Trains would be subject to disruption from a range of obstructions that included 'weasel ahead' and 'dementia on the line', to name a couple, and this would leave passengers waiting for minutes, hours, or even days at a time. With Darsham station unmanned, there was no physical means of communication. Despite constant calls for the installation of a display board that would indicate a train's status, the local train operators refused to comply on the grounds of sheer incompetence.

Finally arriving at Darsham station still represented a journey in its infancy, however, as Peasenhall residents then had to complete the thirteen-mile journey to the village using a taxi or the locally operated bus service.

Mike staggered out of the Darsham station exit with a ragged copy of *The Evening Standard* under his arm.

"Taxi!" he shouted, at an empty car park.

The grocer had been in London for the day, attending a pig welfare conference with Holly. She had a spare ticket and thought it would be nice if her dad would go along with her; Stuart and Josh could hold the fort for the day. It was a Wednesday, so Mike hastily agreed, having no problems shutting the shop for a full day's closing.

"Dat sign says you're shut tomorrow, begorra!" Father Mackenzie pointed to the notice propped up on the shop counter.

"That's right," said Mike cautiously, trying not to irk the priest. "I'm heading into London with my daughter."

"So, what de feck are the rest of us s'posed to do? Starve?"

"Oh, I don't think me being shut for one solitary day will leave folk starving, Father," chuckled Mike.

"Yer supposed to be a feckin' pillar of dis community, ye Godless moron!" screamed the cleric.

"Oh, don't you start," pleaded Mike. "I've already had Doctor O'Flanagan in here giving me grief about it. He reckons I'm just going off on some all-day binge drinking session."

"You've a responsibility to the people of dis village!" He wasn't going to stop. "What would folk tink of me if I didn't turn up for work?"

"But you only work one day a week!" Mike argued. "You're probably tossing it off the rest of the week!"

When they met up, Holly had been distressed to see her dad with such a nasty bruise on his cheek, but after Mike dismissed it as nothing the young swineophile was thrilled he'd made the trip.

The conference wasn't exactly Mike's cup of tea but he enjoyed the time spent with Holly, who made some contacts at the event and picked up a good deal of information that was going to help the business. As she was staying in town later to catch up with a friend, Holly waved her father off at Liverpool Street. Mike climbed on the Six Finger Express, found a seat and, happy with his day's effort supporting his daughter, purchased a couple of tins of *Bite Me*, a new lager brewed specifically for the teenage market. On arrival at Ipswich station, however, it was unclear how long he'd have to wait for a train to Darsham.

"Excuse me. What time's the next train to Darsham?"

"Yeah. Oi'm not sure. But there will be one."

"Okay. Any idea at all? A ballpark time is fine."

[Exhales dramatically] "Oi reckon on…soon."

"Soon?"

"Ish."

By the time the Lowestoft train arrived, Mike had been in the licensed platform café for three hours and was off his tits.

Through the mists of his drunkenness, Mike could hear a tooting noise. That's a horn, he realised after the third blast. Once he remembered how to turn his head, Mike saw the number 196 bus sat next to one of the barriers of the level crossing. It was lit up like a bus with its lights on.

"Taxi!" Mike bellowed again and the bus slowly trundled over.

The 196 bus operated by *Beet Route Travel Limited*, ran between Darsham and Peasenhall, pointlessly visiting the communities of Yoxford and Hemp Green en route. The most extraordinary thing about the service was that it only ran one way, which resulted in a lot of the company's buses, and the passengers on them, permanently stuck in Peasenhall.

Despite an additional 'y' in his surname, the driver on board Mike's bus, Jeremy Barnyard, claimed to be a direct descendent of the driver killed in the 'Westerfield Train Incident' at the turn of the twentieth century.

Shortly before nine on the morning of 25th September 1900, a GER Class locomotive came to a stop at Westerfield's level-crossing. As it prepared to move on the locomotive's boiler exploded, killing both the driver John Barnard and his boiler man William MacDonald. The boiler was projected over 100 feet in the air and landed 40 yards along the westbound platform. As Suffolk County Council couldn't be bothered to move it, the boiler was converted into a tobacconist, which remained operational until the smoking ban.

Jeremy Barnyard always blamed the boiler man for the death of his great-great-great-relative, angry at the fact he never got the chance to meet him.

"Peasenhall," demanded the inebriated grocer.

"Four quid," demanded the bus driver.

"Do you take AmEx?"

"No," said Jeremy. "Are you drunk?" asked the Meatloaf look-alike.

"No," said the drunk. "Are you wearing a full Ferrari F1 outfit?"

"Yes," said the bus driver. "Four pounds," he demanded again.

"Look," slurred Mike. "I own the Peasenhall shop at Peasenhall. Take me home and I'll give you anything you want in Peasenhall's shop to the value of…how much is the fare?"

"Eighteen pounds," said Jeremy.

"To the value of eighteen pounds," agreed Mike. "You can choose your items while you're waiting for the pick-up truck to fetch your bus back."

With the deal sealed, Mike bounced down the bus and fell into a seat behind the only other person on board: the masseuse, Roxanne Leathers. As Jeremy set the wheels in motion, the grocer grabbed the phone out of his clutch bag and checked it for messages. Over the last week, he'd sent Jules two texts a day, opening his inbox again he saw she still hadn't replied to any of them.

Misery coursed through him like transfused blood in a Tour de France cyclist. With his belly full of booze, Mike curled himself into a ball on the seat, pulled his jacket over him for a makeshift blanket and quickly drifted off. An otherwise peaceful ride home was only interrupted by the unavoidable potholes that shook the vehicle violently. As each impact pitched Mike forwards, he would wake briefly and cry out, "There's a tom on the bus!"

JEFF

"Have you got Mickey's mobile number, Graeme?"

Jeff held up a printed copy of the email he had received from Pete at pete@pete.com and waved it at the jumper king. "We're in!" he exclaimed. "We get judged two weeks from today!"

"Fantastic!" Graeme punched the air. "What do you need Mickey's number for?"

"To let him know the good news. I've tried him at home, but he must be in the studio working or something."

"Okay," agreed Graeme. "It's zero-sausage-sausage-mushroom-sausage-beans-egg-beans-mushroom-double-toast."

"What the...?" Jeff's finger remained poised over the buttons on his phone.

"Sorry," said Graeme. "I can only remember his number as a fry up. Take the first letter of each breakfast or brunch item and use the corresponding number."

Jeff shook his head as Graeme repeated the sequence of the classic trucker's meal and the number connected.

"Hello, Mickey?...Yeah, it's Jeff...You okay?...Sounds like you're making a trifle. Anyway, we've had our entry to the open mic competition confirmed... Yeah, great news, eh?...The judges are doing us in a fortnight...Too right! So, we need to get a wiggle on...Okay, Mickey, just thought I'd let you know... Sure...See you later...Ooh, what's that groaning in the background? Oh, he's hung up!"

"Right, well, all systems go." Graeme's thin smile betrayed a much deeper concern.

"Smile like you mean it," Jeff protested. "We're gonna knock 'em dead!"

"So, when you bringing Shirley into the loop?"

The launch of a competition between the open mic pubs in the region had gone down sensationally well. It was an inspirational idea that began to get some real traction with the local media. The *East Anglia Daily Times* had already committed an intern to cover the event and local pop station, Town 102FM, had agreed to feature the best-performed tracks across the fortnight with the eventual winners invited to play live on the *Steve Horlicks Breakfast Show*. News that The Peasant had also been accepted into the battle quickly reached Carl Fleming and he promised an editorial update feature in *PQ* every week. Determined not to miss out, Roger Barnett agreed to interview as many of the performers who were booked to play on the night at either village pub on *PeasPlease FM*.

Pete, the organiser, had received twenty-eight entries each with a cheque for three hundred pounds made out to *Pete Enterprises Inc.* It was a nice, convenient number. Not only did it net him two grand after prize money and expenses were taken out, but it also meant Pete could judge two pubs a night and the job would be done in a fortnight. As the judge, he reckoned on being treated like a king in each of the venues, so he wouldn't have to worry about shelling out for too much food and beer over the two weeks. And he may even get the odd phone number from a young admirer or two, the unemployed chiropodist thought.

Via the emailing of the acceptance letters, Pete explained to the contestants the criteria he would be employing to find Suffolk's best open mic pub: effective use of venue layout and available equipment; strategies to build atmosphere; audience engagement; quality of performances; evaluation of the host's skills; refreshment choices and variation of entertainment formats. Pete also added some recommended guidelines. A list of do's and don'ts which included: DON'T keep your best performers on continuously, the judges will see through this and DO ensure to keep all pets attending with performers quiet and on a sturdy lead.

As he looked down his schedule, Pete – a man who only brushed his teeth with cold water for a large part of his adult life – sorted his journey plan across the fortnight. The furthest south he needed to go was *The Horse Hive* in Sudbury; he would do that first along with *The Spoon* in Monks Eleigh. The furthest north was the village of Peasenhall. He would judge there on the last night and it looked like there were two pubs: The Startled Goose and The Whipped Peasant. They would go head-to-head on Thursday the 15th October.

"Don't worry, Graeme. I've sorted Shirley."

Jeff's decision to keep his wife in the dark was, in the humble opinion of his partners in crime, ill-thought-through. Shirley's temper was now a recognised weapon with patrons of The Goose, so when she said no, that was generally taken as gospel. Jeff had been blinded by the pub's recent success and truly believed, with Mickey and Graeme's influence, that the five grand was in the bag. He couldn't allow Shirley to stand in the way of 'free cash' – as he kept referring to the prize money – and an opportunity to really put The Goose on the map. What's more, he wanted to show his wife – who, to be fair, did rather enjoy condescending her husband – that he was *sometimes* capable of making the right decision for the good of the business.

"On my suggestion, she's arranged to have some time down at her sister's," explained Jeff. "She lives on the base at RAF Mildenhall and I think the pair of them are planning a spa day, a bit of golf and some taunting of any passing airmen."

"So, she still hasn't got a clue?"

"Nope."

"Well," said Graeme. "I hope you know what you're doing. I've got a funny feeling this could turn round and bite you in the arse."

Jeff smiled nervously and glanced down at Cloak & Spanner, who were both furiously salivating and seemingly keen to assist in that last suggestion.

Mike's phone pinged. Jules, he thought, but it was only a text from Hector.

We're on, now get your thinking cap on!

JULES

"No, Patrice. I would stay over, but I still think it's too soon." Jules was talking on her phone as she opened her front door and walked in after an exhausting day. "Well, I can't do anything about that," she said. "Maybe you should take a cold shower…or try watching *Pointless*."

After telling the Frenchman she would see him later for open mic, Jules went to hang up, but the intermittent broadband did it for her. Inside *Atora Corner* was cold; autumn was deepening and the mornings and evenings had an edge to them. The midwife went over to the thermostat and twisted the dial until the central heating kicked in with a *thwump!* She dropped her bag on the table and headed upstairs to change out of her uniform and apply some steroid cream to her arms. They were in pretty bad shape after wrestling with a breech birth in Sizewell. The mother was a worker at the nuclear plant in the area – its golf ball silhouette a constant presence on the heritage coast – and, for the duration of her labour, maintained it was the radiation that had caused her baby to turn around. Through the pain she screamed revenge on her operations supervisor as soon as she was back to work.

A breech normally warranted a caesarean, but this was the women's fifth child and she was, as Jules pointed out, as slack as a construction chute, the family decided to stay with the home birth option.

Jules thought about what she was going to wear that evening. She dug out a pair of ripped jeans and an old Black Sabbath t-shirt and slipped them on. She then added a long cardigan for warmth. Suddenly realising she was hungry, Jules headed downstairs to make something for tea. The leftovers from last night's supper were on the kitchen top; Patrice had walked over with a plate of shepherd's pie that was on his menu. It was sweet of him and he sat and chatted with Jules as she ate. The portion was huge and, as tasty as it was, she couldn't finish it. He kissed her goodnight and went back to The Goose to finish clearing up. Right now, though, an almost empty fridge stared back at the midwife and the prospect of a filling meal from half an onion and a half-used tin of peaches seemed remote. The bread bin was empty, and when Jules looked into the cupboard under the sink, all she could find among the J-cloths, plungers and half-empty tins of Glade air freshener was one sad, sprouting potato.

"Damn you, Mike!" she whispered. "Miss you in more ways than you know."

Thinking she was probably able to blag a free meal at The Goose, she grabbed her banjo and headed back out the front door.

"So that's it then."

"They're just good friends, Mike." Janice was still in the shop after Mike had closed for the day. Her twins were back home with her husband, Alan, playing with a skip construction kit he'd bought on the BA flight back from Lisbon.

"Yeah, I get it." Mike felt crushed but suspected there was a bit more to the last ten days of white noise than just a midwife with the hump. He had played it too hot and then too cool; he'd only himself to blame.

"From what oi understand talken to Jules, oi don't think they're...yer know..." Janice tried to remain as discreet as possible, but someone had to tell Mike what was going on and she had no time for that chef – no matter how good his dumplings were.

Mike had been so busy getting the shop updated and ready for a new era of village retailing (he was already considering an advertising campaign in *PQ* and had some initial thoughts on PR thrown at him by a guy called Nick Crabbs), that he'd effectively failed to spot the village's worst kept secret: Patrice and Jules were walking out together. Nobody was prepared to tell Mike outright, but Janice liked Mike and thought enough was enough.

"You can spare me the details, Janice," said Mike.

"My point is, Mike. I know Jules, and if she's not fully on-board, ahem, then summit's not roight."

"Even so, I'm too hard to handle, Janice. Patrice is free of any family commitments. Free of any desires to put on women's clothes. He's probably feeding her meals she's only dreamed about before and…he's probably hung like a fucking baboon." God, Mike thought, baboons keep stealing my girls. "If they haven't already…then it's just a matter of time!" the grocer blurted out.

"Oi'm tellen you, Mike!" Janice argued, "this int over by a long chalk!"

"Janice, she's made her choice. It's time for me to move on from this little episode. Look around you!" the shopkeeper told the stuffing queen. "This place is the mutt's nuts now. I'm gonna focus on the business and Holly and get my shit together."

"But Jules…!" Janice protested.

"I don't need Jules!"

OPEN MIKE

It was Thursday night...etc.

Confidence in The Peasant and its remorseful landlord was improving all the time. The jury, however, was still out on whether Hector's faith in Mike as the new open mic host was justified. Indeed, many patrons showing up were a tad disappointed to find the quiz night wasn't on again – particularly after the dramatic conclusion the previous week.

The Grieving Parents had come out on top, but only after a tiebreaker between them and team 4, *The Elder Statesmen of a Bygone Era*. FW had neglected to consider there might be a tie at the end of four hundred questions, but there they were, both teams with three hundred and twenty points each. FW hurriedly thought of a quick and easy question to separate a winner so everyone could finally get home to bed.

"What's the capital of Holland?" the will writer blurted out.

"Amsterdam!" came a shout from *The Grieving Parents*.

"And you're the winners!" declared FW.

"Hang on!" There was a collective cry from *The Elder Statesmen of a Bygone Era*. "Amsterdam is the capital of The Netherlands. Not Holland."

"Same thing," claimed *The Grieving Parents*.

"Same thing," concurred FW.

"I beg your pardon!" said *The Elder Statesmen of a Bygone Era's* team leader, clearly outraged by the dismissiveness of the question master. "Holland is a province of The Netherlands made up of separate north and south regions whose capitals are Haarlem and The Hague respectively. It is NOT the same thing, sir!"

"Yep. Same thing." FW wasn't interested. "Now fuck off home!"

Mike set up his gear in the usual spot next to The Peasant's original doorway. He studiously set the levels on his amplifier, got his guitar tuned and went through the night's opening number in his head. He had practiced the tune repeatedly and felt if the nerves would hold, he could smash it out the park.

"Evening, folks," said Mike stepping up to the mic. "Thanks so much for being here!"

"Woo!" came a cry of encouragement from the averagely sized crowd.

"I want to start tonight with a version of a Kylie Minogue song about someone unable to encourage their loved one away from a dismal town in the south-west. This is *I Just Can't Get You Out of Minehead.*

Mike took a deep breath and dived into the cover. No bangs, no sparks: he was up and running. Fingers were moving across the frets of his guitar smoothly and the voice was holding a sensible key; the nerves were intact. He was emboldened further when several members of the audience joined in as he sang one of Kylie's more prophetic set of lyrics: "Na, na, na…na, na, ne, na, na! [reprise]"

He nailed it. And the audience roared its approval. "Wow!" mouthed the grocer over their heads to a delighted Hector, who offered him a solid thumbs-up.

Suddenly, the news about Jules wasn't burning his insides quite so painfully.

Next up was Jeremy Barnyard who, as Mike discovered while helping him bag up a large selection of groceries yesterday, was an accomplished acoustic guitarist and harmonica player. Accepting Mike's invitation to come over, the bus driver treated The Peasant to two tunes. The first was his own composition, *Boilerman Blues*, and the second was a hauntingly beautiful cover of Elizabeth Cotten's *Freight Train* and was on a par with Joan Baez's 1982 version of the song.

Freight train, freight train, gorn so fast…

Jeremy's eloquent playing and sweet voice produced a standing ovation from the audience; rarely had they witnessed such an accomplished performance, particularly from a man in motor racing apparel.

Gail Frogmarch, snubbed too many times by Graeme Nash, had stayed loyal to Hector and now she had been given the opportunity, delivered a pitch perfect set on her harp. And FW, who was going nowhere now there was half a chance he could stick quiz master on his CV, stepped up and grappled with two songs of mild interest. However, without the defecting Roger Barnett present to offer the diverse element of poetry to the evening's fayre, Chloe Bramwell offered to step in his shoes and provide some of her own prose.

Hector had tried to dissuade his daughter for the best part of a week, warning Chloe that if people didn't 'understand' her poems, they could be quite hurtful in terms of their appreciation of them. Chloe remained resolute, however, focusing on the task for several hours that week. She'd sought the advice of her father regarding a number of rhyming couplets that she was having difficulty with. When he could offer no suggestions as to what could possibly match 'orange', 'club foot' or 'Helvellyn', she remained undeterred and returned to her scribbling. She can't go up, Hector repeatedly told himself, she'll get ripped to shreds.

"Stop being so over-protective," Chloe told her father as Mike introduced her up to the mic.

"Darling, I'm just trying to save you from yourself," he pleaded.

"Dad, that makes no sense whatsoever," she said, pulling her arm away from his tight grasp.

A few nervous coughs greeted Chloe and her two sheets of A4. As she took a hold of the mic, you could have heard a pin drop.

"Here's my first poem," she declared. "My first EVER poem!"

Hector couldn't look and disappeared into the kitchen.

"There was a young man from Leeds," Chloe began. "Who refused to eat his greens…"

More exaggerated coughs circled the room. Chloe had stopped.

"Oh, no, that doesn't work, at all," she muttered to herself and then quickly scrunched up the first sheet before tossing it behind her. "Forget that one," she announced. "Let's try this one instead."

The crowd heaved a collective sigh and Jeremy Barnyard set himself for the arrival of a real train wreck.

"Dawn.

I wake with your countenance beside me,

Dreamlike in every aspect, you are a lifetime away.

And yet, right here.

I touch your skin. Its warmth on my fingertips is desire found,
And I ache for those eyes which keep me alive.
I wait for your gaze, like the sun's first rays.
But you sleep. So sweet.
And I won't deny you."

"Oh my God!" Hector had re-emerged from the kitchen, his eyes brimming with tears for the daughter he'd doubted so badly; his body racked with shame and unexpected joy in equal measure.

And then the crowd went wild.

Open mic at The Goose was a decent night.

Favours done, a few of the bands Mickey had persuaded to come, help and support hadn't bothered to turn up so there were a few gaps in the line-up. Fortunately, they were filled by a few of The Peasant regulars who had finally finished sitting on the fence and decided to pop in and play.

That included Alan Hedgeworthy, Dave Neal and, of course, Jules – who played two of her mother's songs from her 1980 album, *Dieser Hund wird als Ralph*. She played elegantly and the songs clearly held a poignancy for her. As she sang of life and love in her mother's mother tongue, the only slight distraction was Sammy Grossefinger's insistence on doing Nazi salutes and shouting "Sieg Hiel!" as the words flowed out of her.

As the players played, Jeff, Mickey, Patrice and Graeme consulted regularly across the evening regarding their planned approach for The Battle of the Bands.

After all, it was only two weeks away.

PEASENHALL

Someone once said: "Two weeks is a long time in village politics."

Word quickly got around that Peasenhall's two hostelries would go head-to-head on the last night of judging of the Battle of the Pubs and excitement built steadily across the next two weeks. Even news of the sale of *muckysupermarket.com* (a price comparison website for pig slurry) for three and a half million pounds by its owner and local entrepreneur, Fanny Datchett, failed to surpass the interest generated in the 'Win or Death Night' – Carl Fleming's latest headline designed to fan the flames a little. Carl also placed a picture of each pub sign in his paper and encouraged readers to cut out their favourite and put it up in a front room window as a show of allegiance. Overnight a mosaic of peasants and geese appeared across the streets of the historic village.

It was like a general election but without the interminable drivel. (And exactly how Shirley Timberlake missed all of this remains a village mystery to this very day.)

Jeff and his band of merry men quickly confirmed their line-up and set up a series of practice nights which, given The Goose was out of bounds, had to be done over at Mickey's studio. (This required Mickey's removal of a collection of stark, framed photographs to avoid any revelation of his day job.) Sting had regretfully declined the chance to play but Penny had come up trumps by convincing Radio Suffolk's resident band to play on the night. The tunes from *Hair on a G-String* were hugely popular on the station's *moosic* programmes, and because the band members all had faces for radio, the judges wouldn't recognise them as ringers.

With Patrice due to be out of the kitchen and on bar duty for the evening,

Jeff had recruited the services of Andrea at *Fantastic Baps*. He had asked her to put together a few ideas for a themed buffet for the gig and told her she'd get an additional twenty per cent payment on top if she agreed not to service any requests from The Peasant. Andrea did not want any part of 'such nonsense', but as soon as Jeff gently reminded her he had a little more information on her assistant, James Seville, than was healthy, she grudgingly acquiesced. The unfeasibly large-breasted bun maker got back to him a few days later with some food themes that included 'rocktail sausages', 'head bangers' and 'the mash pit'. Jeff was thrilled. "This is a cake walk," he said to Mickey with a week to go. Cloak & Spanner just salivated.

Graeme got to work on his delivery. He decided to watch *Gladiator* again to see how Cassius, played by David Hemmings, achieved such grandiosity when introducing the deadly duels inside the coliseum. Graeme even considered fashioning his eyebrows in the same pointy-style that the late Hemmings exhibited. While he remained unsure about the eyebrows, Graeme was determined to have a jumper that generations would talk about for years to come. He pulled a production brief together of what he desired and emailed it to Horse Noblett, his most trusted knitter. She thanked him for his order but warned Graeme that, due to other commitments, the jumper wouldn't be available before the night of the competition.

Mickey was in charge of light and sound. He'd recruited additional help from some of the maintenance guys at Ipswich mortuary – they knew a thing or two about bringing something to life with the odd halogen spot – and worked out what he could salvage from his old production kit to boost the PA for the night.

Things were taking shape nicely.

"Unexpected item in bagging area!"

"So, cuz yer so feckin lazy, we've gotta scan our own bastard groceries now, 'ave we?!" raged Father Mackenzie.

Mike didn't know what to say. "I've just tried to modernise things a little." He gestured towards the huge automated checkout till. He'd had to remove the entire counter, including the sweet display, to fit it in. "I'm trying to move with the times."

"Feckin movin' with de times, me hole!" The priest failed to scan a tin of tuna and the machine repeated its bagging area warning. "Feck you!" cried the Irishman. "It's staying where it is! If you can't feckin keep up, dat's your fault!"

Mike scratched his head. "It's okay, Father. Don't worry about it."

The priest passed a *KitKat* across the scanner, which then duly beeped. "Now was dat feckin unexpected, ya cont?!"

"No, that's fine." The language turned Mike crimson again. "But, Father, you can have another one of those for free."

The priest rounded on the shopkeeper. "What am I to ye? A feckin charity case?"

"No," Mike tried to explain. "It's BOGOF."

"You feckin bog off, you little weasel!"

"Buy one, get one free. It's a special offer."

The priest drew up to his full height. "Are ye mockin' me, son?"

"Good Lord, no," said Mike, who then panicked because he wasn't sure if he'd just taken His name in vain.

"Let me tell ye somet'ing Jesus said," the priest growled, "before I remove myself from dis den of iniquity."

"Please," Mike was shaking. "Feel free."

"He said, 'He who dresses like a whore, shall be royally fecked up de ass!'"

"Did he?" Mike seriously doubted that.

"And 'e want talkin' about no donkey!"

Hector sipped at a cup of coffee on Mike's settee. It was a familiar seat because he had sold it to Mike about two years ago for a score.

"Can anything be done about that insane priest?" asked Mike, putting a teaspoon in the sink and joining Hector on the three-seater.

"Father Mackenzie?"

Mike nodded.

"Ah, his bark is worse than his bite," Hector said indifferently.

Mike ran a finger along the bruising that was still faintly visible on his cheek. "Sure," he said, realising there was very little point in pursuing that line of conversation.

"Anyway." Hector popped his tea down onto a tiled coffee table. "How are you doing?"

Mike knew what the publican was alluding to. "It's all good, Hector."

"You sure? If there's anything I can do…"

"You're doing it," Mike interrupted. "You're the one putting faith in me."

The pair smiled knowingly at each other.

"Okay," said Hector. "So, where are we at?"

Mike pulled out his to-do list for the competition. It was three days away. "Well, the bad news is we're still a bit light on performers. Jeremy Barnyard is still trying to change his shift, while FW is trying to contact his call centre to move the appointment they made for him over in Creeting St Mary."

"Did you hear he finally got arrested in Marks and Spencer last week?"

Mike was wide-eyed. "Seriously?"

"Got done for resisting a dress."

"Shit," said Mike. "Is he being prosecuted?"

Hector took a big gulp of his coffee. "That was a joke, Mike." It took a while for the penny to drop, but even then, Mike failed to enjoy the light banter.

"You know," said Hector. "I need you to relax a little bit, my friend. It's only three hundred quid, Mike. Besides, it's my money and I've already written it off. I want us to have a laugh doing this…not get all bent out of shape. The pub's trade is recovering and once I get the bloody food situation sorted, all will be back on track."

Hector's attempts to get the pub menu back to pre-Patrice-buggering-off standards, had been frustrating to say the least. Damien Cartwright called in response to Hector's advert in the Woodbridge Job Centre, but not only turned up stoned to the interview, he was also wearing a neon-green mankini. Two more chefs came and tried out for a few days and, while they were okay, they were nowhere near as gifted as the gigantically handed Frenchman. Hector informed them he would make a decision in a day or two. Or three.

"But we can't just let The Goose win," Mike argued. "We'll never live it down."

"Who cares?" laughed Hector. "I'm really not that bothered. It's hardly a matter of life and death is it?"

No, thought Mike, it's more important than that.

THE BATTLE OF THE PUBS (DAY)

It was Thursday 15th October. It was open mic night and this time…the gloves were off!

Daylight broke over Peasenhall; this small, medieval village hunkered down in the rolling plains of the Suffolk countryside. Unassuming and uncaring, there were very few signs that this commune would ever progress past the Middle Ages. But the day had arrived which would prove to be monumental (or possibly just mental) for the residents of this rural parish.

"Okay, darling, brilliant stuff!" Mike was on his mobile. "Yep, no problem…Bye…Love you!" Holly had rung early to wish him luck on the big day and to let him know she wasn't going to make it down on account of the fact she had a date with Josh, her assistant. In fact, it was a third date. (It transpired he hated *Emmerdale*.)

The day could not have started better, Mike thought, and as he munched through a bowl of fruit and fibre. He'd had a mild epiphany overnight: Hector was right, the competition really didn't matter. He was going to do the gig and just enjoy an evening with no pressure and lots of laughter. Tonight would cleanse Mike from the crap of the last few days; he would simply reboot and begin the new chapter he'd promised himself.

The shopkeeper picked up a copy of the *East Anglian Daily Times,* which had just been delivered along with the other newspapers, and turned to page three for the latest update on The Battle of the Bands.

"*…and with one more evening of judging to go, at 2-to-1, The Startled Goose remains the bookies firm favourite to take this year's title as Suffolk's Best Open Mic Pub and that fantastic top prize of five thousand pounds…*"

Above the article sat a picture of Team Goose, arm-in-arm, they formed a cheery line just brimming with confidence. And there on Patrice's left arm was Jules.

"Good luck to the pair of you," Mike said aloud as a solitary tear inched down his cheek. So much for my reboot, he thought.

"Jeff?" Shirley called out. "Have you seen the *East Anglian Daily Times* this morning? I want to take it with me in the car."

Jeff came through from the restaurant. "No, love, I can't remember seeing it yet." He shot a backward glance at Cloak & Spanner devouring the gravy-soaked pages of the day's edition of the popular local newspaper in an obscured corner of the pub. "Maybe the paper boy's off sick?"

"Typical," Shirley tutted.

"Anyway, you need to be off!" urged Jeff, almost forcing the over-sized rucksack onto his wife's back.

"Blimey," Shirley remarked. "Someone's keen to get rid of me. You got a fancy woman coming round or something?"

"Yeah, I've got dozens of nymphets from *Escort in the Act* coming over while you're gone!"

Shirley blinked. Did her husband really just say that? A decade ago the couple's marriage was nearly done and dusted thanks to the nymphets of *Escort in the Act*. Jeff had taken a liking to the 'establishment' and its personnel, and was one of a trio of lads from traffic who began to sojourn there while on duty. A planned kiss-and-tell by one of the girls was quashed with a rapidly acquired injunction, and the only reason the officers kept their jobs was to ensure the scandal didn't hit the papers. Shirley stood by her man and the subject was never mentioned between them again. Until now.

"You know I was joking, right?"

"Take me to the station."

Jeff dropped Shirley off at Darsham station a good ten minutes before the Ipswich train was due (where she would wait a good eighty minutes for its arrival) and headed back to The Goose. Patrice was already in and busy arranging his cocktail bar on the landlord's return.

"Let's hope everyone likes liquorice," Jeff observed.

Patrice chose to ignore the small man with tiny hands as he organised bottles of Absinthe, Pastis, Ouzo, Absinthe, Pernod Ricard, Chartreuse, Raki, Galliano, Sambuca and Jägermeister along the length of his allocated spot behind the bar. The chef-cum-mixologist then erected a small sign that he had worked on the night before. It read: *Aniseed Will Do.*

"Sweet," encouraged Jeff.

"What time are ze uzzer two cretins turning up?" asked the ever-patient Patrice.

Mickey was committed to a full shift at Ipswich morgue and wouldn't be around until five at the earliest. Jeff was decidedly uncomfortable with that – conscious that the sound and lighting were crucial elements to the night's victory. He'd demanded to know what Mickey had on that was so important it would keep him away until the evening. The mortician simply said he had a funeral to go to, which appeared to satisfy Jeff. Graeme said he would be available earlier but as Thursday was housework day, he was unlikely to be at the pub much before one o'clock.

"I think Penny's doing the early morning weather slot today," said Jeff. "She should be around early afternoon as well."

The misogynistic Frenchman shrugged as if that was of little importance. "Is Shirley still, 'ow you say, oblivious?"

"Oh, yeah," Jeff smugly nodded. "Right, keep an eye on the place, Patrice. I'm off to see Roger."

"With just one night left, the quest to be Suffolk's best open mic pub reaches the final stage of judging tonight when the Battle of the Pubs hits down in Peasenhall!"

Steve Horlicks was being particularly shouty on his breakfast show. The local DJ had already shouted about how teabags always seem to take longer to brew when you're in a hurry. He had also yelled about an hilarious incident when he and his celebrity chums sat on a dog and promptly fell off, and he bellowed about why, oh why, did Suffolk County Council feel the need to notify him (by letter, which he had to open himself!) of forthcoming road repairs and possible disruption on *his* street? "Not interested!" he screamed. "Now here's Brian May with *Save the Badger, Badger, Badger!*"

(A spokesman for Suffolk County Council later rang into the show to point out that the letter Mr. Horlicks had received actually said they *may* be making repairs to his street.)

Carl Fleming had followed the *East Anglian Daily Times'* lead and published the bookmakers' odds on who was favourite to scoop the prize as part of *PQ's* regular update on events. But today was the biggie, and two photos of Jeff and Hector filled the front page with the superimposed image of a combine harvester between them. A bold, provocative headline over the montage leapt off the page: *Threshing Time!*

At *PeasPlease FM*, Roger Barnett introduced the first of his two guests for the morning. "Good Morning, Jeff Timberlake."

"Hello, Roger," said Jeff confidently. "Nice to be here." Jeff had been a big fan of the failed Liberal Democrat leader, Nick Clegg, and considered his media approach one of the smoothest around at the time; he was determined to emulate his style for this, his first radio interview.

"How are preparations going for tonight's big occasion?"

Jeff eased nonchalantly back in his chair. "Very well indeed, Roger…"

"I'm sorry," Roger jumped in. "Would you mind getting closer to the microphone?"

"Oh!" Jeff sat back up. "My apologies. I neglected to…"

"Yeah, just get on with it."

"Okay," frowned Jeff. "Well, as most of your listeners will know our *Rocktail* night is all ready to go and we're very excited about putting on what we believe will be a fantastic representation of the true, creative spirit of Peasenhall."

"Sounds like BS to me, Jeff," Roger challenged the landlord.

"What?" squeaked Jeff.

"The true, creative spirit of Peasenhall?" smirked Roger. "It's open mic!"

"But…it is." Jeff was at a loss. "That seems strange coming from you, Roger, seeing as you're one of the performers."

In his efforts to be considered as a hard-hitting – and potentially Sony-Award-winning – radio journalist, Roger had clearly forgotten this salient fact.

"Yes…" he backtracked. "And The Goose has really embraced this event! And, from what I've heard, it's in great shape to wipe the floor with the competition."

That's better, thought Jeff. "Well, that's not for me to say," he said modestly. "That's down to the judges and the fans."

"Fans?"

"Sorry, audience," Jeff corrected.

"And should you win the top prize when it's announced in a couple of weeks, what will you do with the cash?" Roger asked the question Jeff had handed him the night before.

"Well...we haven't considered that possibility," lied Jeff. "But should, via some minor miracle, we happen to snatch the title from some very worthy opponents, I'd like to think The Goose could set up a trust fund for the all the abused farm children in the area."

"That's a fantastic cause," said Roger, sincerity oozing out of every pore.

"Well, let's keep our fingers crossed the judges feel our open mic is worthy of such an opportunity."

"Well, the very best of luck for tonight's Battle of the Pubs, Jeff, from all of us here at *PeasPlease FM*."

Somewhere on the streets of Cowlinge, Pete of pete@pete.com got into his car, turned on the ignition and listened to the silence of his vehicle failing to start.

"Any luck on the food front?"

Mike had closed the shop for an hour to come over and see Hector for a quick update (much to the annoyance of Father Mackenzie, who found the place shut when he needed milk).

"Liam Lewis has come through for us." Hector polished glasses while he explained how Liam had agreed to fetch a catering pack of Brendan Matthew's turkey pieces. All Hector needed to do was heat them up and serve them; piece of piss. Other than that, it was open mic as usual for The Peasant. No fancy lighting inside, no elaborate sound system and, other than Steve and Maddy, certainly no ringers.

"They'll take us as they find us," was Hector's view.

"The Goose's posted its line-up on Facebook!" Chloe called from the kitchen, where she was using the laptop to find a YouTube video on warming poultry.

"They're keen!" Mike smiled. "Can you bring it into the bar, Chloe, so we can take a look?"

There was a pause. "But it's attached to a plug in the wall?"

"It's okay, darling, you can unplug it!" Hector looked up, waiting for the inevitable response.

"But the light will drain away?"

"No, it's got a battery, darling!" her father explained. "Just bring it through, precious!"

Graeme had uploaded The Goose's schedule on social media around noon, once the last artist had texted confirmation of their availability. It was an impressive array: *Zumba Wumba, Radio NaNa* (the pseudonym for *Hair on a G-String*), Dan Naysmith, Alan Hedgeworthy, Roxanne Leathers, *Superating Wound*, Roger Barnett, Dave Neal, Sally Womber, *The Hashtag Lads*, Paul Pickering, George Raft, Dorothy Wellman and, last but not least, Julie Wiseman. They had guitars, drums, acapella, Jew's harp, poetry and…banjo.

"Looks good," remarked Hector.

"Still relaxed about the outcome tonight?" said Mike, raising an eyebrow.

"Mikey!" Hector smiled. "We get a bit of publicity and have a thoroughly good evening, what's not to like?"

"Best ply the judge with a few drinks. That could help."

"Forget it!" Hector shouldered his tea towel. "Look, The Goose is pulling out all the stops for this thing and I'm sure they'll be on a massive charm offensive as soon as that Pete fella comes through the door. I'm just going leave him to it."

"You really are chilled out about this, aren't you?"

Hector smiled. "But now I've got a date with PeasPlease's finest."

"Welcome to my second guest, Hector Bramwell."

"Hello, Roger," Hector said breezily. "How's your mum?"

"Um, fine," said Roger, a little thrown by the familiarity.

"She okay after that nasty bout of shingles?"

"Yes, fine. Thank you," said Roger, getting testy. "Now, how are preparations going for tonight's big occasion?" he snapped.

"Great. We…"

"And how are you reflecting the region's active gay and lesbian community in your show tonight?" Roger grinned deviously across the studio table at his guest. Answer that and stay fashionable, he thought.

Hector considered Roger's unwarranted interjection for a moment. "That's a good question, Roger."

Is it, thought the presenter?

"You'll know, as a regular open micer at The Peasant before you deserted ship like the rat you are…"

"Now, hang on!" protested the architect of murky poetry.

"Let me finish!" barked Hector. "As you know, we are thrilled and proud to have Gail Frogmarch, a brilliant harpist and singer, and Bill Fearnley-Whittingstall, a pillar of this vibrant community, performing for us not just tonight but on a regular basis."

"And?" Roger was confused.

"Well." Hector shook his in astonishment. "They're both gay, Roger."

"FW? Gay? Fuck off!"

"Seriously?!" screamed Roger's producer.

"I'm shocked you didn't know that, Roger," smiled Hector.

Roger paused briefly as his earpiece continued to bristle with his producer's demand for an apology. "I'd just like to apologise for any offensive language our listeners may have heard just then." The words almost chocked him.

"So, we're all set and looking forward to greeting any Peasenhall residents who fancy a night of good moosic and fried turkey." Hector was enjoying himself. "Oh, and of course, best of luck to The Goose!"

THE BATTLE OF THE PUBS (NIGHT)

"D'you know Plato said that *moosic* is a moral law?"

Jeff stopped and looked hard at Sammy Grossefinger. "Do you know what, Sammy?" said the landlord still coming to terms with what had just come out of the villager's mouth. "I think it's going to be an exceptional night."

It was seven o'clock and The Goose was filling up nicely. Jeff had spoken to Shirley an hour earlier from the relative quiet of the pub car park; she and her friend had finished at the spa and were having pre-dinner drinks. Jeff told her to have fun and not to worry about contacting him for the rest of the evening. He told her he would be busy with another run-of-the-mill open mic night but didn't expect any mad rush. Shirley sounded like she was over the nymphets' gaff and thanked her husband sweetly for the chance to take a night off. She rang off with a kiss.

Jeff winced slightly when he got back inside; Mickey was still fiddling with the PA system. He'd been delayed by traffic getting back from work. It was pension day and the A1120 was awash with retirees.

"Everything okay, Mickey?" Jeff asked, waiting for the gift of sound and vision.

"One, choo! One, choo!" The mic was on. "Yarp!"

Mickey's colleagues from the mortuary had done a great job with the lights and the room was looking its moody best. There was one awkward moment when Mickey had to step in and prevent one of the lads showing pictures of an autopsy on his Samsung to Patrice. Now, everything was in place and a prompt seven-thirty start was assured. There was, however, one small problem.

Barry Noblett had just dropped off Graeme's jumper. His wife, Horse, was too exhausted after finishing eight knitted garments in a single day to deliver it in person (a feat later ratified by the *Guinness Book of World Records* as a...world record). Exhilaration turned to despair when Graeme pulled the new pullover out of its brown paper wrapping. The image of a goose playing a Flying-V guitar had been captured superbly on the front of the jumper by Horse's close-knit knitting. The problem, however, was that the thing was half the size it should have been. In an unprecedented mix up of sizing patterns, Horse had constructed Graeme's jumper to the dimensions of local schoolboy, Nathan Hunch. Consequently, Nathan's mum was wondering why her son's new jumper looked more like a burka. It was a disaster.

"I can't get my breath," wheezed Graeme.

"Oh, calm down, you big girl's blouse!" Penny grabbed the jumper. "I've got an idea."

As far as big girl's blouses went, Mike had excelled in his choice of eveningwear.

For the big night he'd picked out a chic, nautical ensemble and was clad in a pair of white skinny jeans and a Breton-striped, navy blouse. He had even made an effort to put on some eyeliner and a touch of lippy. Rather than splash out on the price of a bottle of aftershave or perfume, Mike would usually drive into Ipswich, pop into *Boots* and then cover himself with scent from one of the testers. He'd found half an hour in his afternoon schedule to get out and landed on a sample bottle of Dior's new *Parsnip!* and doused himself liberally. His heels were a second-hand pair of Jimmy Choo's from the St. Elizabeth's Hospice charity shop on Woodbridge's thoroughfare.

The smell of reconstituted turkey filled the pub as a steady crowd mingled and discussed the likely permutations for the night.

"I took a look at the running order for The Goose tonight...have to say it's impressive," FW told Gail Frogmarch.

"Well, that Graeme Nash is welcome to the prize!" snapped the bitter harpist. "It'll be a Pyrrhic victory seeing as half the performers belong here!"

"Here, here!" said Hector, overhearing Gail's staunch defence of his pub. He placed a plate of steaming turkey cock onto a table (Liam had neglected to mention which turkey pieces he could lay his hands on).

"I don't think I've seen Hector so relaxed for some time." Catherine Bush was talking to Janice Muffler who'd decided – once she'd found babysitters for the twins – to split her time between the two pubs on account of her allegiance to both Jules and Mike. (And on account of her husband, Alan, being away at an *Apps for Skips* brainstorming session in Bucharest.)

"Oi'd 'eard you'd never set foot in this pub again after Hector's outburst." Janice hadn't much liked the fete organiser's overt, public defamation of Hector. An eye for eye makes the whole world blind, she'd been reminded by Father Mackenzie in a recent sermon (minus the expletives).

"Oh, I don't hold a grudge for long, my dear," Catherine lied. "People always need a second chance!"

Truth be told, Hector had visited Catherine at home to make a personal apology and offered to run the mulled wine stall at the Peasanhall Christmas Fayre for free and give all the profits to a charity of her choice.

Other assessments of the likely outcome of the evening flew around the pub like a wasp in a jar. Carl Fleming texted his wife to say the whole village appeared to have turned out for this historic event. The outraged reply from his missus suggested predictive text had done for him again.

"I really hope The Peasant can do it tonight, don't you, darling?" said Gaynor Bradley.

"Absolutely," her husband replied. "Shall we slip out the back for a quickie?"

Maddy and Steve watched as the pair disappeared out the east-by-east door.

"I'm still quietly confident Hector's goin' to pull this off the neet," suggested one half of *Dog-Filled Pantry*.

"For goodness sake," tutted the other half. "I've already told you *exactly* who will win."

"Good Evening, Peasenhall!" crowed Graeme, dressed in what could best be described as a cable-knit crop top. The audience was suitably impressed by the detail of the rocking goose on its front, but somewhat sickened by Graeme's ample paunch poking between the jumper and a latticed belt holding up his corduroys.

Somewhere on the streets of Cowlinge, Pete of pete@pete.com was still trying his car to start.

"Good Evening, Peasenhall!" beamed Mike and the audience gave a huge welcome to their cross-dressing grocer. "Well, here we are, and all I can say is, win or lose, we'll 'ave a booze!"

Cheers went up and Mike got ready to play.

"Here's a song about seasonal vacations in Liverpool. Put your hands together for *Wirral Going on a Summer Holiday*!"

The crowd, filled with expectations heightened by the build up to this moment, needed no encouragement and soon began singing along to Cliff's brooding and emotional lyrics: "Do, do, de, do, de, do, do, dooo! [reprise]"

Somewhere on the base at RAF Mildenhall, Shirley's friend switched channels over to *Anglia News* on the TV as she was drying her hair in readiness for their night of fun. She turned up the volume as a female anchor handed across to one of their outside broadcasters reporting on 'the last night of the county's big *moosic* competition'. She turned to her friend, who was sat on the bed doing her nails and could only point at the television.

"Thanks Karima. Well, I'm outside The Goose pub in Peasenhall for the climax of the Battle of the Pubs and, as you can see, things are hotting up inside!"

Shirley picked up the remote and clicked the telly off. "Can you call me a cab, please?" she coolly asked her friend. "I'm going home to kill my husband."

"Good Evening, Mr. Wooluff." Hector had quietly slipped out back as Mike kicked off the evening, his mobile phone in hand. "Is everything still on?" he asked the person on the other end. "That sounds perfect. Thank you."

Radio NaNa were on fire. Their ability to reproduce a CD-like quality of songs was awe-inspiring and they treated The Goose crowd to flawless covers of Boney M's *Brown Girl in the Ring* and the Kaiser Chief's *Ruby*.

Jeff saluted Penny across the pub as a mark of respect for her ability to pull a few strings. Penny mouthed, "You're welcome" back and blew a kiss.

"'Ave yer seen any judges yet?" asked Mickey above the noise of the crowd screaming "Ruby, Ruby, Ruby, Rubeee!"

"No, they're probably doing The Peasant first." Jeff nudged the corpse handler. "Saving the best 'til last, eh, Mickey?"

Patrice laughed.

"What?" said Jeff. "There's no debate!"

"I laugh because I sink The Peasant will 'ave zeir hands full wiz uzzer zings, and ze judges will be ze least of zeir troubles."

"You sly French dog," smirked Jeff. "What have you done?"

Jeremy Barnyard was halfway through an elegant, bluesy version of Bon Jovi's *Homebound Train* on a sumptuous steel guitar when Hector spied the familiar pink and green helmet of the *Speedy Pizza* deliveryman as he pulled up outside The Peasant's south-by-north door. The suspicion of foul play quickly formed in the landlord's head. He quickly excused his way through the throng in an effort to get outside and cut the delivery man off at the pass.

"Good evening," said the pizza deliveryman, his words thick with a Lithuanian accent.

"Hello," Hector smiled. He'd managed to halt the man's progress halfway along the smokearium. Hector glanced over the man's shoulder at the moped stood on the road in front of the pub that looked like it had a replica of the Twin Towers perched precariously on the back. The landlord had rightly sensed some tomfoolery was at hand. "Are they for me?"

"Yes," the man said, sounding more like a Mysteron than a pizza dispatch rider.

"Hm," mused Hector, pinching his bottom lip between thumb and forefinger as he regarded the two giant stacks of pizza boxes held in place by a collection of coloured bungees. "And I ordered these, did I?"

"Yes," came the reply, deeper than before.

"And did I, by chance," Hector wagged a knowing finger at the man, "order these in a thick French accent?"

"Yes."

Ooh, you clever sod, Patrice, thought Hector, affording himself another grin. There must have been at least fifty boxes per stack; at eight quid per pizza, this prank was going to cost him. Hector needed a way out.

"I assume you've got my order correct?" Hector asked, buying himself a bit of time to think.

"Yes."

"Margherita, pepperoni and Quattro Fromagi in a forty, forty, twenty split?"

"Yes," the deliveryman replied, but then hesitated. He slowly removed and consulted an order slip that was tucked in his jacket pocket. After carefully scanning the illegible scrawl on its surface, he finally looked up and said, "Yes."

"Dammit!" Hector stomped a foot; Patrice knew him so well.

"And they are all thin crust?"

"Yes," the Mysteron's impassive face was becoming a tad disconcerting.

"And they're all gluten-free?"

"Yes. Er...no!" The deliveryman's expression changed for the first time from glazed to slightly glazed.

"Ah, well," Hector nodded towards the crowd in the pub behind him. "This is a private party for the *Suffolk Lactose and Gluten Intolerant Society*. If I feed them those," he pointed to the swaying towers, "they'll have irritable bowel for weeks. There's every chance they'll sue you, my friend. Understand?"

"Yes."

"Sure?"

"Yes."

"Listen," Hector popped a hand on the shoulder of the pizza man. "You're not going to have time to cook all those again, so let's just leave it for now. I'll be sure to get back to you with an order for our next event. Okay?"

"Yes."

And with that, Hector turned and returned to his patrons.

Somewhere on the streets of Cowlinge, Pete of pete@pete.com managed to start his car.

Somewhere on the platform in Ipswich station, Shirley waited for the train to Darsham; the timetable said it would leave in twelve minutes.

"Okay, just zis absinthe and then you will 'ave completed my famous aniseed run!"

Patrice and Jules were cosied up on the end of the bar. Despite her initial reluctance, Patrice had convinced Jules to take the ten-shot challenge. As he was tending bar for the evening, Patrice was 'sadly' unable to partake. Jules put on her famous 'whatever face' and quickly downed shots of Pernod and Ouzo – the ensuing jolt to her brain effectively masking any degree of self-consciousness. Jules felt good.

After sinking the Raki, Pastis and Jagermeister, Jules looked at Patrice through sleepy eyes. "If I didn't know you better, monsewer le Clef, I'd say you were trying to get me drunk."

"'Ow dare you," said the chef in mock offence and handed her a sixth shot. Zis could be my lucky night, Patrice thought. As the midwife grew increasingly unsteady on her feet, the chef continued to ply Jules with shots, encouraging her the whole time to complete the challenge.

"So, just zis tiny absinthe to complete a memorable achievement, my love." Patrice handed Jules the tenth shot glass.

"An den done?" Jules was incoherent. She swayed, her face sweaty and bloated from the alcohol.

"And zen done," confirmed Patrice, who promptly and proudly applauded the midwife as the absinthe disappeared.

Jules went to put the shot glass on the bar but missed and careered into a couple of bar stools. "I sink someone needs a little lie down."

"Been a long time since I rock and roll!"

FW smashed an A-chord on his guitar, which buzzed and fizzed its way around The Peasant. Mike had found a distort button on his new amp, which he let FW use with impunity. The grocer was in raptures at the will writer's performance. "Where the hell did he get this from?" Mike kept asking the assembled onlookers. He was a born-again rocker!

The flagstones once again became an impromptu dance floor. Hector was jiving with Catherine Bush (he didn't mind a little hypocrisy, nobody was perfect after all) and alongside them, Chloe and Trevor Gibb were doing a strange robotic dance together. Trevor, who had shown up with his father, Trevor, was a reluctant attendee. He had intended to spend the evening watching repeats of *Midsummer Murders,* but his dad wanted some company at the pub. They arrived just as Chloe was starting her second poem, *The Exquisite Inevitability of Love.* Trevor had been transfixed.

"Yer read so lovely loike," declared Trevor. "Oo wrote that?"

"I did," replied Chloe.

As Hector and Catherine danced, he felt his trouser pocket vibrate. He quickly pulled out his phone and glanced at the on-screen message. He grinned and spun Catherine even harder, the pair laughing in unison.

"Ooh...my head." Jules was stretched out on Jeff and Shirley's bed. She was barely conscious; passing out wasn't far off.

Much to Graeme's dismay, Patrice had carried Jules away from the madding crowd. The chef explained she suddenly felt peaky and thought it best she got her head down for a bit. Regrettably, it didn't look like she'd be fit enough to play tonight. Through the mists of noise and excitement of the gig, Graeme couldn't see how drunk his charge actually was. He gave Patrice a look which said, poor girl, bless her.

Patrice stood at the bottom of the bed. The room was hot and seemed to pulsate from the energy of the stage passing up through the house. He stared at the midwife and her vulnerability on the Timberlake's mattress.

"So zis is where ze magic 'appens, is eet?" he said softly.

"Eh?" Jules opened her eyes and briefly lifted her head a fraction. "Is that you, Mike?"

Patrice wrapped his huge hands around the metal bedstead, his eyes ablaze.

Then the lights went out.

As Mr. Wooluff walked evenly across The Goose's car park, Pete of pete@pete.com turned in and found a parking spot.

Steve and Maddy slowed things down with a stunning rendition of *Don't It Make My Brown Eyes Blue*, turning The Peasant from public house to teenage party.

Mike watched as a full-on smooch fest ensued and Greg and Gaynor Bradley, who were both down to their underwear, were setting the standard. The erection section, Mike chortled to himself.

"Thank God you had this in the car!"

Alan Hedgeworthy switched on his battery-powered busking amp and The

Goose was back in business. "Looks like the kingfisher will be in Dubrovnik earlier this fall," was his response to the numerous slaps on his back.

Torch in hand, Jeff had gone upstairs to find the fuse box. He tried resetting them all and then the master switch, but to no avail. It must have been an external power failure, he surmised. As he went to go downstairs, he caught sight of Patrice in his bedroom. "What the fuck are you doing in here?"

"Jules is sick," he replied.

"Oh, well, I need your help downstairs."

"Okay, I'll be zere in one minute."

"Now, Patrice!" Jeff demanded as he headed back to the bar.

"Merde!" hissed Patrice.

Downstairs, Mickey had found the stash of candles Jeff told him to dig out of a kitchen cupboard and was placing them around the room. Graeme was behind him lighting each one with Penny's zippo. As each candle took hold, the gloom lifted and the bright flames brought a magical feel to the place. Once Dave Neal picked up his Bodhran drum and began to tap out the beat to an instrumental number he'd penned called *Estuary*, an intensely intimate atmosphere descended on to the audience.

"Jeez!" Mickey's mind was blown. "A disaster has just turned into a triumph."

"Pure gold dust, my friend," said an electrified Jeff.

At this point of almost absolute purity, Pete of pete@pete.com walked into the pub, his face registering total wonderment. As he stepped in further, the judge passed a welcoming Cloak & Spanner, who wagged their tails furiously at the arrival of the latest guest.

And toppled over a lit candle in the process.

"'Ere, oi think all the loights have gorn out over at The Goose!"

It was Liam Lewis who received Steve Naysmith's text: *Lights out. Sat in dark. No moosic.*

As the news spread, cheers and laughter filled the pub as *Dog-Filled Pantry* rocked on.

Liam's phone buzzed again: *Scrap that. Candles in play. Fucking magic!*

So what? was the general consensus to the new news, everyone in The Peasant swas having too good a time of it to worry about events down the road.

Liam glared at his phone when it went off for a third time. "Leave me alone, Steve!" he shouted at it. The screen flashed up another text: *Shit! Come quick! The place is on fire!*

By the time the patrons of The Peasant arrived at The Goose's car park, flames had engulfed half the property.

Hector quickly found Jeff. "Is there anything I can do?"

Jeff was visibly shaken. "We tried to get it under control with a couple of extinguishers, but it just took a hold and started ripping through the place…"

"Is everyone out?" asked Hector, scanning Jeff's face.

"It was going so well…"

Hector shook his compatriot. "Jeff! IS. EVERYONE. OUT?"

"Yes." Graeme was behind Hector. "A lot of people had to leave personal belongings, but we got everyone clear."

"Thank God, Graeme." The landlord put a conciliatory hand on the MC's shoulder and gave him a warm smile. "You did good."

"Oi think the fire brigade's about foive minutes away," Mickey informed the group. "That's dependen on traffic, of course."

Then Mike rushed across the car park to join them. "Where's Jules?"

Patrice was sat on the grass verge that framed the pub's car park; he had his head in his hands and was gently sobbing.

"Patrice!" Mike dived over and booted the Frenchmen directly on his shin.

"Ow!" he bawled.

"I can't find Jules! Where is she?"

The chef hesitated, gripped with a fear that was etched all over his face. He seemed to take an eternity to lift an arm and point towards the Timberlake's bedroom on the first floor.

"You fucker!" said Mike and sprinted to the front door of the pub.

"Mike, wait!" shouted Graeme, but the grocer was gone.

The fire was in full throttle on the west side of the pub and the ferocity of the flames quickly repelled him. He scuttled round to the back door, where the fire was equally brutal. "Think!" he demanded of himself. Just then he caught sight of two door handles in the ground five feet away: the cellar drop! With veins full of adrenalin, Mike had the doors open in seconds and was peering into the lightless hole. He couldn't figure out the height of the drop through the darkness but the top of the skids was just visible. "I hope the pig was left in place after the last delivery," he said to no one. Mike lowered himself on to the top of the skids and then executed a perfect roly-poly onto the waiting cork sack at the base.

Through the pitch black of the cellar, Mike scrambled and stumbled until he found stairs leading up to the restaurant. Seconds later, he was up and through the kitchen. The going was easier as light from the fire illuminated the way. He rounded the door between the kitchen and the restaurant but was beaten back from the foot of the main stairs by flames and smoke pouring out of the main bar. The grocer took another few seconds to way up his options. He dived back in the kitchen, swiftly changing his very combustible polyester blouse for Patrice's whites. He then grabbed a pile of tea towels, soaked them in the sink and threw them over his head and hands for protection. The next step required no subtly, he simply charged at the flames and launched himself through the inferno and onto the staircase. As he spotted the dive, his forehead cracked against a step halfway up the flight and his world spun for a few seconds. The smell of singed hair quickly brought Mike to his senses; he dragged himself up and scaled the remaining steps.

Jules was prostrate on the bed; the room was full of smoke.

"Please don't be dead!" Mike begged. "Please don't be dead!"

He entered the bedroom, choking on the acrid smoke. He tried to shield his nose and mouth with the crook of his arm, but it offered no respite from the smoke's effect. Climbing onto the bed, he rolled Jules on to her front to see he could determine her condition. He was no first-aider, but he knew how to find a pulse, a clumsy finger on her wrist revealed she was still alive. Unconscious but alive.

"Thank you, thank you!"

Mike went to pick her up but the smoke was debilitating, he could barely function. Open a window; get some air. Thankfully, his mind was still alert and he stumbled over to the bedroom's large bay window.

The double-glazing was securely locked.

"Fucking coppers!" he hissed just as a massive crack ripped through the house.

Mike could almost taste the falling masonry: the building was starting to collapse. He ran to the stairs and saw the fire steadily making its way upwards, its heat splintering and shattering the structure of the house on its inexorable path. There goes our way out, Mike realised. Back in the bedroom, he searched frantically for some window keys but found nothing in the darkness. There was only one thing for it, he'd have to pitch Shirley's dressing table through the bedroom window.

Mike couldn't manage the full weight of the table, so, in between trying to take lung fulls of what air remained, he removed enough of the side drawers so that he could get the thing off the ground. With one final superhuman effort, Mike hurled the table directly at the large central window pane. The PVC framework absorbed all the energy of the impact and the table bounced back into position like a basketball off a backboard. There was hardly a mark on the window.

Smoke enveloped Mike.

"How could you possibly leave her upstairs?!" Graeme screamed at Patrice. "Are you fucking inhuman?!"

The Frenchman cowered as a tirade burst around him like November fireworks.

"Two people are stuck in that building and probably going to die because of you!" Jeff pulled the Frenchman's head back using his ponytail. "Why didn't you get her?"

"I wanted to…" the Frenchman babbled uselessly between sobs.

"What do you mean you wanted to?" Penny was now letting the chef have it. "What does that mean?"

"I wanted to…but…"

The west roof cracked and imploded in on itself showering the night sky with a million embers.

"Oh, Lord," said Graeme. "Tell me Jules is in the bedroom on the left." He also now had a hold of the chef's hair.

"Oui," Patrice confirmed.

"Where the hell is the fire service?" Hector was pacing, panicked.

Mickey was going to mention the possibility of slow traffic again but thought better of it.

"WHY THE HELL DID YOU LEAVE OUR BABY IN THERE?!" Penny

was hysterical and began lashing out at the chef. Hector and Graeme quickly grabbed her and pulled her off the Frenchman.

"It's okay, love…he's not worth it." Graeme's attempt at soothing words failed and his wife dissolved into a heap on the floor.

"I wanted to but," Patrice tried again to explain. "But I was terrified for my life. So, I just ran wiz everyone else."

"You stinking coward," said Jeff.

"But…" Penny whimpered from her heap on the floor. "Why didn't you just tell someone else you didn't have the balls to go up? Graeme would have done it. Jeff…Mickey…anyone…"

The three men nodded their heads in agreement.

"I was embarrassed," Patrice confessed. "You would question if I was a real man."

The air around the group seemed to crystallize at that moment. It felt like time suddenly ground to a halt and they would all be a hostage to this revelation forever. The inevitable horror of death was upon them…trapped in a hell with nowhere to go…all life and love drained out of them…

And then the entire first floor bay window fell out of the brickwork and crashed to the floor.

"Well, that's Suffolk tradesmen for yer!" said Mickey.

As the air rushed into the bedroom, Mike was quickly revitalised and, given the absence of any firemen, he grabbed Jules in their trademarked lift.

It was time to jump. Thanks to the presence of mind of the villagers, a crash pad of mattresses had already been sought and built below the window should the need arise. The need had most definitely arisen. Again, there was little time for an elegant approach and, with flames licking at his back, Mike drew up to the edge of the bedroom floor now fully exposed to the elements, and just flipped Jules off his shoulder. She did a perfect Frosbury flop and landed safely in the middle of the improvised mat. When Jules was carefully plucked out of the way, Mike took off through the hole in the wall as the roof on the west side began to collapse. As he fell, he could see the blue lights of the emergency services crawling up the A1120.

"Is she okay?" asked Mike as soon as he was back by Jules' side. It had taken him a minute or two to cut through the crowd, which had deliriously descended on him when he landed.

"I've got her on oxygen, Mike," said Doctor O'Flanagan. "Let's give her a moment."

"Good to see you, Doctor." Mike held the old man's arm. "She's in the best hands now."

"You haven't been drinking again, have you?"

Before Mike had a chance to protest, the arriving paramedic team moved into position. "Thank you, doctor. We can take it from here," said one of the ambulance crew.

O'Flanagan happily passed Jules over to the expert care of the paramedics. "Are you okay?" he said as he turned to Mike, aware that he too might have sustained an injury.

"I'm fine," replied Mike. "Let's just get her fixed."

"Hello, Julie!" the paramedic shouted once she'd ascertained Jules' name. "Can you hear me? Can you just squeeze my hand if you can hear me?" Nothing. A few minutes passed and the frowns deepened on the ambulance crew: she should have been responding by now.

The crowd around them was still, every breath held. The only voice above the silence was that of Father Mackenzie.

O'Flanagan moved across the car park to where the priest stood muttering to himself. "You should probably stop reading the last rites, Father. I think it's upsetting a few of the locals."

"But I 'ave to administer dem, it's me feckin job!" griped the cleric.

"Granted. But I don't think anyone is in imminent danger of dying."

"Besides, it should be dat fecker about to croak." The priest pointed towards the grocer. "Feckin heathen!"

Mike stared hard at Jules' face; it was all puffy. Something was amiss.

The grocer looked up and searched the faces of the crowd for Graeme. "What did Jules eat at the pub tonight?" he urgently asked on spotting him.

"No idea, Mike." Graeme looked baffled.

"What was on the menu?"

"Sausages!" Mickey said, recognising Mike's train of thought. "With sage!"

"Brilliant! Thanks Mickey!" Mike turned to the paramedics. "She's in anaphylactic shock," he told them and breathed again. "She's allergic to sage."

"So, she can't eat stuffing?" In the midst of the crowd, Janice Muffler was appalled.

"If you've got an EpiPen, a quick jab and she'll be right as rain." Mike turned and smiled at Penny and Graeme who were embracing each other.

"Thank you," Penny mouthed to Mike.

One of the paramedics recovered a pen from a bag inside the ambulance and stuck the short needle into Jules' leg.

"Come on, sweetheart," urged Mike. "Open your eyes for me."

One minute. Two minutes. Five minutes. No change in Jules. The effect should have been instantaneous.

"Oh my God, she's brain dead in a coma!" someone in the crowd wailed.

Mike's jaw slackened. He was suddenly numb all over.

"Nah, she's not!"

Mike looked up. "What?" It was Sally Womber.

"She's pissed," Sally said with no dramatic effect. "She did the aniseed run with Patrice tonight. Ten shots, with the last one being absinthe. I saw him drag her upstairs, she was off her tits."

"For Christ's sake, Sally!" Mike was on his feet and ready to take a swing at crystal woman. "Jules is lying half dead here and all you can do is…"

At which point, Jules started snoring.

Loudly.

The fire brigade continued to fight the blaze as the ambulance headed off to Ipswich A&E with Jules inside – she would still need monitoring for smoke inhalation. Mike was perched by her side in the back of the vehicle.

Virtually the whole village was on the High Street to witness the final demise of The Goose; it had fought its last battle.

"Valhalla, I'm comen," Mickey said as the brigade slowly got control of the pyre and it started to diminish. The entire building was now gutted and only four scorched external walls of the pub remained.

"Well, I didn't see that one coming." Maddy glanced across at Steve. The fiddler shrugged, put an arm around his clairvoyant partner and they strolled back to The Peasant to pack up their gear.

Hector came back to the car park after using Doctor O'Flanagan's toilet, and found Jeff staring at the smouldering remains of his livelihood. "I'm so sorry, Jeff," he said. "You're more than welcome to stay at mine for as long as it takes to get back on your feet."

The fire's dying flames danced in the fixed eyes of The Goose's landlord. "If only the lights hadn't gone out."

Hector felt sick. He was the cause of this mess. His actions – his cowardice – were worse than Patrice's and could so easily have resulted in the death of two people he loved. "This is my fault," he told Jeff. "I had someone cut off your electricity supply. This tragedy is on me."

Jeff was still transfixed on the blaze. "What was that, Hector?"

Thwump!

The crowd turned around at the sound of the rear door of a taxi slamming shut. Next to it stood Shirley Timberlake; the shock of her face for all to see.

"Jeff!" Hector tapped the landlord's shoulder. "It's Shirley!"

"Hm?" Jeff said vacantly and, finally taking his gaze off the fire, turned around.

"It's Shirley," Hector repeated.

"Hm?" Jeff looked over the sea of onlookers to where Shirley stood with her rucksack. He shot a hand high in the air and waved ecstatically. "Hi, darling!" he called out. "Nice time?"

PEASENHALL

"Anything else, Janice?"

"No, just the stuffing and pastry thanks, Dave," said Janice Muffler. "Oh, Clive, put that back!" she scolded her son who had taken a bottle of Drambuie from the spirit section.

"Three-fifty, please, Janice."

Janice put the change on the shop counter. "I hear Hector got a suspended sentence."

"He was lucky not to go to jail, by all accounts."

Freddie Stevens had arrested Hector the day after the fire, charging him with criminal damage and reckless conduct endangering life. He was convicted at Ipswich Magistrate's Court but let off an additional charge of arson as the ensuing fire was shown to be the fault of a double-headed dog. The prosecution pressed for a jail term but, given his impeccable record and services to a number of communities, the magistrates chose to be lenient and gave Hector a two-year suspended sentence and forty hours of community service. He was told to pay costs and had his personal pub licence revoked for five years.

Despite news of his punishment, Janice couldn't hide her delight. "I know. At least he can now go to Chloe and Trevor's wedding. Missen that woulda killed him."

"Sure," grumbled Dave Neal, who'd lost his favourite Bodhran drum in the blaze.

"But, anyway!" Janice squealed. "How's all this goen, mister grocer man?" she said, glancing around the shop that still had 'GROTTY STORES' on its awning.

"It's good," beamed Dave. "Oi've now incorporated the butchers, so…"

"Yeah, I believe yer old place is gorn a be an art gallery."

"Apparently," said Dave. "That'll be great."

"Come on!" Janice baulked at the remark. "As if Suffolk needs another fucking art gallery!"

Jeff opened up the letter from the insurance company confirming that it would only be paying out seventy percent of the rebuild costs of The Goose; he then opened the envelope containing the divorce papers he was required to sign.

"More good news?" Graeme's irony wasn't lost on his temporary lodger.

"Well," Jeff cursed his luck. "If The Goose is ever going to be rebuilt, it won't be by me."

Graeme placed a cup of tea in front of him. "I reckon there was only ever room for one pub in this village."

"Good to know." Jeff stroked Cloak & Spanner's heads.

"What about the filth...er...the police again?" said Graeme. "I hear Shirley's going back in a civilian role."

Jeff sighed and picked up a copy of the *PQ*.

The front-page headline screamed: *What's on the menu? CHICKEN?* Underneath it was a picture of Patrice le Clef working in a restaurant kitchen in London. Carl Fleming had kept tabs on the Frenchman as soon as he'd cleared out of Peasenhall, monitoring his Twitter account to see where he would eventually turn up. He'd had the headline up his sleeve for some time, confident he would find an appropriate moment to use it. It was a shoe-in as soon as Patrice tweeted the image with the message:

lovin new job at #WingHo #Wembley Chinese co-workers real nice #itshotinhere.

Like a ghost from the past, Carl favourited the tweet and grinned at what Patrice's reaction might be.

Jeff dropped the paper. "Think I'll take Cloak and Spanner for a walk."

"Are you sure you're ready?"

"Absolutely. I wouldn't say if I wasn't."

"Okay. I'll put a note on Facebook tonight."

"Good. Now I think FW needs a drink."

Mike turned and smiled at the will writer. "Another pint of *Balding Bovine*, FW?"

FW nodded. "Um, I couldn't help overhearing," he said. "Was that Jules agreeing to start open mic nights again?"

Whether he was going to jail or not, Hector knew his time with the folk of Peasenhall was over. When he was bailed out from Ipswich nick (the officers thought Chloe was joking when she arrived with a trailer of compacted hay), he spoke to both Mike and the brewery about the grocer taking over; he would be perfect as The Peasant's next landlord. While the brewery had no problems – pending Mike taking the licensee exams, the northern lad had one condition he needed to confirm before he would accept.

"I want you to run The Peasant with me," he told Jules while still in her hospital bed. (She was perfectly well after sobering up, but the doctors wanted to keep her in – she was proving a great case study for multiple allergies.)

Jules took a couple of days to think about it and, after speaking to Holly – who thought it was a brilliant idea when asked, agreed. She would keep *Come On, Spit it Out* going until the Suffolk NHS could find her replacement, which it somehow managed in an unusually short space of time. The pair moved into the historic pub on the 5th of November. It was a day to remember for two reasons. Firstly, their inaugural night as joint landlords included a little matter of hosting Holly and Josh's engagement party.

Secondly, the *Horse Hive* in Sudbury was crowned the best open mic pub in Suffolk.

EPILOGUE

The BBC News anchor turned to face camera three. "And it's over to our financial correspondent, Suzanne Hills."

"Thanks, Hugh," said Suzanne. "Before we look at how the markets have fared so far this morning, let's start with the astonishing news that *Screw Ewe* has made a successful bid to take over *Robert Dyas*. The Suffolk-based independent ironmonger is reported to have agreed a deal worth over two hundred million pounds and will increase its retail operation from one store to over a hundred.

"In an exclusive interview with the BBC, which viewers can see in full on *Newsnight* later this evening, *Screw Ewe*'s CEO, Carl Fleming, said the deal is great news for the UK retail trade and is an example of if you aim high enough, sometimes you can reach the stars. He then had to dash off as he'd just sent an errant text to his wife."

--- THE END ---

Lightning Source UK Ltd.
Milton Keynes UK
UKHW040652130319
339001UK00001B/59/P

9 781912 601790